The Hooligan

Teddy Bart

PublishAmerica
Baltimore

First printing

This book is a work of fiction. Names, characters, businesses,
organizations, places, events and incidents either are the product of
the author's imagination or are used fictitiously. Any resemblance to
actual persons, living or dead, events, or locales is entirely
coincidental.

ISBN: 1-4137-8707-X
PUBLISHED BY PUBLISHAMERICA, LLLP
www.publishamerica.com
Baltimore

Printed in the United States of America

...A time will come, wherein the soul shall be
From all superfluous matter wholly free:
When the light body, agile as a fawn's,
Shall sport with grace along the velvet lawns.
Nature's most delicate and final birth,
Mankind perfected shall possess the earth.
But ah, not yet! For still the giants race,
Huge, though diminished, tramps the Earth's fair face;
Gross and repulsive, yet perversely proud,
Men of their imperfections boast aloud.
Vain of their bulk, of all they still retain
Of giant ugliness absurdly vain;
At all that's small they point their stupid scorn
And, monsters, think themselves divinely born.
Sad is the Fate of those, ah, sad indeed,
The rare precursors of the nobler breed!
Who come man's golden glory to foretell,
But pointing Heavenwards live themselves in Hell.

"Sir Hercules: from *Crome Yellow*"
Aldous Huxley

Part One

Chapter One

Jerry Cooper hated Nashville. He desperately missed the political juice of Washington, "a company town" he called it, where the company product was politics. He yearned for his small group of cronies who took part in the daily drinks-and-dinner bonding rituals that political junkies wallow in.

Cooper had enjoyed Nashville in the old days. He had come there several times on various producing assignments when he worked under Millard Hampton at NBC News. Later on as Chief Assistant to Iowa Governor Albert Packard, he relished the Music City campaign stops and fund raising appearances when Packard ran for President. A slew of country music stars threw their support behind Packard, which made the Nashville visits special from the sameness of the rest of them. After Packard became President, Cooper tolerated the Nashville meetings with Packard's bible belt backers so he could go and hear some real country music at night in Printer's Alley saloons and other "shit-kickin' joints," as he called them.

"Nashville had a style all its own back then. Now, its a big-city pretender," he griped to a pal over the phone more than twenty years later. He detested pretenders of any stripe.

Cooper missed Washington almost as much as he missed cigarettes, booze, and his typewriter. When his last ulcer flare-up nearly took him out, he promised his doctor he would give up his beloved Camels and Jack Daniels. Reluctantly, he kept his promise. No longer able to find ribbons for his cherished Underwood, he abandoned it for a PC, to which he leveled a loud "fuck you" upon hearing the welcome chime when he turned it on.

It had been two weeks since Cooper grudgingly said yes to an offer from the Jefferson Institute in Nashville as Scholar in Residence. The Jefferson Institute was a think tank endowed with ten million dollars to study how to establish democratic governments all over the world. The founder and CEO was a former Nashville newspaper editor whom Cooper admired because of the pro-civil rights stands the newspaper took when Cooper was starting out in the '60s. The ensuing years failed to diminish that personal admiration even though *The Nashvillian* vigorously endorsed Albert Packard's opponent, and even more vigorously waged editorial warfare on every policy and program of the Packard administration with the notable exception of their strong stand for universal human rights.

Jerry Cooper had a hard time accepting the cushy assignment. He had leaked tips to his newspaper pal in Nashville during his years in the White House because he respected and trusted him. He viewed those leaks, and the leaks to others in the media, as a quid pro quo, sufficient unto itself. The idea of pay back didn't sit right. Nor was he comfortable dining on the dole of a tax-exempt institution. As a conservative true believer Cooper held The Jefferson Institute and most all of its IRS 501 (c) 3 counterparts as shams: "Like limousine liberals in the '60's, who'd drive to a civil rights demonstration in their

Lincolns, get out and yell 'Right on, brother', get back in and drive safely away," he used to say to his Washington drinking buddies.

But the reality was that he was sixty-four years old, out of work, unhealthy, nearly broke, and oddly, unemployable. Logically, having been Special Advisor to a President, especially one as controversial as Albert Packard, should have been a ticket to fame and fortune. However, Cooper had no appeal on either the lecture circuit or the talk shows. His delivery was terrible, he looked worse, and he hated the spotlight. He had managed a couple of campaigns for a couple of long shots. They both got trounced. His heart wasn't in their campaigns or with them. He had written a half dozen or so forgettable articles for political journals, most of which don't exist anymore. He even took a position as the editor of a new travel magazine. He hated everything about that job, most of all the people with whom he worked. Under his leadership, the magazine folded within eighteen months. Then the Jefferson Institute offer beckoned. Other former White House staffers who found themselves as yesterday's commodity and today's trivia question had found sustenance at the Jefferson Institute. So to Nashville he came, to the J.I. he reported, to the bank he went, the pique he repressed.

Cooper's assignment was to organize a symposium on what the media was now calling Packardgate.

For years after he left office, Albert Packard was all but forgotten. The press and the public had other interests. Then about a year ago, a tabloid ran a cover story under the headline, "Albert Packard...The Shocking Facts." However, instead of investigating the truly shocking events that lay hidden beneath the Packard presidency, the tabloid obtained an interview with a former nurse who had cared for the former President up until recently. She was quoted as saying, "He exists in a zombie state."

The tabloid had attempted unsuccessfully to get a comment from all the key players in the Packard administration including

Jerry Cooper, who told the reporter to "fuck off" and hung up on him.

However, the story was picked up by *Hard Copy*. CNN then got some former low-level Packard staffers to appear who talked about some of Packard's eccentricities and speculated about what may have happened. Other talk shows followed which fed the public appetite for more. Since none of the principals in the play would grant interviews, Packardabilia took on a mythical life of its own. Conspiracy theories abounded, web sites, blogs and chat rooms devoted to the enigma proliferated. The media and the public became fascinated by Packard, the man and the mystery.

Yet, the central question remained unanswered: What happened to former President Albert F. Packard?

Cooper's Nashville benefactor had decided The Jefferson Institute was the appropriate laboratory in which to search for the truth about the Packard affair, and the man who was once so close to Packard that the press referred to the two as "Coopard" was the person to lead the search.

At first Cooper was skeptical. "Look," he told his old friend and new boss, "I don't know all of it, for Christ's sake. I know what I know, what I saw, but the goddamn thing was a riddle. As much as I've turned it around in my head over the years, I never learned all the pieces."

"Look, Jerry, just organize the thing. Get the best panelists you can…witnesses, investigative journalists. File a Freedom of Information suit; run a…shit, what am I telling you for? You know how to do it. You may not know the whole story, but you know a hell of a lot more than most of us."

Cooper nodded his agreement, and his friend left him alone with his thoughts. With an unlit cigarette dangling from his lips, Cooper stared out of his office window as afternoon traffic began grid locking on West End Avenue. He contemplated: *Maybe this would help to finally launch an investigation into the death of Freda Tucker? Maybe it will help reveal the truth about the disappearance of Yuri Belov. Or who he was.* Then, cupping his hands over his eyes, he thought, *and maybe this will end the dream.*

Cooper had suffered from a recurring nightmare since shortly after the whole Packard thing happened. In the dream, he is frantically running across a cornfield chased by a funnel cloud. He tries to dodge it and vary his path, but the funnel cloud follows him no matter how frantically he tries to elude it. He hears it hiss. He trips and falls and the cloud comes upon him. From the funnel a giant tongue emerges which violently sweeps him up into the cloud's hissing mouth. He wakes up terrified in a pool of sweat.

Using a felt tip pen, Cooper began to make a list of possible panelists on a yellow legal pad.

He printed Millard Hampton. *What a coup if we could get Millard here! We'll see. Who knows? He owes me one. Jesus H. Christ, does he owe me one!* He printed "locate" by Millard's name.

Next, he printed Bernie Frank, *Hell yes. Got to have Bernie.* He printed "moderator" beside Bernie Frank.

Then, he thought of McKenna. *Bet he's head of some goddamn militia nuts in Idaho,* he chortled, as he sketched an America flag by his name.

Next on the list, he printed David Strauss. *You devious old son of a bitch, I wonder if even this place can afford you? Shit yea they can. Wonder how many secretaries I'll have to go through to get to you?* Beside David Strauss's name, he printed "the key," and boldly underlined it.

More names were added: journalists, historians. Deciding to frame an outline for the event, he turned on his computer and heard it chime.

"Fuck you!" he shouted, and began scanning his memory back to a time before Letterman and Leno, when the Cold War froze hearts and minds on both sides of the Iron Curtain.

Chapter Two

As a child, Jerry Cooper was the adult he became. While his schoolmates played sports, listened to 45s of Eddie Fisher or Patti Page and talked about girls, he was glued to "Person to Person" with Edward R. Murrow and anything that Walter Cronkite did and Brinkley and Jack Paar, and he would dream of being their producer. Years later he would often recall a school field trip to a TV station and the feeling of bliss while watching the producers and directors in the control room sitting behind the panels of lighted buttons and overhead monitors calling the shots, determining what viewers would see on their screen. He knew better than to dream of being Murrow or Cronkite: As his mother used to say in a kind tone, "Jerry was rewarded with other attributes than looks." Most noticeable, Jerry's left eyelid drooped nearly closed.

So while the other kids wore tee shirts, dungarees and brown penny loafers with white socks, Cooper would show up everywhere wearing a wrinkled dress shirt, a sharpened pencil sticking out of the pocket, and a tie, which hung from his neck like a loose noose.

Even his jargon and attitude was Hollywood reporteresque: gruff, abrupt, aloof, and cynical. Constantly the butt of jokes from the other kids, Cooper shrugged it off. Having a quasi-family connection to the famous television producer Millard Hampton gave the young Jerry Cooper a fantasy escape route from ridicule to reality.

Hampton was once married to Jerry's mother, Sheila. She had told her son that Hampton divorced her shortly after he went overseas near the end of World War II; although court records indicated that their marriage had been annulled a month after their wedding. Jerry was the offspring of his mother's second marriage. He recalled his mom and dad sharing some secret joke whenever Hampton's name would appear on the credits of a TV show. Young Jerry would fall asleep wishing Hampton had been his father.

The reasons for the derision Cooper suffered growing up became assets when he went to college. In little time, he was producing programs for the university radio station. Although courses in TV production were not offered then, he volunteered at the local TV station and soon became valued for his ability to handle just about any production chore.

One day a candidate running for Mayor of the college town came to the studio to film a spot for his campaign. Cooper, who was on hand to run the audio board, noticed something on the screen he thought could be done more effectively, a missed smile or gesture opportunity, and he approached the candidate with the suggestion.

"Son, I wish you were older, " the candidate said, putting his arm around Cooper's slouching shoulder, "I'd hire you."

The incident piqued Cooper's interest in the showmanship aspect of politics. He became a member of the Young Republicans. He chose the republicans because they were less eminent on campus than the democrats, and he felt he could contribute more to them. Immediately he became recognized and sought after for his ability to organize and strategize the campaigns of republican candidates for student government.

When he became editor of his college newspaper, he decided it was time to attempt to connect with Millard Hampton and meticulously composed a letter requesting that Hampton grant him an interview for the publication. He had considered inviting Hampton to speak at the college, but opted for the print interview so that he could meet one-on-one with his hero.

Hampton, who was an executive producer with NBC news in Washington, wrote back and agreed to be interviewed, "not because you're Sheila's son, but because the samples of your work that you sent me show some potential." Cooper grinned his one-sided grin as he read Hampton's letter.

The interview took place in Hampton's office at the NBC news headquarters in Washington. It was Cooper's first visit to the nation's capitol, and he immediately felt the same sensation he had felt during his boyhood visit to the control room of the TV station.

Cooper's high got higher upon entering NBC. Shuffling down the narrow corridor leading to Hampton's office, his head pivoted from side to side so that his good eye could catch glimpses of the people in small offices frantically typing finger-pecking style or talking on the telephone. Like a baseball fan at Cooperstown, Cooper recognized them all.

Hampton waved him in and pointed to a chair while barking something to someone on the phone cradled between his shoulder and his ear. He was holding a pipe in one hand and a pencil in another. While everyone else Cooper saw seemed to be dressed in shirtsleeves, Hampton was wearing a tweed sport jacket over a crisp white shirt with a perfectly knotted polka dot tie nestled within an English tab collar. Although winter was approaching, his face was tanned.

After very little small talk, Hampton picked up the phone and told his secretary to hold his calls for thirty minutes—a device Cooper would often use in the future as an indirect way of letting visitors know how much time they will be granted.

After the interview ran in the paper, Hampton wrote a note to Cooper thanking him "for getting most of it right," and invited him to look him up when he graduated. "I may have something for you if you're interested," Hampton wrote.

Cooper thought of framing the letter but decided against it. *Too sappy*, he thought. Instead, he began a weekly ritual of writing to Hampton, often including articles he had written, tapes of radio pieces he had produced, recognitions he had garnered. He kept his common ground with Millard Hampton plowed, seeded, watered and fertilized.

After he graduated, Hampton kept his promise and hired Cooper as an associate producer. For several years, Jerry Cooper learned at the foot of the master how to spot, secure, and deliver a story to television. He worked the gamut of stories from human interest, entertainment, sports and politics—the latter for which he demonstrated a particular knack.

Hampton would caution his disciple against excess when producing a story about a public figure. "Between the extremes of vice and virtue," he would say, "flows a dense vapor of gray."

Hampton did not lecture or pontificate; he taught by example. His programs reflected his attitude, his approach, his special gift. Rather than going for the jugular, he deftly probed for a glimpse of the heart.

And while Hampton, always debonair and perfectly coifed, would rib Cooper about "appearing as if you slept inside a washing machine," he was pleased that Cooper's product didn't look like Cooper, and he gave him choice and meatier assignments as the years went by.

The association was all strictly professional. No "how you feeling, lad?" or any indication of interest in Cooper's state of being. Cooper was never invited to Hampton's apartment socially, but then, neither was anyone else on the staff. In fact, it puzzled Cooper that Hampton never inquired about Sheila, Cooper's mom and Hampton's ex wife. He tried to excuse Hampton's lack of interest in his mother as a quality of the consummate professional journalist. Still, somewhere inside himself, Hampton's lack of some curiosity about his mother annoyed him.

Hampton's disinterest in Cooper's well being changed without warning on a frigid winter day in Iowa.

Hampton and Cooper were working on a story about the candidates for president seeking the endorsement of the Iowa caucus. One of the delegates, a huge square-jawed businessman farmer cornered Hampton during a break in the politicking, grabbed him by the arm, and said, "I'm going to be running for Governor, Brother Hampton; how's about joining the crusade?"

"Sorry, Al," Hampton said. "King Richard left me with a bad taste for them."

It was a typical Hampton quip: dry, subtle, and historically based. Packard certainly didn't get it, but then, Packard didn't get much.

"However my protégé here, "Hampton added, while uncharacteristically patting Cooper's cheek like a Poppa proud of his accomplished son, "he may be interested. Say hello to Jerry Cooper, Al."

"How's about it, Jerr? Packard said enthusiastically. "Want to join the crusade?"

Before Cooper could utter a word, Hampton told Packard to call him at his hotel in the morning and he'd let him know "if Jerry will accept your offer to be your Administrative Assistant!"

After Packard lumbered off, Cooper hooked his arm around Hampton's elbow and dragged him outside. Never before had Cooper dared to be so aggressive with his benefactor. The January wind was whipping up its usual late afternoon bluster as the two men stood in their shirtsleeves on the frozen steps of the Iowa schoolhouse.

"For Christ sake, Millard," Cooper screamed. "What in the hell are you doing with my life? You all but appointed me the administrative assistant to some guy I don't know who says he's running for Governor of Io-fuckin'-wa!"

Hampton's eyes veered upward to the slate gray sky as if in search of something. When he found what he was looking for, he spoke. "Lad, there is a strange conflagration of forces developing in this land. It is an energy formula fed by fear and anger melted with social conservatism and fundamental religion. Never before have those volatile forces combined into a viable political entity in this country. I believe a time is coming very soon when they will collide and fuse into the damnedest political movement this nation has ever known. The only missing element necessary for it to erupt is a leader."

"What the hell has that got to do with me and what we're up here to do, Millard?" Cooper shouted, as he tried to rub some blood into his numbing arms.

Totally focused on the issue, Hampton seemed oblivious to the chilling wind.

"Lad, that man," Hampton said, pointing to Albert Packard, "he could become that leader. He's got the presence of a Billy Graham and the brain of a Billy goat! He is just charismatic enough and vapid enough to become the centerpiece of the coming political current."

"Great! Then why in the hell do you want *me* to go to work for him?" Cooper begged. "Me, a fuckin' agnostic! I'm happy doing what I'm doing. Why are you trying to get rid of me, Millard? Hell, *you* accept his offer! He asked you first anyway," Cooper said while pacing back and forth.

"Wouldn't work," Hampton said calmly. "They'd never buy me. I'm a known commodity. They'd suspect something was fishy, and move away from Packard. No, it's got to be you."

Cooper stopped pacing, and said, "Who? Who wouldn't buy you?"

"Them, the religious right. The ones who will coalesce with the social conservatives and rally 'round that bumpkin over there," pointing to Packard, "and use him to achieve their agenda."

Hampton put his arm around Cooper, another first, and guided him out of the freezing Iowa wind and back into the rear of the schoolhouse where a candidate was speaking to the caucus. While personally befuddled over the sudden sea change in his career, enough of his mentor had rubbed off on Cooper so that he instinctively knew that guiding him back into the warm schoolhouse was, like the pat on the cheek in front of Packard, not an act of endearment but a Hampton theatrical ploy. In this instance, Hampton needed to keep an eye on the video crew taping the candidate.

Positioning his body to Cooper's so he could look him in the eyes while glancing at the progress of the taping, he said, "Mark my words, lad: Albert Packard will be the next Governor of Iowa. One day he could become the President of the United States."

Cooper nervously grinned, and wiped his chin with his hand. Hampton continued:

"Then there is you, Jerry Cooper, about the only political conservative I know in the news business. Setting aside the religious drivel, the truth is that you are philosophically in league with one ingredient of the recipe that will propel Packard to the Governor's office and possibly to the White House. Look at you, lad: I read the stuff you wrote in college, I noted the beliefs of the candidates you managed. I'm aware of your convictions today. Now, to me it really doesn't matter who is ruling the roost or what they stand for just so long as I have access. But you…you are a conservative true believer. You are as perfectly fitted to be Al Packard's other self as Hopkins was to FDR. I don't want to get rid of you, lad; I'm merely shepherding you to a more fertile pasture. Signing on with Packard is your ticket to Pennsylvania Avenue with a seat to the right of the throne."

Cooper lit a cigarette, and rubbed his droopy eyelid and thought: *So Millard wants a mole. He's betting on a gut feeling about Albert Packard and he wants an inside source if it pays off. Hell, he's got them placed everywhere else. He cultivates sources like these shit-kickers out here do soybeans. That stuff about advancing my career is bullshit.*

"Look, son," Hampton said, still another first, "If he gets elected Governor, you'll have a good job, one that's fulfilling and meaningful according to your beliefs, away from the political throat slashing of broadcast bureaucracy, and maybe a future ride to the White House and back to Washington. If he loses, I'll take you back."

During the years he worked under Millard Hampton, Cooper had often witnessed him doing his schtick. There were variations depending on the requirements, however each application had one common element: He would say and do what ever it took to get a yes. It was what made Millard Hampton a great producer. Standing in the Iowa schoolhouse gym, Cooper mentally flashed back to others he had seen on the receiving end of the Hampton treatment. *I'm in good company*, he said to himself.

Looking up at Hampton, Cooper said, "I want to talk to Packard before I make a decision. And Millard, I want to talk with him alone."

Hampton smiled and nodded okay and patted Cooper on the cheek again. Cooper's wanting to meet with Packard was Hamptoneese for an inquisitive fish wanting to examine the bait.

The City Café in downtown Dubuque was bustling the next morning when Jerry Cooper arrived. One could easily identify the out of town political staffers from the locals. Aside from the locals' bib overalls, flannel shirts and caps with some feed supplier's name on it and the politico's dark suits, dress shirts and ties, the difference lay in the hands. The hands of the locals looked like patches of parched earth. The political staffers hands looked like a surgeon's after a scrub.

Except for the occasional booth hopping, flesh pressing, "Hello, I'm so and so and I'm running for President" by a candidate, there was no mingling; each person felt comfort within his own tribe. For the moment, the political junkies were finding their fix in Iowa. The following month they would migrate to New Hampshire.

The locals discussed farm commodity prices, the cost of equipment, and their kids while drinking hot coffee from fat mugs that never got empty thanks to a smiling buxom honey-blond waitress named Dora. Essentially, the locals ignored the out of towners, viewing them like visiting rich relatives — soon to return to their own world leaving the locals to clean up after them.

After looking around and not spotting Packard, Cooper sat down in a cracked vinyl covered booth. He had a newspaper with him, but he wasn't in a mood to read it. Hampton had set the meeting for 8:00. The deadline disciplined Cooper got there on time and decided to give Packard ten minutes. He hoped he wouldn't show up.

"Want the special?

Dora was standing over him with a big smile.

Cooper looked up, stopping first at her chest, and then panning up to her farm-fresh face.

"It's two, any way you like 'em, bacon and biscuits for a dollar ninety-nine. Home fries are extra."

"I'll just take coffee, please."

Just as Dora turned and headed for the coffee pot, Cooper felt a heavy hand gripping his slumped shoulder. He had to turn his head nearly all the way around so that his good eye could see whose hand it was. It was the biggest hand he ever saw. He recognized it from the night before.

"Mornin', Jerr," Albert Packard said, as he removed his hand and slid his huge frame into the booth across from Cooper. "Sorry I'm a tad late. Had a cow decide to drop her calf just as I was leaving."

Cooper immediately observed the reaction of the City Café's local clientele when Packard arrived. There were a number of "Howdy Al" greetings, a few good-natured jibes evoking friendly laughter from the others including Packard, and a tone of respect and admiration. *These folks like this guy,* Cooper said to himself. *Hampton may be right.*

"Jerr, I'm not one for small talk," Packard began. "So let's get right to it."

Cooper nodded agreement and waited, a tact he learned from Hampton.

"I know you have a good job. I'm offering you a better one. I know you like what you're doing. You'll like the one with me better." Packard paused, obviously waiting for Cooper to say something. He didn't. He knew Packard's opening was rehearsed and memorized *probably while pulling out that calf,* he thought.

Packard squirmed slightly and continued: "You probably want to know who Al Packard is. I'll tell ya. He grew up in these parts. Farmed all his life. Made a good living. Wants to give a portion back. How? By serving. He believes in less government, lower taxes, personal responsibility, the United States of America, and the Lord Jesus Christ."

Cooper dropped his head and grinned, joking to himself he had just attended his first Rotary Club meeting. Packard thought Cooper's grin signified how impressed he was, so he returned it with his own broad, proud smile.

Sitting across the small round wooden table painted over with countless coats of shellac, Jerry Cooper's inherent and protective cynicism temporarily softened in favor of serious consideration of the facts before him. Packard continued talking, something about his family background, but Cooper tuned him out and listened, instead, to the content of his own thoughts:

Millard's motive may be disingenuous but his radar screen was clear. Packard does indeed have a shot. The guy radiates. And the people here, these Norman Rockwell poster-people, they love this guy! Shit, what's not to like? He's a natural. His beliefs? Millard's right: They echo my beliefs precisely—with the exception of the Jesus stuff. Bull shit, the Jesus stuff is part of the package. It fills out the resume'.

I can live with it. Hold on: Why do I want to give up the job I've wanted since I was a kid? Okay, think: What's the most enjoyment you ever had? Not fun…enjoyment. Think back. Be honest. Whoa! I'll be a son of a bitch. Running those college political campaigns. That was it! Nothing topped it. I loved it. And it meant something; at least I think it did. Shit, I've had my fun. Maybe it's time to do something with meaning again instead of trying to please Millard. Shit, taking this job would please the hell out of him! Let him think he's got a mole. If that keeps his pipe lit, fine. Once I sign with Packard, if I sign with Packard, there ain't no way I'll undercut him. Millard never learned that about me. One thing: If I'm going to cast my lot with this guy, I need to know I've got the authority to do what we both need to get done. If he hesitates, I'm gone. If he agrees, I'm in. Here we go.

Cooper waited for a lull in whatever Packard was saying, and said, "As I understand the offer, Mr. Packard,"

"Call me Al, Jerr."

"Okay Al, that is until I call you Governor."

Packard thought for a minute, then, wide-eyed, he said, "Gover…does that mean you're hitchin' up your wagon?"

"Just about. But before I say giddy-up, I want to affirm my understanding of your offer. I am to be your chief administrative assistant. Right, ah, Al?"

"Right, "Packard said, with praying hands.

"No one between us. Right?"

"Absolutely. Right. With the exception of the Lord, of course."

"Of course. And if—no—when you are elected, I will be deputy Governor. Is that acceptable?"

"It is, Jerr. It certainly is. You will be my Joseph."

"Fine, then, Al. We've got a deal."

Cooper extended his hand and grinned, then suddenly grimaced after Packard took it and nearly crushed his fingers.

Packard ran for Governor and Cooper ran Packard. He became his handler, his advisor, in essence his producer. In time,

Cooper grew to like him, to feel warmly toward him. His relationship with Packard was much the same as it had been with Millard Hampton: strictly professional, no socializing.

The night Albert Packard was elected Governor, the media touted him as Presidential material. Physically, he had it all: Six feet-three inches tall, a ruddy complexion that required no TV makeup, and a head of thick gray hair that did the right things in the wind. Even his voice was a natural for the electronic voter— resonant, with just enough preacher to give comfort to his evangelical flock.

Jerry Cooper orchestrated his presidential campaign to accentuate Packard's star quality and minimize his lack of knowledge on the issues. No one really listened to what he was saying. He looked and sounded so good saying it that it didn't matter. His supporters heard what they saw.

By the end of the campaign, Cooper's daily telephone conversations with Millard Hampton decreased in frequency. Soon they became an occasional courtesy. A few mornings before election day, Cooper read that Millard Hampton was leaving NBC news for a job with a new network. Hampton's assignment was to create, format and lead the production of a new late-night talk show. Cooper knew the challenge was awesome, going up against Johnny Carson and others. Cooper appreciated the account in the article of who the host of the new show would be and how he was chosen. *So Millard's dubbing another knight*, he laughed to himself.

Seems NBC had sent a news crew to Atlanta for a feature on Dr. Martin Luther King, Jr. The producer was Millard Hampton. One day Hampton was a guest on *Mid-Day In Atlanta*, which was hosted by a popular local personality named Bernie Frank. About a month later, Hampton telephoned Frank and said he was leaving NBC and was going to work for World Television to start up a new national talk show. He asked Frank if he wanted to host it. "He offered the job in such a matter of fact way, I thought at first he was putting me on," Frank said to the reporter. "When I asked Mr. Hampton if he was serious, he replied, 'Lad, I am as serious as Hiroshima.'" Frank said.

Cooper's good eye brightened and he burst out laughing when he read Bernie Frank's response to the question of whether he and Millard Hampton are close personal friends.

"No one is buddy-buddy with Millard Hampton. I don't even know where he lives."

"Amen, brother!" Cooper said out loud.

A few days later, just as Millard Hampton had foretold, millions of evangelical Christians coalesced with the social conservatives. Thus, Jerry Cooper moved back to Washington, this time as Special Advisor to the President, Albert Packard.

Jerry Cooper was the second most powerful man in the Packard administration. The man who knew it all.

Or did he?

Chapter Three

The second best thing about coming to work in the morning was seeing the gift that Bernie Frank had bought her the day she began working for him. Just a strip of plastic that slid into a wooden holder with FREDA TUCKER painted on the surface, the kind any clerk has on the front of his desk; yet to her it said, "you've come a long way, baby," or as Freda liked to put it, "I has arrived!"

The *best* thing about coming to work was coming to work—until recently. Since coming on board *The Bernie Frank Show* as Millard Hampton's production assistant, she was always the first to arrive and the last to leave. Her professional passion was not only because the job required it. Freda was one of the chosen few whose fantasy materialized. She became what she dreamed. Freda's lot was different from most of the chosen who find disillusionment at the end of the rainbow. To Freda, the joy was in the destination.

Next to her nameplate was a gold frame containing a photograph of her father. How she wished she could have a talk with him that morning, maybe call him up and invite him for lunch and say, "poppa, here's the problem; what do you think I ought to do?"

That morning she took a few telephone calls and shuffled

through the morning mail, but her eyes kept returning to the photograph. After several more attempts to do the regular routine of organizing the thousand elements required to get a nightly show on the air, she finally gave in to some force beckoning to her. Slowly picking up the frame and holding it in front of her like a church hymnal, she leaned back in her chair and allowed the evaporation of time.

Nineteen Sixty-Three was a terrible year for Freda Tucker. Her father, Malcolm R. Tucker, was a Sergeant with the Atlanta Police Department. He prided himself on his recent promotion even though it was given grudgingly to satisfy demands of the local NAACP.

On a sweltering June afternoon, a mob gathered at Johnny Rebs, a restaurant on Peachtree Street. A rumor circulated that the Rev. Martin Luther King, Jr. and some of his followers were going to try to enter the place and asked to be served. The truth was that Dr. King was out of the state at the time, but no one knew it except King and, of course, the FBI.

The longer the mob waited the angrier they became. The animalistic fever that pervades when individually anonymous misfits find an identity with a mob escalated into an ugly mood.

Sgt. Tucker was off duty that day. He had slept late, ate a good breakfast, and looked forward to taking his daughter to a movie in the afternoon. First, he had to drive downtown to leave off some department paper work at the courthouse.

He felt the mob even before he saw them as he drove by Johnny Rebs. He'd felt it before. The air had a taste and smell of its own when hate gathered. Sgt. Tucker used to think of it as "ugly air." He'd smelled it when he was a boy growing up in Marietta. His stomach would always warn him about a gang of white kids coming over to beat him up ten minutes before they got there. He felt it in Korea hours before the blaring trumpets and blinding searchlights signaled another onslaught of swarming Chinese soldiers. He'd say to his buddy freezing along side of him, "I'm breathin' ugly air, baby. There're comin'." And sure enough, they came.

Sgt. Tucker pulled up along side Johnny Rebs just as the TV cameras arrived. Five A.P.D. black and whites and two vans rolled along side and unloaded their squads of riot control officers. His first impulse was to assist his fellow officers. Dressed in a pair of khakis and a blue striped half-sleeved sport shirt, he grabbed a bullhorn and asked the crowd to disperse.

"Atlanta is a peaceful law abiding city," he hollered, "let's not have any trouble." The other police knew who he was and appreciated any help they could get. The mob thought he was a member of the King entourage.

"Go to hell, you black mother-fucker!"

It rang from out of the horde. He knew that the first one brings a second, and a third, then worse.

"Get your black ass out of here and back in the cotton fields."

A white officer yelled to him. "Malcolm, get back in the car, for Christ's sake."

His sense of duty overcame his sense of reality. He shouted again into the bullhorn for the crowd to disperse.

"Are we goin' to mind some nigger?" a voice shouted from the mob.

More units arrived with sirens shrieking making the white officer's cry inaudible.

"Duck, Tucker. Watch your head!"

The bottle caught him flush between the corner of the right eye and ear. The thrower had filled it with sand so that it landed with the impact of a glass brick. Sgt. Malcolm Tucker's life pumped out of his head in blood-spurts until he lay dead on the mat in front of Johnny Rebs that warned, "WHITES ONLY."

Back at Sgt. Tucker's home, little Freda waited. When two A.P.D. officers unexpectedly appeared on the front porch, she ran to her room. Somehow, she knew something bad had happened to her daddy.

Freda was an only child. Her mother died giving birth to her. Her mother's older sister, Sarah, kept house for Freda and her daddy. Freda wished that Aunt Sarah would leave or get married or something because she felt that only she could properly care for her daddy, whom she idolized. Sarah understood. That's why she told Freda that her daddy had been killed protecting Martin Luther King.

"He's by the side of our Lord, Jesus Christ," the preacher said at the funeral. Freda tried to picture that in her mind. She liked the picture. He looked handsome there in his favorite black turtleneck sweater and old worn army pants. Jesus was dark-white in her mind picture.

Freda didn't cry too much at the funeral, even though everyone else was wailing. Some place inside of her a protective cushion from pain had already been formed. Sitting in the back seat of the patrol car on the ride home, she heard Sarah keep saying something like, "Pres'nt Kennedy will stop all this. Pres'nt Kennedy'll make this right."

When they got home, Sarah asked Freda to turn on the TV to her favorite show while she put out some food friends had brought over. While waiting for the set to warm up, Freda looked over at her daddy's chair and to her astonishment thought she saw him sitting in it. She blinked three times. *Still there*! He looked so real, and he was smiling. She blinked again, and he disappeared. Disappointed, she turned to look at the screen and there he was again! On TV! She blinked. And he was still there!

"Aunt Sarah, Aunt Sarah. Come! Look! It's daddy! Daddy's on TV!"

Sarah hobbled in from the kitchen with a bowl and a spatula in her hand.

The official A.P.D. photo when he made Sergeantwas framed in a corner of the screen while Sarah's favorite "TV man" talked:

"This world is full of heroes, my friends. Not the famous

athletes, or movie stars, or medal winners in battle; I'm referring to the little people; unknown, ordinary people."

"Is he talking about daddy?" Freda asked wide-eyed.

"Hush, chile. Listen to the man," Sarah said.

"Men like Sgt. Malcolm R. Tucker. The Malcolm Tuckers are the true heroes, friends. And no mob of racists, not a million bigots, not even a gang of bottle-throwing cowards will stop the good works, the courageous deeds, and the heroic acts of one man like Sgt. Malcolm Tucker." He paused, then concluded, "That's *Mid-Day In Atlanta* for today. Till tomorrow, I'm Bernie Frank. So long, everybody."

Sarah gathered little Freda into her frail arms and pressed her tightly to her shrunken body and together they rocked to the rhythm of Sarah weeping. Curiously, Freda didn't cry.

All that summer each day at noon, she watched Bernie Frank on TV with Sarah. At some level, Bernie Frank's interviews impressed upon her that questions were the key to acquiring knowledge and information When school started back Freda Tucker was the marvel of her class. Her teacher was especially amazed with her curiosity. It was insatiable. Why this? Who that? When did?

Like millions of other people, November 22nd of that year changed Freda Tucker's life. Samuel Jarvis, the principal, rushed into Freda's classroom, hurriedly whispered something to her teacher, then half-jogged out. Freda's teacher gasped and clenched her hands together in front of her mouth and closed her eyes. Then in tears, she said, "Boys and girls. Our dear President John F. Kennedy has been killed." She paused for a minute, and then went on, "Let's pray for the soul of our beloved President Kennedy and for his family."

Sgt. Malcolm R. Tucker would have known something bad was going to happen in Dallas that day. He would have felt the "ugly air."

At the Hopewell Elementary School in Atlanta, of the twenty-eight kids in the fourth grade, twenty-seven were in sobbing prayer. Freda Tucker neither sobbed nor prayed. She wanted only to ask, *why?*

When Freda ran into the house that day, Sarah was weeping in front of the TV. "Lord Jesus," she cried, "he was our hope. He would've made things right. Why'd you need Pres'nt Kennedy?"

Freda envisioned Kennedy with Jesus just as she had her daddy. Jesus was holding a microphone.

Sarah and Freda spent the weekend in front of the TV watching President Kennedy's funeral ceremonies. The little girl welcomed returning to school Monday morning. Her teacher gave the class an assignment: "On a clean sheet of notebook paper, I want each one of you to write a letter to Mrs. Kennedy and tell her how we feel, and that we are praying for her. Just write how you feel about what happened so she'll know that we are thinking about her. Now begin."

Of the millions of messages to the Kennedy family, Freda Tucker, age eight, was adding hers—and shaping her destiny with every word.

The only telephone at Hopewell Elementary School was in the principal's office, and it didn't ring often. Sam Jarvis, who taught sixth grade arithmetic and science as well as serving as principal, answered the first ring.

"Mr. Jarvis?"

"Yes, this is Samuel Jarvis," he said.

"This is Beverly Shannon with WATL TV's *Mid-Day Show*."

Almost like an amen in church he said, "Yes!"

"We were wondering if your school is doing anything special or maybe had some event scheduled with respect to President Kennedy's assassination. If so, we'd like to do a feature on it on tomorrow's program. We're trying to show how children have reacted to the terrible news."

Sam Jarvis was taken aback. Television stations didn't call him or Hopewell unless there was a fight or a flu epidemic.

"You mean, like some sort of special project?" He inquired.

She jumped on the word "project" as that was right on target. "Yes, yes. That's right. Anything the children have been assigned or asked to do regarding the tragedy," she explained, in her Atlanta accent.

Jarvis shuffled through some papers on his desk. Maybe the answer would be in a teacher's note to him. Near panic, he saw nothing except requests for supplies. Beads of perspiration formed on his forehead as thoughts of losing his pension flashed before his eyes. After twenty-seven years in the Atlanta Public School system, he needed only three more years to retire. The school board would love an excuse to fire him for something like not instructing the teachers to give the kids a special project about Kennedy's death, he thought. Frantically, papers were being hurled off his desk as if a winning lottery ticket had been misplaced. Suddenly his eyebrows rose to the middle of his forehead. Eureka!

"Why, yes, Miss Sharron."

"That's Shannon, Mr. Jarvis."

He thought, *Damn. Why didn't I write her name down? White folks are so sensitive about their names.*

He said, "I'm sorry, Miss Shannon; the tragedy, and all. We're all somewhat confused, I think. But yes, as a matter of fact, we have several projects planned about the awful incident. One in particular you might find interesting."

Jarvis had suddenly remembered what the fourth grade teacher sobbed to him as they were leaving school together last Thursday. She planned to have the students write letters to Mrs. Kennedy.

His voice took on a more sonorous tone as he continued. "I suggested to the fourth grade teacher this morning that she have her pupils compose letters to Mrs. Kennedy telling her how sorry they are for her and the children."

"That is exactly the kind of thing we're looking for! I wonder, Mr. Jarvis, if you might select about three letters that you feel are the best and bring the children to WATL for tomorrow's *Mid-*

Day In Atlanta Show? We'll have them read their letters on the program."

After receiving directions and arrival time, Sam Jarvis leaped from his chair, shook his hands above his head in jubilation and exclaimed, "Good Lawdy, Miss Claudy!" Then he composed himself, straightened his necktie and headed out the door toward the fourth grade classroom.

Freda expected her letter to be selected. Even before she was told she'd be on *Mid-day in Atlanta* to read it, something inside her prompted her to memorize it for recital rather than read it. Such intuition and confidence had already become a part of her nature.

At 10:45, three little people — two in suits and ties and one in a yellow dress — piled into Sam Jarvis' white '57 Ford Fairlane. The top didn't fit to the sides letting in the cold air in the back where the kids sat. Jarvis and the teacher sat up front.

During most of the ride, Jarvis railed against "the Jew who sold me this junk for two hundred dollars more than it was worth. Serves me right for doing business with that kike."

Embarrassed, the teacher turned her head toward the window hoping that the kids didn't hear him. Freda heard him and wondered what a Jew was.

The studios of WATL Radio and Television were located in a white column building on Peachtree Street. Jarvis pulled around to the back entrance as he was instructed to do.

"Now, no one say nothin' less you asked to, you hear?" Jarvis commanded.

As the group made their way from the loading dock up the metal stairway used for deliveries while Jarvis kept stage whispering, "don't ya all make no noise," Freda's heart pounding with anticipation. When the door to the lobby opened and they walked in, she drew a deep breath and held it a few seconds. Her eyes widened. It was magic land. The lobby was so white, so clean, so perfect. Freda felt bathed inside.

After the receptionist welcomed them, she buzzed and Beverly Shannon greeted them with a toothy smile. She was an attractive tall red head with four million freckles. She extended her hand and said, "You must be Samuel Jarvis." He held his hand out tentatively until she found it with hers. Atlanta was making an effort to be known as the new south. Jarvis was a product of the old.

After meeting the children, Beverly pointed to two rows of metal folding chairs on the side of the studio. "Take a seat over there and I'll come and get you when it's time for you to talk with Bernie. And don't forget: Speak up nice and loud when you read your letters."

Freda Tucker took it all in: The bright lights hanging from connections to the ceiling, how much smaller the studio looked than it did on her TV, the kitchen area, the curtains and scrims near the walls, the gray painted floor. And the people, they all looked like it was Christmas, so happy. A new world. A lovely world. She'd never forget this moment. Never.

Jarvis leaned over to the group, motioned with his head, and said, "There's the man himself."

Freda's mouth dropped open. Be it child or adult, there is always a rush seeing someone in person you know only from the screen.

The program began and time seemed to drag by for Freda. She wasn't nervous; she was anxious. Finally, Bernie set up the segment and introduced Freda first. After a few simple questions, he asked her to read her letter to Mrs. Kennedy.

She stood, although she wasn't asked to, and with her letter clutched in her small hands, looked up and, in a clear voice, recited: "Dear Mrs. Kenn'dy. I'm sorry about what happened to President Kenn'dy. I know your little girl must have cried a lot. My daddy got killed, too. I cried when my daddy got killed, but I don't much anymore. Your little girl will stop crying, too. I b'lieve we should still try to do good even though' we might get killed. Say hello to your little girl. I hope you are not too sad. Love, Freda Tucker."

When the program ended, Bernie thanked Mr. Jarvis, the teacher and the two boys. He turned to Freda and said, "Would you mind stepping over here a minute, please?"

A pang of fear shot through her. *Had she done something wrong, she wondered?* Jarvis cocked an eyebrow at her.

Escorting her over to a metal stepladder, he asked, gently, "Freda, was your daddy an Atlanta policeman?"

"Yes, sir," she said quietly.

Squatting on his haunches, about eye level with her, he said, "Freda, your daddy was a great man. I talked about him one day on TV, but I knew him before he got killed."

"You knew my daddy?" she asked softly, her eyes wide.

Bernie went on to tell her about the time he interviewed Stokley Carmichael and got a threatening phone call. His boss took it seriously and called the A.P.D., who sent Malcolm Tucker to guard him at the studio and at his home. "He was so proud of you and he loved you more than anything in this world. I know how proud of you he must be right now. I want you to know you did such a good job on the show today, and I just know your daddy was watching and smiling that great big smile of his."

Freda just looked at him for a moment. Then came the tears. Bernie's arms held her tightly to him. Then came the love.

In a minute or two, she stopped sobbing. Bernie stood up and asked, "What do you think you want to do when you grow up, Freda?"

She didn't hesitate. "Help you," she said.

"Tell you what," he said. " You get your education. Try as hard as you can to learn everything you can. Go to college. Then, when you finish, come to see me and I'll give you a job. Work hard, go to college, then you'll work with me. Promise?" he asked, eyebrows lifted.

"I promise," she said.

"Remember, there will be rough times. Times when you want to quit, to give up. When it happens just think of yourself as a runner. Like Wilma Rudolph. You know how they run as fast as they can till they come to a hurdle. Then they jump over it and run as fast as they can to the next one and jump over it? That's what you have to think like. Do you understand? I'm saying, don't let anything stand in your way, and you'll win the race. Now, give me a kiss and go back to your principal."

Freda Tucker never forgot what Bernie Frank told her that day. Not at Fulton County High School where she competed in every forensic competition she could enter. Not when she applied for and was awarded one of two scholarships WATL was sponsoring to deserving black students at the University of Georgia School of Journalism. She remembered the hurdle lesson when one professor told her he'd flunk her unless she slept with him. She slept with him. And she determined to hurdle the surprising news that Bernie Frank had left Atlanta for a national show in New York. Sure enough, Freda Tucker jumped every hurdle—and landed on her feet, grounded and focused.

Finally, her day had arrived. Bernie Frank burst from his office seconds after his receptionist notified him. Scanning the tall, svelte, gorgeous lady sitting on the white upholstered sofa, he said, "Freda?"

Extending her hand confidently, she said, "Hello, Bernie Frank. When do I start?"

The format of "*The Bernie Frank Show*" was essentially the template used by Steve Allen, Jack Paar, Johnny Carson and others: A glib host, a band, a studio audience, and several guests. Rarely, but occasionally, Millard Hampton would scrap the usual format and produce a special *Bernie Frank Show* built around the body of work of one prominent guest and originate the program at an appropriate location.

Initially, Hampton didn't want to hire Freda. However when Bernie told him her story, he not only acquiesced, he mentored. Patiently, and always referring to her as Ms. Tucker, he demonstrated how to put the elements of the show together. "The key is Bernie: he's the salesman." he taught, "We supply his goods."

Hampton demonstrated the daily art of providing Bernie's merchandise for his opening monologue. "The more trivial the better," Hampton advised as he demonstrated how to scan the newspapers and neatly clip tidbits to be placed in a folder labeled "Today's Show."

"Be watchful for items involving government mistakes, or nonsense," he said while going through the exercise. "Ah, perfect," he exclaimed, pausing at a passage in the *New York Times*. "Look at this: HEW has approved one-point-two-million dollars for a study on why dogs eat grass when their stomach is upset. That's grist for our mill, Ms. Tucker. We'll get the writers to suggest several punch lines, I'll consult with Bernie on the best, and he'll hit it out of the ball park."

Freda caught on quickly. Because she was generationally more attuned to the audience than Hampton, she even improved on the element as the years went by. The one element of the show Hampton did not relinquish was the selection of guests. That was his domain. He chose, Freda booked.

Because Millard Hampton and Freda Tucker were the cultural antithesis of one another, she, like Jerry Cooper before her, made a study of the man. Her best resource was provided by Cooper's college interview with Hampton. She underlined Cooper's epilogue to the piece: "To many, Millard Hampton is the best at putting the ingredients of a story or program together for broadcast. His formula is etched on every program he produces: Fascinating guests, good research, and resourceful hosts who could shift gears when needed." Bernie, Freda, and Hampton, or "The Wizard," as she thought of him, comprised the family she had always craved. She loved being part of that creative climate.

Hampton's mentoring method with Bernie was like his technique with Freda, the technique it had been with Jerry Cooper, and who knows how many of others. He was their guru. Using Freda's research, which she would put on four by six blue index cards, Hampton would go over the show with Bernie. He seemed to smell what might happen on each show and his nose was usually perfect.

"You might have to shift gears early on if this one…"

"She might resist talking about…"

"Hang in there with him and keep prodding gently, eventually he'll tell you about the…"

"He's going to go religious on you. I have a feeling he's another fading star trying to…"

"Don't let her get away with…"

Such was Hampton's way.

The Wizard knew he had a receptive pupil in Bernie Frank. He possessed the required gene: intuition. The initial high ratings only confirmed what Hampton knew: He had done it again!

Night after night, intuition guided Bernie though his show. While Hampton's index cards provided a map; his own inner voice provided entrances and exits, hazards and visibility. Life often blindsided Bernie Frank; a guest never did.

Intuition was Freda's salvation as well. Unlike Bernie's, who's got him safely through a show, hers got her safely through life. It was the kind her father had. The kind he described as "ugly air" when intuition warned him.

While it hadn't gotten to the "ugly air" stage, Freda began picking up something after about two years aboard *The Bernie Frank Show*. Subtle at first, nothing specific, the kind of feeling that makes one wonder about one's own balance, view point and state of well-being, or dismiss as changing weather.

The weather *was* changing. As the days went on and the

troubling feeling increased, she finally acknowledged to herself, *somethin' ain't right.*

More and more Hampton challenged her selection of items for the monologue, and he did it in a way that embarrassed her in front of the other staff. One day he lashed out at her saying, "You think this is good material, Ms. Tucker? Its worth about as much as that Woolworth ring you're wearing, my dear Ms. Tucker." Freda tried to put the gasping staff at ease after he left the room.

"Who said men don't get PMS?" she asked, mockingly.

The following day, the weather changed again, and he was the same mentoring Millard Hampton again. Nonetheless, she was sensing enough dark energy from him with enough frequency to be warned of impending danger. *The lull before the storm*, she thought.

Also symptomatic of a problem festering, one worse than Hampton's tirades and mood changes, was the obvious lowering in the quality of the guests Hampton was selecting. As Bernie said to her, "When announcing the line up is the funniest spot in the show, you know you've got a problem!" Worse, no one challenged Hampton choices. How could they? He was Millard Hampton, the living legend. He wrote the book on producing a show.

To everyone else, there was no warning, no yellow caution flag, just a crash. No one saw it coming, except Freda who walked into the production meeting, took her seat at the conference table, and definitely sniffed the "ugly air."

After giving Freda his list of people he wanted booked on the show the next week— "The Book of Boredom" Freda had begun calling it—Hampton went through the final questions and quips for the evening's taping. Everyone was sullen. Hampton asked if there was anything else.

Earlier, Bernie promised Freda he would broach the guest

subject. Politely, he asked, "Millard, is it more difficult getting name guests than it has been?"

He kept his promise, Freda thought sadly, *and wimped out doing it.*

"Tell you what, lad," Hampton shot back, "I'll make a deal with you: Don't tell me who should be on the show, and I won't tell you how to be dull. Deal, lad?"

Before Bernie had a chance to reply, if he would have replied, Hampton continued. "Why do we have these bloody production meetings if you are going to strike out on a path of your own?"

Both Freda and Bernie looked at him in amazement. What did he mean?

Bernie attempted to speak. "Millard, I, I…"

"Yes, lad? Go ahead, now is your time to ad lib. Not last night, when you completely digressed from the index cards with Howard Baker and pursued a line of conversation for which you were totally unprepared." Hampton's face was purple with anger.

Freda was stunned by not only the extent of the venom, but by the incongruity of the charge. Actually, the Baker interview was one of the finest Bernie had done once he shifted gears from politics to dealing with unfulfilled expectations. Bernie's performance was in the purest tradition of Hampton's Law on interviewing. Bernie called an audible at the line of scrimmage rather than run the play sent in from the bench and scored a touchdown. Hampton should have loved it.

Instead, Hampton said, "From now on, lad, stick with the cards. Period."

Finally, Bernie spoke up. With a half smile, he pleaded, "But Millard, I don't understand. I mean this is crazy! Why all of a sudden are you changing our deal?"

"Deal? Your *deal,* to use your typically pedestrian word, is that you follow the instructions of your producer. Your producer happens to be Millard Hampton. Your key to success is behind this door," he said, tapping his forefinger on the side of his temple. "I'll repeat: Never, ever stray from the questions and the direction which I lay out. You are not operating in the sticks any more. Y'all come back—let's set a spell and visit—was fine for Atlanta. This is Hampton country, ladies and gentlemen. I expect and demand absolute obedience."

Freda felt as if a spear had been thrust into her heart. *Why,* she thought to herself, *does everything I love always have to blow up?"* Her heart ached for Bernie. *Surely he's not going to take that kind of abuse,* she thought. *Not the man who talked on television in Atlanta against bigots and bullies.*

Bernie sat stunned, shaken, and afraid. He was well aware of being the current and perhaps last of the lineage of great broadcast personalities for whom Hampton had produced. He now doubted he measured up to his predecessors. *Hampton must be seeing some weakness in my performance,* he scolded himself. Oddly, that doubt hurt the worst. Still it was also the place to which he ran. Throughout his life, he would search within himself for some personal deficiency whenever adversity arose. Never luck or someone else, he was always the source of his suffering. Self-blame was strangely comforting to him, even when he instinctively believed otherwise.

Chapter Four

Bernie Frank's office was all white. White walls, white leather sofa with two white wingback chairs in front of a white desk.

He really didn't like the way his office looked; nor did he want it decorated like that. Like all parts of his life, however, he commissioned others with the responsibility of deciding for him. The only judgments he felt comfortable making were those within the parameters of his professional performance. Decisions required outside his performance, no matter how trivial or inconsequential, caused him great distress.

So when the president of World Television, during a welcoming party in Bernie's honor, escorted him into a barren room, and said, "This is your office Bernie. Have it decorated any way you feel it will make you comfortable," Bernie nearly went berserk.

He called Beverly, his former producer in Atlanta, to seek her advice.

"I'd put a big picture of the virgin Mary on the wall, Bernie. You're going to need a miracle." Beverly said. Bernie gratuitously laughed.

Other friends back in Atlanta had similar advice, all based on the heavy odds against him. His former bandleader suggested a picture of the Last Supper while his barber, Shorty, said, "My advice, my boy, is to rent!"

In desperation, Bernie called Millard Hampton, who had instructed him to call only if there was an emergency. When Bernie told Millard what his problem was, Millard said, "Lad, Noah had an emergency. Julius Caesar had an emergency. Paul Revere and Jim Lovell had an emergency. Do you read my message, Lad?"

Finally, Bernie appealed to Stanley, the program's set designer. Bernie's soft and gentle way with everyone must have conjured a delectable fantasy in Stanley's imagination.

"What would you like me to do for you," Stanley asked, almost panting.

"Decorate my office," Bernie pleaded.

A slight pause, then: "How?"

In a tone even softer than usual, Bernie said, "Do it the way you see me."

"I will, Mr. Frank, I will. It will be my best work. I swear it."

The first time he saw what Stanley had done, he felt a familiar sense of anger at himself for avoiding a decision. He said to Peggy, "I feel like Billy Bigalow in the opening scene in Carousel."

Bernie Frank and his wife Peggy lived in a modest Manhattan apartment within walking distance from the studio.

The Bernie Frank Show was taped at 6:00 PM for airing the same night. Up until a few months ago, he'd walk from the studio to his apartment rather than use the perk of a network provided limo. He enjoyed being recognized, signing autographs, chatting for a few moments. It made him feel like the person he dreamed of becoming.

These days he used the limo. The comments from the people on the street had turned from, "Love your show, Bernie" to "Hey, Bernie, what's with the show these days?"

Peggy knew not to ask him questions or make him be anything other than he felt when he first got home. Tonight was no different as Bernie, absorbed in his problems, and Peggy, absorbed in him, prepared for their nightly ritual:

40

"And finally tonight, the official soviet news agency, TASS has announced that the soviet government will soon grant freedom to one of its imprisoned dissidents and allow immigration if requested. Just whom the soviets have selected for release was not disclosed in the announcement.

And that's the news, weather, and sports tonight. Stay tuned for the tonight show starring Johnny Carson.

Good night, everyone"

"Okay, are you ready?"

"Ready, Commander."

"You're going to have to be quick."

"Honey, have I missed once in nearly two years?"

"Let me think. Hmm, yep! There was the time during the writer's strike when…"

"Tell me later, baby; right now I've got to concentrate. Here we go."

"It's the Tonight Show starring Johnny Carson. Johnny's guests tonight are Dr. Henry Kissinger, Bruce Springsteen and comedian…"

"Switch!"

"Merv Griffin will be talking with Bill Cosby and First Lady…"

"Switch!"

"Walter's guests are former Israeli Foreign Minister Abba Eban and PLO chief Yassar…"

"Switch!"

"Bernie Frank's guests tonight are the United States Ambassador to Iceland and band leader Les Elgart."

Peggy Frank slowly lowered the television remote control panel and cupped it in her hands pressed to her chest. Closing her eyes for a brief moment in the prayerful hope of selecting the precise words needed for the man who was both in bed beside her and on the TV screen in front of her, she said, "Bernie, honey, why don't we change the rules next time: You do the channel thing-a-ma-jig business, and I'll holler 'switch!' How'd we get into this routine anyway?"

The trim body resting on his side with his head propped up in his left hand didn't react. He seemed to be staring at a spot to the side of the TV set. He heard his wife try to kid him out of his gaze, but it felt too good in there to come out yet. A long time ago he learned not to come out of himself until he was ready.

Peggy knew the game, too. If she aborted the effort after only one attempt, her husband would sink a level deeper, and the rescue would be more difficult. So, she persisted.

"I've got a better idea," she said, bouncing on her bottom like a child who just decided what she wants for Christmas, "why don't we hire an umpire to come in every night and do the switch bit?" She searched his prone body for any sign of reaction. A twitch would do. Nothing. "Preferably about twenty-five years old, six feet two, dark, not too dark, but he'd have to be…"

"Soft," Bernie said.

The trampoline act ended abruptly with the performer flat on her back looking up with expectation into the eyes of her audience. *Bingo*, she thought. *I did it again. He's coming out.*

"Soft? What's soft?" She asked.

Disconnecting the circuit between his eyes and the lamp beside the TV set, he leaned down and kissed her lightly on the lips. Then, in a whisper to them, he said, "The scrambled eggs you're going to fix for us; I want mine soft."

Peggy Frank's eyes suddenly moistened when she saw that certain smile that only appeared on her husband's face when they shared a special moment together. It was his smile for her — different from the one he could synthetically create with variations for the TV camera. The smile for Peggy was born in his heart, and it spoke to hers. This time it said, *I'm back; I'm with you again.* What she was unable to hear it say was the secret it shared only with its maker: *I despise myself when I withdraw, but I cannot bear being unsure of myself.*

The only time he was sure of himself was when he was behind a mike, looking into a camera, on the air. That was before the Hampton blow-up. Now, even his professional confidence was gone. What she heard, however, was enough to grant her relief for that night. Time had been her teacher. She knew this was only another curtain in closing a play of a thousand acts.

Peggy hopped out of bed and donned a full-length eggshell colored robe that matched her silk shorty pajamas and winked at Bernie as she headed toward the bedroom door. Suddenly, she paused in the doorway, turned, and said simply, "Bernie, I love you."

He cocked his head slightly to the right and smiled her smile. He needn't say anything. She knew he loved her deeply.

"I'll be in the kitchen in a minute, baby," he said.

With movements older than his 48 years, he got out of bed and walked to the TV set. Manually flipping the channels back to WNBC, Bernie stood directly in front of the set as Kissinger was telling Carson, "Nixon was the kind of person who..."

Click.

"Merv, I've never told this to anyone: My honest feeling that first night in the White House was..."

Click.

"Barbara, the Egyptian President once confided to me personally that..." Click.

"Mr. Frank, let me tell you a little bit about the Eider Duck, a most important bird to the Iceland economy. Perhaps your viewers didn't know that. Of course, if the Russians invaded..."

Click-off.

Nearly plunging again into that inward pit he used as a protective vacuum to shield against hurt and disappointment, Bernie was shocked back into reality by the unexpected ringing of his unlisted telephone. Peggy answered, and after a few minutes of whispered conversation, brought the cordless to Bernie, who was still standing in front of the TV as if he was daring it to accost him again.

"It's Freda, honey." Peggy said, looking concerned. Freda didn't call during his show unless there was an emergency.

"Hey, kid, what's up?" Bernie tried to sound laid back as his heart raced in anticipation.

"Bernie, I know Millard booked the Eider Duck man because he said a CIA source told him the Russians have a secret plan to invade Iceland, but I had all I could take. I turned on the radio for some music, and as I was fishing around for a station, I stopped on Larry King when I heard your name mentioned. A caller must have asked about you, or the show, or something, and King says he hears that, now I don't want to freak you, Bernie, but King says that he hears that the network...now, Bernie, this is just a radio man who probably..."

"Freda," Bernie said as controlled as he could fake, "just tell it. What did King say?"

Bernie's stomach started to churn. This was a familiar churn. The one called fear. He knew it well. It had been gnawing at him all day since Hampton's vebal assault.

"Okay. King says that the network is already looking for a replacement, a whole new team. King said, 'Trust me. I know about this.' as if to tease that he's the one they've talked to."

Bernie grimaced and turned pale. He took a deep breath, and found a voice level that seemed natural. He said, "Thanks, Freda. Get some sleep. Don't worry. I've seen guys try to position themselves for a spot if they think a show is wounded before. It's the broadcast version of a PR plant in a column. I'll see you tomorrow. Good night."

Bernie hung up the telephone hoping that what he said eased Freda's anxiety a bit. He wanted so much for her and the rest of the staff to respect him. They'd seen him at his worst today. He hated the feeling of looking like a *schlemiel* to those who were to look up to him.

But then, he thought, *there was truth to his analysis of her Larry King report.* He's done it himself: dropping a hint on the air about someone in trouble and implying that he knew because he was the replacement. He thought about Larry King. *No way, the brass would never go Jewish a second time.*

Turning back to confront the TV, he pointed his finger accusingly at the screen and said, "Millard, you're killing both of us."

Putting on his maroon velour robe with the gold B. F. monogram that Peggy gave him for Chanukah, Bernie walked down the short hallway to the kitchen. Be it his boyhood home in Coaltown, Pennsylvania, where he dreamed of stardom, his home in Atlanta, where he and Peggy started a life together, or his Manhattan apartment where the star of a syndicated talk show and his wife lived, Bernie never felt quite as good as he did in the kitchen. The kitchens of his homes were places of decision, strength and comfort. He engulfed Peggy with his arms as she stirred the eggs.

"Hi there, sexy," she teased.

"Who, me?" he responded as he reached inside her gown for her breast.

Peggy felt his body respond to the feel of her. After 24 years of marriage, she had learned long ago that her husband got turned on watching her cook by the stove. Once or twice early on, she wondered if he might have an Oedipus complex after she heard someone discussing it on a talk show. She let it go.

"Look, fella," she squawked in a bad Brooklyn accent, "you want eggs or you want sex? You get one or the other here—not both. Make up your mind, huh?"

He loved it. *How in the hell did she always manage to handle his feelings, his failings, his trips and his moods so appealingly?*

"Ah, does toast come with both?" he drawled.

She shook her head no.

"Then, ah b'lieve I'll take the eggs, ma'am."

They both snickered. Bernie took his place at the round oak table that had been in their dining room in Atlanta. The presence of the sturdy oak table reminded Bernie of the professional stability he once had. His Atlanta talk show years stirred a kind of myth-like sensation within him. Like the warming thought of one's great love, it's always there some place inside.

In Atlanta, he and Peggy had as normal a life as possible in a public business. His program was the most watched local TV show, and he had a connection with the audience that left the competition bewildered and the guests impressed. He owned the town. While everyone said, "You ought to be in New York, You ought to be national," his instinct said no. Then, the seductive melody of the big-time beckoned, and he submitted. For Bernie it was less a case of being seduced, and certainly not of wanting to take a risk. It was more a sense of being afraid of not giving the publicly expected response to the offer.

Peggy set down two plates of steaming scrambled eggs and toasted bagels. He waited for her to be seated before he began to eat, an unconscious imitation of his father. Biting the cream cheese slathered bagel followed by a forkful of eggs brought a reflective mood to his eyes.

"Honey?" he inquired.

"Too much salt?" she anticipated.

"No, no, the eggs are delicious. That's what I want to tell you."

"So tell already," she said.

"Listen, this is very significant. Do you realize that the way a person fixes scrambled eggs is just as identifiable as their fingerprints? Now, I've come to this conclusion after many years of tasting scrambled eggs all over this land. No one cooks them alike! There is always a tinge of difference. You could blindfold me in a room of a hundred cooks, and I'd pick out your eggs. Not your fried eggs, mind you, just your scrambled eggs. Isn't that fascinating?"

He was serious.

Looking at him in a manner feigning intense interest, she said, "Bernie, you're beginning to sound like the guests you've been having on your show lately."

The instant the words were off her lips she regretted saying them. Peggy Frank hadn't made many mistakes in all these years of living with this finely tuned instrument. When she did, it was an Edsel.

Reaching out to touch his hand, she said, "I'm sorry darling." She struck ice.

"Honey, come on. I was only trying to joke. I'm sorry. Let's eat some more."

He was off again to that place where painful reality sends him. Peggy hated herself for personally kicking him back into the pit. If poor ratings, the competition, the fast-track pressure of New York made him dive inside himself, so be it. However, the shove shouldn't come from the one person to whom he looks to as a life preserver. Peggy cursed herself for violating the cardinal rule for wives and lovers of performers: Never try to amuse them with the truth. If *they* want to joke or indulge in self-effacement, allow it; but don't participate. For sure, don't instigate it, no matter how solid the bond. Bernie didn't go all the way to the basement on that trip. Somewhere between the mezzanine and the lobby, he sensed the awful pain his wife was feeling. Loving her too much to indulge himself at her cost, he decided to come up.

"That's the last dissertation on scrambled eggs I'll ever give," he chided.

Peggy's relief was expressed in a deep sigh. Teary-eyed, she took both of Bernie's hands in hers, and said, "Darling, I'm so sorry. I know how much the pressure with the show is getting to you, and how much you have put in to your career. You don't know how many times I've wondered if we wouldn't have been better off staying in Atlanta where you didn't have the weight of the world on top of you every day. But you were asked to do this thing in New York, and I suppose it was right to come here..."

The tears were more profuse now. He knew he needed to take control, yet in a way, he resented the responsibility.

"Peg, dear Peg. It's okay. Everything's okay. I'm too sensitive these days, and I know it. As far as leaving Atlanta, I don't know if it was right or wrong, but we left and that's the way it is."

Actually, he didn't buy the fatalistic attitude he was consoling Peggy with. In his heart of hearts, he now wished he never took the New York gig.

He watched in disbelief as Peggy took a bite of a bagel. He had assumed all appetite in her had vanished. *She probably didn't even know she was eating,* he mused.

He changed to a more assertive tone of voice.

"Okay, the show is in trouble. Big trouble. Carson and the others are clobbering us every night, and I've got a legend for a producer who went ballistic on me today. It's Millard! Millard Hampton brought us up here, and Millard Hampton is running us out."

Peggy smiled slightly, pleased that he told her about Hampton's attack.

He finished by saying, "I'll find a way, Peg. I always have."

Standing behind her, he put his hands gently on her shoulders, and said softly, "Now, let me help you with the dishes and we'll go to bed."

"Let's just leave them here. I'm tired," she yawned.

Peggy had heard it all before. The realization, the resolve — followed by no action. Patting his hands with hers, she prayed silently that her husband would find the courage to do what was required to save them both.

They walked down the hallway together; brushed their teeth over the bathroom sink together; and Bernie got into the bed while Peggy remained in the bathroom. He resisted the temptation to flip on the TV. *No,* he re-considered, *enough punishment for one night.* Instead, he turned off the light.

In a matter of minutes, Peggy's silhouette appeared in the bathroom doorway. Her robe easily slid off, and she tossed it over the velvet chair near her vanity. Then the pajamas. Climbing naked into bed from the foot to the head — the way he loved to watch her do — she lay close to him silently for a few moments holding hands.

Then Bernie asked softly, "Honey, you know the two choices you offered me in the kitchen?"

There was a pause for a reply. None was spoken so he continued: "I want to change my vote."

The next morning, Freda positioned the framed photograph of Sgt. Malcolm Tucker precisely under her desk lamp as she did each morning. Coming to work was not the joy it had been. Each day recently has been like heavy lifting. After yesterday's row, last night's show, and Larry King's comment, today felt like a bad hangover. Sighing deeply, she ploughed into the first newspaper in search of monologue material for tonight's show.

To herself, she softly ruminated, *Nothing on the front page, or page two. Something about a Soviet dissident being released on page three. Screw that. Nothing funny there. Hold on, here's one: 'Rare Mussel Said Endangered...Holds Up $190 Million Dam In Tennessee.' Bingo. Got one for ya, Bernie, baby. Nothing here, or here. 'President Packard to Hold Press Conference Today'...certainly nothing funny there, that's for sure. Nothing here, here, or here.* The pages were flying now as Freda scanned her way into Section B. *Hey, here's something: 'Dr David Strauss Voted Third Sexiest Man in the World!' All right! That's a winner. Nothing here, here. Wait a minute! Oh my Lord!* Freda's expression instantly changed from focus to shock, as she read the headline, "'What's Wrong With *The Bernie Frank Show?*'" As one would read her own obituary, Freda glued on to John Collier's important television column in the *New York Times*.

> Personally, I like Bernie Frank. He is an empathetic interviewer who neither attempts to impress the viewer or his guests with his vast intellect, nor his puckish wit. Thus, he transmits both intelligence and wit as opposed to his late night talk show competition.

At the moment Freda Tucker was reading John Collier's column, Bernie Frank was having his second cup of coffee with the Times while waiting for the limo to pick him up and take him to the office. Having just finished the sports page, he turned to the TV section. Seeing the headline, he grimaced, then read,

> Bernie was never afflicted by the chronic disease of interviewers: Not listening. And that, with his bonhomie, made him a refreshing addition to the predictability of other talk show hosts. Because his guests were doing the talking instead of the host (sorry Johnny), telling about themselves from a level deeper than when they're next playing Vegas, (pardon me, Merv), Bernie Frank developed a loyal following here in the schmaltz capitol of the world. However, over the past several weeks, a gradual, darkening veil has enveloped *The Bernie Frank Show* to the point where it now airs in living shroud.

Millard Hampton was reading the Collier article in the cab to the studio. The driver had to glance in the back several times to make sure the seat had not caught on fire. The smoke was billowing from the constant deep puffing of his passenger's pipe.

> Last evening, the veil took a name. Bernie's guests were the Ambassador from Iceland, and Les Elgart. After twenty minutes this writer could not distinguish one from the other, nor did he try. By the end of the program, Bernie looked as pained as his viewers felt when he heard for the seemingly billionth time from one: 'Big bands are really coming back, baby.' And from the other: 'We are a proud land.'
> *The Bernie Frank Show* had all the charm and effect of drinking a bottle of Go-Lytely before a colonoscopy.

The bell to the Frank apartment rang, signaling the arrival of the limo.

"Wait just a goddamned minute, will you?" Bernie yelled, uncharacteristically.

Gripping the sides of the newspaper as a wrestler grabs the shoulders of his opponent, Bernie finished the article.

"Here we are. That'll be eight dollars and seventy five cents," the cabby said to the smoke.

"One minute, my good man. I want to finish reading the comic page," Hampton said, sarcastically.

"Freda, what is it?" the receptionist said, as she brought some messages in. "You look like you've seen a ghost."

"You better believe it, sweetie," Freda replied, without glancing up from the newspaper.

> What's wrong? For starters, the guests. Last night's line-down was no exception to the bill of fare of late served up on the Frank Show. Guests for a talk show are like food to a hungry man. In the last six weeks, the Frank Show has been offering a light snack. It seems like the venerable Millard Hampton, the illustrious producer of the program in question, is searching the world for the dregs of the earth and seats them beside Bernie Frank for an hour. Frank, in turn, appears as interested as an atheist in the Vatican. I'm bored too, Bernie, but can't you at least fake some interest!
>
> The mystery is why? Why is the combination of a Mensch-like host and a wily old producer giving birth to a nightly hour-long wake?
>
> Oh, yes. I said the veil has a name: Dull, as in DULL.

"Hey, pal, I hate to disturb your reading time, but if you don't finish I'm going to have to turn the meter back on, ya' know," the cab driver said.

Laying down the newspaper, Hampton took a contemplative look at the entrance of the World Broadcasting Building. Putting his left hand into the breast pocket of his tweed jacket, he withdrew a thin brown leather covered flask. Holding the flask in his right hand with his pipe, he unscrewed the cap, put the flask to his lips, and took a quick swig of its contents.

With a slight sigh, he leaned up closer to the front seat, and said, "359 Park Avenue, please."

The cabby turned around quickly. "Dat's where I picked you up, right?"

"Precisely, my good man," Hampton responded with a head nod.

"Okay, pal," the cabby said, as he jerked the gear stick into drive. "It's your nickel."

How unoriginal, Hampton thought, as he consumed the remaining liquid in the flask in desperation that it would drown the demons that had beset him since his secret world had shattered.

The following day, Bernie sat in his white office silently wallowing in his dreary fate when Freda walked in.

"Is Millard here?" Bernie asked.

"My lord has yet to make his entrance, " Freda replied in a mock British accent.

"I guess you read John Collier this morning," Bernie said.

Hurting for Bernie, Freda said, simply, "Yes, I saw it."

Freda had become indispensable to Bernie. His need for Freda went beyond the description of her job. She was his professional completion, dealing with the myriad of emotional and interactive particles that, left unattended or exposed, would impede the flow of his natural talent. His dread and avoidance of confrontation was among them, and Freda was his firefighter.

Bernie reached over and picked up a sheet of paper. "Would you look at this guest line up, would you?"

Freda didn't have to look; she was told to book it.

He stood, and as if reading from a proclamation, Bernie announced, "Tonight: a blind wine taster, an expert on the snail darter, and presidential candidate John Anderson. Wednesday: author Frank Yerby, Dr. Benjamin Spratley on acne, and a goose-plucker. Thursday: wildlife artist John Left, songwriter Harry Tobias, and former Under Secretary of State Joseph Sisco. Isn't this exciting? TV fans, if you think that was something, get this: Friday: to top off one exciting week, we present the president of the National Gourd Society to discuss swapping gourds for fun and profit, to be announced, and General Raoul Hrierez, second in command of the Bolivian army! Can you believe it? We can't even get the head honcho! We get his deputy! Freda, do you know what: If Bolivia attacks the United States and you and I are taken prisoner, we can't be guaranteed we won't be shot! Do you know why? We don't know the top guy!" Bernie was hollering so loud that Freda worried the vein on the side of his neck would explode.

Crumbling up the sheet of paper his career was dying on, Bernie fastballed it toward the white wastebasket. He missed.

"John Collier, you are so right," Bernie said to the copy of the *New York Times* on his desk. "And Larry King probably is, too," he said.

"Let me see if the former Wizard has come in yet, " Freda said, as she walked out. In a couple of seconds, came back in.

"Nope, he's not here yet. That's strange. He's usually here by now listing goose pluckers and gourd swappers for me to book," she said sarcastically. "Tell you what: I got a feelin' he won't show. Don't know why; something' just tells me, " Freda said, shaking her head back and forth.

Darting into Hampton's office just to make sure for himself, Bernie returned and anxiously said to Freda, "Go find him. Accounting will have his address. Go find him and find out what's wrong. I'll put the show together tonight."

Then he headed out his door toward the bathroom, turned after a few steps, and, with a look of desperation, said, "Go find him, Freda."

Freda picked up the phone and dialed 72. "Hello accounting."

Chapter Five

Within the Byzantine atmosphere of the White House, no one was more devious, and more vexing to Jerry Cooper, than Dr. David Strauss. Strauss was the National Security Advisor to the President and wielded enormous influence by virtue of his intellect and personality. While feigning loyalty, he operated as an independent contractor within the Packard administration. Thus, he neither countenanced nor fathomed Cooper's unique position with the President. His secret service code name was The Prince; Machiavelli would have approved.

The one thing The Prince detested was surprise, to be caught off guard, to be blindsided by political events. Yet, few men, when confronted with the unexpected, processed and managed the matter with the duplicitous skill of David Strauss.

Upon hearing the TV news item the previous evening, Strauss placed a call to the Soviet Ambassador, Anatole Molenski. He was told the Ambassador was asleep. Strauss left word that he would like the Ambassador to come to see him in the morning.

"The Soviet Ambassador is here to see you, sir."

The famous face behind the gigantic desk had the receiver of one of his three telephones braced between his right ear and his shoulder. Without removing his propped feet from the pullout extension of the hunk of oak, he motioned a quick "come here" to the statuesque feminine figure at the door. Naturally, she obeyed and stood in front of the desk between the two visitor chairs straightening one of the corner-to-corner piles of papers while he finished his conversation.

"You did finish reading the information I sent over to you then, did you?" (pause)

"Oh, very well, I understand." he said, rolling his eyes, "but I must urge you to read the material I prepare for you, especially with the Summit conference upon us, Mr. President. Preparations are nine-tenths of the game. I assure you, Chairman Pavlovsky will be prepared with all the minutia regarding ICBMs, Intermediate range missiles, troop strength, and…" (pause)

"Yes, yes, I understand what you do Wednesday nights, however I would be derelict in my duty, sir, if I did not urge you to study at this time especially…What?" (pause)

"Yes, I heard that on the news last night." (pause)

"You're exactly right, Mr. President." (pause)

"Yes, I thought the same thing: We spend billions of dollars for intelligence and hear about the release of a dissident on the 11:00 o'clock news! What?" (pause)

"No, I didn't laugh." (pause)

"You laughed? Well, I suppose it is amusing, in an absurd way, sir."

Strauss shook his head in disgust, as the President told him that Cooper thinks he ought to call Molenski and ask him what's up. Strauss's face flushed. He wanted to tell the President to tell his one-eyed flunky to mind his own business.

Instead, he said, calmly, "As a matter of fact, I called him last night, sir. He's outside now waiting to talk to me. I thought I'd hear what he has to say—maybe find out who they're letting go and what they expect us to do in return, and so forth." (pause)

"Yes, sir, I will, and I'll drop by your office and fill you in after he leaves…I'm sorry, sir, what did you say?" (pause)

"Oh, speculation? My impression at this point, based only on supposition without any factual data, is that the other side wants to nullify your human rights position before the Summit so as to proceed on pragmatic issues. By releasing one of the dissidents." (pause)

"Thank you, Mr. President. We'll see if I'm right. Goodbye, sir."

As many times as she had heard her boss speak, Marsha Kushman was still fascinated by the accent. As his student assistant at Princeton, his research analyst at the Brookings Institute, and now as his administrative assistant at the White House, she was still enthralled by the accent.

Strauss waited for the click of the President's phone. Then he threw his receiver toward the telephone cradle. It missed. Caroming off the desk, it dangled over the edge like a body from the gallows. She knew a tirade was coming. She continued to sort papers as the first salvo flared.

"My God, what a fool he is! What a fool! Can you imagine? I prepare a detailed briefing for him on the possibility of Soviet aggression in the North Atlantic area—a sophisticated, delicate issue that will require his thorough comprehension when he confronts Pavlovsky—and do you know where he was when he should have been studying? Do you know where in the hell the man was? Teaching a Bible class at Wednesday night prayer meeting at his church!"

She watched as he pounded both fists against his forehead while he repeated his supplication, emphasizing each syllable: "TEACHING A GODDAMNED BIBLE CLASS!"

He paused, as if to find the precise entreaty. Then, he closed his eyes, put his hands together in prayer, tilted his head upward, and said, "God help us if the world is run by moralists!"

Marsha Kushman had heard such ill considered, non-sequiturs from Dr. David Strauss before. "Goddamn bible class" was bad enough, but "God help us if the world is run by moralists" was one of his most memorable. If she weren't so captivated by him, she'd leak it to the Washington Post as an example of the dialectic of the man considered by some as the brightest man in the world. She also was aware that he would know who leaked it, and fire her.

"Dr. Strauss, may I get you something?" She asked formally.

Reclining in his black leather chair, he folded his hands behind his head and looked up at her for the first time since she entered the room.

"Yes, Miss Kushman, you can. You can get me the Soviet Ambassador by walking very slowly to the door so that I can closely observe the movement of your remarkable buttocks." His accent was more apparent when he was trying his best to be cool.

Marsha nodded affirmatively. Well aware of his fascination with her derriere, she purposely wore tailored skirts and blouses in his presence. As his fetish was for intelligent women with small breasts and rounded fannies, Marsha Kushman was a perfect 10—intellectually, emotionally, and structurally.

Leaving his door open for a few seconds, she soon reappeared with his visitor. Marsha always felt awkward in the presence of both men. She was nearly three inches taller than her boss was and at least six inches taller than Anatole Molenski.

"The Soviet Ambassador, sir," she announced.

David Strauss got up smartly and came around the right side of his desk with his arms extended.

"Anatole, my dear friend, how are you? Good of you to come. How is the family?" Strauss could care less.

Molenski, mid-sixties, rosy cheeks and a broad smile featuring widely separated brown stained teeth, rolled across the room with his arms extended like a toddler taking his first steps. Bear-hugging each other, Strauss caught a glimpse of Marsha's fanny as she closed the door behind her. His brief fantasy was cut short by the unmistakable aroma of onions from the panting ambassador's breath.

"Fine, David, just fine. My wife has gone back to Moscow to prepare for next month's festivities. You know how it is when our two heads of state get together. Ah, but what do you know of such domestic duties, David? You have the privilege of bachelorhood, how do you say, the pick of the litter?"

The Soviet Ambassador chortled at his joke, and three layers of cheeks responded.

"It's not all that rosy, Anatole," Strauss replied. "As the saying goes, one must pay the fiddler if one wishes to dance. Frankly, my friend, if I were as active as the media say I am, I would not have the energy to run the foreign policy of the United States."

One of David Strauss's lessons to his students of diplomacy was to always lead frivolous conversations to a higher level from which substantive discussions can be launched.

He said, "Which brings me to my reason for asking you to come over here at this early hour. I'm referring, of course, to the television news announcement last night."

Ambassador Molenski removed a fat Cohiba cigar from his shirt pocket, grappled off the cellophane wrapper with his stubby fingers and crumpled it in an ashtray. He viciously bit off the tip and wiped the moist brown morsel off his tongue with a white handkerchief. Reaching into his left coat pocket, he produced a gold lighter that he clumsily flicked, producing a huge flame. Billows of gray smoke nearly obliterated his face for a few seconds.

Waving the smoke aside, he asked casually, "What television news announcement, David?"

Strauss would have none of that charade. Only a sudden blitz would end it. Otherwise, they would be playing cat and mouse all morning.

"You know goddamn well what TV news announcement," Strauss blurted loudly, so as to appear piqued. "Don't sit here smoking that foul smelling Castro missile and play innocent! That contemptuous woman on the 11:00 o'clock news said you are letting a dissident go. Now, I want to know what the hell is going on?" Strauss pounded his knee with his fist to the beat of, "is going on." He sat on the edge of the beige overstuffed chair across the coffee table from Molenski's matching sofa.

"David, David," the Ambassador began, but changed course between "Davids." These were two cold warriors jousting for position. Molenski presumed Strauss was performing one of his infamous tirades for effect; with David Strauss, however, one was not absolutely certain. Molenski decided to play it straight. Strauss won that round by ending it.

To demonstrate deference, Molenski set his cigar aside, placing it in the crystal ashtray on the side table while looking at David as if to say, "okay, let's get down to business."

In a lower, more formal tone, the Ambassador said, "David, what you heard on the television is true. TASS was given the story and apparently we were neglectful by not giving it to your ambassador simultaneously."

David knew this to be false. The Soviets couldn't get a crop of wheat to market, however they did manage news better than anyone else. For their own purpose, they wanted it on American TV before American diplomats could study it. He let Molenski continue.

"For that I beg your apology. Now, in the larger sense the story is this: Your President Packard has made quite an issue out of the denial of human rights in certain nations. As you know very well, David, we object not only to his intrusion in our domestic policies, but in the selectivity aspect of the issue as well. That is to say, for example, on what basis does your President judge our domestic policies as repressive while voicing no objections against the human rights policies of some nations from whom America buys it's oil? Be that as it may, we are very concerned that the Summit Conference will become dragged down by nebulous and unproven charges of Soviet denial of human rights, and therefore ignore and neglect the basic and pragmatic issues threatening the very existence of our two nations."

How Molenski wished he could take one deep puff from that now cool cigar at that moment. *Ah, the sacrifice of national service,* he thought, then continued speaking.

"Therefore, David, so as to preclude any obstacles to substantive discussions, we decided to release one of the so-called dissidents to prove to you that our heart is in the right place on the issue, or non-issue, of human rights. That is the truth, and those are the facts, my dear friend."

Strauss felt pleased. He had accurately assessed the event for the President not twenty minutes ago simply on deduction. Calculations like those confirmed his belief that he was endowed with those qualities incarnate in the greatest of historical diplomatic tacticians.

Fundamentally he was satisfied with the ambassador's explanation. In fact, in the deep recesses of Strauss's duplicitous mind, he not only hailed the Soviet's motive and method, he shared their disdain for the application of human rights as a geopolitical issue. He held the position that human rights are a policy for Popes, not Presidents. To his utter dismay, human rights were a Packard for President campaign plank that became foreign policy. Strauss was well aware that the person who designed, delivered and installed the plank was Jerry Cooper.

"Certainly, Anatole, I can appreciate your government's failure to communicate the news through proper diplomatic channels before notifying the press. In this country, it usually happens that way inadvertently, by leak or design. As for the release of the dissident, I can only offer my congratulations to you. Such a move is a step in the right direction. Although it does not solve the many objections President Packard has regarding Soviet denial of human rights to all its people, it will encourage the President to go forth to the Summit with confidence and faith in the knowledge that your government recognizes the importance of the issue to him personally."

Strauss carefully couched the issue of human rights as personally important to the President and not to his administration so as to exclude himself from personally backing the issue. He assumed Molenski caught the distinction.

Molenski reached over to the side table for his half-burned cigar without searching Strauss's face for any sign of disapproval. Of course, the sly fox caught the message sent by the leopard. The two had reached common ground.

Strauss reached casually under the right arm of his chair and pressed the end button. Outside his office, a green light flashed atop the doorway leading to Marsha Kushman's desk. Seeing it, she stopped her typing and opened the boss's oak door.

"May I order a beverage for you gentlemen?" She asked.

"How about it, Anatole? Have you had breakfast?"

Strauss knew the answer before he asked. The whiff of onion breath was all too vivid in his mind

The Soviet Ambassador patted his tummy and waved off the suggestion by saying, "And how I had breakfast! I would welcome a cup of tea if you don't mind."

Marsha had walked over to the seating area while the Ambassador was speaking and stood between the two world powers. Molenski's eyes focused on her chest, then her eyes.

Smiling pleasantly, she said, "I don't mind at all, Mr. Ambassador. Do you still take sugar?"

Making a stubby-fingered peace sign, he replied, "Two lumps—on the side, please."

As was his usual social habit, Strauss pretended not to be noticing the niceties by reaching into his pocket and pulling out a slip of paper, glancing at it, and replacing it. In reality he was seeing every gesture, hearing every word, aware of every nuance. To Dr. David Strauss, attention to the seemingly inconsequential was often the lever in an untenable negotiation. Everything was data filed and set aside for use at an opportune moment.

Looking down at him, Marsha asked, "And you, Dr. Strauss?"

She knew what he would reply. Strauss always ordered what his guests ordered, no matter how he detested the choice. One night while she was having sex with him, she asked him why, and he told her: "In diplomacy, any area of agreement is a step forward."

"I'll have the same, Miss Kushman. Thank you."

Marsha turned, and Strauss took a look at her behind—peripherally noticing Molenski lighting his cigar. The door closed behind her.

"Fine lady, David, but terribly thin, don't you think?" He inquired, blowing out gray smoke.

Strauss was well aware of Molenski's preference in women. CIA photos and recordings of call girls performing at the Soviet Embassy indicated his fetish for blonde, buxom, and hefty bed partners, usually in pairs. Strauss and Marsha spent one unforgettable weekend in bed together reading dossiers of the sexual habits of foreign ambassadors to the United States he had ordered from the CIA. They laughed until tears rolled down their faces at the Molenski file. The vivid document described that ferocious bear, who rattles sabers of nuclear devastation during every crisis possessing a fetish for call girls feeding him soup from a spoon while holding him in their lap. Following the soup, he asks to be burped in the over-the-shoulder manner and sung a Russian lullaby. When they tell him they don't know a Russian lullaby, he coos while they sing anything close to a lullaby. Then he tells them he still can't sleep and needs some warm milk. The hooker then unbuttons her blouse and removes one breast, which she affixes to his mouth cuddling his head in her arms. According to the CIA report, he achieves an orgasm in this fashion, without any manual, oral, vaginal or anal contact with his penis. If there is another girl, he repeats the same process. He likes to be kissed goodnight on the forehead when it's over.

"Perhaps a bit thin, Anatole. Yet, to every man his own fantasy," Strauss said.

"I suppose you are correct, David. Mrs. Molenski and I have just celebrated our thirty-ninth wedding anniversary. Quite an achievement, no? Thirty-nine years with one woman, David. She has been my constant and only companion. Ah, you don't know what you're missing by not having a partner like that, my friend. Fantasy? Fantasies are for the unfulfilled. For me, mine was fulfilled thirty-nine years ago and has remained so."

Strauss thought to himself that he just heard the perfect example of dialectical materialism when the steward from the White House mess gently knocked at the door and carried in a sterling silver pitcher of tea between two bone china cups with the White House seal on the side. Strauss nodded thank you while Molenski did not acknowledge him at all.

Both men leaned forward as Strauss poured for the Ambassador. Molenski placed one sugar cube in his mouth and schlooped a drink of tea.

"Ah, that's good," he half-breathed. *Schloop.* "Delicious."

Strauss took a sip of his tea, a very small sip. He really didn't want any. He craved a cup of black coffee. However, he also wanted to learn more about the release of the dissident. So he drank tea hoping that bond led to information.

"Tell me, Anatole, who is the lucky person to be released?"

He couched his question in a friendly, matter of fact tone.

Schloop. "Pardon me, David. I didn't hear you," he said to the cup.

Here we go again, David thought.

Attempting to maintain the two guys in a pub atmosphere, Strauss reiterated, "I inquired about the name of the fortunate person selected by your government for release, Anatole."

He expected more delay, more contrived evasion. Instead: "His name is Belov, Yuri Belov." *Schloop.* "Now, David, I really must be going. Thank you so much for your kind invitation to visit. It's always a pleasure seeing you."

Molenski put his cup and saucer on the coffee table and stood up by pushing his arms against his thighs with an "oof" sound.

Strauss arose more abruptly than he normally preferred to appear to escort the Ambassador out of the office. Vaguely familiar with the names of prominent Soviet dissidents, the name, Belov, didn't ring a bell. Strauss felt uncomfortable, at a disadvantage.

"It's always a pleasure to see you, Anatole. I'm delighted we had this brief opportunity to clear up any lack of communication we might have had in this matter. Again, I want to say that your government's action is a step in the direction of harmony between our two countries."

Strauss still felt defensive and off balance.

Molenski paused mid-way to the door and turned to Strauss with a peevish glint in his eyes and said, "I'm gratified that you see the good faith shown by our action, David. If there is to be a lessening of tensions between our nations, I think that it would be imperative that extreme caution and utmost discretion be exercised in the manner with which your country treats this matter."

What was he getting at? Strauss wondered. How he despised the feeling of being baited. *Molenski you old devil, what are you telling me?*

Strauss watched as Molenski ambled over to a window and looked out at Lafayette Park. Strauss joined him and the two small giants peered out the window together in silence. Strauss's hands were in his pockets as the skin around his fingernails absorbed the punishment his psyche was taking.

Strauss spoke first: "We are always discreet in matters of negotiations, Anatole. Have no fear about that."

It was a general statement fashioned to miss the point inoffensively, thus provoking clarification. Strauss waited. He had given Molenski no option other than to spell it out.

In a tone a shade shy of threatening, Molenski finally said, "What I am suggesting is this: When Belov arrives in America, which is where we presume he will want to emigrate, it would not be in the interest of lessening tensions before the Summit for him to become a hero. As much as you can, I would discourage that, understanding the lack of restrictions on your media, of course. Perhaps factions in your country will recommend a hero's welcome, speeches by him, perhaps an invitation to visit the President. I would advise you to use your influence to

65

discourage that as well. You see, this man, Belov, he is unlike the other so-called dissidents. They are traitors. He, Belov, is a simple troublemaker—a hooligan. He borders on lunacy. Otherwise, he would not have been arrested in the first place. He has done certain things, said certain things that are disturbing beyond the usual criticism of our political system. Given a voice by your media, he may tend to make certain statements that would not be conducive to lessening tensions between us. He is not one of the ones that have had an organized international movement supporting or promoting his release. He is, as I say, inconsequential. As such, however, he is potentially dangerous to both of us."

Molenski's then concluded in a delivery that seemed to Strauss as if rehearsed or memorized. "In other words, my friend, do not permit the Soviet government's show of good faith to be used as a weapon against us. If you do, it could prove your undoing as well."

With that, Molenski abruptly patted Strauss on the arm and walked to the door and out.

As Strauss headed toward the Oval Office, he thought, *So that was it: Molenski didn't want the Soviets made to appear to their people and their satellite nations that U. S. policy on human rights bullied them into releasing a dissident. Belov was the Soviet's token to Packard. They expected reciprocity in the form of substantive discussions rather than moral ones at the Summit. Fine. Accordingly, they don't want this fellow Belov to become a media darling. Well, if I were in their shoes, I'd expect the same constraints. But what's all this about Belov being different? Not a traitor? A troublemaker? And why would the ramblings of this unknown hooligan who I never heard of and apparently, no one else has either, be perceived by Molenski to be dangerous?*

As Strauss reached the Oval Office, his mind was spinning a hologram of hazy possibilities, none of which revealed the clear picture Dr. Strauss wished to see.

Chapter Six

The night the Soviet dissident release story broke, Jerry Cooper had planned on watching the Kissinger interview on TV, ordering a pizza, having three or four shots of Jack Daniels, and getting a good night's sleep in order to get to the office early the next day. Packard had a press conference the next day, and that required note taking and Packard prepping. Instead, all he consumed was the booze. After the story ran on TV, his telephone rang incessantly, which put him in an even more irascible mood than normal when he got to work the following morning.

Walking into the Oval Office unannounced as usual, a privilege given to him alone, Cooper said, "Good morning, Mr. President." Taking his normal seat to the right of the President's desk, he said, "Ready for the sharks at eleven this morning?"

Instantly, Cooper knew Packard wasn't home.

After several minutes of silence, Packard said, "Jesus makes it quite clear: In Matthew chapter 5 verse 3, Jesus clearly says, 'The poor in spirit and the pure in heart will enter Heaven.'"

Packard assumed the praying hands pose and cast his closed eyes upward, and repeated slowly, "The poor in spirit and the pure in heart."

Lowering his head and opening his eyes, Packard looked at

Cooper, and said, "That's why this Summit conference must not fail. That's why I will need all the energy, all the inspiration that God can provide when I meet with Pavlovsky. Do you understand that, Jerr?"

Perhaps it was the lack of sleep, or too much Jack, but Cooper felt oddly out of balance, with a sense that something has changed. He replied acerbically, "No, sir, I do not. What I know is we've got a press conference coming up, and I've got to prepare you for it, especially since a major development has occurred overnight."

Like a return to the body after a near death experience, Packard jolted as if slam-dunked back into reality. With that patented smile his evangelical followers loved, the one which Cooper labeled his "shit-eatin' grin," he said, "I guess I've confused you, Jerr. Read Revelation tonight, okay? Now let's get going."

Questions that Cooper anticipated would be asked by the press were written out on the yellow legal pad affixed to a clipboard on his lap. After all the years together, they had the system down pat. Cooper talked; Packard listened. Press prep time was a chore Cooper relished. It made him feel like a producer again.

"They are going to go heavy on the economy, probably in the beginning," Cooper began. "The latest figures including today's wholesale price index are on your podium. Emphasize the downward trend in unemployment for black teenagers. The number is circled in green. Thank business leaders for finally getting your message about the need to hire black youth. After you do that, quickly take another question and maybe no one will pick up on the rise in white teenage unemployment. If they do, I've written some quip lines. Get on top of the sound of the laughing and use it as a bridge to the next question. Remember, all the joke lines are printed in red by subject just like always at the left corner of the podium."

Sitting with his feet propped up on the pullout slab of his desk and his chair tilted about sixty degrees horizontal, the President listened carefully. Cooper's coaching had brought him too far too well for him to ignore these sessions.

"Any questions, so far, sir?" Cooper asked.

Packard just shook his head no.

"Great. Now, if CBS gets a shot at you, they'll most likely ask you about more arms shipments to Saudi Arabia. They put something on last night about our selling more planes to the Saudis 'according to an informed source at the White House'. I don't know how they can continually put on erroneous information and credit it to so called 'informed sources', but you…"

"It's true," said the voice from the reclining chair.

At that moment, Jerry Cooper understood why he was feeling like his tires needed rotating. The rules had changed. His first urge was to shout, *"What the fuck is going on, you stupid son-of-a-bitch?"* However, you didn't handle Packard like that.

Collecting himself, taking a deep breath, then exhaling, Cooper said, "That is an alteration of our previous position, is it not, sir? One that we publicly stated!"

Still nearly horizontal, the President replied, " Jerr, I'm sorry I didn't tell you I changed my mind. As you know Strauss has wanted me to take a position in favor of selling planes to the Saudis, and brought the subject up again yesterday. And after I prayed over it, I acceded to his position."

Cooper's mind raced. In and of itself, the Saudi issue was not crucial to him. But the occurrence did demonstrate a sudden sea change in the current between he and Packard and that was disturbing. Had Packard decided to cancel the deal they made in the City Café in Dubuque Iowa years earlier that there would be no other gods before him? Must he now vie not only with David Strauss, but with the word of the Lord, as well?

"Alright, sir. When asked about the arms sale, I strongly suggest you set a viable *political* response to the inevitable question of why you changed your mind."

The President remained silent.

"Now, the biggie. I'd bet that Sam Donaldson asks what effect the release of the Soviet dissident will have on the Summit, or something to that effect," Cooper said.

The President turned his head to look at Cooper and up-righted his chair and himself behind his desk. After pressing a button on his phone, a woman's voice immediately said, " Yes, Mr. President?"

"Send Dr. Strauss in, please, Mrs. Thoman."

In an instant, the door to the Oval Office opened and in walked the man who once told adoring reporters that when he first heard the song, "He's Got the Whole World In His Hands," he assumed they were singing about him. It was the kind of quip that made the press love him and his staff ulcerate.

"Good morning, Mr. President, I come with news," Strauss said proudly. He nodded to Cooper, who simply said, "David."

Strauss always had difficulty concealing his resentment of Cooper's most favored status with the President. *How could a person with no hidden agenda and no paranoia occupy such a revered place?* he fretted.

"What is it, David? Did you meet with the Ruskie? Packard asked.

Strauss detested Packard's favorite appellation for any Soviet official; but he ignored it.

"Just as I presumed, Mr. President, the Soviets are releasing a dissident—a minor one—but nonetheless a dissident, as an pre-Summit indication of their sensitivity to our objection to their policy regarding human rights. Now they figure you and Premier Pavlovsky can move on to more pragmatic issues."

"In other words, they're trying to buy you off, Mr. President," Cooper said.

"Whatdaya mean, Jerr?" The President asked.

Cooper said, "They let some nobody go and expect you to bow and say, 'Oh thank you, thank you. Now I won't bring the subject up any more. Now, what do you good people want to discuss?'"

Strauss fumed. "There is a difference in diplomacy between acts of good faith and bribery, Mr. President. Your assistant here seems to believe the President of the United States can be bribed!"

"Shove it up your ass, Strauss. You know damn well that's not what I'm saying," Cooper shot back.

Jerry Cooper cared deeply about the issue of human rights. Because freedom of religion was an aspect of the issue, Packard easily and ardently bought into it.

"What this shows, Mr. President," Cooper began, "is that our human rights position has had an impact on the Soviets," and turning to Strauss, he finished, "despite the strong criticism you've received from our enemies, as well as some of our friends."

Piqued by Cooper's subtle cut, which went right by the President, Strauss cleared his throat and, in a voice somewhat more thickly accented, said "There is no question, Mr. President, that *our* attachment of the issue of human rights to *our* foreign policy has indeed had a profound effect on the Soviets. We should not overlook, however, the fact that although they recognize how sincere we are, the practical and pragmatic problems of the world are as critical to the Soviet Union as they are to the United States."

Cooper knew that that sonorous voice from the mouth of the master of ambiguity was speaking as much for his benefit as it was for the President's. What he did not know, could not know, is that David Strauss and Anatoli Molenski had just privately colluded an understanding to maintain control of events connected with the release of the dissident, and prohibit it from becoming larger than a Soviet diplomatic courtesy.

Throughout the ensuing polemic between Cooper and Strauss, the President sat behind his desk looking back and forth at each man as they spoke. He was trying to keep up.

They both looked at their leader for a reaction. He said, "I concur."

Strauss glanced quickly at Cooper. In an instant, their eyes shared a secret cognition. Both were aware that when conversation became too subtle, too sophisticated or nuanced, Packard would say, "I concur." Whether he really concurred or didn't was irrelevant. It was a way of saying something when he had to, or of terminating the conversation.

Nonetheless, for Cooper and Strauss, Packard's "I concur" was one of those rare albeit satisfying moments when opposites caught in the heat of rhetoric unite.

The President then added, "What we know is one lucky soul is getting out of that God forsaken place, rather, I should I say, place where God has been forsaken." He smiled, obviously pleased with his juxtaposition. Then he asked, "By the way, do we know who it is, David?"

"The man is named Yuri Belov," Strauss said. "He seems to be different, according to Molenski; not your normal dissident. The best I could understand from Ambassador Molenski is that he's more of a troublemaker because of some ideas he has rather than an insurrectionist."

"Does that name ring a bell with you, Jerr?"

Cooper had researched the dissident file when he arrived at the White House that morning and found nothing on Yuri Belov.

"No, sir, and that's precisely my point. They release a third-rate dissident, one even their Ambassador can't describe as more than a troublemaker, and say 'whoosh' and expect the human rights issue to disintegrate."

The President thought for a moment then pressed the same button that produced David Strauss twenty minutes ago.

"Yes, Mr. President?"

"Mrs. Thoman, find General McKenna and tell him I want to see him at once."

"Thank you, Mr. President."

Packard said, "If anyone knows who Bel...Bel...What's his name again?"

"Belov. Yuri Belov," Strauss responded.

Packard smiled confidently, and said, " If anyone knows who Belov is, McKenna does. Right, boys?"

"I'm certain that is true, Mr. President," Strauss replied.

"After all, Jerr, here it is 10:45, the press is out there with their loins girded, and we don't know diddlie-squat about the man."

The President's colloquialisms always made Strauss start chewing on his fingernails. To irritate him more, Cooper added, "Nope, Mr. President, we don't know a hill of beans about him."

Just then, the door to the Oval Office opened quickly, and the President looked up gratefully. Cooper started writing on a yellow pad. Strauss started chewing on his fingernails.

Attired in his customary black suit, black tie, mirror polished black shoes, the diminutive man snapped a crisp salute, and in his pinched, nasal voice said, "Good Morning, Mr. President. "

"Good morning, General McKenna, the President responded slowly.

Abruptly glancing at Cooper and Strauss, as if he had a picture of them in bed with the other's wife, he said, "Cooper. Strauss." He accentuated the sound of "rauss" in Strauss whenever he said the name.

Strauss nodded, and Cooper said a cool good morning to General Andrew Jackson McKenna, the Director of the Central Intelligence Agency. Like a bandy rooster changing directions, McKenna turned and sat down in a chair to the side of the President's desk. He had been holding a red file folder in his left hand. Laying it in his lap, he raised his head in anticipation of his Commander In Chief's orders.

"Gentlemen," the President began, "the question is: Who is Yuri Belov? What do we know about him? What do I say to the press in fifteen minutes? Do you have anything on him, General?"

Glancing at Cooper, then Strauss, McKenna smirked and said, "I certainly do, Mr. President. I do indeed."

Neither Cooper nor Strauss was surprised. When Albert

Packard was elected, the one appointment his right-wing evangelical supporters insisted they designate was the Director of the CIA. General Andrew Jackson McKenna was their man. McKenna was not only the head spy for, but Strauss suspected, *of* the United States.

General McKenna methodically opened the red file folder, obviously enjoying his advantage over Cooper, and especially, Strauss.

Cooper said, "General, can we get on with it? The President doesn't have much time."

McKenna bristled; his body seemed to hop in the chair.

"I'll proceed with haste, Mr. President," McKenna shot back. "This file contains information on all the reported Soviet dissidents. Dissidents such as Sakharov, Bukovsky and Nudel have rather lengthy dossiers. They are quite active and have support groups petitioning for their freedom all over the free world. When we come to Belov, Yuri, we find only a newspaper clipping, one that is five years old, from the *Jerusalem Post*."

"Wait just a minute, General McKenna," the President interrupted. "That's all you have? One five-year-old newspaper clipping? Is that the best you have to offer, General?" The President's face reddened.

McKenna bolted out of his chair and snapped his five foot four frame to attention.

Cooper and Strauss savored the moment. Each would have relished the dressing down more had not Cooper been concerned about the imminence of the press conference and Strauss concerned with the imperative to finesse every aspect of the Belov in accordance with his pact with Molenski.

Walking over to the still vertically prostrate General, Strauss asked, "May I see the article on Belov, General?"

McKenna's eyes darted to the President for approval. At first uncertain what the puppy-dog look meant, it finally registered in him. "Oh," the President said, "yes, of course. Show it to him, General. And, would you mind sitting down?"

McKenna saluted and returned to his chair, poking the clipping at Strauss without looking at him.

Strauss read the article. Nodding his head in agreement with himself, he said, "Just as we thought, Mr. President. Belov is a nobody."

"David, have Jerr read it, please." The President said.

McKenna pursed his thin lips.

Cooper read it quickly, and said, "Looks about like a third string dissident. I agree with David. Here, you take a look."

Taking the clipping in his huge, earth worn hand, the President read out loud:

> JERUSALEM (WPA) – KGB officials arrested a man in Red Square last night following a speech in which he denounced the denial of religious and human rights to the Soviet people. The man was identified as Yuri Belov, described as appearing about 30 years old.
>
> Sources say he condemned "atheistic communism suffocating the soul of Russia." He reportedly said that those who are oppressed will be as free birds while their oppressors would lose their nests.
>
> According to POST sources, crowds gathered for the fifth consecutive night in Red Square to hear Belov speak. As the plain-clothes officers took him into custody, Belov was reported to have pleaded with his followers to do no violence on his behalf.
>
> TASS, the official Soviet news agency, issued a brief statement saying, "Yuri Belov, a persistent hooligan, was taken into custody last night after delivering an obscene speech laced with threats against the Soviet people."
>
> Prior to last night's events, Yuri Belov was an unknown to those who monitor the dissident movement inside the Soviet Union. The National

Conference on Soviet Jewry and the National Jewish
Community Relations Advisory Council in New York
report that they have absolutely no data on Belov
whatsoever.

A top Israeli official, who asked not to be named,
indicated that since Belov is not from the academic,
literary or scientific community in the USSR, his
chance of mercy under the Soviet system is slim. As
the official put it, "It is easier for them to get rid of a
self proclaimed prophet than a Nobel Prize winner."

The President looked at McKenna, stood and said, "Anything
else?"

"Just this, Mr. President," McKenna said in his nasal staccato
voice, "I'm not quite certain I'd accept the theory put forth here
today that Belov is a token dissident set free to appease you. I'm
not sure I'd readily accept that, Mr. President."

"What do you mean, General? Please get to the point. Jerr, it's
almost time, isn't it? Holy Jehosephat, General, if you have
anything of substance, say it, for goodness sake," Packard said,
as he headed for his bathroom.

"All right, I'll say it. I'll say it straight away. I think there is a
likelihood that this Yuri Belov fellow, or whatever his real name
is, may be a Soviet agent!"

Strauss hit his forehead with the heel of his hand while
closing his eyes. Cooper began gathering his notes.

McKenna turned to Strauss, and screamed, "Beat your breast,
Strauss! But let me tell you something!"

The President glanced in the mirror to check his hair. Perfect.
He emerged heading for his door. Everyone stood while
McKenna ran to get there first to have his say before everyone
left.

"This administration, and every previous administration,
deals with the Russians as if both parties were of honorable
intent. The Communists are no different now than when Lenin

wrote his Manifesto. They are out to destroy us, gentlemen. *Out to destroy us!* Belov may very well be a trained, highly sophisticated KGB agent under the guise of being a dissident. The lack of information about him only makes the theory more plausible."

The President put his hand on McKenna's arm and gently moved him away from the door to the Oval Office. "Excuse me, gentlemen," he said. Motioning to Cooper, he said, "Let's go, Jerr."

"Would you like me to write out a response to the Belov matter, Mr. President, Strauss said anxiously.

Packard's man Friday had already done it and placed the index card in Packard's coat pocket during McKenna's tirade.

"No, thanks, David. I'm sure Jerr's got me covered," the President said. "We'll talk more later."

Strauss clawed at his fingernails. McKenna saluted as the President headed for the East Room of the White House for the press conference.

"Mr. President, would you comment on the Soviet announcement that they intend to release one of the dissidents?"

"Sure, Sam. When we came into office eleven months ago, we committed this nation's foreign policy not only to the practical best interest of America, but to our spiritual best interest as well. We said that the human rights of every man, woman and child in the world are of concern to us. And we urged consideration of those human rights by other governments when dealing with the United States. Although the Soviet Union has accused us of meddling in their domestic affairs, they were getting the message." At this point, Cooper had printed, DO THE DADDY MULE STORY NOW. "Or, as my daddy used to say when he'd smack our ol' mule a lick or two on the behind when he'd get ornery and stubborn, 'He might not agree with me, but he sure knows my point of view!'" After pausing for a few snickers among the press from this Packardism, he changed his facial expression, as the card said to do, and adopted what Cooper called his "Uncle Sam face."

"Seriously, with the release of Mr. Yuri Belov—incidentally, that's his name—the Soviets are demonstrating their acknowledgement of human rights as a viable international issue. Frankly, I feel that a new day is dawning between our two nations. A day of mutual respect for our people and theirs, a day of inalienable freedom and dignity is at hand. As I prepare for the Summit, I feel we can negotiate the harsh realities of this world in an atmosphere of greater understanding. I commend them for their action; and so do all freedom loving people of the world."

Off to the side of the stage, stood a beaming Jerry Cooper. Moments like these reminded him why he took the job, and why he remained, in spite of Packard's religious obsession. The electrical impulses that drew him to Packard and kept him aligned must have been hot enough to ignite at that moment. He would never have guessed that it was all about to change.

Pacing the floor of his office as he watched the President on television, Dr. David Strauss worried that today's statement would send the wrong message to his Soviet soul mate. Anatoli Molenski's words echoed in Strauss's mind. *Do not permit the Soviet government's show of good faith to be used as a weapon against us. If you do, it could prove your undoing as well.*

Part Two

Chapter Seven

Rabbi Julian Zoya was one of the most highly respected Rabbis of Vilna in 1941. His synagogue was not only a house of prayer, it was also a center for discussion of Talmudic and philosophic thought by most of the intelligentsia. To be included in the audience—not to mention in the discussion—of a Rabbi Zoya session was tantamount in Vilna to strolling the corridors of the Lyceum with Aristotle. Reb Zoya's fundamental position was that man is capable of incredible good and incredible evil, and that God intervenes in the affairs of the world when man does more evil than good.

Unlike her father, Ksana Zoya was neither curious about the world nor philosophic about its unfolding. She had a deep and abiding faith in God and her religion, which she accepted rather than questioned. Neither a theorist nor a sophist, Ksana's consummate and unambiguous outlook on life was, what is, is.

In part, her philosophy—or lack of it—was born of her lot. Her mother died of tuberculosis when Ksana was twelve, and she became Rabbi Zoya's housekeeper and cook, as well as being Ksana, his child. As she grew and developed, her responsibilities to her father increased. His clothes, his robes and prayer shawls, his food, his tea, his wine, were all within the province of Ksana's world.

In spite of the responsibility of being Rabbi Julian Zoya's daughter and housekeeper, Ksana managed to finish high school in the top five of her class. She never studied much; at examination time she somehow recalled whatever she was lectured.

Ksana was lovely. So lovely, that boys of her age were put off by her. A grace, a gentle serenity, a natural calm constantly emanated from her. To sixteen-year old boys such a quality is disarming. To men: tantalizing.

When she was not at school, she was home preparing and doing for Rabbi Zoya. Other times, she would be at the synagogue teaching the young children the traditional Yiddish songs. She loved that part of her life the most. When the lessons were over, she would sing to the class some of the *dainos* –Lithuanian songs that have never been written down, some going back more than a thousand years. She had learned them from her mother. How the children's eyes would sparkle when they watched Ksana, with her chestnut hair pulled tightly back and wrapped into a bun, sing the ancient and simple songs in her clear, soothing voice. To them, she was as a movie star in their midst.

The ravage of Poland by Germany was the daily topic of conversation in Vilna in 1941. Two years earlier, Lithuania had signed a mutual security pact with Russia. A year later, Russia overthrew the democratic government of Lithuania and established a communist regime. The only value of living under Soviet communist oppression was the comparison to the alternative. Some, who managed to get across the border from Poland — either by bribery or luck — told the horror stories. The rumors, the speculations, the idle gossip monopolized the conversation of Vilna's populace.

"We are safe, aren't we, Reb Zoya? A student asked. "After all, Stalin has a non-aggression pact with Hitler."

Reb Zoya, who was ordinarily apolitical, looked over the top of his small glasses, and responded, "When a leopard makes a pact with a lion, the agreement is automatically invalid."

July 12, 1941 was Ksana's seventeenth birthday. It was also the Shabbat, the Sabbath. Reb Zoya remembered it was the Shabbat, but forgot it was his daughter's birthday. Like most scholars and philosophers who contemplate the world, the needs of those closest to them go often unattended.

"Did you remember the wine for the Kiddush cup?" Reb Zoya asked, as he dabbed his bearded mouth with his linen napkin.

"Yes, Poppa. Everything is in order. Did you enjoy the chicken?" Ksana asked.

"Chicken's chicken," he said dismissively. "Now hurry or we'll be late for synagogue."

Ksana had already taken most of the Shabbat dishes off the table and put them into the sink. She would wash them when Shabbat was over. She didn't have to change clothes for shul; she was already wearing a crisp white linen dress that one of the women made for her last week. Ksana loved the way she felt in it. Her breasts were more than ample for her graceful young body and somehow this dress subtly outlined them in a way that made her feel blossomy.

Maybe it was the dress, or the magic of her birthday, or maybe even the Shabbat—which temporarily made the awful rumors subside—whatever it was induced Ksana to tug several times on the coat sleeve of her father just as he was about to open the front door of their house. The unexpected gesture nearly made him drop his white tallit bag, his prayer shawl.

Turning with a look of surprise and impatience, he said, "What is it, daughter? What is it?"

Ksana Zoya looked up at her venerated father and placed her delicate hand on his face. Her hand felt warm on his bearded cheek. Reb Zoya was taken aback for an instant, but the calm emanating from her countenance mellowed his anxiety.

She said, "Good Shabbat, Poppa. I love you."

Reb Zoya took her hand from his face and pressed it into both of his. Slowly bringing her hand enveloped in his to his lips, he gently kissed it. Then he said, softly, "I love you too, Ketzally. Good Shabbat to you, too."

They stood for a silent moment looking at one another in the light that magnificently glows when two hearts touch.

"Come now, daughter. What will the congregation say if the Rebbe is late for Shabbat?"

Ksana didn't care that her father broke the moment and became Reb Zoya again. He had just given her birthday present. How she loved to hear him call her Ketzally, the pet name he used to call her when she was a child. It said so much this time: I love you. I appreciate you. I need you. You're a good girl. Happy birthday. You're smart. You're beautiful. You're everything you want to be and feel. It was all conveyed in "Ketzally."

Ksana nearly danced across the courtyard from their home to the synagogue. She was so happy.

The crowd milling around outside the synagogue caught her up short. *Maybe it's too warm inside*, she thought. *No, there's something else.* She didn't like the feeling. Where was the magic she felt a heartbeat ago?

Reb Zoya didn't notice them as soon as Ksana did. His mind was probably discoursing on a transcendent Talmudic issue with Rabbi Akiba, who was to Reb Zoya as the wind to a sail.

Moshe Kaminsky noticed them coming and ran up to them. "Reb Zoya, Reb Zoya, the Germans are already in Kaunas and Kaisladorys." Moshe suddenly pressed his hand to his abdomen. His hernia hurt from running. He stayed in the Rabbi's face as he continued walking the rest of the way with the Zoyas. "The Russians have nearly evacuated Lithuania. How's that for our great defenders!" he shouted, while grimacing at the pain below his gut.

By the time Reb Zoya and Ksana reached the steps to the synagogue entrance, the throng was milling around them. Their voices intermeshing into the likeness of a babbling chant, the words indistinguishable.

Finally, Lev Belov, an outstanding young Polish soccer player ran up to the top of the steps of the ancient synagogue and shouted, "Quiet, everyone! Quiet!" Lev had escaped from Lomsia disguised as a nun the day before the Germans invaded. His presence was commanding. The chanting faded to tacit.

Lev spoke: "Listen. The Germans should be in Vilna within hours—at least by morning. You know what they did in Poland. They will do the same here…to you, to me, to us all."

The indiscernible voices started building again. Belov caught the fortissimo in mid-swerve. "Listen, for God's sake! Listen to me! The women will be relatively safe at first. I'm going to the forest, and I want every able bodied man to go with me. There we will be safe. And we can fight back! WHO'S WITH ME?"

Immediately five men in their early twenties ran up the steps and joined Lev. Animated and boisterous arguments ensued between husbands and wives, fathers and mothers and sons. Then a few more joined, maybe twenty, thirty in all, no more.

"Anyone else?" Belov demanded.

Silence. Then weeping.

Belov and his followers jaunted down the steps, pausing beside Reb Zoya and Ksana. They bowed their heads, and the Rebbe extended his arms over the warriors, and, in a solemn tone, chanted, "May the Lord bless thee and keep thee. May the Lord life up His Countenance and shine upon thee; and be gracious unto thee, and grant thee peace."

They jogged off before his arms lowered, vanishing in to the twilight to the accompaniment of sobbing and pitiful good-byes.

After they were out of sight, Rabbi Zoya ascended the steps of the synagogue slowly. Turning to the rattled assemblage below him, he said, softly, "My friends, it is the Shabbat. Shall we enter our synagogue and celebrate the Sabbath?" He turned, Ksana beside him, and walked in.

For one reason or another, many fled to their homes. Others, perhaps one hundred and fifty, remained at the synagogue.

After opening the service in the prescribed manner with the wine Kiddush, Rabbi Zoya added an improvised prayer for the band of partisans who followed Lev Belov into the forest, referring to them as Maccabees.

Ksana sat in her usual place upstairs with the women, the pew nearest the pulpit. Remembering how good she had felt earlier, she wondered if she would ever feel that way again.

However, her feelings of personal misgivings dissolved rapidly as she became aware, first in a subtle way, then with escalating clarity of a unique and splendid spectacle below. Standing behind the pulpit was that same frail man that had always stood there. Yet, this was a different man! She watched him as if enraptured. With that rare and noble blend of humility and resolve, seemingly undaunted by fear, Rabbi Julian Zoya was calmly ushering in the Sabbath. Ksana marveled at the sight of that strength. Wise, he'd always looked. Thoughtful, contemplative, intense...yes. But strong? Strident, but never strong—until that Shabbat of July 12, 1941.

She looked around the synagogue and saw some of the men below beating their breasts, and women upstairs softly whimpering. Then her eyes returned to her father, and again, even more than before, she saw that special dignified strength. The discovery made her smile and just at that instant he looked up to her with a gentleness, as if to say, "Ketzally."

Suddenly the doors to the sanctuary crashed open. Ksana looked down and saw a squad of black uniformed SS troopers storm down the aisles. A shriek from the congregation reverberated against the synagogue walls. One man tried to run out, only to meet the butt of an SS rifle crushing his nose. As he fell, the soldier viciously kicked him in the groin. He screamed. Blood spurted from his nose as he lay in a heap, his body jerking as if it were being poked by an invisible cattle prod.

The soldiers ran up to the pulpit and aimed their rifles at the men, who froze as in a still life. Several of the troopers raced upstairs to the women's section. The women wailed in assorted sirens.

After a moment of holding their captives at bay, an SS colonel strode slowly down the aisle and up to the bema. His presence stilled the noise in a collective gasp of breath. Tall, lean, confident and typically Aryan, he said nothing for a moment — standing with his black leather gloved hands on his hips surveying his catch. Then, he turned to Reb Zoya. "Come here, Jew pig."

Rabbi Julian Zoya slowly approached the colonel and stood before him.

Suddenly, in a wild frenzy, the SS colonel grabbed Reb Zoya by the beard with his left hand and began brutally smacking his face. First forehand, then backhand, forehand, backhand, again, and again, and again. As the congregation gasped, the soldiers raised their rifles and clicked the bolts. The blows continued for at least three minutes until the face of the Rabbi was a bloody mat of skin and beard.

Upstairs, Ksana screamed, "Poppa, Poppa, Poppa." She grabbed her mouth to try to stop the vomit. When the SS colonel finally stopped slapping, he glanced at his hand painted with Reb Zoya's blood. With wild eyes, he screamed at the Rabbi, "Jew pig, how dare you bloody the uniform of a German officer?"

Walking back to the ark containing the Torah scrolls, he reached in, grabbed one up, and brought it back to the front of the pulpit where Rabbi Zoya was still standing, although unrecognizable. The colonel flipped off the silver amulets covering the wooden handles, yanked off the felt cord securing the scroll, and pulled away the silk maroon cover. Then, he unraveled the sacred Torah on the floor of the bema. With a flick of his wrist, as if directing traffic, he shouted, "Lie down on it, Jew pig!"

Reb Zoya's lacerated mouth began uttering the *Sh'ma*, the

sacred affirmation of one God, over and over. He desperately wanted to die with the sacred affirmation of one God on his lips. He didn't hear the colonel's command.

Infuriated with rage, the colonel pushed the Rabbi down on top of the unraveled Torah and kicked him over to one end. Gripping the handles, he wrapped that end of the parchment around Rabbi Zoya, rolling him over and over inside the scroll until it tightly enveloped him. All that was visible was a bloody head on one end mumbling the Sh'ma and knees to the feet on the other. The SS colonel tied the cord tightly around the center of his package and stood it on its feet. It fell with a thud! He stood it up again. It fell over again, and this time the soldiers laughed. One more attempt to prop the human scroll on its feet failed and the soldiers laughed louder. The swollen lips of Reb Zoya barely continued to affirm God.

The congregation sat frozen by the horror. Upstairs, Ksana's face was buried in the heaving shoulder of Moshe Kaminsky's wife. A steady "Poppa, Poppa" came from her trembling lips.

On the bema, the colonel was feeling fatigued from his ordeal and was tiring of the sport. Disappointed that the package wouldn't stand upright for further torture and humiliation, he withdrew his revolver from its black holster, put his polished boot on top of the Torah as it lay murmuring on the bema floor, aimed, and fired three loud rounds into it.

The Torah bled.

Standing over his kill, his gun smoking and his jack-boot mounted atop his prize, in the pose of an African game hunter who has just bagged a cat, the SS colonel turned his head to face the gaping congregates.

"This is your leader, ladies and gentlemen." His voice had a shrill bite to it. He spoke slowly and enunciated each word carefully. "He lies under my boot as a symbol of the new order. The glorious German nation needs to be cleansed from such trash as this."

Waving his pistol toward the heap on the floor of the bema,

he motioned to the squad of SS guarding the audience and bellowed, "Now take this garbage out to the gutter and burn it!"

Two of Germany's finest stepped forward and fixed their bayonets to their weapons. Standing over the Torah-wrapped remains of Reb Zoya, one soldier speared it cleanly through the neck, the other through the groin. Hoisting up the blood-oozing scroll above their heads on the third count of a whispered "Eins, Zwei, Drei," the two soldiers marched down the steps of the bema, turned, and marched down the aisle of the synagogue with Reb Zoya skewered to their bayonets.

For the members of Reb Zoya's synagogue, the night of July 12, 1941 was the start of their nightmare.

For Rabbi Julian Zoya, it was the night he met Rabbi Akiba.

Within days of the *Einsatzgruppen* invasion, thousands upon thousands of Jews in Vilna and hundreds of other towns and tiny houses called *shtetls* in Lithuania disappeared in raids. It was said the Jews were taken away for work. By mid-July, reports of mass executions of the Jews at Ponary filtered back. In September, the SS rounded up Vilna's remaining Jewish population and confined them to a ghetto.

Among those forced to live in the crowded ghetto was Ksana Zoya. She lived with the Kaminskys since her father was martyred. The constant threat of death, the deprivation of food, clothing and medicine plus the shock of events did not permit her the luxury of grief. By day, she taught the children in one of the ghetto schools. With the children, she found some solace and usefulness and a sense of removal from reality. Teaching the children about their heritage, Ksana felt inspired and somehow strangely linked to the Maccabees and Simon Bar Kochba. Where only weeks before her life totally revolved around keeping her father's house, she now found herself curiously fascinated with events of Jewish history just before and after the life of Christ.

In the evening, she would curl up in her bed in the cubicle

provided for her in the cramped apartment of the Kaminskys, and study the lesson she would teach her children the next day. Always hungry, and with the damp cold of Vilna's winter approaching, her last thoughts would be that of her father. She found it amazing how much of their conversations and his teachings she retained.

One vivid recollection originated two years earlier while Reb Zoya was preparing his sermon for the holiday of *Shavuot* on the responsibility of maintaining one's Jewishness amid adversity. He had looked across the room at her, and said, "Ketzally, do you know what our name, Zoya, means?"

"No, Poppa," she said, while drying the last supper dish. "What does it mean?"

"Zoya means life. Life!" he said, a little louder. "Always choose life when presented with the alternative. Remember. Life. Always." He returned to his sermon; she to her dish. A forgotten moment suddenly remembered became the cherished imprint in Ksana's heart every night before drifting into the freedom of sleep, there in the Vilna ghetto.

Late in the day on the eve of Yom Kippur, October 1, 1941, the ghetto suddenly swarmed with German storm troopers. The Kaminskys and Ksana had just finished the last of their chicken-less chicken soup. Moshe Kaminsky had no sooner said, "Let us have a good Yom Kippur fast," when the door flung open, and a burly Lithuanian with a club hollered something about work permits and moved them out into the street.

Hundreds of others were already standing in long rows two abreast. German soldiers and some SS stood nearby, obviously in charge, using the Lithuanians as their surrogates.

Slowly the lines began to move forward. Moshe Kaminsky, a printer by profession, half turned his slouched back to make sure that his wife and Ksana were behind him. He was walking with Gershon Spetzler, who ran a florist shop before the German occupation.

"Turn around, Moshe," his wife scolded in a firm whisper. Moshe smiled at her. The scolding from his wife was life affirming.

Dark had settled over Vilna that Yom Kippur eve as the seemingly endless row passed through the old city, known as the Jerusalem of Europe because of it's veneration for learning and study, and out through the gate in the direction of Ponary.

It was an eerie, surrealistic procession, with thousands of Jews holding candles to light their way as darkness rapidly descended.

Meanwhile, the Lithuanian guards kept the pace moving through the darkness with shouts of "Keep moving; we'll soon be there; keep moving."

Someone asked a guard, "Where are we going?"

"To re-stamp your work passes, " he answered, without looking at the questioner.

Frequently, a German soldier would thunder toward the rear of the column on a motorcycle; then moments later, he would return in the other direction.

"Shame on them for riding on Yom Kippur," Moshe Kaminsky said to Gershon Spetzler.

"Let's hope God doesn't forgive them," Gershon replied. Both laughed to themselves.

Ksana was wearing the linen dress she wore the fateful Sabbath of her 17th birthday. Although the Nazis had turned her father's synagogue into a latrine, she dressed up for Yom Kippur. She appeared strangely serene and lovely amid the macabre procession. Hearing the sobbing children and being unable to comfort them caused her the most concern.

Suddenly, as if drifting back from the front of the plodding column on a stream of warm air, the soothing strains of a familiar chant floated through them. Gershon looked at Moshe. Both were startled. It was *Kol Nidre!* Someone up ahead was singing the traditional chant of the ages for the Day of Atonement at the top of his voice. Instantly the melody touched a dormant fiber in everyone, and Ksana sensed a mist of hope envelop the motley procession. After a moment, Ksana and the others were humming the melody as the anonymous Cantor chanted that most sacred prayer in Jewish liturgy.

Not even the revving engine of the German motorcycle racing toward the front of the procession penetrated the cosmic fabric woven from soul to soul by the mystical Kol Nidre.

As the Cantor's voice rode the musical crescendo to the final passage of the ancient chant, instead of culminating with the Sh'ma, his voice suddenly became a shrieking scream. The movement of the procession halted involuntarily from the jolt of the piercing sound, which rendered the Kol Nidre incomplete. Another scream—not as loud, nor as shrill. A moan. Then, nothing.

Ksana, perhaps a few others, finished the Sh'ma. The seemingly impregnable mist of hope collected and returned to where hope comes from. Certainly not from Vilna. Prodded by the clubs and shouting of the Lithuanian guards, the column began to trudge forward on the path through the forest.

Ksana looked down at him as she passed. So did Moshe and Gershon. Mrs. Kaminsky couldn't bear it and turned her head away. He lay in the fetal position on the ground, beaten to death.

Michael Frankel was the best tenor in Vilna. Everyone believed that the sixty eight-year-old artist had the ability to perform at La Scala and the Metropolitan Opera. Michael was happy to just sing opera in Vilna. God gave him a voice that he used to the fullest, and to the end.

"His greatest performance," Moshe tearfully said, as he *schlepped* by him.

"Flawless," agreed Gershon, the florist. "Flawless."

"At least he knew his brother escaped to America, thank God," Moshe said.

Ksana felt spirited with a strange energy after looking at Michael Frankel curled up on the ground. She thought: *Such a fine man. So talented. He was always so kind to me. He used to tell me I sang pretty. Imagine, Michael Frankel, the Vilna opera star, telling simple Ksana Zoya, the Rebbe's daughter, she sang pretty! How kind. And so brave. To dare sing the Kol Nidre tonight—now! With the Nazis in front and behind us, and every thug in Vilna to the side of us, Michael Frankel had the courage to sing the Kol Nidre—tonight—just to lift our spirits. Poppa would have been proud of him. He tried to live—or did he? Maybe he knew he'd be killed for daring to sing a Jewish song. Or maybe he just dared to, whatever the consequences. Perhaps he was telling us to live! Was that it Michael? Were you chanting the Kol Nidre as a message for us to live? Or to try to live? Did you know we're going to Ponary to die, Michael? My God! We are going to die! We're walking in a funeral procession to our own funeral! God, Michael, is that what Kol Nidre meant tonight? To live? Ksana Zoya, live!*

Mrs. Kaminsky didn't even see her flee; she tore away that quickly. The Lithuanian guard saw her though and turned to take out after her. By then the column was five miles from Ponary and death. The woods were thick with underbrush. The leafless trees stood like grotesque demons enticing her into the pitch-black night.

She ran with the swiftness of a gazelle. The stocky Lithuanian guard was no match for her, and he dared not call for help lest his German superiors beat him for negligence. Letting a Jew escape Ponary was punishable by death at Ponary. After running several meters, the Lithuanian cussed and headed back toward the column. He'd beat someone's skull in for restitution.

Through the underbrush and thicket ran Ksana. "Live, Live, Live" was the rhythm she ran to. With no idea where she was headed or how far she had been running, Ksana realized that she had the oddest, almost intoxicating sensation. It was of total freedom. Never, even before the Nazis came, had she felt quite as totally liberated. Further and further she ran, urged on by Joshua, Bar Kochba, Judah Maccabee, Reb Zoya and Michael Frankel.

Finally, the four months of mal-nourishment suffered inside

the Vilna ghetto caught up with her and drowned the energy rush of the moment. Ksana collapsed with exhaustion in a bed of leaves. She was breathing so loudly she thought the whole of Vilna would awaken.

Suddenly, she heard a movement in the brush behind her. *Was it an animal?* She could hear her heart pounding beneath her heaving chest. *The dress! The white dress!* she moaned silently. More rustling movement, now to the left of her. Her head darted toward the sound. She tried to stifle the noise of her panting breath by putting both hands over her mouth, but she grew quickly dizzy and put them instead over the place she thought her heart was. She sensed people! *Nazis? Lithuanians?* She imagined the worst for herself if she was discovered. Her father's battered face atop the Torah zoomed in and out of her mind. She dare not move; dare not blink. The movement came closer. The sounds of leaves and twigs breaking under booted feet became louder. Now she could make out the silhouette of a figure with a rifle—and another—and another!

Dear God, help me.

The largest of the three figures approached the leaf bed and stopped a short distance from her feet. The other two took positions about ten yards on each side of her and pointed their rifles at her. Ksana began to whisper the Sh'ma. For a brief instant, the dark clouds parted, exposing her larger captor to the dim light of the moon. Wide-eyed, Ksana looked up toward heaven; then suddenly she erupted into an outpouring of tears.

Lev Belov crouched down beside her and took her into his arms. Gently rocking her back and forth as she wept, he turned to his two companions.

"It's okay. It's Rabbi Zoya's daughter.

The two approached her and leaned down. One offered her a sip of water from his canteen. The other held out a piece of bread.

"I can't," Ksana said, between sobs. "It's Yom Kippur."

The three partisans broke into spirited laughter.

After a minute, Lev said, "Now that God has saved you from a bullet, I think He would be pleased that you don't die of starvation."

Ksana took the bread, said the proper blessing, and ate it ravenously.

Still kneeling beside her, Lev asked, "After all you've seen and been through, why do you still say a blessing for the bread?"

Retrieving a small sliver of crust that fell in her lap and putting into her mouth, Ksana replied with a slight smile, "Because the Germans are doing what they are doing doesn't mean that God approves."

From that moment on Ksana entered Lev's heart. He didn't try to understand the way he suddenly felt for her. Self-analysis was a luxury for those with predictable lives, not for the hunted on the outskirts of death.

Since leaving Vilna moments before the Nazis arrived in July, Lev and his band became partisans, living in and off the forest. His group comprised about twenty-five in number; among those, three were women. Their goal: disruption. As a partisan, he had ambushed German troop carriers, sabotaged rail lines, blown up bridges and other acts that created disorder among those for whom order was preeminent. His zeal and courage would have gladdened the heart of Judah Maccabee.

That night in the forest, while kneeling in a bed of moist leaves in front of seventeen-year-old Ksana Zoya, the Zealot was momentarily a lamb.

"What's your name, anyway?" Lev asked, while pretending to issue an order.

"Ksana."

"Mine's..."

"Yours is Lev Belov," she said, softly.

"Yes," said Lev tenderly, his pretense disarmed by the grace of his companion. "Are you feeling better?"

"Much better, Lev."

Ksana now had a chance to look at him. His face was closer

than any man's had ever been to her aside from her father. *It is a good face,* she thought. He was motionless before her, as if entranced. She roamed his face with her eyes, which kept returning to his nose. *It must have been broken,* she thought. *Must have happened during a soccer match,* she concluded. It curved slightly to the right from the center to the tip—not much, so slightly one wouldn't notice ordinarily. It gave him a sort of rugged yet gentle look. She wanted to brush his light brown locks away from his forehead. *His hair is much too wild,* she decided *but what else could one expect after four months in the forest?* It was his eyes that finally absorbed her. His eyes hadn't left her since her blessing for the bread. She couldn't tell the color of his eyes in the dark, yet looking into Lev Belov's eyes, Ksana Zoya felt a stirring within her she had never felt before. *My God,* she said to herself, *I love this person.*

As if drawn by some magnetic force, Lev leaned forward and gently kissed her soft lips.

A gruff voice from the side broke the spell of the moment.

"Lev, we'd better go. Is she coming with us?"

Ksana raised her eyebrows as if to ask, "Am I?"

Lev offered her his hand, and the four vanished into the night.

Ksana Zoya's life as a partisan began concurrently with her love for Lev Belov. Her once cleanly regimented life as Rabbi Zoya's daughter suddenly shifted to the ungoverned ruffled universe in the forest.

Lev and Ksana's days were filled with skirmishes with Nazi patrols, espionage to disrupt the German army's communication, and perhaps most dangerous of all, smuggling food, ammunition and medicine inside the Vilna ghetto.

The nights were for treating the wounded, moving to yet another hideout, and finally lying together in the shared warmth of each other's body. There, in some cave, or, if they

were fortunate, some abandoned hunter's shack, Ksana and Lev would talk and dream of the future.

Ksana looked forward to the nights—cold as they were, for they dared not signal their location with the light of a fire—the nights were a haven from the fright and the fighting and the fury of the days. The nights gave her the stars; and the stars gave her hope.

Before the Nazis came, Reb Zoya's daughter would never permit herself to lie so close to a man. All she was taught, all she believed would have prevented it. Yet there, in that universe, it was different. It didn't have to be explained to her; the conditions instinctively changed the boundaries. There, on that universe, the rules were set by only one creed: Life!

"When the Americans and the English come," Lev would begin, "we'll go to Eretz Israel."

"Yes, my love," Ksana would smile slightly. She loved this dream of Eretz Israel, the land of Israel.

"Eretz Israel, Ksana," Lev would say, with more intensity. "All of us who will live through this will go there. We'll build a Jewish nation from the ashes of our people. Never again will any beast like Hitler rise up. If he does, we shall annihilate him before he has a chance to strike."

Ksana could feel Lev's body tense as his Zionism raged within him. Sometimes, when he spoke of the Jewish nation in Palestine that would be forged from the fire of the Jews in Europe, his voice would become too loud. Then Ksana would gently brush her small, soft hand across his lips, as if to say, "Hush, my handsome zealot, or else Israel will never receive us."

"You'll see, Ksana, the day will come when you and I will go to Israel. The day will come when all Jews will go to Israel. You'll see. We will carve an invincible paradise as we are destined to do."

Ksana shared Lev's dream for reasons of her own. Lev dreamed of the nation; Ksana longed for its spirit. Zionism was not at the heart of Ksana's dream. Israel for her was where God

revealed Himself to man at Mount Sinai; where she could pursue her ghetto-born craving for knowledge of Torah and Talmud.

Lying in the arms of her warrior gazing at the sky, Ksana would form a picture from the stars. Early on, the form was of her father. Of late, it was of a child.

Just before sleep overtook them, Lev would clench his fist and silently vow. Ksana would open her heart and silently pray.

Chapter Eight

Yuri Belov loved to hear his mother tell him stories about the war. He heard them before he was born. From the instant the shock of realizing she was pregnant abated, Yuri's mother felt strangely compelled to tell her child about the man he would call his father and about her brief life with him. If what she suspected were true, he needed to know it all and know it from his mother. Regardless, he should know it anyway. She was careful, gentle. At first, only the love parts were important to tell. There would be enough time, when he came of age, to add the horror. Eventually, he must know it all.

So, from the first instinct of an awakening, Ksana Belov talked to the life inside her. It always began the same way, putting her hands over her abdomen, she would say, "I loved Lev with all my heart and soul, and he loved me the same. It is because of that great love that you are inside me. You are the reflection of the light of our love."

After Yuri was born, when she felt he could comprehend, Ksana added to the love story. She would tell her son about her life fighting and surviving the Nazis—the battles, the heroes, the victims, and the vanquished. By the time he was ten, Yuri knew the stories about the martyrs, those who resisted the Nazis and paid with their life. It was important for him to know that some

97

Jews did not walk like sheep into the gas showers; that there were some who resisted. Early on, she told him of their dream under the stars of one day going to Eretz Israel. Lev would want him to know.

Of Lev's death, Yuri was told only that he died of injuries sustained while a prisoner of the Germans.

"He was captured by the Gestapo," Ksana told her young son. "They tortured him, but he would not reveal any information. Although they hurt him terribly, he managed to escape and found his way back to us. But the wounds were too bad. God spared him from dying with them. He died in my arms. Now he and your grandfather are with God."

It was a story Yuri heard hundreds of times. He imaged his father as his mother described him: sand colored hair that wouldn't stay off his forehead, light complexioned features above a strong, athletic frame. Yuri could see him, bruised and battered from the Nazi beating, dizzily stumbling through the woods to rest finally in the comfort of his mother's arms.

That last night they probably talked about going to Israel, he would picture.

His mother never told him what they talked about.

Along with the stories about recent history, as seen through the eyes of his mother, Yuri was taught Torah and Talmud. Ksana wanted him to be totally Jewish, to be a connection from the nightmare to the dream. If Rabbi Zoya's life and Lev Belov's life—the two men she cherished most—were to be manifest in Yuri, he must study, learn, and then study and learn more.

So, she taught him. She had to do it; it had to be from her. Ksana believed that no one else could teach him with the care and love this child deserved and required. She didn't want him to know only the names and places; Ksana wanted him to know about God. If Lev had lived, he would have taught Yuri about Israel—the nation, its struggles and its purpose. Ksana would still have had to teach to teach her son about his religion, for Lev had no room for it in his mind or his heart. Ksana didn't want her son to be the disenchanted agnostic Lev was. Jewish liturgy came easily and comfortably to Yuri. Somehow, it seemed to him that he was learning what he already knew. He only needed to be reminded.

Vilna, the name now Russianized as Vilnius by the Soviets, was desolate after the war. Charred, burned, waste and deprivation covered the ground once so fertile with music, art and knowledge. The Jerusalem of Europe was like a burned out star uselessly clinging to the sky.

By then the Soviet army had reoccupied Lithuania and life became a different form of terror. The "Final Solution" of German Nazism was replaced by the malignancy of Soviet Communism. One brutally fast; the other brutally slow. Both had the same goal.

Because she spoke several languages, Ksana secured a job teaching the children of Russian army officers garrisoned in Vilnius. That gave her the opportunity to earn enough money for her and Yuri, and time enough to tutor him at night. She was allotted a small apartment adjacent to the school, which was located next to the remnant of the opera house. Ksana never passed the site without remembering and telling Yuri about Michael Frankel chanting the Kol Nidre that death-march night to Ponary.

Strangely, all that happened in Ksana's life since her world exploded that Shabbat night in 1941 did not take its grim toll on her appearance as it had on everyone else. In fact, if one studied her closely, she had acquired an almost ethereal beauty. Her eyes, which witnessed so much, became radiant deep pools. Her hair was still brown and soft. In the forest, she kept it rolled up tightly and wrapped in a bun over the crown of her head. Since returning to Vilnius, she let it down, and it seemed to dance on her shoulders in celebration of its freedom. Unmistakably, the spellbinding quality of Ksana was in her smile. Ksana's smile was infinity materialized.

As a boy, Yuri Belov had the sensitivity and spiritual nature of his mother along with a keen insight of his own. When he was not being tutored by Ksana, he found comfort in being alone.

By the time he was thirteen, he knew he wanted to emigrate to Israel, and said as much in his Bar Mitzvah address. There were eleven guests present in the only synagogue in Vilnius, each one knowing they were giving up their full food allotments for a month because of their attendance at a Jewish ritual.

However, this was Ksana's boy—Reb Zoya's grandson. They were not left wanting. Yuri read his bar mitzvah portion of the Torah with the self-assurance and confidence of an experienced Rabbi. Then, dressed in a white robe that his mother had sewed for the occasion, he spoke to his first congregation:

"My dearest mother, my fellow Jews, today I become one of you, according to Jewish law, an adult with authorization to read from the Torah and to participate in Jewish services and ritual. Another Jew is added to the role. For this privilege, I am grateful not only to you, my dear mother, who has lovingly taught me and guided me since I was born, also to those who came here today. You, who risk your food, your jobs, perhaps even your lives, to be with my mother and me on the day I become a son of God's commandments. You will some day know God's special blessing for your bravery and your spiritual devotion.

Unfortunately, all over Lithuania, and everywhere else that Soviet communism has buried, Jews are renouncing themselves and their God for the emptiness of the state. Hitler took millions by force. Stalin is taking millions by omission. I tell you, those Jews who give in to the disease of Soviet communism and renounce their religion are worse than those who control the system. I will not give in! I was a Jew. I am a Jew. I will die a Jew!"

Yuri's eyes blazed as he glared at his small congregation for a few seconds then turned and took his seat beside his mother.

The eleven were stunned.

At a brief, hurried wine and sweets reception after the

service, Yuri accepted the congratulations of his congregates modestly before they quickly vanished. All of them went to their houses feeling oddly inspired by a thirteen-year-old boy. However, one of the eleven went to Red Party Headquarters and told what he had heard. From that moment on, and for the rest of his life, Yuri Belov was suspect.

Yuri practiced Judaism with fervor. Wrapping the phylacteries around his arm and forehead every morning was not a burden; it was performed with spiritual and emotional passion. The scrolls on which the prayers were written, housed within the square black boxes, seemed to penetrate Yuri's body and seep into his bloodstream. His brain and his heart picked them up like a thirsty plant sucks in water. They enlivened him. He loved prayer; he loved the communion he felt when he prayed. And when Yuri prayed, he prayed with enthusiasm. He seemed to feast on the prayers, savoring every word like an Epicurean.

As there was no Rabbi left in Vilnius, Yuri Belov, at age sixteen, became the acting Vilna Rabbi. In the tradition of the legendary Vilna Goan, and with the devotion of his grandfather, Yuri Belov dedicated his life to the study and teaching of Jewish ritual and law. The fire in him raged constantly. It burned when he walked, spoke, laughed, ate and drank; a tempestuous flame that he neither understood nor questioned. He could not read enough, teach enough, learn enough nor pray enough to satisfy its insatiable need to burn. Yuri's Judaism embodied the practical use of man's mystical relationship with God. "As above, so below," he taught.

In addition to teaching and officiating services, Yuri performed the traditional rabbinical duties of visiting the sick, comforting the lonely and bereaved and acting as a confidant and confessor to those in need. One forgot how young he was when they looked into his eyes—deep, penetrating, empathetic, knowing, assuring and incredibly loving.

It was while visiting Bluma Ketsherginski's flat that Yuri found out something about himself, something that he had only suspected. Bluma had been a rather attractive girl before the war. Auschwitz changed that.

As Dr. Joseph Mengele was making his selection of who shall live and who shall die by the flick of his hand, he temporarily stopped the human procession when Bluma presented herself. With the eye of a vulture, Mengele waved over an SS guard and whispered something to him. The guard yelled at Bluma to follow him. Blonde, buxom, and large-boned — the materialization of Teutonic lust — Bluma was marched to a building slightly removed from the main complex marked Officer's Recreation Center. Bluma was deloused, scrubbed, bathed and perfumed by two enormous SS guards. "Lie down and be ready," they shouted laughingly as they left.

Bluma Ketsherginski became a member of a harem from hell. All through the day and night, German officers, men as well as women, used and abused her body as a spoil of war. Early on, the other women in the building advised her, "No matter how obscene, how barbaric they treat you, flatter them, compliment their manliness. They are German. You must make them think you like it, what ever you have to do. If not, they get mad, and you go to the ovens, what is left of you."

Bluma lived at and for the pleasure of the SS men and women guards at Auschwitz until nearly the end of the war. The Nazi "recreation center" was closed as the allies battled closer. Times became so bad for the Germans there that they had to abandon the pleasures of the flesh for the exclusive task of burning it. The other women from the brothel either died of typhus or were gassed. Bluma somehow survived, but not without the experience taking its toll. She was blind. The doctor who examined the emaciated shadow of a woman diagnosed her blindness as the result of extremely high fever due to typhus.

It was in that condition that Bluma returned to what was

Lida, a small town not far from Vilna, now Vilnius. Yuri made Bluma Ketsherginski one of his flock when he expanded his visitations to the sick outside of Vilnius.

On one remarkable day visiting Bluma, Yuri was gripped by an intuition, a prompting, an inner whisper that he had heard before but had stifled. He prayed to God silently. A warmth flowed throughout his body. His hands felt hot. He looked at Bluma and saw, not the bedraggled, worn out sightless creature sitting on a wooden chair in front of him, but as she once was. He saw her robust and attractive. The warmth in his body was nearing a simmer. He resisted himself no longer.

When Yuri Belov left Bluma Ketsherginski's small flat that day, Bluma could see.

Word of Bluma's healing miracle spread throughout Lida, although Yuri had asked her not to boast nor disclose what had happened. Yet Bluma could not restrain her impulse to tell people.

"Bluma, Bluma," they would ask in amazement, as she would shop in the market, "you can see! What happened?"

"We have among us a *Tzadik*. Reb Belov," she would say with awe.

"Reb Belov? Yuri Belov?" they would ask doubtfully. "Smart, wise, a scholar, yes. But a Tzadik? A maker of miracles? Come now, Bluma. Tell us the truth."

Eventually, Bluma was believed, and the word spread from Lida to Vilnius that Yuri Belov could heal the sightless. As if carried by the wind, the message blew forth in all directions that there was a Rabbi in Vilnius who performed healing miracles. Almost instantly, and without preparation for such attention, Yuri was attending to a steady stream of visitations from people with every known and unknown ailment. They came from all over and then from further and beyond to be treated by the "miracle Rabbi" in Vilnius. From Pabrade to the north, they limped to him. From Aisiskes to the south they crawled to him.

From Varena, and Lazdijai, and Alytus, and Vievis and Svencionis they made their way to find Reb Belov—Yuri Belov, "the son of the heroic partisan of the Nazis days, who wipes out disease like his father killed the Germans."

With only his mother there to greet the decrepit and crippled and the rotting who made their way to his tiny shtetl, Yuri attended to them with all the fervor and energy he could muster.

Not all were healed, yet many were. Some believed that they were healed—such was the vibrancy of his personality, and that was as good as being healed.

Yuri's only annoyance was that the healing preempted much of his time for study and attending to services for the healthy.

"Mother, they are too many! I have not studied for weeks, and I barely have time to prepare for the Sabbath service, not to mention my neglect of the children at religious school. With such demands on me, how will I ever officiate Rosh Hashanah and Yom Kippur with any degree of preparedness?"

When Yuri spoke to his mother, he spoke as a child. From that first instant in her womb when he felt her voice, he loved her unconditionally.

Ksana, in turn, understood her son, although the dimension of his capability continued to surprise her.

"Yuri, trust God. What you are doing is good. He would not have you doing what you are doing unless He wanted you to."

When she spoke to him, he calmed. She would take both of his hands in hers, and look the words into him as well as say them. As he gazed into the infinity of his mother's eyes, a strange sense would overtake him. He felt as if they had loved before.

"I will trust God, mother."

God responded through the person of Viktor Abramov.

"Sit down, Comrade Belov. Make yourself at home. Care for some tea?"

"No, thank you, sir. May I ask why you sent for me?"

"Ach! Such a hurry. You young people are always in such a hurry."

"I am not in such a hurry, Mr. Abramov."

"Call me Comrade, please. It makes me feel so much better."

Viktor Abramov, a disavowed Jew, had worked himself up from a Communist Party worker with the postal service to become Party head of Lithuania's largest city. He was short and had a nose that looked like an apricot seed. Three fingers were missing from his left hand. He held his glass of tea with his right. A sarcastic smile matched the tone in his voice. He had that certain air of confidence devoid of grace that marks the big fish in the small pond.

Yuri's anxiety was not from fright or apprehension. He had appraised Viktor Abramov carefully when he entered his office.

"I am not in such a hurry, Comrade Abramov; I would quite enjoy a visit with you. My home is filled with the sick, however, and I must attend to them."

"Precisely why I asked you to come, Comrade Belov." He inflected the word Comrade so as to imply doubt about Yuri's political leaning.

Abramov continued. "The incident in Lida with, what's the name of that old whore?"

Yuri bristled, but composed himself quickly.

"Bluma Ketsherginski."

"That's right. Bluma! Quite a piece of ass that one used to be, before she decided to fuck for the Nazis. Anyway, when the coincidence of your visit and the regaining of her sight occurred, the Party thought all the excitement was temporary. Unfortunately, the proletariat has a penchant for the spectacular. Curiously, even when the spectacle is obviously fraudulent, the gullible people continue to want to see the trick performed.

"I am not entertaining them, Comrade Abramov," Yuri said, with some defiance.

"But you are fraudulent, Comrade! And that is politically unhealthy!"

Viktor Abramov was becoming unnerved. He had depleted his patience for posturing. Yuri sensed his insecurity.

"Comrade Abramov, people—poor sick, hopeless people— have come from all over the Baltic, and even from Minsk, to ask me to help them. That is not fraud."

Abramov screamed, "What do you charge them? How much do they pay you? Do you know it is against the law to practice medicine for a fee without a medical permit?"

"I charge nothing."

"Nothing?"

"Nothing."

Viktor Abramov remained silent and did lip exercises while drumming his two fingers of his left hand on the old brown desk. It had a crack running lengthwise across the middle. As if on film, a scene formed in Yuri's mind of a Jewish prisoner being savagely beaten by the Gestapo. The top of the desk cracks under the force of the blows. Psychically, Yuri could feel the cries of agony still surrounding the desk twenty-five years later.

Abramov stood up and paced the floor to the right of where Yuri sat. His lips were still exercising.

Yuri looked at his left hand, and said, "It didn't hurt you as much as you thought it would when they sliced off your fingers, did it?"

Abramov stopped short and almost stumbled. His short legs weren't pivoted properly for an involuntary turn.

"No, it didn't." He had meant to say, "How did you know?" The sudden memory of the torture rocked him.

Yuri continued, "The third finger, they did slowly, stopping halfway through to light cigarettes while you bled. You thought they might let you bleed to death."

Breathing heavily, sweating profusely, Abramov's lips started to quiver, like a child expecting the worst of his father's wrath.

"They finished the amputation, and again asked you to reveal information about the partisans. At first, you refused; then they said something, and you told them what they wanted to know."

The calmness of Yuri's voice only made the replay more unbearable for Abramov. Sobbing uncontrollably, he stammered, "They...they told me they would slice off my testicles next." A flow of unrelenting tears and near convulsions followed.

There were other people present in the mental picture in Yuri's mind of Abramov's ordeal, but their image was blurred. Not until years later, in meditation, would Yuri see the others.

Yuri got up and walked slowly to the weeping leader of the Communist Party in Vilnius. Standing over him, Yuri put both of his hands around the sides of Abramov's plump face. Abramov's frightened eyes gazed upward into Yuri's.

"Why did you tell the Gestapo what they wanted to know?" Yuri asked calmly.

"I didn't want to die," Abramov answered, with the blank innocence of a child.

Yuri said, "Neither did Bluma Ketsherginski."

Abramov's eyes closed as the meaning registered in his tormented mind.

Yuri said, "Bluma gave the Germans what she had to give to live. You gave them what you had to give to live. Tell me, sir, which one of you is a whore?"

Yuri removed his hands from Abramov's face slowly and walked toward the door of the office. He stopped before opening it and turned to Abramov who was still sitting dazed on the couch. His mind was making the return trip from then to the present.

"May I go?" Yuri asked respectfully.

There was no response

"May I leave, Mr. Abramov?"

He heard him that time, not the first. Taking a deep breath, he looked at Yuri, and his expression changed completely from a daze to a shattered look of *how could I have been so stupid*? However, Abramov, being Abramov, decided that Yuri didn't know the full story. *Otherwise*, he figured, *Yuri would have mentioned it*.

"Yuri," Abramov began solemnly, "Your father back in those days…a brave man. Braver than I, believe me. A Zionist first class. What they did to him, the bastards! And your mother, what a lovely woman she was…still is. How they loved each other! We used to make fun of them, those two. Always holding hands, you know? Ach, your mother! She would insist we say morning and evening prayers. I gave all that up even years before the war; never even had a bar mitzvah. I was a young Communist through and through. But for Ksana, I prayed. Ach, what a woman! I wish she hadn't told you about the torture, you know, how they took my fingers off. I didn't think she knew, really. Someone must have told her. Maybe Gershon Spetzler. He escaped with your father. Those two were quite a team. Always planning to go to Israel some day."

With a slap of his hands on his pudgy thighs, he jumped to his feet and strode to his desk. He sat and looked at the trim robust figure in the doorway still waiting for permission to leave.

"You are right about Bluma. We all did what we had to do in order to live back then."

He paused, looked at his left hand, and continued directly. "Yuri, now is now, and we must address ourselves with now. Now says that too many people are coming to Vilnius to see one Yuri Belov, a Rabbi without diploma, a doctor without license. It creates a public nuisance. Now also says that I honor the memory of Lev Belov and love your mother. That's why Yuri Belov is getting a reprimand and not a trial—now."

Getting up and rolling to the door to stand in front of Yuri, he continued in a voice a decibel higher than a whisper. "Yuri, leave Vilnius. Go somewhere. Study. Learn a trade. But leave before your reputation becomes your indictment. Since your bar mitzvah, I knew one day I'd have to deal with you. The next time, the past won't intervene. For the present," then in his normal voice, "Good-bye, Comrade Belov."

With a last kiss from his mother, Yuri left Vilnius at dawn one April morning. His destination: Kiev—six hundred miles southeast of Lithuania, a large city, and a center for learning. He planned to travel the distance by foot, stopping over in any town with a Jewish population to preach in the synagogue and, hopefully, collect a few rubles to take him to the next town.

His first stop was Minsk. The complexity of the first large city he had ever seen at first perplexed him. However, the massiveness of Minsk did provide benefits for him. Minsk had three synagogues and several libraries. Yuri provided food for the souls of the congregates; they provided food for Yuri's belly.

He continued studying the Talmud, Kabbalah, the Prophets, and traditional and mystical Jewish literature. Beyond that, he found an insatiable interest in other religious doctrine. He could not satisfy his thirst for knowledge about the reciprocal relationship between God and man. That thirst led him to visit churches to hear other ministers. Some of it pleased him. Most of what he heard disturbed him.

Yuri remained in Minsk for three months. Feeling the time was right to set out again, he walked the country road to the town of Bobruysk, a rural town on the west bank of the Berezina River. Bobruysk had virtually no Jews, so Yuri spent most of his time lying near the Pripet Marshes watching the tadpoles and nesting birds taste life. A nearby farmer fed him for caring for his invalid wife while the farmer worked his field. The woman was paralyzed from a fall during the past winter. Yuri Belov got to know Yuri Belov very well while sitting beside the Pripet marshes. When he left the farmer's home early one morning for his next destination, he left his host a gift: His wife could walk.

Following the Berezina River south to Gomel, he felt as if the pieces inside him, which so often seemed in disorder, were comfortably settling. He stayed in Gomel only two weeks healing twelve children suffering from hepatitis during his stay.

From Gomel, he walked fifty soggy miles to Chernigov and went into utter seclusion in an abandoned hunter's hut. The time he spent in Chernigov was deeply significant for the forces at play within him. To his unwavering dedication to Jewish discipline, he added the practice of deep and profound meditation. Emerging from each meditative session was a Yuri Belov renewed in strength, faith, and a clearer sense of self-awareness.

Finally, in September, Yuri arrived in Kiev. It was there that he set his course. Yuri was immediately awed with the vastness and the complexity of this major Soviet metropolis. It was quite a departure from the simplicity and rural solace he had come to appreciate along the way since Minsk. Standing high on a cliff overlooking the Dnepry River, he understood why he was in Kiev. Kiev promised him his destiny. Its National Library, Academy of Sciences and museums rounded the shape of his development by providing the intellectual assets to compliment his ample spiritual resources.

Additionally, Kiev had Jews and a building they used as a synagogue, at their risk. That was vital, for somewhere between the paralyzed farmer's wife, the stricken children of Bobruysk and the hut near Chernogov, Yuri resolved that he would heal the sick when and where he could regardless of the personal consequences, and that he would preach uninhibitedly of God and His expectations of man, when and where he could no matter the personal peril.

Preach and heal he did. When he was not comforting his flock, he was at the library or the museum, always studying. World events began to interest him. His avenue of interests expanded beyond the confinement of Torah, Talmud, and mysticism to include how they interact with the pragmatic secular world of mankind and nations. More than ever, he affirmed "As above, so below."

In time, Yuri expanded his pulpit from the small makeshift synagogue to restaurants, subway depots and street corners. Following his remarks, the ill, the lame and the wretched would come forward for healing. Informers were everywhere.

One night, while preaching and healing outside a sporting arena, the KGB arrested Yuri Belov. He was taken to a detention center where he was interrogated continuously for four nights and four days, kept awake with powerful thrusts of ice-cold water on his naked body. He was then brought before a judge and told to stop his foolishness for good.

The four nights and physical abuse solved his only remaining riddle about his life. He understood his purpose.

The next morning, Yuri Belov set out for Moscow.

Eight months later, the KGB arrested him after giving a speech in Red Square.

Chapter Nine

The late Sgt. Malcolme Tucker would have been proud of his daughter as she stepped out of the taxi in front of 359 Park Avenue. He wouldn't have understood, but he'd have been proud. His vision of his little Freda, as she'd fall asleep in his lap, was one day becoming the woman her mother was – "good-looking and good-cooking." The times had changed, however, and Freda grooved right in there with them. She was the personification of what her daddy died for. Freedom was a credo for Sgt. Tucker; a dream for Aunt Sarah. To Freda Tucker, freedom was now.

"Keep the change," she said, as she handed the driver a ten-dollar bill. The fare was eight twenty.

The cabby looked at the ten spot in his hand like it had suddenly developed leprosy.

"I hope the John in there tips you a lot better than this," he said with a smirk, as she headed for the door.

Freda's first inclination was to turn and tell him what he could do with the ten-dollar bill. After an instant assessment of the situation, however, she thought, *stay with the program, girl,* and she resisted her impulse.

The wind was blowing softly off the Hudson River, pressing her orange ultra-suede skirt against her thighs. Her recent tightly curled permanent behaved like it was meant to; not one curl around her face or the bangs over her forehead was displaced. Her black leather coat covered her sheer black blouse; otherwise, the doorman would have surely stopped her. Flashing him a wide smile, he returned it with a tart, "Good day, ma'am." She sauntered past him, knowing the next obstacle was the severest test.

Wealthy middle-age folks who knew all the words to "Moon River" occupied the 359 Building. Nothing was young about that building except the Disney-like scene every morning, evening and Sunday afternoon when everyone came out the front door holding a leash with a miniature dog attached.

There were several blacks in the fold, but none was ever known to wear an orange skirt. The security officer eyed Freda up and down at least three times as she stood before his desk. He reminded her of a doll she made out of a pillow when she was a child that she named Turnip. She stifled a giggle while he perused the shapely orange and black visitor standing over him. Collecting herself and waiting for him to say something, "she looked him down good," as Aunt Sarah used to say.

Finally, "Can I help you?"

His voice was high pitched, like how she used to make Turnip talk. She was going to explode if she couldn't let the laugh come out. Somehow, she managed to contain it.

Freda wanted to say, *Buster, you couldn't help anybody.* Again, she controlled her impulse.

Instead, she said, "My name is Freda Tucker. I'm with *The Bernie Frank Show.* I'm here to see Mr. Millard Hampton, our producer."

Turnip's eyes widened. Then, instantly, he returned to the role of security guard.

"Is he expecting you, Miss Tucker?"

Leaning down so that her two hands braced herself on the front edge of his desk, she talked to his face about eight inches away.

"How do you know I'm not married? Have you checked? Maybe I'm a Mrs. How do you know, sir? Why the Miss? Maybe I'm a man in drag! Why not Mr.? Or, haven't you heard: we've come a long way, baby." She tweaked his nose on "Baby." There's a new word around, pal. It's Ms...Ms. Try it. Ms."

Turnip got in a whispered, "Ms." As he sat there stupefied by the diatribe of Millard Hampton's assistant, and pupil. "When pursuing a guest," he often coached her, "be aggressive, clever, and resourceful."

She continued. "Now, do you want Bernie Frank to come on television tonight and say, 'Folks, I want to tell all of you that the security guard at 359 Park Avenue is a male chauvinist pig!' Is that what you want, buddy?" She glared in his eyes to let it all sink in. Then she stood upright.

Immediately, the guard picked up the phone and dialed a number. It rang, and rang and rang. Freda could hear it. With each "braaang," she realized she'd have to use her ace. She had to see Hampton! *Be aggressive, clever, and resourceful.*

"No answer in the Hampton apartment," he hesitated, "Ms. Tucker."

Freda took a deep breath.

"Then let me in to his apartment; I'll wait for him," she said, coolly.

Turnip had started shaking his head "no" even before she finished; not an authoritative "no"; more like, "Oh please don't ask me to do that!"

"I'm sorry, Ms. Tucker. That's strictly against rules and regulations. I simply can't let you in without written permission from the tenant."

"But you must let me in. You must." She demanded.

He picked up a notebook. "Here, look at it yourself. These are the rules of the building. See, here...I've found it. Look...read it yourself: It says right here in black and white, see, look." She wouldn't take her eyes from his face.

"Okay, I'll read it to you myself. 'No admissions shall be granted to...'"

114

Freda slowly pushed the notebook down with one slender index finger. When it touched the desk, she said in a low, soft tone of voice, "Sir, do you love your country?" His eyes glazed with bewilderment.

"Huh?"

"I said, do you love your country?"

"Of course I do," he said, in nearly a boy soprano register. "What's that got to do with letting someone into…?"

"You've already indicated your tendency to discriminate against women. You might even be a closet racist. But even with all your repugnant prejudices, I do believe you love America."

He was now completely destroyed. All he could do was put his hand near his heart and say, "I swear I love America, Ms. Tucker."

"I tend to believe you," she said compassionately. "Now you have an opportunity to prove your devotion. I thought you would let me into Mr. Hampton's apartment without me having the show you this. Since you won't let me in, I'll have to let you see it. You must give me your word you won't breathe a word of this to anyone. If you tell a living soul what you are about to read, Bernie Frank will tell the nation what I tell him about you. Now, do I have your word?"

Raising his right hand, with his eyes wide, he said, "I swear."

"Very well, then. You may read this."

Taking a yellow envelope from her purse, she handed it to a devastated Turnip.

"I thank you, and your country thanks you," Freda whispered, as the security guard turned the key to the door of Millard Hampton's apartment. She waited to make certain he got back on the elevator, and then she carefully entered Oz.

Freda stood for a moment in the small entry hall. It was dark. Dare she turn on a light? *No, not yet. Get your bearings first, girl. Size up the joint.* Her eyes gradually adjusted to the dark. She took two more stealthy steps into the apartment. Finally, she could see well enough to make out a room, a rather large room, fully furnished, recessed about three steps down from the left side of the entrance hall. She paused at the top step.

"Mr. Hampton?" she called, as if asking a question.

No answer.

Again: "Mr. Hampton?" A bit louder.

Nothing.

For a fleeting second, she considered making a fast exit. *After all, I'd gotten in and found he wasn't home. That was the mission, wasn't it?* she rationalized.

No, no. She knew that wasn't the mission. She was sent by Bernie to "Find Millard, Freda. Find him." To leave now went against her instructions, her nature, and her training.

Carefully placing her foot on each carpeted step, she descended to the living room. An end table held a huge porcelain based lamp. She reached under the pleated shade for the switch. Almost magically, the light unfolded what appeared to be a 1940's Hollywood sound stage. She'd seen enough of those melodramas on late night TV to feel that the only thing missing in the Hampton living room were Charles Boyer and Bette Davis. *Nobody lives in a living room like that*, she thought. Like anonymous actors from central casting, every piece was costumed, set in place, and directed to hold it. Not daring to sit down on either the tufted 18th century Italian provincial sofa nor the deep rose colored velvet upholstered Queen Ann chair, Freda slowly strolled around the room.

The walls were finished in a nondescript subtle green tone which, when combined with the pinks and reds in the Oriental rug, seemed to fill the space with a kind of mistiness. The heavy brocade drapes embellished the effect.

In front of the sofa was a cherry wood coffee table with very precise engravings, like large deep veins down the legs. A silver cigarette box, a brass silent butler, and a silver mint dish were satellites to a bowl containing silk flowers of iris, roses, and a sprinkling of baby's breath.

Freda's tour stopped in front of the gas log fireplace. Looking at the paintings of jockeys—an original Degas—above the mantel, Freda said, nearly out loud, "That figures." She recalled Hampton professing his love for Edgar Degas' work one time during one of his office seminars on the need for journalists to remain unbridled and independent. "Take Degas," he offered, "there was a man, born into wealth, who had neither the need to be subsidized, nor the motivation of hunger; yet he motivated himself. He courted no one, neither the impressionists nor the critics. In other words, he stayed away from the special interest groups and was thus able to capture scenes from everyday life honestly and vividly." She remembered he concluded with, "We could use a few Degas in television these days."

Freda left the set of *Dark Victory* and went back up the three stairs and turned left down the hall, this time flicking on a hall light switch.

A door. She opened it. Seeing a made-up bed, she closed it. Another door. The bath—clean and vacant. *Would you look at all those cologne bottles?* she observed to herself. *Who lives here: Calvin Klein?* she laughed.

The kitchen was off to the left. It was papered in bright yellow with deep brown mahogany cabinets high and low. Freda never saw a kitchen so clean. *No one has a kitchen this clean*, she thought. Turning to leave, she stopped, and said, *I gotta do it!*

Since she was a child, Freda never went into anyone's kitchen without taking a peek into the refrigerator. She could not resist seeing what folks kept in the icebox, as it was called back home.

Freda explained her fridge fetish to friends by telling them that one could learn more about people by reading their icebox than any other method. "There's only two sure fire ways to find out what a dude is really like," she would say, "and if you don't want to do that, open his fridge."

Millard Hampton's refrigerator was a Eugene O'Neil play. Dried up cheese and vodka bottles; wilted lettuce and scotch bottles; the spoiling carcass of a turkey and wine bottles. Freda's lips whispered, "Waste."

She closed the door slowly, sadly. A feeling of pity swept over her. It took her by surprise. Pity and Millard Hampton were inconsistent terms until she read his refrigerator.

More than that, there was something about the place, the whole apartment, which gave Freda a dispirited feeling. Absent were all the apparent signs of life that distinguish every home, rich or poor. Nothing in this place breathed; nothing laughed or cried. As if in a coma, it all just seemed to be there, wasting.

The last door was at the end of the hallway. She opened it. The late afternoon Manhattan sunlight found a crack between two adjacent buildings and streamed into the room. Like a laser beam targeted perfectly at a subject, the figure of a man in a robe, slumped in a worn leather chair. Freda studied the spectacle for a frozen moment, and then clumsily groped for a light switch on the wall. It flooded the room and dissipated the laser beam, still leaving the man looking dumped in the chair.

Rushing to him, Freda put her ear to his gray-haired chest. The heart was beating. He wasn't dead. He was dead-drunk.

"Hello, Bernie? Freda. I found him. Drunk as a skunk."
"Drunk?"
She kept her eyes on Hampton as she talked to Bernie. This was not Millard Hampton, but it was. Not the man she both admired and despised. Here slumped a hopeless, yet strangely handsome pretender.
"Bernie, you ought to see this place!"
"What's he drunk for? I mean, Millard's not a *shikker*."
"Newspapers all over the place, Bernie. Piles! No, not really; just a mess of newspapers and magazines all over the floor. And glasses everywhere! He's not a what?" Her thoughts were racing; her mind just caught up.
"I just can't believe it," Bernie sonorously grumbled, as if oblivious to anything Freda reported after, "He's drunk as a skunk."
"Millard's not a shikker."

"There, you said it again! What's a shikker?"

"Shikker. It's Yiddish for boozer...drunk...sot."

"Oh."

She quickly added shikker to her list of Yiddish terms Bernie used whenever the emotional impact of a situation required a more graphic term than English avails.

"Yea, well, he's shikkered all right. And from the looks of this place, he's been shikkering for quite a spell."

The room was a hazardous waste dump. Newspapers, dropped where they had been read then carelessly kicked to another spot again and again, were everywhere.

And glasses everywhere, too; all kinds of glasses, everyday glasses, goblets, tall ones, short ones, some with a swallow or two of booze remaining. Obviously, a new glass was used for every round, and then it was deserted, or forgotten.

The cups were apparently used after the glasses ran out. Cups with remnants of stale booze, some resting on their sides like small vessels, victims of a storm at sea, tossed recklessly aground on desolate islands of *Washington Posts*, *New York Times* and *USA Today*.

Freda knew messes. She could date messes like she could read refrigerators. The neighborhood she grew up in endowed her with mental imprints of every domestic environment conceivable – from the squalor of a ghetto shack to the faked simplicity of a college-town cathouse. When it came to how long has this been going on, Freda Tucker was a basic black carbon-dating system.

"He's been living like this for about a month I'd say, Bernie," she said.

"Well...do what you can for him. I pretty well have the show together for tonight. Call me later, all right? Damn, I can't believe this!"

"What am I suppose to do, Bernie? I mean, like he's out cold, and I..."

"Just handle it. Okay, Freda? Take care of it. Talk to you later. Bye bye."

Freda looked at the phone receiver like an astronaut stranded on the moon who had just received instructions from Mission Control to get back the best way he could. "Over and out."

Like always, Freda's instinct assumed control. First, she studied the scene. Slumped in front of her was a legend. Or was it a myth? None of the Millard Hampton stories ever portrayed him a drunken sot. On the contrary, he was always the impeccably, self-assured captain who stayed the course throughout challenging storms; the poster model for Rudyard Kipling's "If."

The full head of combed back gray hair that never looked like it needed trimmed, or that it had just been trimmed, remained basically intact. However, the black-rimmed half-glasses that normally perched on the middle of his prominent nose somehow got unperched so that the rims were resting on top of his parted lower lip. The lens fogged from the snoring. Like inebriation, snoring seemed uncharacteristic of Millard Hampton.

Freda carefully removed his glasses, and Hampton inhaled a snore while mumbling something that only his subconscious understood. Then he swallowed and fell deeply into a stupor again, one hand dropping limply over the edge of the chair. Freda gently placed it over the other one on top of his stomach. She wondered why she never noticed his perfectly manicured nails before.

His silk robe was parted at the chest. A gothic MH was monogrammed on the lower right sleeve. *Leave it to Millard not to have the monogram on the traditional place,* Freda thought. Fastened with a bowed belt, the robe was unusually long, covering most of his legs, which rested on the ottoman where Freda sat. His hairy muscular calves and exposed chest evidenced a man to whom dissipation was a recent denizen. Brown leather slippers covered his feet.

Freda reconnoitered the room. This was Hampton's study. Near the window was a desk with an old Remington typewriter parked in the center surrounded by piles of scripts, papers, notes, jottings and the necessary disarray of the working journalist. A closer look revealed that the desk was a table.

Freda stood up. She felt warm. Taking off her jacket, she haphazardly tossed it on the black leather sofa that fit the wall across from where Hampton slumped. Above the sofa, attached to the dark mahogany paneled wall were four gold-framed glossy photographs. Freda moved closer to see whom, after such an illustrious career of covering the greats, Hampton had selected above all others for the high honor of adorning his wall. She looked, and then looked more closely. They were all Hampton with the same man. Freda didn't recognize him. *Only Millard would put a guy on his wall that no one knew but him!"* She thought.

Back in the corner, nestled between two large, starving plants, was a baby-grand piano. As if possessed, Freda immediately ambled to the kitchen, filled a pitcher with water and scurried back to feed the neglected Cyprus and thirsty Fiascoes. They sucked up five pitchers full a piece. "At least somebody's glad to see me," Freda said to the grateful rubber plant.

The piano looked inviting. Freda couldn't play but she had always wanted to. Sitting down to rest on the piano bench after her phytological mission of mercy, Freda pantomimed playing a lively song without actually striking a note.

The pantomimed performance made a sudden transition to an andante passage as Freda's eyes caught the familiar face of Perry Como on a sheet of music in front of her. She liked Como's face. It made her think of Bernie. Above Como's photograph was the title, "Precious One." Beneath the title: "Words and music by Sidney Wade."

"Precious One" became the next selection in Freda's quiescent concert. She liked the song, although when it was popular most of her college friends thought it was awfully square.

Resting on the slant board next to the Como song was a red folio with a long list of song titles down the front of the cover. "Twenty Hits Written by Sidney Wade." Freda read the titles. Most of them were hit songs of the forties and early fifties. One or two were popular within the last ten years.

Freda recalled noticing the articles about the death of Sidney Wade about six months earlier while perusing the newspapers one morning. He was one of those innocuous American composers of whom people say, "I didn't know he wrote that one too," after he dies. She remembered that Bernie wanted to do a "Salute to Sidney Wade" on the show and even wanted to sing some of Wade's songs himself, but Hampton vetoed the suggestion with that tone of finality which, when interpreted, said that to argue is to die a swift death.

Thinking about the incident, Freda inadvertently stopped her mute version of "Precious One," and picked up the folio, and turned to the first page. There was a full-page of Sidney Wade. *A little pudgy*, she thought, as she looked at the bespectacled man in the pinstripe suit sitting at a grand piano in the traditional "I'm writing a song now" pose. Returning the folio to its place next to Perry Como, Freda mused, *Guess Millard likes his songs."*

Suddenly she froze. Then she gasped. Grabbing the folio, she raced to the black sofa and gazed at the photographs above it. Each photo—all four—was of Sidney Wade! There, framed in gold, were a young Wade and Hampton, wearing flying togs, standing by a World War II vintage airplane. Hampton, his face straining, carrying a portable typewriter in one hand and camera gear, slung over his shoulder in another. In another, Wade smiling gleefully, his hands extended, pantomiming how light he is traveling. The next, a somewhat more mature Wade and Hampton lying on beach chairs on what looks to be the Riviera or elsewhere in Europe. Hampton is remarkably well built. Wade already has a paunch and double chin. The third is at a restaurant. Both have wine. Hampton's pipe is resting in the ashtray next to Wade's cigarette. Hampton there looks like

Hampton now. Wade's face has rounded to its genetic intention. The fourth photo is recent. They are sitting on a park in Central Park. Hampton is wearing a tweedy overcoat and muffler – no hat. It is late Fall. Wade's face is not as pudgy – somewhat less shiny. The eyes are set deeper. A Russian fur hat seems to be too large for his head; it comes down too low. He's wearing a dark, heavy fur coat and his hands are jammed in the pockets. This is the only photo of the four without a smile on Wade's face.

Freda returned to sit on the ottoman by Hampton's feet. *He'd love this if he was sober*, she smiled, *me at his feet like a good nigger woman*. For the first time she noticed the pipe rack on the side table beside his chair. *Must be fifty pipes in that rack*, she estimated. Actually, there were about as many on the floor, and lying on tables, his desk, and wedged in between cushions on the chairs and sofa. Like the glasses and cups, his pipes were used once, and then abandoned. Only the piano remained free of any debris, newspaper, or briar-and-stem. Aside from the hulk in the chair, the rest of the room could be either read or smoked.

As the melody of "Precious One" played in her mind, Freda got up again and furiously began to gather the newspapers on the floor. "Be a good nigger woman and clean this white man's 'partment up," she chided out loud. "That's it, nigger, jess like it was cotton," she said, laughing, as she moved around the room gathering bales of paper. "Careful now, don't catch up masser's pipe in one of these here bales, nigger. You know what masser will do if you lose one of his pipes." She was nearly hysterical now, bowing and shuffling around the Hampton plantation, carrying all the paper she could to the newsroom size trashcan beside Hampton's desk. When it was full to the top, she turned to her imaginary boss, and asked, "What I do now?"

With her hands on her hips, and a stern look on her face, she said as a white man, "What you do now, nigger? You set your black ass in that can and push it down so you can get more in, that's what."

And that's what she did. Bracing herself on the rim of the

receptacle, she hopped up, and sat down on the can. Tears were streaming down her face from laughter as she wiggled her rear end round and round pressing the newspapers a little further down with each gyration.

"If I learn to wiggle real good, maybe masser will come and fuck me some night like he do de udders. Yes, sir, I gotta learn to be a good fuckin' nigger woman."

By then, she had wiggled and giggled and pressed the newspapers at least two feet into the can.

With her legs dangling over the sides, and her skirt hunched back to her hips, she screamed with laughter, "Now I'm a good nigger woman. I done bailed all da cotton, and I wiggled my black ass into dis here can so masser can fuck me good!"

Her head was thrown back in convulsive laugher. When she brought it forward, her face froze in wide-eyed shock.

"MS. TUCKER, GET OUT OF THAT CAN!" the voice from the leather chair bellowed. She couldn't believe her eyes…or her ears. She just stared at him. He hadn't moved from the position he'd been in since she found him. Only his eyes had opened, and they were fixed on her.

'I SAID, MS. TUCKER, GET OUT OF THAT CAN."

It seemed even louder this time.

"Oh my god, Mr. Hampton, I'll be…I'm just…I came over to…wait…"

Placing her hands on the rim for leverage, she tried to boost herself out, but she didn't rise. She pushed against the rim harder this time. Still, she didn't budge. Feeling his eyes burning a hole in her, she tried once more. No use, she didn't rise an inch. Noticing her orange skirt exposing her black bikini panties, she quickly pulled it up her legs, but it slid down to her hips again.

"Mr. Hampton," she said meekly.

"What?"

"I'm stuck."

He said nothing; his eyes remained sternly fixed on her.

She attempted one more effort to push out. No lift off. No give at all. So she started to rock back then forward, slowly, back then forward.

Finally, the can tipped over, and out plopped Freda Tucker on the floor, with a resounding crash.

Her impulse was to laugh, then cry. She did both. His voice interrupted her brief outpouring.

"Now, get up from the floor please, and come over here and tell me what in tarnation you are doing in my apartment."

Freda got to her feet slowly, tucked in her blouse and straightened down her skirt. Dutifully, she came over and stood by his chair.

"We hadn't heard from you, so Bernie and I decided…"

He tried to wave off her explanation with his hand, but all strength failed him and the hand fell limply over the side of the chair, where it hung lifelessly.

"Will you fix me some coffee, please?" The tone was different. It was softer, yes, but needing, too. She never heard it quite like that.

"Of course I will, Mr. Hampton. Now you stay right there; I'll be right back."

"I assure you, Ms. Tucker, I am not going anywhere." He didn't smile. She did.

Freda felt oddly happy as she threw heaping spoonfuls of some of Hampton's Kenyan coffee into the percolator. The situation she found herself in was so utterly bizarre; she had run the emotional gamut from fright to euphoria. The result was an uninhibited sense of pleasure.

"COFFEE!" bellowed the slightly craggy voice from the study.

She liked that too.

"Ready in a minute, Mr. Hampton," she yelled.

Some sort of low grunt emanated from Hampton's room that no one except Hampton would understand.

As she leaned against the side of the mint kitchen countertop, impatiently tapping her long maroon-painted fingernails against the top of the wooden doors beneath, Freda's mind zigged and zagged with disconnected thought patterns. Right then, she concluded, she liked who she was and what was happening. She was needed. Serving, rather than servitude, gladdened the heart of Freda Tucker. At another level, in the orbiting of their souls, an attraction was pulsating drawing the unlikely pair closer.

Finally, the first perk meekly responded to the heat in the pot. Then the second and the third. Freda joined in and did a few disco steps to the beat of the Hampton Percolator Band. Within seconds, she was really boogying in the kitchen when the conductor suddenly stopped the music. The coffee was done. She applauded the pot, washed two heavy mugs, and filled them with coffee. Not bothering to ask how he wanted his—he needed it black—she took hers straight as well.

Hampton hadn't budged since she left him. His arm still hung like a tree limb damaged in a storm, and his head continued to face the spot where she fell off the can.

"You rang for room service, sir?" Freda said, with mock black coquettishness.

Hampton didn't respond either with amusement or disgust. This was Freda's first try ever at light-heartedness around the wizrd, and she didn't feel threatened with the role. So disabled was he, so grounded was she, that keeping in her place seemed ridiculous. Actually, frivolity seemed the natural posture at that moment.

There was no way he was going to hold his coffee mug. He did try to lift his dangling arm. It barely moved. His eyes conveyed his helplessness. His voice didn't quite concede.

"Ms. Tucker, I believe I am in need of some assistance."

She looked at him and smiled, as if to say, "Man, you'll never say 'Uncle', will you?"

Placing her steaming coffee mug on the side table beside the enormous ashtray filled with half-smoked pipes, she knelt down beside his chair. Putting her hand behind his head and nudged it forward to meet the lip of the mug. He sipped and slowly swallowed. It burned a little. He sipped and swallowed again. Then he cleared his throat.

She leaned away to give him and his palate a chance to savor the trusty reviver. Then she repeated the process, after placing his dangling arm back on his lap. Doing so parted his robe slightly at the thigh.

Several more sips of coffee. Then, perhaps in an effort to steady himself, he inhaled an enormous breath. The sudden rush of air into dormant lung sacs sent him simultaneously coughing and lunging forward, followed by what seemed to him to be an ax splitting his head open. He grimaced with agony and stifled another cough so as to thwart the residual aftershock.

Gradually, the cerebral timpani retarded, and he rested again against Freda's hand. She carefully assessed the remains. Magically, he seemed to be slowly resuscitating—enough, anyway, to notice his robe had fallen distastefully from his leg. He corrected it. Running his reanimated hand through his disheveled hair, he looked quizzically at Freda.

"Thank you, nurse," he said, in a soft low tone. "I think I can handle it the rest of the way."

Freda didn't want to take her hand away from his head, but she did. Hampton took the mug from her and caressed it with both hands. The warmth of the cup was as comforting as the contents. His head rested on the back of his leather chair. He eyes scanned the ceiling.

They didn't say a word to each other. Freda didn't know if she should talk or not. All she was sure of was that the feeling of feeling good was still inside her. She knelt by Hampton's chair, watching his face for a clue, and sipped her coffee.

Without warning, his lips stretched to a smile; then they parted. Still studying the ceiling, he suddenly burst into a boisterous belly laugh—so loud and cachinnating that Freda was afraid he would spill his coffee. She reached out to take it from his hand, but he moved it away to his side so she couldn't reach it. He wanted everything the way it was—the laugh, the coffee, and her right there.

Finally, he put the words inside the laughter.

"Just like Clancy Bascum! Just like ol' Clancy!" The words made him laugh harder, louder. Now the tears were running down his cheeks. It occurred to Freda, as she gently brushed them away with her slender hand, that those tears must have been at least 86 proof.

She asked softly, "Who's Clancy Bascum?"

"Just like ol' Clancy. I knew I had caught that act somewhere else!"

Freda considered the possibility of Hampton hallucinating. Wizard or wino, she'd seen what too much booze can do to the brain.

"Mr. Hampton, who is Clancy Bascum? Was he a performer?" she asked, in all innocence.

Hampton relinquished the ceiling and turned to look at Freda for the first time. The expression of wide-eyed innocence set him off again into another salvo of wild and uproarious laughter. Finally, he calmed down to a point where he could utter a complete sentence, although the words were separated by gasps of laughter.

"Clancy Bascum was a belly-gunner on a Flying Fortress. I knew him when we were both stationed in England. A little guy, they all were; they had to be to fit into that upside-down dome they flew in. Anyway, early one morning, right before sunrise, after we had been out drinking at the officers' club all night, we had finished the mission briefing and were getting ready to board the craft. I was going along to cover the mission as a stringer for Shirer...William Shirer?" he said, as if to say, "You know him, don't you?" forgetting Freda hadn't been born then.

To keep the story flowing, she nodded, "uh, huh," and Hampton continued: "Leaving the briefing room, we walked outside for a last smoke before take-off. Some of the boys sat down on empty oil drums. They had been stacked upside-down by the door to be picked up and taken away. Clancy hoisted himself up on one, but it hadn't been turned over, and nearly fell into the damn thing bottom first! You should have seen him," Hampton's laughter was building again, and Freda, now in on the joke, started giggling too, "with his legs kicking against the side of that damn drum, and his arms flaying about screaming 'Get me out of here! Get me out of here!' We watched him for a while, then a couple of the boys rocked the barrel back and forth till it fell over, Clancy and all!"

By the time Hampton finished telling the story, Freda was matching him laugh for laugh. Her act, twenty minutes earlier, sent Hampton back over the years to another world.

"Ms. Tucker, never reject the theory that history repeats itself. It did in this room, didn't it?"

"Just call me Clancy," she said, with a "that's all there is to it" gesture.

Hampton looked at her for a brief second, then nodded approval.

"Okay, Clancy, I think I will; even though ethnically, it's inconsistent."

"There you go stereotyping," she replied, with a "you're a bad boy" shake of the finger.

He laughed. "I knew you'd say that. Got to keep that guard up against we fogies of the old school, don't you?"

Now *she* felt like a stereotyper. "I'm just kidding, Mr. Hampton," she said.

"I am too, Clancy," he said warmly.

The laughing explosion and the story telling took its toll on Hampton's limited energy supply. Freda noticed he looked drained. The grip on his coffee mug loosened, and his head fell back to the chair again. As he closed his eyes, she took the cup from his hands. That time there was no resistance. She didn't want to leave his side.

"More coffee?" she asked.

Just a "no" nod was her reply.

"Are you hungry?"

A grimace was her answer.

Now she felt compelled to talk. Intuitively, she believed that Hampton needed her to say something…something more than small talk.

"Mr. Hampton," she began, with measured words, "Bernie and I thought that…"

"That was the last time I ever saw Clancy," he interrupted, without opening his eyes.

"I'm sorry." *What a dumb thing to say*, she thought.

"He was killed on that mission. I wrote to his mother in Chicago. She scrubbed floors in an office building on the Loop. Nice lady, Mrs. Bascum."

"I'm sure she was, Mr. Hampton."

"Go on. What were you saying?" His voice remained low and sonorous.

Freda regrouped her thoughts and began again.

"Bernie and I thought that since the ratings were…"

"Oh, yes, Bernie. Bernie Frank. My star. How is Bernie today, Clancy?"

She started to say the conventional "fine." Instead, she seized the opening to reveal the motive for her visit.

"Not so good, Mr. Hampton. You see, he's suffering, and I'm suffering for him, because, well, no doubt you read…"

"Did he ever tell you how we met?"

"No, well, I think it was during the King…" A sudden urge to throw the cold coffee on his lap flitted across Freda's mind.

"We had come down to Atlanta to do a story on the aftermath of the King slaying. I happened to tune in his show in the motel room, and he was interviewing a candidate for Governor of Georgia. The man, a farmer, was difficult to interview and more difficult to understand. Nevertheless, Bernie persisted, and drew out of him emotions and impressions and views that were apart from the normal politician interview. He made a very average, inarticulate guest become interesting and human. Sitting in that motel room, I saw in that boy the qualities necessary to get people talking. Then I did a spot on his show myself. Intentionally, I held back…made it tough…gave him nothing. Confronted with a bad guest—me—he dipped into a reserve—himself—and made the segment entertaining and informative. I knew then that he was special. So, when World Television discussed putting together a talk show to buck the late night menu of Carson, and the rest, I touted Bernie Frank, and they bought the package." Then his voice trailed off as he said, "I guess we did all right for a while."

"Yes, for a while, Mr. Hampton."

"You see, Clancy," he continued his soliloquy, "I have always separated my professional and personal life. I've been that way all my life for my own reasons. I've always worked best by maintaining distance not only between myself and those I work with, but by remaining totally unaffiliated. Non-attachment provides an uncompromised broadcast, but a lonely life. Clancy, I want you to understand that I love Bernie Frank."

Freda couldn't believe what she was hearing. She reached for Hampton's hand without thinking.

"And you love him, too, Clancy. You love the person to whom you hitched your wagon, and I am the person to whom he hitched his. Odd, isn't it? Both wagons left from the same town and arrived at the same destination."

"Mr. Hampton, I…"

"And that is why I agonize from the core of my heart over the effect that events in my own life have had on him and his career."

Hampton stopped there, leaving Freda empty. There she sat, gazing at a man journalism professors lecture about, of whom broadcasters trade stories, whom fledglings in the media fear, whose austerity and pomp disarm, and whose word is law. Now he lies in his lair, dissipated and semi-sober, holding on for dear life to the sepia hand of his assistant, who was always made to feel inconsequential in his presence, while extolling his affection for the star of a show he is destroying.

Freda realized that the basis for this paradox had to be rooted in some dreadful and painful wound. This Hampton was not the one of the legend; this one was the one God knows — a suffering and tormented soul. Her dilemma was the mode of treatment.

Do I dare probe at that spot in him that is the source of his agony? she pondered. *Would exposing the wound to the sunlight devastate him; or would the verbal exorcism cleanse and heal him?*

Freda searched Hampton for an answer. Finding nothing, she looked around the room, to the ceiling and the walls, as if to spot some invisible angel with the answer. Her eyes found the piano.

Gently rubbing his hand with hers, she said, "Tell me about Sidney Wade."

Only a slight flinch in his fingers gave an indication that the question landed. She was not about to repeat the question. The words nearly gagged her the first time. The wait was interminable. His breathing seemed quicker, uneasy, with stabs for breath.

Finally: "Ms. Tucker, I believe you have overstayed your welcome."

Where did Clancy go? she wondered. She decided to send "Mr. Hampton" away with him.

"Millard, tell me about Sidney Wade."

He rose up, as if lifted by kinetic energy — stiffly, unnaturally, but to Freda, miraculously — and sat on the edge of his chair. She moved to the ottoman to face him, and reached for his hand. Abruptly, he withdrew it.

"Why? Why?" he yelled. "Why tell you? Why tell you anything? Who are you anyway? Do you know? You are a product of legislation. Without legislation, do you think you would be in here? Working for me? Were it not for quotas, affirmative action, black caucuses, and no-gut white politicians, you would still be on your hands and knees like…"

"Clancy Bascum's mother?" Freda asked, gently.

It stopped him momentarily. She was sure now. She had touched the spot. Now, can she remove it and stop the bleeding in time?

"You...you come into my apartment—no, *break* in to my apartment—scrounge around for goodness knows what, elicit my most private thoughts while I am weak and in no condition to protect myself, and now, you—you mercilessly, blatantly, and without the slightest bit of human compassion, probe my soul for the sake of your own curiosity? Or is it for the sake of your own career? Is that it? Yes...yes, that's it! Get Hampton to spill his guts out. There must be something in his regurgitation I can use to get his job! All that's left of his life, his career, is feces anyway. Might as well finish him off with some awful sin he has committed, if only I can locate it. My black sisters and brothers will surely reward me for nailing Millard Hampton—the last whitey left standing. So rub his hand, give him coffee, start him talking, and get his job! Hallelujah, brother! Right on! Another whitey bites the dust—a victim of his own sin, and my civil rights."

Freda sat silently for a few seconds. Then, she calmly asked, "Millard, was Sidney Wade your lover?"

He looked at her as if, for an instant, all of mankind's suffering since the dawn of the world had just flashed before his eyes. Seconds passed. Then, he closed his eyes, and the tears flowed profusely.

Freda cradled Millard Hampton in her arms and slowly, steadily rocked him back and forth, back and forth. With every weeping tremor, a part of the painful spot was expurgated.

Freda knew this process. Inherently, she knew that pain and agony suppressed must eventually be expelled by tears. The alternative is disintegration.

At least fifteen minutes passed. Fifteen minutes of solid, heart-rending weeping, rocking, and silent consoling. Then, a deep, shuddering breath and Millard eased back from Freda's body. She ran to the kitchen, soaked a towel with warm water, wrung it out, and ran back to wipe the salty wet face of Millard Hampton. It felt good.

"Let's go make more coffee," he said.

"There's lots more in the pot; I'll go get some for both of us."

"Okay, but I'll come with you," he insisted gently.

She got up and extended her hand. He took it and, for the first time in many hours, Millard Hampton was on his feet.

Freda poured two mugs of coffee and handed one to Hampton. Only their eyes communicated. At that moment, talk for either one was inappropriate. He motioned her back to the study, and she followed, making sure that he got there.

"This was his piano, you know. So many of the things he wrote in the fifties and sixties were written right here. Let's sit down for a moment."

They sat on the piano bench together. Hampton hit a note or two nervously.

"Did you write that, Millard? It's short, but pretty."

Hampton laughed.

"Actually, it's one of my better pieces. The others are not as elaborate."

Freda laughed.

As a few silent moments passed, Freda waited. Hampton remembered.

"I met him when he was assigned to Special Services in England. His job was to make arrangements for the entertainers who performed at the camps. He had been drafted right out of tin-pan-alley where he had already made his mark as a successful songwriter. I figured he would make an interesting sidebar story so, I interviewed him. I knew that one of the radio correspondents or papers would pick it up. It was a natural: "Sidney Wade, From Tin-Pan-Alley to GI Joe." Hampton gestured the headline.

"We hit it off right away; my *chutzpah* and his sensitivity meshed beautifully. The catalyst was creativity. Both of us, in our own way, were creative. We began to appreciate each other as human beings caught up in a place we didn't want to be yet some how knowing that we need to be there for some reason not yet illuminated. Let's go over to the sofa may we?"

To her amazement, Hampton extended his hand. She smiled and accepted it graciously. They moved across the room slowly. He paused at the sofa, and waited for her to be seated before he relinquished her hand and sat down next to her. Cinderella at the ball darted through her mind. He began to talk again, but something was wrong. She couldn't look straight in his eyes. Freda was annoyed with the positioning. She preferred him in the chair and she on the ottoman.

"Excuse me, Millard," she said, and rushed across the room. Pushing the ottoman like a railway porter pushing a baggage cart, she plopped down on it in front of his crossed legs.

"Sorry. Go," she said.

She waited. He continued.

"Sidney was not married; I was." Freda's brow lifted, widening her eyes in surprise. "It wasn't much of a marriage— there wasn't enough time for us. Sheila was my high school sweetheart, and we married right after graduation. The war came six weeks later; I'm in Texas, and she's in a defense plant. We kept in touch by letter as best we could. After a while, the letters were shorter and less frequent. Not hers as much as mine. I developed sort of a love-hate relationship with the war. I hated it for what it did; but loved it for what it was. The war, all of it, gave me a world to explore—a world to find me. From the first day of boot camp it was like that. The stories! The people! Fascinating from the first. There was a spirit, a juice that flowed throughout the thing of which I drank heartily.

Freda asked, "And your wife?"

"Sheila? Sheila was Sheila. Nice girl. We had the marriage annulled actually, cheaper than a divorce. She remarried, had a son, who, incidentally came to work for me and has since gone on to bigger things. Jerry Cooper—heard of him?" Hampton asked, nonchalantly.

"President Packard's main man? That Jerry Cooper?" Freda asked.

Hampton answered, "Precisely. Anyway, without the war, and me in it, Sheila and I would have been okay, maybe. At least I could have faked it for a time. However, the emotions that the war evoked compared to what I felt for Sheila was like a Dr. Grabow to a Dunhill. Both are smoking pipes; there the similarity ends."

The ease with which Hampton constructed his metaphor convinced Freda that his mind was clearing. It remained lucid as he told of his growing friendship with Sidney Wade. Sidney, it appeared, was the teacher; Hampton the student. Sidney taught Hampton the things he craved to know: art, refinement, music, taste, and life—as it is lived by those fully aware of its potential.

Before long, the Merlin-Arthur relationship between Sidney Wade and Millard Hampton provided the incentive that ignited Hampton to sniff out, often by incredible devices, some of World War II's most beguiling stories. The thirst for Wade's approval constantly challenged Hampton to exceed himself. By and by, Sidney had wangled transfers to where ever Hampton was, and Hampton was where the action was.

"Sidney was nearly indispensable after a while. You see, Sidney understood. That's a very simple sounding yet complicated, rare virtue. Sidney understood. He understood because he, too, was an artist. I painted verbal descriptions for broadcasters. He painted musical descriptions for performers. He realized how difficult mine were to create, as I grew to understand how agonizing it is to search for the precise note, the exact word. And when you find it—Eureka! Sidney understood. Do you follow me, Clancy? This is a very sensuous business we're in. Creativity. All of it; art, music, journalism, what have you. When one produces the precise ingredient at the precise moment to make people respond emotionally, my dear, what you have produced is tantamount to an orgasm. Sidney's music, much of it, was orgasmic. Many of my finest moments in broadcasting were orgasmic. The greats achieve it frequently. They probe, they excite, they fondle, and then, like magic, they intuitively sense the moment and strike the right note, the incredible question, the irresistible word, gesture, color—then suddenly, the volcano erupts. Then, all the stars in the universe smile. For they too, had their moment and know how gratifying it is. Sidney understood that. More than anyone I had met, Sidney knew the orgasmic-like elation of producing something well."

Symbolically seated at his feet, Freda was fully absorbed with Hampton's sexual metaphor. She sat enraptured. The concept was novel to her. Sex in broadcasting, or any endeavor, was an issue, a tactic or a weapon used just as she had been used by so many. She had learned to live with the things she had to do in order to get where she wanted. However, with Hampton claiming that the joy of a properly executed creative endeavor is the equivalent to the ecstasy of the sexual climax, Freda's deep-rooted self-disgust mollified. And sex, like love, appeared more as a precious flower than an obligatory weed.

Impulsively, she felt a compelling urge to bend down and identify with the joy of a properly executed creative endeavor.

Closing her eyes for several seconds to ponder the possibilities, she opened them to find her answer in framed in gold. Suddenly her erotic fantasies dissolved, and into focus on the wall behind Hampton's head, hung a photograph of Sidney Wade. Her temperature normalized; her lust abated, her stomach knotted.

"Clancy, I need a pipe. Would you mind getting me that Meerschaum? Hampton asked.

Freda welcomed the abrupt change of energy and mood. Walking to the huge pipe rack with a few remaining pipes still at attention, she asked, "You say Meerschaum, Millard? Would that be its breed or religion?"

Hampton laughed, and brought his hands together, applauded and said, "I love it! I love it!" Still laughing, he said, "one with a white lining in the bowl."

"That figures," Freda said. He laughed at that too, as she handed him the pipe. Freda also knew that the pipe was a delaying tactic. She knew that shtick. It was time to prod him along, get him to go on with the story she wasn't sure she wanted to hear but knew he needed to tell.

The rich aroma of Hampton's special tobacco mixture permeated the study. It found its own level and hovered in a gray cloud near the window.

She began cautiously. "Millard, were you and Sidney in love lovers? I mean, was it just...?

"Does that matter?"

Freda replied quickly. "It matters. Yes, it matters. It matters because I'm trying to find out what's wrong with you, which is what is wrong with Bernie, which is what's wrong with our show. Yes, Millard, it matters a lot."

He nodded thoughtful approval of her monologue. Taking one quick, then one deep puff from his pipe and slowly blowing the smoke to the air above Freda's head, he said, "All right, I'll answer your question. I agree: It is important for you, and maybe for me, to tell you. It would be a hell of a lot easier if I had a drink, though. I don't suppose you would..."

"No way!" she said implicitly.

He held his thumb and index finger an inch apart near his face and said, "Just a tiny sip? This much?"

Freda defiantly shook her head no.

"Well, so be it," Hampton replied resolutely. "You see, Clancy, lovers can be defined several ways. I'll save both of us the embarrassment of not defining the obvious. However, I will, for the sake of the grounds you delineated a moment ago, attempt to clarify the relationship between Sidney and me. I will be as honest and graphic as I am able. Ready?"

Freda feigned a confident look, and said, "Lay it on me." Inwardly, she felt tentative.

"Sidney Wade had a sensitivity about him that I have never known in any man or woman. Sidney cared about essence, about craft. He was successful in the field he loved, but he was unimpressed with success. He would often say, 'If the craftsmanship of a work is faulty, any accolade is meaningless. His sensitivity manifested itself in nearly perfect taste, personally and professionally. He used to define taste as 'moderation'. 'Poor taste is excess,' he would say. How many times he would scold me in that sensitive manner of his for exceeding the bounds of good taste."

Hampton paused to re-light his pipe. When he was satisfied that the entire bowl was glowing, he continued.

"That sensitivity remained constant in his personal life as well as the way he wrote songs. As you can tell, he was not a particularly attractive man. Yet, when you got, or I got, beyond the impishness of his appearance, I saw unfictitious beauty. Sounds amusing, doesn't it, Clancy? Look at him on those pictures. Do you see anything beautiful up there? Hmm?"

Hampton wanted a break in the action for a moment. As he did with his programs, he was now orchestrating the play for maximum audience effect. As his disciple, Freda was aware of the tactic. Out of respect, she acquiesced.

"Well," she said, playing along, "you look pretty good, but Sidney Wade? Definitely a face for radio."

Hampton laughed. Holding his robe snug to his lap, he re-crossed his legs, and then continued.

"Sidney cared for me in a different way than I cared for him. Sidney Wade was in love with me. He was a homosexual—had been, he told me, since he was about nine years old. He didn't swish, didn't mince around with a limp wrist, or talk with a lisp. He didn't try to make certain there was no mistaking it. It was just the way it was with him. We had known each other about four months when he told me. It was in a bar in Rome near the last part of '44. We had buddied around a lot by then, plenty of fun and good conversations. So when he calmly and characteristically confided to me that he was a homosexual and that he cared deeply for me, I didn't find it repugnant at all. It's strange, I can still hear him say, 'Millard, if what I say to you is repugnant, be honest enough to tell me straight away so that our friendship can traverse a different path.' At the time, under the circumstances, it seemed perfectly natural. Isn't that odd, Clancy? Can you understand it at all?" Hampton leaned forward, his eyes pleading for her understanding.

Freda was having a difficult time understanding. The legendary Millard Hampton was macho-man. He dressed, ate, spoke, and walked macho. Everything about this man exuded panache. He would chide those around him: "Tone up! I do fifty pushups and fifty sit ups every night!" He'd bore you with his tales about hunting and deep-sea fishing, and quote Hemingway and Faulkner with the zest of Billy Graham quoting Matthew and Luke. Such was the persona of Millard Hampton to every one with whom he had contact. Looking at him plead for her understanding of his love affair with a man—sexually consummated or not—asked for more than Freda was capable of giving. She had absolutely no qualm with gays; she had contempt for hypocrites.

Yet, she realized that complete honesty at that point would stifle the priority to get to the bottom of Hampton's problem. Consequently, she resolved to do what she resented: She would placate.

"Yes, Millard, I can understand," she said.

Studying her eyes for a brief moment, he went on.

"I told Sidney I like him very much, respected him, cherished his friendship, and needed him in my life. I told him, too, that I had never had sex with a man, and that I doubted that I could. I was not repelled by the thought, I explained to him, neither was I stimulated. Quite frankly, sex to me always interfered with a relationship rather than enhanced it. It just didn't mean very much in my life, ever. Odd, isn't it, Clancy, considering that I've applied the components of sex to every program I've produced. However, for its own sake, sex was never meaningful nor, quite frankly, fulfilling to me.

"Anyway, Sidney told me he understood and suggested as long as I understand where he stood, he would make no sexual advances unless I indicated I was ready. After the war, we both came home to New York. Sidney and I found this apartment, and we shared it until he passed away six months ago. He continued to write songs through the fifties; when rock and roll killed music, he more or less retired."

Hampton's voice faltered a bit. His eyes glazed.

Freda asked, "And you?"

"You know what I've done. I became the big bad wolf and ate people up while becoming a legend. However, when the camera was turned off, when the star took his final bow, when the director yelled, 'That's a wrap. Nice program everybody.', I'd go home to Sidney. Sidney would care. Do you know how important that is? To have someone who cares—not for support or security or toadying elation—to care because you love that person without reservation, without conditions, even without commitment. To care. Sidney cared like that. For me."

Allowing a few seconds to elapse, Freda asked, "Millard, did Sidney have a heart attack?"

She really didn't give much thought to the question. In fact, she remembered as she asked it that the clipping said he'd died "after a long illness." She was merely trying to keep the story going until its conclusion.

Hampton answered gently, as if to a child.

"No, Clancy, Sidney had cancer. We learned of it after he underwent what was supposed to be minor surgery to relieve an ulcer. They found a tumor on his pancreas. They gave him ninety days at the most. He lived five months. During that time—the period of his illness up to the end—I stayed with him as much as possible. There wasn't much that I could do. In the beginning, we played a lot of chess. I read to him, played music for him. We didn't watch television; he despised most of it. 'Crass' he called most of the programs. Anyway, the chemotherapy thoroughly debilitated him."

Hampton's pipe became a useless object at that point. Freda removed it from his hand. His eyes teared, but he held up his hands to gesture don't stop me now.

"It was during that period that our show began to slip. I found myself totally engrossed with Sidney. The show, Bernie, nothing meant anything. His pain was my pain, his weakness my weakness, his failing life my own life. Beyond that, I was totally wracked and helpless myself. You see, I had always controlled events. I conned, manipulated, out-foxed, and at times, nearly broke the law in order to develop and produce a program. But there, during Sidney's illness, I was totally at the mercy of an unmanageable and malignant event. Worse yet, it was devouring the only person I ever loved, and it was thus devouring me. You cannot imagine how absolutely devastated I became. When Sidney died, he took me down into the grave with him. He took my zest; he took my spirit. Millard Hampton died when Sidney Wade died. Only Hampton doesn't rest in peace."

He paused, breathed deeply, blinked several times, and then continued.

"Anyway, I decided, after Sidney passed on, to play it safe. Actually, I didn't decide; it was the only way I could function. I was literally petrified to get the great guest, to tackle the controversial subject, to build the provocative show. Safe—that was the way to play it. Play it safe. Sidney's illness—that unmerciful malignancy that I couldn't control, manipulate or orchestrate out of the script—stripped me of the very fiber of my essence, of my soul. As a result, I booked safe, sterile, boring people on the program. In so doing, I became my own assassin and the instrument of Bernie Frank's destruction. My battle with that irreconcilable enemy—an enemy that resisted and defied wit and savvy—destroyed with one death the accumulation of countless victories. My only comfort was the bottle. And you know, I guess I would have continued to exist in that state were it not for the awful truth in John Collier's column this morning.

He hit it right on the nose. I am the producer of the worst sin in the business: dullness. My God, that poor boy! I pull him out of Georgia—where he was happy—and bring him up here in New York, and then slowly, methodically, strangle the life out of him. My god, can he forgive me?" The sudden gush of tears was squeezed against Hampton's face with his two hands. He wept disconsolately.

Freda leaned forward and held him as she had earlier in the afternoon. Rocking him, as her ancestors had done for other white children, she let him weep.

The story Millard Hampton couldn't shape, finesse and produce zapped him of the stuff that made him go. He could make a program turn out the way he wanted; reality, however, blew his mind. Other people's deaths, other people's victories and defeats, successes and failures, wins and losses were fuel for his professional furnace. His death, his loss, was unbearable because it was the bloody truth—impervious to a story line, rewrite, edit or other video varnish. The master of the theater of the mind was destroyed by the theater of the heart.

Holding the sobbing gray head to her breast, Freda tried to reconcile the sauntering Hampton, the authoritatively pompous Hampton, the my-way-or-the highway Hampton, with the package in her arms.

She thought, *Was it all a fake? Was this Wizard from Oz a carefully calculated, impeccably designed, nattily attired, masculine image to camouflage a sensitive, caring, tenderhearted homosexual?"*

One deep sigh quelled the tremoring sufferer in Freda's arms.

Smoothing back his ruffled hair, she asked, "Feeling better?"

With a slight touch of his former self, Hampton said, "To paraphrase a tired bromide, Ms. Tucker, your breast hath charm to soothe the savage music."

In *The Bernie Frank Show* offices, such Hampton offerings nearly evoked applause from the obsequious staff. Here, Freda Tucker felt no obligation to feign any appreciation for anything she didn't feel merited it.

"Millard, that sounds clever, but I don't get it," she said boldly.

Looking at her for a brief second, Hampton leaned back against the sofa, and sighed, "Ah, such is the price one pays for venting one's soul to another: Once perspicacious, he becomes instantly a fool."

Freda sprang to her feet and leered down at the fallen hero. With her hands on her hips and her head slightly cocked, she said, "Oh, is that it? Now that you are a tad more sober than when I found you here half-dead, are you inching back into the world of Millard Hampton? The world where no one is quite worthy enough to comprehend the complexity of your genius? Five minutes ago, when my black tits were your comfy blankets, you didn't complain about not being comprehended. Well, let me clue you in about my ability to comprehend. My comprehension of Millard Hampton is that he is a sensitive, caring man, who loved another person—who happened to be another man—more deeply than most people ever love. And that in order for Millard Hampton to cope with what he felt was a defect in himself, he built another layer of personality around him. The original layer is made of goodness, decency, and kindness. The second layer—the one called The Wizard—is constructed from piss and vinegar, and a shovel full of bullshit!"

Standing there like Wonder Woman, she defiantly kept her eyes fixed on his. He returned a look of utter amazement.

"Clancy," he began, defensively.

She interrupted, "I'm not finished!"

He mutely said, "Oh?"

She began pacing back and forth in front of her prey on the sofa mentally arranging her thoughts. When she had them organized, she said, "Now, you can grieve and booze till you croak, if that's what you want. What I want is for you to either fix Bernie's show, or get off the pot! That's what I came here for, you know, to find out what the fuck is going on! Well, fella, I found out, and I'm sorry. I'm really sorry, Millard. But the point is that Sidney

Wade is dead and gone to heaven. He's okay—better off than us. But you? You're in hell, and you ain't even dead yet! Worse than that, you're pulling Bernie down there with you! And, not that it matters, but lately I've been feelin' a little hotter than usual myself! Now, you either have to live or die, Millard. If you die, die alone. If you live for God's sake, LIVE! If you need the bullshit image to pull it off, go ahead. I'll never tell. But don't allow one real death of a good person to kill two more. Don't, Millard!"

Hampton gazed at the impassioned svelte black figure with a sense of awe. A frozen silence gripped the study as the two searched one another with their eyes. A knock at the door cracked through the perfect stillness.

He said gently, "Do you mind?"

Freda's smile was his answer. She walked out of the room and down the hall to the front door.

"Who is it?" she asked.

"Telegram," said an adolescent voice from the other side.

"Just slide it under the door, please."

A pause. "You Millard Hampton?"

"Yes, I am."

"Figures," muttered the tip-less messenger.

Freda waited for the yellow envelope to stop sliding till she bent down to pick it up.

"Thank you," she said to the door.

Hampton was sitting behind his desk when she came back into the study. Freda stopped short for an instant. Except for the robe, this was the Hampton portrait that greeted her with such authority every morning since she came to work for him.

"Let me have that," he said, in that stern official manner she had come to despise so. His head was looking down at some papers.

As she stretched her arm out with the telegram in her hand, she disappointingly thought, *The Wizard lives again.*

Instead of grabbing it without acknowledgement, as he did so often throughout the course of a day, he slowly looked up at her. Taking the yellow envelope gently out of her hand with his right hand, he let it drop lazily to the top of his desk, while holding her outstretched hand with his left. Moving his head close to where he held her hand, he closed his eyes and tenderly kissed her slender fingers. Freda watched in stunned surprise.

Raising his head to find her face, while caressing her hand, he said, "I have decided to live, Clancy."

Freda's eyes welled up with tears, but she didn't cry. Her smile conveyed her deep joy.

"Now, why don't we celebrate me being born-again by you fixing us something to eat? I'm starved," Hampton said robustly.

In mock subservience, Freda said, "Ah, sorry boss, but the only thing you got in your fridge gets poured into a glass or studied under a microscope. Ain't nothin' edible in there."

"Well, then, my first decision as a reconstructed legend will be to take us out to dinner."

Freda clasped her hands in prayer pose as she looked toward heaven. "I don't believe it. It's another miracle! Me, Freda Tucker, actually going to break bread with Sir Millard Hampton."

"Don't push your luck, kid," Hampton said, with a pretended swat to her behind, as he strode out of the room in his familiar swagger. "I'll be ready in a moment. Open that telegram for me, will you?"

Freda ripped the seam of the Western Union envelope with the long nail of her right index finger. Reading it slowly, she swallowed a sudden gush of saliva to keep from gagging. Slowly, she walked to Hampton's bedroom. The door was open, and she caught a glimpse of him draped in a towel, still a bit moist from the shower. He was powdering his body.

"Millard," she called uncertainly.

"Just can't stay away from me for a minute, can you, dear?" he answered whimsically. "All right, come in; but believe me, I can not be rehabilitated. I gave up on that years ago."

The message went right over Freda's head. Sex was the furthest thing from her mind. She came in and sat on the edge of the bed. Hampton was deliberating the shirt selection in his closet. A plain white won. Tan slacks had obviously been decided upon in the shower, as there was no indecision there. The tie was no contest either: navy blue. He didn't need a mirror to tie it. The knot turned out perfectly.

"Courtesy of the United States Army," Hampton said, motioning to his tie. "You have to learn how to tie a perfect knot in the dark."

Sticking his knee-length brown stocking feet into a pair of Bally slip-on loafers, Hampton dislodged a navy blue blazer from its hanger and slipped it on. Pulling at the sleeve of his shirt, he said to Freda, "Eight minutes flat. Pretty good time, right? Okay, let's go." He reached for her hand, but got the telegram instead.

Taken aback somewhat by the exchange, he looked at Freda and saw an empty gaze. His glasses were in the study so he held the telegram at arms length and read:

MILLARD HAMPTON AND BERNIE FRANK:
DUE TO CONTINUING TREND OF SLIPPAGE IN THE RATINGS, PRODUCTION OF *THE BERNIE FRANK SHOW* WILL BE TERMINATED EFFECTIVE THIRTY DAYS FROM TODAY. STOP.
REGRETFULLY, R.T. EDMONDS,
VICE PRESIDENT FOR PROGRAMMING, WORLD BROADCASTING NETWORK. STOP.

Hampton looked down at the sullen Freda, thought for a moment, then said, "The time for decision has arrived, my dear."

Disconsolately, she said, "What do you mean 'time for decision'? There ain't no decision! We're screwed. Gone. Cancelled. Kaput!"

Who said anything about the show? It's time to decide where we're going to dine! French? Italian? Chinese? What's your pleasure? We'll talk about the show later." He reached for Freda's hand, and she extended it and stood up.

Shocked by Hampton's spunky resilience, she said, "Aren't you concerned?"

"Concerned? Yes. Worried? Somewhat. Lost? Heavens, no." Taking her arm, he guided her toward the door.

She stopped, and asked, "What will we do?"

Thoughtfully, he responded, "I'll tap that reservoir of piss and vinegar and a shovel full of bullshit."

"And Bernie?" she asked.

Checking his wristwatch, Hampton said, "Ah, yes, Bernie. Let's see how the poor boy is faring tonight. Flip it on, Clancy. It's right behind you on the dresser."

Freda turned, and there was a small 13-inch color set placed at an angle facing the bed. Hampton stood beside her as the set instantly provided a picture. There was Bernie, in his usual host's seat, with a man in a loud Glen Plaid, wide-lapel sports jacket. Freda's mouth dropped open as she focused on what appeared to be a gigantic penis standing erect and perfectly rigid from the guest's crotch.

Turning up the sound, she heard, "No, Mr. Frank, you can't eat this. It would kill you. Only very young Dishcloth gourds are among the few that can be eaten. So beware. Now, gourds grow easily, you'll be pleased to learn. The seeds need only be planted in a sunny location after the danger of frost has passed. Here, would you like to hold this?"

Freda slowly reached over and turned off the set. Her eyes were moist. Turning to Hampton, she saw that his were, too. They stood silently for a moment.

Then, Hampton said softly, "More than all of the rest, and I've worked with the best, Clancy, that boy is special to me. It's the way he works. He almost cybernetically reflects my conception of how it should be done. No one has ever been the extension of my conception of a program like Bernie. Do you understand that, Clancy? It's so rare!" He paused for a brief moment, then turned to Freda and said, "Clancy, I am contrite beyond words. Not for myself; but for that boy."

Freda backed away so that he could see her face. No tears now; her eyes were clear. She whispered, "I know." And now she did.

Hampton took a deep breath of self-composure, and placed his arm in Freda's. Slowly turning her toward the bedroom door, he said, "We'll call him later tonight. Let him talk this thing out with Peggy for a while."

He guided her down the hall to the front door.

Again, she halted. "And me? What happens with me?"

Putting a finger to his lips in deep thought, he paused, and then asked, "How did you get into my apartment?"

"I sent a wire to you at the office telling you President Packard needs to talk to you right away about a matter of urgent national security and signed it Dr. David Strauss. The guard downstairs let me right in when I showed it to him and swore him to secrecy." Hampton burst out in a loud, bellowing laugh.

"Lovely, just lovely, Clancy. You see, you've got some piss and vinegar and bullshit in you, too. Welcome to the club. We're now a team. Now, let's go and eat. I've got some calls to make tonight."

Chapter Ten

The Catoctin Mountains of Maryland, where the Presidential retreat Camp David nestles, was resplendent that May. Avatars and spiritual masters had metaphorically as well as spiritually gone up to the mountaintop for communion with God for centuries. For President Albert Packard, Camp David was the best of both worlds.

"David, how do you think the American people would react if I made Camp David my headquarters for the remainder of my term? I do enjoy it here so much."

David Strauss peered over his glasses at the trim figure standing by the fireplace of the small cozy den of Aspen Lodge. He, Jerry Cooper and General Andrew Jackson McKenna had been in a prep session for the Summit for eight hours. The President was bored after two. His abstract question was a certain indication that his mind was wondering.

"I don't believe, Mr. President, that they would be too thrilled with it. In the first place, they want their President in the White House. It gives them a sense of security. Like when you were a child and you were alone in your bed at night, it was comforting to know Poppa was in the house. In the second place, Camp David should not be over-used, Mr. President," Strauss advised. He spoke in his monotone voice that he affected when he was a professor so that his students would focus totally on the substance of his lecture.

He added, "They perceive and approve this to be a place where the President retreats from the pressure. Not a place where he comes for more pressure."

President Packard continued his study of the fire.

Jerry Cooper, who had been organizing his eight hours of notes, said, "I have to go with David on that one, sir," without looking up from his yellow legal pad. "Anyway, I get to feeling lost in space after just a couple of days here. It's not real, like a damn la-la land for Presidents."

"I disagree with the distinguished Dr. Strauss and Cooper, Mr. President," McKenna staccatoed. "I think you have hit on a magnificent idea."

Unlike the casual attire worn by Strauss and Cooper, the Director of the CIA wore his standard black suit, tie and shoes and white shirt.

"From the security standpoint, Camp David is locked airtight. The military personnel here are absolutely our people, if you know what I mean, Mr. President. No future book writers. No press leakers. No adventurers of any sort. You could run things the way you wanted without concern with our enemies from within, as well as without. No demonstrators, no tours." McKenna smacked his lips, and continued, "Mr. President, I wholly recommend Camp David as the citadel of the United States."

Without looking up from his yellow pad, Cooper said, "Why don't we put him at West Point, General? Or better yet, Ft. Knox?"

Strauss pushed his glasses to rest on his forehead, then suddenly roared with laughter, his shoulders bouncing with each laugh.

McKenna flushed. "Whose side are you on, Cooper, theirs or ours? The President has proposed a solution to governing without intimidation from the cynics who gloat over our inability to control the events of this world, and you jump into bed with the worst of them, as always. I ask you again, Cooper, whose side are you on?"

Half smiling, Strauss quickly interjected, "I don't believe the President inquired from the standpoint of security, General McKenna. His proposal seemed to me to be one predicated on convenience rather than insulation."

Cooper would have preferred Straus not to intervene. He wanted to reply to McKenna's loyalty examination directly. Waving off further comment from Strauss, Cooper looked squarely at McKenna and said, "I'm on everybody's side, General—except yours."

As if someone released the spring, McKenna's feet hit the floor. He screamed, "There! You heard him, Mr. President. You heard him! He finally said it! At last, he admits what I have suspected for a long time. If you're not with us, you're against us—isn't that right, Mr. President?"

McKenna's loose scriptural reference must have invaded the President's mental zone and gotten his attention. Turning from the fire, he smiled that voter-appealing grin and said, "Boys, we're all tired. Let's knock it off for today."

Strauss and McKenna gathered up their briefing books and stuffed them into briefcases. As always, Cooper would remain with Packard until the others left.

McKenna said, "I'll refine and transcribe my concurrence with your desire to establish your headquarters at Camp David, Mr. President, and have it on your desk in the morning no later than 0700." Then looking squarely at Cooper, he said, "I'll mark it 'President's eyes only.'"

"Thanks, General," responded Packard. "There is really no rush on that."

"Don't worry, Mr. President. I'll be up all night on it if necessary."

Packard nodded.

Strauss peered at Cooper. He wasn't smiling.

McKenna strutted toward the door then pivoted instantly when the President said, "Oh, one more thing, General McKenna."

"Yes, Mr. President," McKenna said smartly.

"Anything more on that Russian dissident, what's his name, Bellow?"

"Ah, Mr. President, I have the total resources of the Agency on this. All of our people in the Soviet Union are gathering data. Naturally, it's not too easy because of the way the Soviets have disguised this action, however I assure you, we will know more about Belov, I believe it is, Mr. President, than he knows about himself."

"But, do we have anything more now than we had a day ago, General?"

McKenna's nostrils flared as he pursed his lips.

"No sir, not a lot."

As he did on Cooper's behalf earlier, David Strauss intervened for the President."

"General McKenna, perhaps it would be in the best interest of the President and the nation—perhaps even the world—if you would confine your investigation to intelligence data, and then formulate a theory, rather than attempting to have your theory corroborated by your intelligence."

"Dr. Strauss," McKenna began, with eyes blazing, "I am the Director of the Central Intelligence Agency. Prior to that, I was its Deputy Director. And prior to that, I was a special operative in East Germany and other places. I am not harmonious with the Janus-face of diplomacy, sir. Nor am I accordant with the equivocal nature of politics. What I am expert on, Dr. Strauss, what I am positively convinced of, what I would stake my life on, Dr. Strauss, is that the Soviet Union is the archenemy of the United States. That the Soviet Union is to the United States what the devil is to the Lord."

With his hands and arms in a "What's the big deal?" pose,

Strauss said, somewhat weakly, "General McKenna, you need not defend your patriotism to me or…"

"Just a minute, Dr. Strauss. Allow me to finish. You did not hesitate to offer me the benefit of your vast experience in espionage and counter-intelligence. Granted, Dr. Strauss, any utterance I might render would appear dull, ill conceived, and, if reviewed by the press, comical by comparison. After all, who can compete with the illustrious Dr. David Strauss in a battle of the spoken word, the quotable quip, the facile mind, or, if one believes the rumors, the seductive charm?"

"Mr. President," Strauss appealed, "I think this has…"

McKenna bored in. "Nor do I posses the dubious talent for appearing to be the President's man when I'm with him, only to become the President's detractor when he's out of sight."

His face the shade of the President's shirt, Strauss made a mental memo to have Marsha Kushman's bedroom swept for bugs the next day. Pleadingly, he said, "Mr. President, I insist this discussion has…"

"Let General McKenna finish, David," the President said in his familiar mellow baritone.

"Thank you, Mr. President." McKenna paused to find Strauss's eyes, then Cooper's, in celebration of his moment of triumph. "Dr. Strauss, you counseled data first, theory second. That is sound advice in science, medicine and criminology. In the relationship between the Soviet Union and the United States, however, it is naïve, amateurish, and gravely dangerous. The Soviets, Dr. Strauss, never give us an inch without a mile in return. To be specific, Dr. Strauss, the release of Yuri Belov might be an indication of a friendly gesture to you and other sophisticated one-worlders. To me, Yuri Belov is another Russian weapon. It is my job to find out how it was built, how it works, and how it can be destroyed. In my business, Dr. Strauss, theory first; data second. Now, if you'll excuse me, Mr. President, gentlemen, I have much work to do this night." McKenna about-faced and clicked out of the room.

After McKenna closed the door, Strauss said, "Why do you tolerate such an idiot, Mr. President? He's dangerous, for all of us. Naturally, I'm not one bit disturbed with his attack on me personally."

Cooper looked at Strauss's fingernails. The skin around them was bleeding.

The President said nothing. Walking back to the fieldstone fireplace, he stretched his strong arms behind his back.

"Missed my exercise today, boys. All this sitting, not good I'll tell you."

Strauss, looking drawn, headed toward the door and said, "Well, if you have no more need of me, Mr. President, I think I'll take in a movie with the press pool tonight. It might help me forget that nincompoop for a few hours."

"Good idea, David," the President said. "What's playing?"

"It's called *Oh God*."

Without looking back at Strauss, Cooper said, "Congratulations, David. So they finally made the story of your life."

The President looked at Cooper quizzically. As usual, he didn't get it.

Brushing off Strauss's shoulder, the President said, "Don't worry about McKenna, David. He means well."

"So did Joe McCarthy, Mr. President. I will talk to you later, perhaps. Good night."

"Good night, David. Thanks for the bang-up job you did on the Summit book. I'll call you later."

Cooper got up, put his papers in his well-worn briefcase, and said, "Mr. President, I think I'll go over to Laurel Cabin and have a bite; probably see the movie. Is there anything else you need for now?"

Albert Packard turned from the spectrum of beauty beyond the glass wall that looks out over the vast mountain to the farms in the distance and thought for a moment.

"Jerr, how about having your dinner with me here tonight?"

Cooper was taken aback. In all the years of serving at the

pleasure of Albert Packard, he was never once invited to dine with the man. Albert Packard ate alone. That was as much Packardabilia as Truman's poker games and Kennedy's libido. In fact, he issued a staff memo just after the inauguration declaring, "information or discussion internal or external regarding the President's menu is absolutely top secret." That the most powerful man in the western world had equated his vittles with the guidance system in a nuclear warhead often made Cooper chuckle.

"Will Mrs. Packard be joining us?" Cooper asked.

"No, Jerr," the President replied. "It'll be just you and me."

Then he slung his broad arms around Cooper's shoulder, and added, "Just like old times, uh?"

Old times, shit, Cooper thought. *This is new times! I've campaigned with this man, coached him, advised him, been embarrassed and proud of him—but never, never has he just shared a buddy moment with me. Now why, all of a sudden, has the cuisine curtain been lifted?*" he asked himself.

"I'd be happy to, Mr. President." Then Cooper added for himself, "Just like old times."

The President guided Cooper to the small dining area just off the living room. The face of the young Navy steward, Ensign Felton Avery, who always served him at Aspen Lodge, flushed to a shade of red that nearly matched his jacket when the President said firmly, "Son, prepare another place at the table for Mr. Cooper, please."

Ensign Avery, selected personally by the President on his first weekend at Camp David shortly after his inauguration, was well aware of Packard's menu embargo.

The secret—at least for that evening—for which poor ensign Avery envisioned his spending the rest of his life in the brig, was pot roast. The President and Cooper ate heaping platefuls of the steaming stuff and hardly talked except for occasional grunts that only a satisfying meal can evoke. Cooper had second and third helpings, smiling often at the thought that he was eating a classified top secret of the government of the United States.

The President, likewise, did himself proud. He must have had five servings, which he absorbed with giant mouthfuls. His beverage was fruit juice. Cooper ordered a Budweiser, knowing but not deferring to Packard's disdain for "spirits."

After the second helping of chocolate cake, the President stood up from the table and said, "Let's move over by the fire, Jerr."

"Mr. President, you must be as worn out as I am, so if you'd rather pack it in for tonight, that'll be fine with me."

Strolling toward the huge roaring fireplace, he said, "Jerr, ol' boy, don't be silly. Come over here, kick off your shoes, and relax a spell. You know me, Jerr, a tea-totler. But if you want something, just ask for it. I'm sure the boys could find something."

Cooper said, "And you know me, Mr. President, a brandy would be terrific."

To the side of Packard's chair was a white console telephone with 16 buttons that occasionally blinked. The last two buttons were red and would buzz if a call warranted the President's attention. He had issued instructions that nothing, short of a nuclear attack on Washington, justified his answering a call when he was "on the mountaintop."

For what seemed to be ten minutes, they didn't say much to each other. Cooper wasn't unnerved; he knew how much difficulty Packard had making small talk. Idle chat with a pal was something Cooper never saw him do in all the years he worked for Al Packard. Campaigning he was the best—affable, gregarious, charming. Anything more intimate, and he was a blank slate, a dry hole.

Then, gazing intently in the fire, Packard said, "Jerr." His words had air around them, like the last words before falling asleep.

"Yes, sir?"

Cooper looked at him. Packard maintained his stare somewhere deep into the fire.

"Do you think those stories about David are true?"

"What stories are you talking about, Mr. President?"

Cooper's request for clarification was legitimate. There were so many David Strauss stories circulating.

"Oh, you know. The ones about his sexual appetite, and so forth."

Cooper took a quick gulp of his brandy. Never had this pillar of Mid-western propriety ever brought up the subject of sex except as it applied to a political issue such as abortion. Dirty jokes were outlawed on the plane or anywhere near this President. Everything he read or watched for his own enjoyment was rated ultra G.

Cooper groped for an answer.

"Frankly, Mr. President, I think most of those stories are press exaggerations. We run a pretty straight shop, unlike other administrations. The reporters love Strauss because he feeds their imagination."

It was the best Cooper could come up with on short notice.

The President didn't seem to hear him. He remained still, silent.

Cooper felt alone in the room. *There's no one there,* was all he could think of as he leaned over for a closer look at Packard. His eyes were open, but they didn't blink. Nothing moved; not a hand, not a finger, not a foot. If his massive chest hadn't been heaving slightly beneath his flannel shirt, Cooper would have summoned his physician. "He's alive. But where?" Cooper wondered.

Cooper leaned back into his chair. His eyes were drawn to the flames in the fireplace spastically jutting, as if commanded to perform by some invisible authority. He felt an eerie chill run through his body.

Once again, Cooper leaned toward the President, closer this time than before. Packard was oblivious, as if in a hypnotic trance.

Suddenly, Cooper shuddered when a voice that sounded like

it was coming from the inside of cave said, "Imagine, Jerr, my National Security Advisor ejecting his seed into the vessel of every tart that beckons. I've been meaning to talk to him, Jerr. I've been meaning to explain to him how his behavior is a damnation to his soul. But the Summit and all the responsibility of dealing with that atheist Pavlovsky has kept me from talking to David. You understand, don't you, Jerr?"

Cooper just watched and listened. Through the years, he had witnessed other Packard diatribes involving his religious beliefs, and dismissed them all. This one was different. *Spooky* was Cooper's description to himself.

"You see, Jerr, the Lord's laws about fornication are clear and irrefutable. Do you know that when Mrs. Packard and I joined for procreation purposes, we never touched one another? I insisted she remain motionless under a white linen sheet so that she was entirely covered. Naturally, a hole was slit so that my rod could enter her vessel. When I deposited, I left the room and prayed that I had fertilized her. I assume she did the same — although the prayers of women are of secondary value to God. Now that her childbearing years have expired, she is no longer capable of completing her part of procreation, which is the only, I repeat, the only reason for man to spend his seed into a woman. That's why Mrs. Packard and I don't share a bed anymore. Were I to engage with Mrs. Packard merely for the sake of my gratification, I would be a fornicator. Therefore, we abstain."

Cooper thrust his arm out to grab the brandy glass, and belted down the remains. He silently thanked the steward for leaving the bottle. He refilled his glass to the rim.

Still motionless, the President continued his hollow monologue:

"Yes, I must speak with David. He must come to realize that all his brains and all his influence will never undo the irreparable harm he is doing by allowing his staff of life to lead him into the devil's den. I know what he is doing. McKenna keeps me informed."

Cooper thought, *So that's how that son-of-a-bitch keeps his job; by peeping through keyholes for the President.*

"Yes, if it wasn't for the Summit, Jerr, I'd have Strauss freed from his temptations. But the Summit is paramount, Jerr. This Summit with the atheist Russian is the second singular most important event in the history of the world. I will tell you why."

Cooper cringed at the possibility, drank some more brandy, and waited silently.

"I am going to offer Pavlovsky a two fisted ultimatum. First, he must publicly denounce the Soviet policy of atheism. Second, he must personally repent of his sins and be baptized in the name of his Lord and savior Jesus Christ. If he refuses, I, on behalf of the Prince of Peace, as steward of Revelation 20:7 will release nuclear Armageddon on Gog and Magog. The black box will be programmed to give Pavlovsky twenty minutes to decide yes or no, during which time I will pray for his soul and those of his people."

Rather than jump up and shout, "You're going to do what!" Cooper remained poised bordering on numb thanks in part to the Courvoisier. His mind flashed back to that frozen late afternoon in Iowa when Millard Hampton introduced him to Albert Packard and Packard said, "Wanna join the crusade, Jerr?" "The bastard meant it! Literally!" Cooper said to himself.

As Cooper sat in bewilderment, the President continued: "Have you ever wondered what current world conditions really mean, Jerr? Why global pollution? Crime? Chaos? Moral corruption? Well let me tell you, brother: Things will worsen before they get better. That is because of the likes of the David Strausses—men whose lust spreads moral decay throughout the world. The human body is nothing but a filthy hulk of rotting flesh, Jerr. Carnal delight is the food of the devil. It is the cause of all our problems. That is why I have taken it upon myself to alter the present direction of mankind from the course mapped out by the Red Beast residing in the Kremlin. Dmitri Pavlovsky is the anti-Christ, the devil's ambassador. It is up to me, Jerr, to seize the Holy Grail and cleanse the purveyor of the devil's will in the name of Jesus Christ. I repeat, Jerr, Pavlovsky accepts Christ for himself and his nation at the Summit, or I will ride the Pale Horse and annihilate the seven heads of the Red Beast in the name of Jesus Christ. That, and that alone, is my mission and my destiny. It is the reason I ran for President. It is the reason I was elected by the will of God

Cooper finished the bottle.

Only the occasional flicker of light from the telephone console buttons gave evidence that a real world was still out there. Within the ghostly atmosphere of the President's citadel, the ranting of President Albert F. Packard shut out time, and life, and joy, and reality.

Before Cooper could coax his brandy-soaked brain to decide how to handle the weird situation to which he was the sole witness, Packard suddenly spoke. This time his voice raised a tone in pitch.

"Jerr, I feel the Holy Spirit, now. Lord Jesus, I feel it, Jerr. Oh, how wonderful! Oh, how beautiful! Yes, Yes, Oh Lord Jesus, yes! Oh, Jerr, if you knew what I feel, what I see."

Slowly, his arms began to rise above his head in hallelujah style. Cooper felt a cold frightening chill all over his body, smothering the effect of the alcohol.

Cooper screamed, "MR. PRESIDENT!"

"No, Jerr, don't. Allow it to enter me," Packard cried loudly, "Don't stop, the, ah, Jesus, rhget tuun ahgumitarabib teruntib stibularim cknebularioum stomwpitop ziparium poynep ahgipelanoymn eympostilov…"

As Packard babbled that indiscernible sequence of sounds, he waved his arms from side to side above his head, while his body slowly rocked back and forth. His eyes rolled around in their sockets. His face bore an expression of supreme ecstasy.

The chatter continued for what seemed to Cooper to be ten hours. Actually, it lasted about twenty minutes.

Although Cooper was in a state of utter shock, he was not

perplexed with what he was witnessing. When he worked with Millard Hampton, he had gone to a rural place in Tennessee to produce a story on "speaking in tongues." He got linguists, anthropologists and others to attempt to explain the phenomenon. One claimed it is an ancient, now obsolete, language that is somehow induced by euphoria from some unexplained memory bank in some people. The surly Cooper didn't buy it. *Folks who babbled were simply fucking nuts,* he had personally concluded. Cooper was drawn to the natural and dismissed the supernatural.

He thought back to that story as he continued to observe the incredible scene unfolding for his eyes only.

The babbling continued: "spectibytim syejtopip boynebuaris hos charyo ventiromopoum chy syrio kentpnoplim."

Finally, with a sighing and protracted, "Auhhhhhh," that Cooper thought sounded like the end of every scene of every porno flick he ever saw, Packard was still.

Cooper searched him closely noticing how drained he looked. His face was devoid of its color and was damp with perspiration. His eyes were closed and his lips were slightly parted. Edging a bit closer, Cooper saw Packard's head tilt then fall to rest near his right shoulder. The President of the United States was asleep.

For several moments, Jerry Cooper reflected upon the staggering events he had just witnessed. Always the objective cynic, he tried his best to clear his mind of the farcical aspect and treat the matter with the crisis management it justified.

Am I the only one who knows the President's plan at the Summit? He pondered.

Surely, I am, he concluded.

Did Packard really intend to give Pavlovsky twenty minutes to renounce atheism and accept Jesus Christ or all nuclear hell will rain down on Russia from the press of the Presidential button, or was this a man who somehow gets high on pot roast and has Paulian illusions of grandeur? Cooper wondered.

Based on what went on in front of him, he concluded Packard was dead serious.

Should I tell Strauss? Certainly not McKenna. Shit, he'd probably like the idea and propose that Packard hold Pavlovsky's head under the Volga for ten minutes!

He then considered informing Packard's wife. He quickly dismissed the idea. *Hell, any broad that would allow her husband to fuck her through a sheet has to be slightly bonkers herself,* he thought smiling his one-sided snide smile.

Cooper reviewed his options for a moment or two more. He even considered calling Millard Hampton for guidance. *Too risky,* he thought. He didn't know where that relationship stood after not hearing from Hampton for so long. Best to keep his own council he mused, as he sat alone, feeling alone, watching the fire burn out.

Suddenly, the cranky sounding buzzer from the telephone console stabbed through the stillness of the Aspen Lodge living room. Cooper leaped to his feet and bolted in front of the vanquished President. Grabbing the receiver so tightly, he thought he heard the plastic crack.

"Yes?"

"Mr. Cooper," the Naval operator's voice was firm and crisp. "Prime Minister Amos Gavron on the line for you, sir. He wants to speak to you before he speaks with the President. He says it's a matter of dire urgency."

Cooper dug desperately into his shirt pocket for the first cigarette he'd had since breakfast. Packard didn't allow smoking in his presence by anyone, however Cooper figured Packard wasn't there to object even though he sat three feet away. With the receiver cradled between his cheek and shoulder, Cooper took a deep drag, and blew the smoke to the ceiling.

All I need now was to hear a fucking war has blown the Middle East apart," he scowled.

"Okay, put him through," he said to the operator.

A slight pause, some clicking, then: "Jerry? Are the telephone lines secure? Is this call scrambled?" asked the slightly hoarse voice of the Israeli Prime Minister, with its mild British flavor.

"Yes, Mr. Prime Minister," Cooper assured him.

"Good, then let me ask you something. How about setting me up with a good *shiksa* piece of ass next week when I'm in New York?"

Cooper's mouth dropped open, the cigarette stuck dangling from his lower lip.

"And, by the way, tell that ass-hole Strauss to lay off my broads, or I'll tell the world how he sodomized a camel the last time he was in the Negev."

Was he drunk? Cooper wondered. *What the hell was happening tonight? Has the whole world gone fucking mad?*

Cooper faked a laugh, and said, "Mr. Prime Minister, this must be a joke. Are you having a party?"

Indignantly, the voice on the other end of the phone replied, "Party? Joke? Who has time for jokes? Arabs here; Arabs there. A *shmuck* in the White House. Who jokes? You must be joking to say I'm joking."

"No, I didn't mean you were joking in the sense that..." he abruptly stopped talking when a thought ripped through his brain. *Only one person would make a call like this. One man in all the world*, he thought. He smiled his half smile, removed his cigarette from his lips, and nodded his head as if to say, *nice job.*

Slowly, Cooper spoke into the receiver: "Millard, you conniving son-of-a-bitch!"

"Hi, lad, how are you?" said the familiar voice.

"I don't believe it. I don't BELIEVE IT!"

"Believe, lad, believe. I needed to talk to you."

"Well, why the hell didn't you just call me?" Cooper didn't say he was thinking of calling him, only a few minutes ago.

"I've been trying all night, lad, but they wouldn't let me

through. They said it had to be an emergency. So, you know, I did what I had to do."

Cooper sang: "And did it your way."

"They told me you were dining with the President, lad. Is that true? If it is, my understanding is that he'll have you tossed to the alligators in the morning. Or is all that recluse business overplayed?"

"Amos, baby, some day I'll tell you the whole story." Cooper hoped Millard would let it go at that.

"I'll be waiting, lad. Say, let me tell you why I called. I know you're busy so I'll get to the point. The boys at the network and I have had a difference of opinion on some things, and I've decided to take my leave. How about finding me something with The Voice of America, or some such uselessness, until I get relocated? I hate to ask you for this, old friend, however reality demands it."

Cooper was aware of Millard Hampton's difficulty making *The Bernie Frank Show* a success. He imagined how hard it was for him to ask anyone to do anything for him, especially one of his disciples. Hampton was the bestower of favors, not the begetter.

"Millard, I'll look around first thing in the morning, make a few calls. I'm sure something will open up soon. Sorry things haven't worked out with World."

He glanced down at the President. Packard was still sacked out somewhere between Camp David and the road to Damascus.

"I'd do it now," Cooper continued, "however things are really hectic tonight." The second he said it, he wished he hadn't.

"Oh?" said Hampton, in that inherently curious tone that only good journalists emit when they smell something. "What's up?"

Cooper quickly reverted to his press briefing tactic of making something of minimal importance seem vital in order to avoid questions about something vital.

"Well, we've been preparing for the Summit, you know, and our work is compounded by this dissident clown the Russians are releasing. How to handle that, and so forth, you know."

"Oh? Tell me more?"

Hampton could get more information out of an "Oh?" than any reporter alive.

Cooper figured he'd feed him some more and find a way to get him off the phone.

"Well, you know how the President has been insisting that human rights must be accepted as an issue by both sides before progress can be made at the Summit?"

"Yes, go on, lad."

"Well, it seems that the Russians have selected some harmless schnook from one of their prisons and are going to set him free. You probably heard about it. It's a terrific PR move on their part and opens the way for the Summit to proceed without them being encumbered with the human rights question. So, we're kicking around our response, you know, whether to see the guy, or not see the guy, praise the Russians, or downplay the deal. You know the drill. Say, Millard, I'll get on the job thing first thing in the morning and call..."

"Jerry, this dissident—what's his name?"

"Millard, believe me, it's no big thing. He's a small time— means nothing. Strictly PR."

"Name, lad."

"Goddamn, Millard, do you want a favor or a briefing?"

"Jerry," Hampton said in a firm, controlled voice, "do we know the dissident's name?"

"Yuri Belov."

"Yuri with an R or an L?"

"R, goddamn it, as in Red-ass," Cooper fumed.

"Jerry, I want you to get me an interview with him."

"You what? You want me to do what?"

The President stirred, snorted and returned to Armageddon.

"Lad, I want you to assist me in the procurement of a diplomatic passport as well."

"You did say what I thought you said. Look, Millard, you call me at five past midnight while I'm here alone with the President of the United States. You get through to me by impersonating the Prime Minister of Israel. You ask my help finding you a job. I agree to find you a job. And, now you say get me an interview with the hottest potato we've got to handle? Millard, that exceeds..."

"Stop, lad. Listen. Cancel the job request. Please forget that I asked. Okay? I want to travel to Europe and Russia without restriction. You say Belov is a nobody. Fine. Then there should be no problem. I sense something interesting there. Who knows? I used to. Now I'm not sure. Back when you worked with me, you remember those days don't you, lad, I would have been certain whether or not there was a story. Now I can only say that I sense something. Will you help me, Jerry? For whatever reason, will you help me?"

Cooper tossed his cigarette in the fire and fumbled for another.

He thought, *Hampton is doing his number on me. It's Iowa all over again! What an awful fucking night!*

"Millard, old friend! The guy might not even come to the U.S. Who knows? He's unknown. No book on him at all. Even McKenna's got very little, and that's unusual for McKenna."

Again, he knew he shouldn't have revealed that to Hampton. *Shit. He has me spilling my fucking guts out!*

"I mean, Millard, they might set him free and all he'll want is a bowl of borscht and a broad. A Solzhenitsyn he ain't, I assure, you," Cooper said.

Hampton said, "Doesn't matter. I'll make my own judgment after I learn about him. You can arrange the interview no matter where he goes. If he's a dissident, he'll want freedom. So he'll want to go to a free country. Probably ours. There aren't that many any more. Just help me get it, exclusively. I'll settle for being first. That's all I ask."

"That's all you ask? First, you ask for a job because you're on your ass. Now you say 'I don't need a job, I need an exclusive interview with the guy who is making the Summit go.' That's all you ask! Millard, I am the Special Advisor to the President of the United States. I owe my loyalty to him and to the country and I've been consistent on that score. You may have thought you planted me in the Packard parade as one of your many faucets, however time proved you wrong. Right, Millard? So the answer is no. I simply can't."

"Lad, when you needed national exposure for Packard's campaign ten years ago, I provided it. When you needed lessons in dealing with the Washington press corps, I gave them. Whenever you wanted something leaked, I sprang it. I got nothing out of that, lad, except the satisfaction of helping you. Remember, lad, it was you who wrote me when you were in college. It was I who offered you a job when you graduated. And regardless of your perception of my sinister motives, it was I who placed you with the President you now so loyally serve. Now, in the spirit of reciprocity—it's a sacred word, lad—I am only asking you to repay in kind a partial measure of the favors you received from me. An interview, Jerry, with Yuri Belov— that's all I ask for my years of service to you, and for the love we both have for your mother. I won't ask again. Figure out a way to deliver that makes sense for everybody. Just consider it, Jerry. If you decline, however, I just want you to know how proud I have been of you, what you have accomplished, and how you have done it. And I know how proud Sheila must be as well."

Cooper couldn't help but smile. He reflected back to his NBC days when they used to call it "Hampton Poker." This time he played the Sheila card. It was the first time ever that Hampton had evoked the name of his first wife and Cooper's mother. *He's probably been saving it like an ace*, Cooper mused, *for just such a time as tonight.*

The thought activated his mind's replay button mind. Watching the tapes of his childhood adoration for Hampton brought on his one sided grin. It grew wider seeing again his interview for the college paper, his job with the network, and the cold day in Iowa when Hampton passed him off to Albert Packard. He interrupted his *This is Your Life* episode to look over at Packard. Still no sign of life from the hulk snoring in the big chair. A shudder passed through Cooper's body and his grin disappeared as he fast-forwarded to the night's events and what Packard planned to do at the Summit. A mushroom cloud hovering over the Kremlin formed in his mind. He shook his head to rid himself of the image.

Cooper sighed deeply, and said, "All right, Millard, I'll try."

There was a slight pause on the other end, then Hampton said almost casually, "Oh, one more thing, lad, if it's not too much trouble, please send anything you've got on Belov to my apartment by White House courier."

"I'll take care of it, Millard. I do not have to describe for you the conditions of this arrangement, do I?"

"No, lad. I understand and will abide. I want you to know how much this means to me and how grateful I am. Thanks again, my boy. I'll be in touch. Goodnight, lad."

"Hello, David? Sorry to bother you so late, however I have an idea on Belov."

"At three in the morning? Couldn't it wait?"

"I suppose it could, but since you're awake, allow me to try it on you."

"Well, go ahead, quickly, if you don't mind."

"Surely. The press is already beginning to request interviews with Belov. With the delicate state of affairs between the Russians and us at this point before the Summit, why don't we restrict the news coverage?"

"Restrict the press! Cooper, I think you're barking up the wrong country. The domestic political ramifications will be outrageous against the President."

Actually, Strauss delighted in Cooper's suggestion. It was just what would please Molenski. Typically, however, he didn't want to appear over-eager.

"Not if the Russians insist on it as a condition of his release," Cooper said.

"What?"

"Look, all we've got on Belov is that he's for human rights. Well, so is my Uncle Oscar. But ask him to define human rights, and he'll get flustered and belt you in the mouth. See what I mean, David? Yuri Belov might be a blooming idiot. Or, he might be an irrational fanatic. Or he might be what McKenna wants him to be. He could be anything. He could be downright dangerous and shoot off his mouth about things to the press that get him headlines and wreck the Summit."

"I see what you mean, Jerry. Go on with your proposal."

"If we could satisfy the press's need, and at the same time protect our interests, everyone would come out all right."

"Go on."

"I've got this friend of mine, Millard Hampton. No doubt you've heard of him"

"Yes, I'm ashamed to admit, but, yes, of course I'm aware of Mr. Hampton."

"Right. Well, Hampton's down on his luck lately. For the past years he's been producing that late night talk show, *The Bernie Frank Show*, and it's really about to go under. Nobody's watching it. Now, supposing Hampton would get a call from us explaining that one of the Soviet dissidents is being released, but that the Russians have put a hands-off on him as far as press conferences are concerned."

"Yes?"

"But, we have been able to convince the Soviets that in the interest of free speech blah...blah...blah, they should at least allow one American journalist an in-depth interview."

"I see. Go on."

"And, that several mutually acceptable names were

proposed, and that because of his legendary name and major contribution to investigative journalism, plus the fact that he filed several pieces favorable to Russia during the war and they trust him, Millard Hampton was unanimously approved."

"Jerry, I like it. I like it very much."

"He'll send Bernie Frank to do the interview. Fourteen people will watch."

Strauss picked it up, "The Soviets make their point. The President makes his. The Summit goes on as scheduled. Jerry, I could kiss you."

"Later, David. First, get in touch with Molenski and set up the deal. I'll call Hampton after that. Oh yea, I better get the President to sign off on it. Shouldn't be a problem. He really wants this Summit."

"Good! I'll call Anatoli right away. He loves late night calls. Makes him think that he's involved in a big intrigue. Also, it gets him out of his wife's bed."

"By the way, Jerry, the eleven o'clock news reported that Belov wants to go to Israel."

"Interesting. Talk to you later, David."

"Fine. Thanks for calling with such an ingenious plan, Jerry. I was just lying here mulling over something similar in my mind."

"Amazing. Say, David, before you hang up: Have you been noticing anything peculiar about the President lately?"

"Well, nothing I haven't thought was peculiar before." Strauss said.

"I see."

Strauss said, "Why do you ask?"

"I had dinner with him tonight and…"

"Now, that's peculiar!"

"I know," Cooper said with a laugh, "but after we ate, he sort of got carried away with his religious feelings and expressed some goals he hopes to reach at the Summit that, well, they aren't part of our briefing book."

"Oh, like what?"

"David, this is something I better go into with you alone. Let's take care of this Belov interview business, and I'll give you the low-down on my dinner date with the President tomorrow. Okay?"

"Very well. Goodnight, Jerry. And, thanks again."

Part Three

Chapter Eleven

"Do you believe sixteen dollars a pound for nova?" Bernie ranted. "It must be part of an Arab plot against the Jews, Peg. First they drive up the price of oil, forcing America to reverse its policy toward Israel, or else we ride bikes, then they drive up the price of lox so the Jews here starve every Sunday morning."

Peggy looked up from the breakfast table she was busily setting and smiled.

"You think I'm kidding, don't you." Bernie pretended, while waving the white deli wrapping paper and pointing his finger at $32 boldly magic-marked in black on its surface. "Kidding, huh? You'll see. Just because a guy bombs out on a network talk show doesn't mean he's suddenly lost the intuitive touch, fella. I tell you: Today the lox; tomorrow the bagel! Then what'll we do: Eat pita? Hell, no. Never!"

Early in his career, Bernie learned that a bit of masochism in a performer made the whims of fate tolerable.

Peggy had grown accustomed to the subtle injection of self-deprecation into nearly everything her husband said since his show was cancelled. If he sunk into some deep depression, she was prepared to intervene. Otherwise, she determined she would just ignore his attempts to punish himself and pray that the catharsis would purify and cleanse him of the terrible pain she knew he was feeling.

Having laid the lox aside, Bernie began to plop twelve tablespoons of Hampton's favorite Kenyan Coffee, into the Mr. Coffee.

"Sleep well last night, honey? Peggy asked.

Pressing his right hand into his groin, Bernie moaned, "Not too well, baby. I've got to see a doctor about this thing. Hurts like the devil, day and night."

Bernie's sudden hernia came on right after the bad news arrived. It prevented him from having sex with Peggy. She knew it was a ruse, or as she kidded herself, "When he's hot he's hot; when he's not he's not." She played along, if that's what he needed to get through it.

Bernie opened the refrigerator, removed the container of cream cheese and sullenly carried it to the kitchen counter where he scooped it out into the glass bowl in the center of the table. He started to leave the room, but he stopped and turned to his wife.

"Peg, there's so much that goes unsaid, unspoken between us. You know what I mean? What I want you to know, darling, is that with all my heart, I love you. I love you, Peggy."

Instantly, her eyes misted. Gently joining his parted lips with hers, they kissed tenderly, passionately, fully.

She whispered, "I love you so much."

They held each other, entranced in the energy of that rare moment when souls speak.

Reluctantly, Peggy interrupted the delicate silence.

"He ought to be here in a few minutes. I better finish preparing the breakfast."

Bernie asked, "Honey, this thing frightens you a little, doesn't it?"

"You mean the cancellation?" She asked.

"The whole business of making it, bombing and going back to Atlanta. I mean. I know what it's done to me. How has it affected you?"

She looked at him in that earnest way that set her apart from any woman he'd ever known.

"Darling, my only hurt about all of this is the hurt that it's caused you. I know much you wanted all this, New York and everything that goes with it. I'm hurt because you're hurt. I see you trying to deal with it, and you're doing fine. But I know my husband. Inside, you hurt so bad; so bad, my darling because your work is your life. It's the hurt in you that I feel."

"And as for you? What about Peggy Frank?"

"Honestly?"

"Honestly."

"Perfectly honestly?"

"Come on, honey. I want to know."

"Well, perfectly honestly, I feel relieved."

"Relieved?"

"Yea, kind of like the pressure's off—more like Peggy's out of Wonderland and back into the real world—or at least she will be soon."

Bernie half-laughed. "You're kidding!"

Peggy sat down at the kitchen table, and lit a cigarette. Talk time for the Franks was rare, especially when the subject was Peggy. She was glad to have a moment about herself with him.

"No, I'm really not, honey. You know I was never thrilled to leave Atlanta and come up here. This was something you wanted. So, I came. And it's been all right—nothing terrible, nothing wonderful—a life. I knew how tough the pressure was on you, and for me that was the hardest part. You see, honey, when a person is directly under pressure, they understand it, deal with it, and devise ways to deal with it, like you are. But when someone loves that person who is under pressure, you don't really understand it, and you don't really deal with it. So it's harder, because you have to try to figure out what's going on that's making that person you love so miserable, and you don't want to ask because if that person is Bernie Frank, he's not going to tell you until he's got the answer figured out.

"One more time, okay? Slowly and with feeling," Bernie said.

"Okay, I'll try to explain. You asked, you know."

"I know. Go ahead."

Peggy took a deep drag and contemplatively blew out the smoke.

Kind of wiggling in her chair, she put up her arms in a boxing pose, and said, "Two prize fighters in the ring, okay?"

"Okay." Bernie said, as he sat down beside her.

"They're really going after one another, okay?"

"Okay."

"One is taking a terrible pounding." Peggy animated the punches. An ash dropped on Bernie's crotch. She quickly wiped it off.

"You'll do anything for a piece of ash, won't you," Bernie quipped.

"That's awful. Now listen, I think I've got it."

"Sorry. Okay. Two fighters going after each other. One is really taking a licking. Kidney punches, jabs, blood all over his face. Right?"

"Right," she said. "Now the camera pans to his wife in the audience, and Howard Cosell says, 'Ladies and gentlemen, the only beating worse than the one Rocky is taking is the one being felt by his lovely wife, as exemplified by the pain and anguish on her face. It tells the story."

"You do a bad Cosell, but I see what you mean."

"Get it, honey? Win or lose, it's your fight. You agree going in that you're either going to come out a champ or a bum. You understand and fully accept the rules. For the one who loves on the sidelines, there's only the pain of seeing you being hurt. It's not my game, not my rules. Just my love that I'm watching being pounded."

"And, now?"

"And now I feel like you've been knocked out. I want to take you away from here, take you where they don't hit so hard, and just…just be happy."

"I understand," he said to his tearful wife. Pausing a moment, he said, "Maybe we should have never left Atlanta"

She replied, "Honey, you know we did the right thing by coming up here. You had a chance and we took it."

Bernie pursued the point. "No, really. Look at all the productive, effective people who do their thing in some town and stay there all their life. They satisfy themselves by doing what they like to do without frustrating themselves chasing rainbows. I envy those people, Peg. Granted, they don't make the money you can make if you catch a rainbow, but it seems that money is not all that important to them. It's the doing that counts. If you want to know the deep down truth, Peg, I accepted the offer not really because I wanted it, I accepted it because it was expected of me. In my heart of hearts, I wanted to turn it down!"

Peggy was surprised. She thought he desperately wanted the opportunity to be a national celebrity. For an instant, she felt hurt. She wished he had confided his feeling to her when he was anguishing over Millard Hampton's offer.

Looking at her husband squarely, she said, "Okay, but some people are not cut out to stay put. Some people are. Maybe it's what's meant to be. I don't know. Bernie Frank wanted to go as far as he could go, or at least at the time that's what he told me, and he took a chance. It turned sour due to a lot of reasons he is not responsible for, but…"

"Now, honey, we agreed we'd hold no grudges against Millard. If it wasn't for him, we wouldn't be here today."

"Amen!" Peggy said.

Bopping her lightly on the knee, Bernie said, "You know what I mean, smart ass."

"All right, all right. I promise I won't say an ugly word when he gets here. But I'll sure think of a hell of a lot of 'em," she said.

Bernie kissed Peggy on the forehead and said, "All I'm saying, baby, is that I have learned that the happy bird is one who sings because he has a song; not because he has to be heard."

Peggy looked at her husband's face searchingly and replied, "But some birds fly higher than others, love."

They got up from the table. Peggy busily put the finishing touches to the buffet, as Bernie went back to the bedroom to comb his hair.

"Does Millard use cream in his coffee, honey? Peggy yelled.

"Who knows," Bernie yelled back, then flushed. "I think so," he said, as he walked down the hall toward the kitchen.

Dipping his finger into the cream cheese for a taste, he said, "Isn't this amazing. This is the first time Millard's ever been to our apartment. Now he comes just when everything's nearly over."

"Sort of like the Last Supper, eh?" said Peggy. "Do you suppose Jesus and the boys had lox and bagels for theirs, too?"

Bernie replied, "If they did, they didn't pay sixteen dollars a pound, I'll tell ya."

He waited for a laugh, then said nervously, "This is unusual for Millard: Usually the guy is as prompt as Old Faithful."

Peggy laid tomato slices around the edges of the white serving plate. Glistening strips of precious lox nestled cozily in the center.

She said, "Honey, when Freda came by yesterday to tell me the inside dope on Millard, I couldn't help but feel that she cares deeply for him. Oh, you know, she tried to jazz up the description of how she found him in his apartment and everything, still there was something different about her."

"Freda caring for Hampton?" Bernie said. "You've got to be kidding. She can't stand the man. Detests him, in fact."

Peggy's preparation was completed. She sat down at her place at the table and lit a cigarette.

"I know, I know," she said. "But people change. Feelings change. Believe me, there's something there."

Peggy actually knew more than she indicated to her husband. Freda had gone through the scenario of her encounter with Hampton with her for an hour on Saturday. Freda left out the Sidney Wade part, however she covered the drunk angle more thoroughly and graphically than she did when she reported her findings to Bernie. She left no doubt in Peggy's mind that she was fascinated with the legend and with the man, whom she now saw as one and the same.

In fact, Peggy believed that if the affair hadn't already started, it soon would. Before she had left their apartment, where they had had their girl-to-girl chat, Freda had told Peggy, "Now, I'm only going to tell your husband that Millard has had a drinking problem that has resulted in his neglect of the show. That's what he sent me there for." Peggy interpreted that to mean that Freda would like Bernie to know that she's enamored with Hampton as an observation from his wife, not from one who tries daily to impress her hero with her professionalism.

"Well, we'll see," Bernie said.

He was in one of those moods when nothing interested him except his own problems. Peggy knew this, but she wanted to plant an idea in his head to circumvent any irrational response when he finds out for himself.

The doorbell rang.

"Finally!" Bernie said.

They both walked to the white door. Bernie peeked through the peephole—a routine that always made Peggy miss the less paranoid South.

"It's them," he said, and opened the door.

"Freda, how beautiful you look! Come in," Peggy said zestfully. And, with less gusto, she said, "Millard, how are you? Come in."

Freda crossed the threshold and kissed Peggy on the cheek as Peggy embraced her.

"Hello, lad. Shoddy pair of trousers you're wearing. Is that the way I taught you to dress?" Hampton said, in that magisterial tone he loved to affect.

Bernie shrugged adolescently. He had vowed to himself that he would not allow the Hampton manner to intimidate him that morning. Yet, there he was, with the home field advantage, and still Hampton was able to put him on a leash with only a brief opening line.

"Welcome to our home, Millard. Let me show you around."

"Lad, the tour of the grounds is unnecessary. I'm sure you live in a suitable apartment. Let's let it go at that, and save me the pain of platitude."

Bernie thought, *As always, Millard is the organ grinder and I'm the obedient monkey.*

Peggy showed Freda to the beige sofa. Above it, on the brown wall, a seascape in shades of sand harmonized the tans and moss colorings throughout the living room.

Freda said, "The room looks lovely, Peg."

"Has it grown lovelier since yesterday when you were here?" baritoned Hampton, as he groped into his tweed sports coat pocket. "Where is that bloody pipe?" He mockingly raged. A plunge of his other hand into the left pocket provided the answer.

"Now, Millard, " Freda said, evoking a simultaneous exchange of glances between Bernie and his wife. He had told Peggy how Hampton demanded being addressed as Mr. Hampton by the staff. Peggy's eyes said *I told you so* and Bernie's nodded acknowledgement of her perceptiveness. "No need to be nasty this early on Sunday morning. After all, back where I come from, most folks are in church asking forgiveness for their sins. Right Peg?"

Peggy smiled and said, "Right. Then comes the church gossip."

Both women laughed and whispered something to each other.

Bernie felt disquieted. His requirement for time to adjust to altered situations, a trait he despised, was clearly demonstrated by his tail-tucked reaction to Freda's obvious status change with Hampton. He had a look of being caught off guard when Hampton leaned toward him, from his brown suede chair, and said softly, "Do you have all the pieces put together yet, Lad?"

Before Bernie could answer, Hampton said, "Allow me to assist you. As a matter of fact, now that we're one big happy family," he spoke somewhat louder so the gossiping girls would pay attention, "allow me to draw a verbal portrait of our condition."

The sharp latakia in Hampton's Dunhill pipe mixture made the living room smell like a caucus room in the British House of Commons. Freda and Peggy stopped their chatter in mid-sentence and turned to Hampton.

"This quartet of coincidence you behold typifies the accidental quality of life. If there be a Presbyterian among us— that might be you, Peggy—one might argue for the predestination of it all."

Peggy winced. Although she never officially converted, she lived as a Jew and wanted so much for people to accept her as such.

"Do not fret, dear Peggy," Hampton said, haughtily, "If there is a God, He will judge you on your thoughts and deeds rather than your breakfast menu."

Freda glanced at Peggy and saw a faint smile; but her eyes showed hurt.

Hampton continued: "Being a devout, proud and practicing agnostic, I can feel secure in my faith of doubt that predestination is as viable a philosophy as mythology. In fact, I should more likely place my trust in Zeus or Athena as in a God who draws a road map for every individual born of woman."

"Millard," Freda interrupted, "if I hadn't been with you every minute for the past three days, I'd think you'd been in the sauce again. Come off this Hampton's Hamlet routine. Okay, sugar?"

Bernie was stunned by Freda's brazen remark. "Sugar?" he said to himself, as if desperately trying to reconcile the changing of the their roles which he thought had been cast for the run of the play.

"Now, Clancy," Hampton said, as Bernie and Peggy looked at each other with puzzled expressions, "Having indeed spent the last seventy-two odd hours with me must have at least taught you that I am not one to partake in idle chatter. Although my remarks may register as plodding at the outset, I assure you that they are well measured and leading to meaningful verbal substance."

"Right on, baby, but get to it, huh? I'm like to starve, " Freda said, patting her tummy.

Peggy stood, and with unnatural vivacity said, "How about if we adjourn to the table and talk there, folks?"

Freda got up and said, "Peg, you're one smart lady. Let's go."

Boogying over to where Hampton was still savoring the sound of his words, she pulled him out of his chair.

"No, leave that smelly thing here," she said, as she pulled his pipe from his hand and placed it in an ashtray. Hampton played the irritated curmudgeon while loving every gesture of this new and essential person in his life.

Bernie still felt somewhat off center. He had not put the pieces in place. In fact, they had multiplied. Not only had Simon Legree become completely enamored with Little Eva, he renamed her Clancy!

More importantly, the casualness and easy humor with which Freda alluded to Hampton's drinking problem nearly eliminated the need to even broach it with him. However, that problem was the root cause of Bernie's perplexity!

Was that all that would be said of it? He worried. *Were Millard and his Clancy so taken with each other that the demise of The Bernie Frank Show and Bernie Frank was but an inconvenience?*

My god!" He thought. *I'm suffering, and they're acting as if they're doing a pilot for Norman Lear*!

All morning he had rehearsed introductory lines. *Millard, I've done hundreds of interviews with experts on the problem, never considering that my own producer…*Or, *Millard, guys have told me about the pressure of this business for years and how booze can get a hold of you. But when it happens to someone as close as your own…*

None of the lines seemed right for the characters.

By that point, Bernie was uncertain of everything. A queasiness enveloped him. After uttering some inconsequential remarks about who should sit where, he sat down across from Peggy and began to pass around the platters, wearing a kind of wimpy grin on his face. He noticed that Hampton seemed to be so comfortable with himself—so together, as if this was his table, his kitchen, his apartment, his guests.

Then Hampton said loudly, "Do you know what I admire most about Jewish men, Bernie?"

Freda gulped. She dared not glance at Hampton. He read the unspoken too well.

"What's that, Millard?" said Bernie, still with that milquetoast grin.

"Their caution."

Freda sighed a sigh of relief and peppered a tomato slice.

"Jewish men seem to posses an innate sense of caution when they are confronted with altered or new circumstances."

Bernie's grin faded.

"It must be genetically inbred through thousands of years of life in the Diaspora. Jewish men have historically had to reevaluate sets of circumstances and select a course of action from limited options. In fact, I would think that the most agonizing of all tortures engendered upon Jews by the Nazis was the gradual elimination of options. To a race genetically conditioned to adjust to any environment, no matter how harsh or brutal, the malignant social claustrophobia must have wrenched the fiber of their soul."

183

Hampton had them now. Bernie, Peggy, Freda—they all listened. This was vintage Hampton. The thinking Hampton. This was not puff or pomp. This was Millard Hampton at his best.

"So it must be a bit disconcerting for you now, as you seek to set your sail to a new wind. 'What's happened? Where am I? Where shall I go?' you ask. I admire the questions, lad. In the main, Gentile men would panic and either bail out, get drunk and try to forget it with a woman, or they would grab the first boat that passes by and jump on board. As a Jewish man, you reach back into the thousands of years of slavery, exile, oppression and unwelcome gates, and taste a stew of intuition, logic and hope. And on the basis of its taste, you make your decision."

Peggy made sure that everyone's plate stayed filled while giving Hampton her rapt attention like the others. As he paused to take a bite, the musical strains of an instrumental version of "Precious One" floated from the stereo. Freda suddenly looked up at Hampton, and he locked his eyes to hers. Telling him with her eyes that she understood, he warmly acknowledged her caring with his.

Bernie missed the exchange. Peggy caught it.

Freda felt a welling, nearly uncontrollable urge to hold him in her arms. Never had she experienced anything near the compelling lust to comfort as when Millard appeared emotionally helpless. During the preceding three days, while she was helping him research the Soviet dissident issue, a word or a photograph would disarm him momentarily. Yet, although they slept together, they remained sexual strangers.

Hampton continued: "Fortunately, lad, you have options. Granted, by virtue, or lack of it, of your gifted albeit chronically inebriated producer, you have become one of the six percent of the unemployed in this nation. Nonetheless, you do have options. Unlike your relatives who perished in the Holocaust, or even the Russian dissidents today who waste away in Soviet forced labor camps or so-called mental asylums, you, Bernie Frank, have options."

Freda thought, *So this is where he was going. Yep, Millard, sugah; you do get to meaningful verbal substance after all. I should have known.*

"Whether your options are by Divine decree or merely happenstance, I leave open for discussion. You already know my position: Chance rules all."

Hampton was trying to draw Bernie out, to resuscitate him from his intellectual coma. Only Freda knew the bottom line; and she observed—like an audience in a Greek drama—with involvement by proxy.

Bernie toyed with the remnants of brunch on his plate and said, "Frankly, Millard, I don't know."

He was beginning to feel somewhat embarrassed. Peggy winked at him for support, which made him feel even more like a *schlemiel*. Taking a deep breath, he determined to belly up to the buzz saw, as they used to say in Georgia, and find the stuff in himself to spar intellectually with Millard. Just as he did as an interviewer, he decided to take a position, whether he believed it or not, and defend it for the sake of the show.

"You don't know? Come now, lad. Just look at yourself: Rescued from the anonymity of an Atlanta talk show by the jolly gray giant of broadcast journalism, who placed you near the pinnacle of your profession, only to be become victim by default from the personal peccadilloes of the same avatar. Bernie Frank, you have been blessed and cursed by the same Messiah! Was it meant to be, lad, or utter chance?"

Hampton's voice seemed to fill up the space of the apartment.

Looking at Hampton intently, Bernie softly said, "Fate."

Expecting a booming reply, he waited. Hampton said nothing. So Bernie, ever the resourceful emcee, filled the gap himself.

"I don't believe in the road-map theory; nor do I believe in the crap shooting theory. I guess I'm in between."

Hampton re-lit his pipe and leaned back to listen. His body language encouraged Bernie to go on.

"If I walk out of this apartment and fall into a manhole, I don't feel that such a precise accident was ordained either at my conception or at birth. On the other hand, I don't necessarily discount the possibility that I fell, in quotation marks, into a manhole to save me from a truck bearing down on me with a drunk driver at the wheel. That is, I allow a measure of reason for every so-called accident."

Peggy smiled slightly, pleased with her husband's rejoinder, although wondering if he really believed what he said.

Hampton raised his chin and said, "And the six million of your fellow Jews, lad? What measure of reason do you allow for their agony?"

The question numbed all present. Freda poured coffee in everyone's cup.

Bernie said, "To even attempt an answer seems to defile their martyrdom, Millard. At this point, I would only hazard to say that perhaps those people were somehow engulfed in a wave of madness—a evil plague—that was immune to rationalization. Then again, that almost seems an over-simplification. Nonetheless the truth is that had there been no Holocaust, there would be no Israel. The mixture of guilt and pity from the West became the political backing for Israel. Maybe that's the reason. Maybe the reason is not yet apparent. Or maybe..."

"Or maybe the rolling ball on the roulette wheel landed on their number. Period." Hampton interjected. "It's all a big poker hand, lad. It's all the luck of the draw."

"Yes, but every hand's got to have a dealer," said Freda, unexpectedly, drawing everyone's attention.

She hadn't really intended to say anything, allowing Hampton to conduct the movement his way, however she lost her control to the philosophic heat of the moment.

Hampton appeared amusingly surprised. "Yes, Clancy. Go on," he said.

"Sorry to butt in, boys, but it seems to me that if everything that happens is pure luck, this world wouldn't have lasted two weeks. On the other hand, if everything were scripted, this would be heaven. Seems to me like man has the inner capacity to do good or to do bad. It's up to him. God, if you pardon the expression, Millard, set man up here with the potential to live like He created man: in His own image. Now, man can say 'right-on, God, I'm going to be as much like You as I can, under these circumstances,' or man can say, 'God, you do Your thing, and I'll do mine.' Like, I'm not boasting or anything, but after my daddy got killed, I could have said, 'I'm going to waste every white dude I can get my hands on.' Instead, I said, 'I'm going to find some way to undo the kind of hate that made that guy throw a rock at my daddy's head.' I know I ain't done it yet, but I tried. Right now, unfortunately, I'm in the same manhole with Bernie."

"I'm there too, Freda," Peggy said softly.

Bernie laughed, and said, "Hey, sure is getting cozy down here."

With a coy smile, Peggy said, "Yes, but you don't mind it, do you honey?"

Bernie looked at his wife. Peggy blew him a kiss.

"All I can say," Freda concluded, "is that I don't see God dotting the Is and crossing the Ts. I believe He gives us an opportunity. The rest is up to us."

"And John and Robert Kennedy?" Hampton asked. "What choice did they have?"

"To serve, which they did," rebounded Freda. "Their assassins made a choice, and the choice of their assassins is what killed the Kennedy's."

Peggy asked, "In other words, you believe that the Kennedy's, or the Holocaust victims, or the imprisoned Russian dissidents are the victims of the evil choices of others, rather than some predestined edict from God?"

"Right on, sister," said Freda.

Peggy nodded endorsement.

Freda continued: "I will agree with Millard that according to the material we dug up last night, all of us have options. Most of those poor souls are locked in. No pun intended, folks."

Hampton had been carefully shaping the conversation into a purposeful form. He was pleased that Freda helped soften the clay.

Hearing the words, "material" and "poor souls" Bernie asked, "What material? What poor souls?"

Rather than answer the question head on, Hampton, the sculptor, diverted:

"Those people probably don't sit around debating whether or not their misery has an author. Most of them relinquished their options when they decided to dissent."

Freda added, "The tales are incredible, Peg."

With a wide-eyed expression of bewilderment, Bernie asked, "You're researching the Soviet dissidents?"

Freda quickly nodded 'yes', then she said, "In a way of thinking, those people are more pathetic than the Jews of Nazi Germany."

Hampton said, "You are correct, Clancy. The gas chamber did not discriminate. All choices were annulled. Hitler's Final Solution was absolute. The Soviet dissident, on the other hand, makes an individual and calculated decision to dissent from the prevailing Soviet political, social or religious policy. Thus, he becomes voluntarily responsible for his plight. The demons that tempt these persons to capitulate to the will of the State and end the torture and agony must be recruited from among Satan's best. Miraculously, few defer from their course of dissent. Their only hope is barter."

"Barter?" asked Peggy.

"Yes," Hampton said. "If, in the politically astute view of the Soviets, a dissident can be swapped for either an imprisoned Russian spy, or for public opinion, such as the Belov release."

Bernie said, "Belov is the guy they're releasing this week, right?"

"Correct," said Hampton, with that patented expression of confidence.

Freda said, "Sometimes they're forced to release someone because of world pressure."

As if he were on a quiz show, Bernie said, "Solzhenitsyn."

"Correct, again, lad," Hampton said, looking even more pleased than before.

"Imagine," injected Freda, "there's a man who withstood the most vicious physical and psychological punishment the Soviets were capable of inflicting, and yet he continued to speak out and write secretly about the poison of their system. Millard, did you bring that outline I typed this morning?"

With a self-satirical tone and posture, Hampton bellowed, "Since when am I *your* grip?"

Freda reached her trim arm across the table, tweaked him on his cheek and said, "Since we stamped you human, sugah."

"Why, Millard, you're blushing," exploded Peggy.

Bernie wished she hadn't said that.

Hampton said, "A slight case of temporary fever, darling. Unpredictably reoccurs since I first picked it up near Bastogne in '45. Dreadful weather, no let-up for 14 days. But, that's another story."

"Sure is, sugah," Freda said coquettishly, while the tip of her tongue slowly licked strawberry marmalade from the top of her spoon.

Hampton cleared his throat. Reaching inside his charcoal tweed sports coat, he removed a folded set of white manuscript papers.

"Whatcha' got there, Millard?" Bernie asked.

"Lad, I hold here a brief account of some of the information I, excuse me, *we* were able to develop about Soviet dissidents. Consummately, the tale is frightening, inspiring and perplexing. Care to hear it?"

The voice vote was unanimous.

For the next fifteen minutes, Hampton read accounts of

heroic men and women whom the Soviets declared to be insane for speaking out against their denial of human rights. For "rehabilitation," they were sent to notorious mental institutions where they endured unimaginable and barbaric methods of physical, chemical, and mental torture. Many were never heard from again. Those who came from the academic or artistic community had organized support in the free world, and were kept alive, barely.

Without any indication of his own reaction to the material, Hampton casually folded the sheets of white paper and returned them to the inside pocket of his jacket when he finished reading. He perched his glasses atop his head, and looked as though he had just concluded the presentation of evidence to a jury and now awaited their verdict. He checked his coffee cup, showing Peggy that it was empty. She could have strangled him.

Freda said, "I don't know about you all, but Freda here needs to stretch her legs."

Freda got up and Peggy followed. She was relieved that the dissident stories, with their graphic description of torture, were finally over. Together they strolled into the living room.

Peggy hollered, "Just leave the dishes there, boys. We'll get them later. Millard, why don't you pour yourself some more coffee?" Freda approvingly patted her on the back twice.

Bernie didn't get up from the table. Neither did Hampton, who was pouring himself another cup of coffee.

Finally, Bernie said, "Quite a story."

"Yes, but incomplete, lad."

"Oh, do you have more?" Bernie asked.

In the next room, Peggy said, "Freda, I want to show you this new plant I bought for the bedroom"

Freda squeezed Peggy's arm and said, "In just a minute, hon. I want you to hear what's goin' down in there."

Peggy looked puzzled then listened as Hampton was saying, "No, I don't have more here. That's the problem. Let me elucidate. In all of this information, all the names, did you notice a conspicuous absence?"

Bernie thought for several seconds. He didn't want to miss this one, yet for the life of him, he could not come up with the answer.

"Think now, lad. Shchransky, Bukovsky, Hanoch, Grilius, Slinin, Nudel and on and on, but no…"

"Bernie! It's BELOV, for Christ's sake!"

Upon shouting the name from the living room, Peggy clamped the palm of her hand over her mouth.

Then meekly, she said, "Sorry."

Freda was doubled over with laughter, and Hampton was obviously amused too. The laser-like leer from her husband left no doubt about his reaction to her blurting out the name.

While attempting to maintain his serious posture, Hampton said, "Your dear wife is correct." Freda's leg-slapping convulsions in the other room didn't help him at all.

"I'm glad she finally got it," Bernie said. "I don't know how long I was going to wait until she finally got it."

Hampton said, "Yuri Belov was not included in any of the reams of documents, news reports and other information we've been gleaning for the past three days. Consider now: The Russians have reported that they are releasing one of their imprisoned dissidents, one Yuri Belov, as a show of good faith prior to the summit. He is not a scientist, not a man of letters, of law, of nothing apparently. It's as if they picked up some non-entity from the street and threw him in prison so that they could release him to the world at the appropriate time. Believe me, I have combed the files of every available agency and interested group that tracks dissidents, refuseniks, prisoners of conscience, prisoners of Zion, what have you, and nowhere does a Yuri Belov appear. I saw where he was arrested in Red Square for preaching about the violations of the Helsinki Accord and the denial of human rights. That was in a five-year-old news clipping. That clipping is the sum and substance of what I am nearly certain this nation and the world knows about Yuri Belov."

Bernie sat silent for a moment, then said, "Amazing."

"It's beyond amazement, lad. It's dynamite! Who is Yuri Belov? Why Yuri Belov? Is Yuri Belov Yuri Belov? In the vernacular of my recently discovered, however already cherished black beauty over there, 'what's shakin' baby?'"

"How absolutely sweet," Peggy said.

"Freda laughed, "I better check his coffee."

Bernie disregarded the secondary plot. He felt a stirring inside himself. He said, "All right, let me put all of this together. No, let me ask you a question."

Hampton puffed deeply on his pipe. Apparently, he was satisfied with his placement of the cannon, but he was not yet ready to light the fuse. He nodded his head for Bernie to ask.

"Why has my producer and his assistant of my terminal television program spent three days researching Russian dissidents?"

Hampton nodded again. Pleased with the phrasing of the question, he leaned toward Bernie, smiled fatherly, and lit the fuse:

"So that you will have sufficient background information about the subject when you interview Yuri Belov."

Freda glanced at Peggy, and thought she saw her lips say, "Oh, shit!"

"Interview Belov?" Bernie asked calmly.

"That's correct, lad."

Again, with calm, Bernie said, "The mystery dissident, Yuri Belov."

"For now, a mystery, yes. That's correct," Hampton replied.

"For what, Millard?"

"Television."

"Whose show, Millard?"

"Ours, lad."

"It's cancelled, remember?"

"Yes, but…it still has three weeks to run."

"And you'll get him in three weeks."

"Or less."

"Oh."

Freda took Peggy by the arm and walked her back to the kitchen. Putting her arms around her husband's neck from behind him, Peggy bent down and kissed his ear.

Freda said, "Millard met with David Strauss at the White House yesterday. His friend Jerry Cooper set it up."

Peggy whispered, "I love you."

"Will he be on 'live'?" Bernie asked.

Hampton said, "No, we'll tape it on location."

"Millard's leaving tomorrow for Russia to dig up the dope on the real Yuri Belov; then he'll meet the three of us for the interview," Freda said.

"The three of us! Where?" asked Peggy, her arms still wrapped around Bernie's neck as he stared off to some distant place.

"You tell 'em, Sugah, " Freda said.

Hampton raised his juice glass and toasted, "To Israel!"

Bernie slowly looked to the ceiling, rolled his eyes back, and said, "Oy Gevalt!"

Chapter Twelve

At the moment Millard Hampton was raising his glass in a toast "to Israel," Jerry Cooper was waiting for the door to open at the Georgetown brownstone house of Dr. David Strauss. Cooper hadn't slept well the night before; he had the first of what would become his recurring nightmare about being chased by a tornado with a tongue.

Earlier that morning, Millard Hampton had called to thank him for "managing the Belov thing."

"It went well with 'the professor'," Hampton reported, "the Frank interview is set." Pleased that he had "figured out a way to deliver,"—as Hampton had pleaded with him to do on the phone at Camp David—Cooper had other fish to fry that morning. He decided to tell 'the professor' what he had witnessed at Camp David.

It was a brisk Georgetown Sunday morning. However Sundays meant little to Jerry Cooper. His blue button down Arrow shirt, maroon knit tie, wrinkled khakis and non-descript sports jacket looked just as shabby Sunday morning as any other day.

By the time Cooper arrived at Strauss's innocuous front entrance, only a few late risers were walking their dogs or jogging. Most of the bulky Sunday *Washington Posts* had already been gathered up and leisurely digested over pots of coffee. For most of the residents of that chic town within a city, that Sunday—like all fall Sundays that year—would be a day for mourning over the lack of any appreciable Redskin offense. Even worse, they were playing Dallas away.

David Strauss could care less. He had the world to run and it didn't stop on Sundays, or when a referee blew a whistle.

A thick wrought iron gated door shielded the door to the house. A surveillance camera tilted downward toward the threshold. Cooper rang the bell, and a voice from the inter-com said, "Yes, prease?"

"I'm Jerry Cooper here to see Dr. Strauss."

"Oh, yes, Mr. Jerry Cooper, Dr. Stlause expecting you."

The gated door opened automatically followed by the heavy wood door to the house. Beside it stood a small Oriental man wearing a white linen servant's jacket and black bow tie. Cooper thought he looked as if he had been hired from B Pictures Incorporated. He felt nervous as the small man helped him off with his coat.

"Forrow me, prease."

Cooper trailed his graceful escort slowly down the long hall lined frame to frame with Andrew Wyeth paintings. Instinctively, Cooper concluded that the snail-like pace was a dictum from Strauss so that visitors would take note of the swank collection. As they crept along, he wished he could hang a sign saying 'Use Burma-Shave' at the end of the row.

"Make comfortable," Cooper's guide said, pointing to the living room. "Dr. Stlouse be here in a moment. I get coffee?"

"Yes, please. Black. Thank you very much," Cooper said, realizing that he had inadvertently bowed. It made him feel like an idiot. Grandeur unnerved Jerry Cooper. He believed people who "made it" are fortunate and owe a debt in return, usually in the form of service.

The living room was Italian Provincial cluttered. No space on the wall, on the tables, at the corners or on the mantel lacked for adornment. Vases, paintings, plaques, sculptures, dry flower arrangements, ornaments, antique and collector this-and-that was everywhere.

On top of what you could see of the lavish Oriental rug, sat an array of sofas, easy chairs, straight back chairs, ottomans, footstools, love-seats and an infinite variety of delicate cherry wood furniture looking as if it were in search of either an auctioneer or a 19th century New Orleans madam.

Cooper was staring at a painting of a fat nude woman by a stream with a nymph peering wantonly up at her when the silence was broken by that unmistakable voice.

"Not bad for an immigrant, huh, Jerry?"

Cooper spun on his heels and saw Strauss standing with a steaming cup of coffee in his hand. Cooper thought he looked more diminutive than he appeared at the White House.

Cooper smiled and replied, "Good morning, David. No, not bad for an immigrant, or a native, for that matter."

Strauss moved toward Cooper and, with a wry smile, said "There are two types that have rooms like this, Jerry: leaders of government and leaders of the underworld. Often it is difficult to make the distinction."

David Strauss never apologized for his success. On the contrary, he would not allow one to ignore it. On the surface, he had that irresistibly charming characteristic of kidding his image; of deprecating the elements that were used to construct him. At a deeper level, he was a poor German Jewish boy who got out of Germany only weeks before Hitler slammed the door on Jewish emigration, to eventually become the second most powerful man in the world. His personal and material trappings masked a terrified boy inside a man.

"Come into the study, Jerry. Staying in this room too long makes me want to invade some country."

The study was off the living room and surprisingly tiny. The volumes, which lined the dark oak shelves, were separated occasionally by glossy photographs of Strauss with some world leader. On nearly all of them, Strauss wore that same smile. Cooper amused himself by mentally captioning one with *Boy, Have I Just Screwed This Guy!* and *Momma, Look Who Your Little David Is Standing Next To!* on another.

As Strauss's servant poured coffee into a white porcelain cup from a silver decanter, Cooper settled into a brown leather chair near the fireplace.

"Something else needed?"

Strauss, who had been standing behind his cluttered desk reading something said absently, "No, Chin, that will be all."

"David, I'm really impressed," Cooper said, while lighting a cigarette. "An oriental house boy! The height of eminence!"

In a low, barely audible voice, Strauss replied, "Quite honestly, Jerry, I have believed for sometime that he is a CIA agent placed in here to spy on me by our mutual friend, McKenna. I say nothing in front of him of any importance, and I have this room swept for bugs every week. Can you imagine, Jerry, the great solace I have in suspecting that an agent of the government I serve is watching me in my own home?"

Not knowing whether to believe him or not, Cooper didn't say a word.

Cooper's eye followed Strauss amble from his desk to a two-seat sofa across from his chair. Strauss's face wore that smile—the one in the photographs—the one Cooper labeled "ambiguity."

"Millard Hampton told me you worked the Belov interview out for him," Cooper said.

Strauss said, "Yes, that is taken care of. I didn't have any trouble with Molenski. He went for it immediately. However, you may find one aspect of my conversation with Molenski of particular interest."

Cooper's street smarts kicked in gear. He didn't react overly curious. Strauss seemed disappointed. The teaser needs his subject willing not insouciant.

He cleared his throat, and said, "I outlined the entire proposal to Molenski carefully. I suggested that to throw Belov to the press would be worse than ten years in Siberia for Belov and potentially as devastating as a resumption of missiles in Cuba for both of us. He readily agreed. So when I suggested that one American interviewer be selected to talk to Belov—you see how I was careful to use the word *interviewer* rather than journalist— he said, "Fine."

"Then when I recommended that that person be someone who has name recognition, but one who is inconsequential in terms of journalistic substance—such as Bernie Frank— Molenski became absolutely livid."

"What do you mean by inconsequential...without journalistic substance? What are you trying to pull here?" Strauss was shaking his stubby finger at Cooper and rattling his cheeks back and forth in a nearly perfect impersonation of the Russian Ambassador.

Then, as himself, Strauss said, "Somewhat taken aback by Molenski's outburst, my first reaction was to regret that I had not taken into consideration that Bernie Frank is Jewish and perhaps Molenski was resenting my suggestion that a Jewish reporter interview a Soviet dissident, with religious freedom being rudimentary to the issue."

Strauss took a quick sip of coffee, then continued: "So, I attempted to smooth out the wrinkle by saying, 'Anatole, by "inconsequential" or "without substance," I was not trying to disguise an apparent flaw in my proposal. I simply meant that the broader purpose would most likely be attained with less anxiety if Belov was presented to the world by someone with more charm and less intellectual curiosity.'"

Suddenly, Strauss bolted from his sofa and began bobbing about the room waving his arms. He was Molenski again.

"'That does it! I've heard enough! You speak of flaw in your proposal? Less anxiety you want? And to top it off, you insult me by proposing that he has no intellectual curiosity?"

Still bobbing about his study like a weighted cupid doll at a carnival, Strauss as Strauss said, "I tried to settle him down, Jerry, however he was too irate. But watch what happens now:"

As Molenski again, Strauss shouted, "'I know what you're trying to do; it won't work, David. You are trying to not only sabotage the selection of my favorite American television figure as the person to interview Yuri Belov, you are attempting— through a most amateurish exercise—to divert me toward someone with less integrity, less credibility; someone, perhaps, to whom you would furnish half-truths or information of an embarrassing or sensitive nature. Someone who may even allow your CIA to compose his questions couched from the convenient barrier reference of a so-called 'informed source,' all under the guise of journalistic freedom! You must be slipping, David. Did you really believe your subtle characterization of Bernie Frank as inconsequential or vapid would turn my thumb down on him? In fact, I watch him nearly every night—unless I have to attend one of your tedious parties. Why, just the other evening, he had a remarkable program about gourds. It was fascinating! After it was over, I turned to my wife and said that I've never seen Barbara Walters or Mike Wallace—with all their KGB methods of interrogating—ever come close to the intellectual prowess of Bernie Frank. Unfortunately, she had fallen asleep—but the point is—that, in my view, Bernie Frank is the most relevant and unfettered television journalist on all of your decadent tube. You insult me, David, with your diplomatically adolescent game. No! I insist! It must be Bernie Frank with Belov—or no one!'"

Exhausted, Strauss collapsed in a heap on the sofa. Cooper burst into an enthusiastic round of applause for the sweating Jell-O-mold panting before his eyes.

Cooper marveled to himself that he had witnessed the President playing John the Baptist at Camp David, and now David Strauss playing the Soviet Ambassador in Georgetown.

Strauss noted his appreciative audience with apparent satisfaction. Then he took a deep breath and thoughtfully added a line after the curtain. "So, you see, Jerry, although technocrats would say otherwise, the actions of nations are still governed by the positive and negative impulses of human passion."

Cooper smiled in agreement, ran his hand through his disheveled hair, and snuffed out his cigarette. Then he asked, "And, with Millard Hampton? How did it go with him, David?"

Strauss whipped a white silk handkerchief from the lapel pocket of his dressing robe and brusquely polished the lenses of his black horn-rimmed glasses, and dabbed the perspiration beads from his forehead, before shoving it back in his pocket. He looked over at Cooper with that professorial expression that implies possession of broader information about a matter than has been divulged.

"An interesting man, Hampton," Strauss said pensively. "An interesting man. Obviously, he thinks highly of you, Jerry. In fact, I sensed a special fondness for you. Or was I imagining?

Cooper's mind said, *Imagining, my ass. Strauss knows damn well he wasn't imagining. It's his method of extracting information. He agonizes when he doesn't have all the pieces put together; and Millard sure as hell never lets any one see all the pieces.*

Instinctively, Cooper let the issue pass by saying, "We go back a long time, David. He gave me my first job, and recommended me to Packard. That's about the size of it."

Cooper knew he was in the presence of a scorpion who exists through suspicion and thrives on knowledge.

Strauss smiled his ambiguous smile, and reflectively nodded several times. In ruminating the Hampton Cooper relationship, Strauss did not eliminate the possibility that Cooper has been Hampton's proxy. He filed the possibility for the moment. Then, in a more convivial tone, Strauss said, "Say, how about a Sunday morning schnapps?"

"Sure, why not?" Cooper said.

Strauss pressed a button on the telephone console on the end table. The door seemed to open simultaneously.

"Yes, Dr. Stlauss?"

"Chin, bring Mr. Cooper and me some brandy, please."

"Light away, sir." Chin bowed and slid out of the room.

"David?" Cooper asked. "Do you really think he is a spy?"

Flicking his hand in a gesture sign of fatalism, he said, "Jerry, one thing is for certain, the President's Director of National Security is very insecure."

Profound and accurate, Cooper thought. He sensed an edge to Strauss, as if his security had indeed been threatened.

Chin slid back in with the brandy decanter, poured a snifter for David and one for Cooper, and bowed out.

Cooper took a sip. The brandy tasted good. Strauss's hook baiting regarding Hampton still bothered him. Why it did vexed him more than his worry about Strauss's motive.

After Strauss took a sip of brandy, and then quickly another, he said, "As usual, Jerry, you handled the President quite well on the Belov interview issue. He's one hundred percent for it. I have often marveled how adroitly you manage him. As a matter of fact, everyone marvels."

Cooper put his glass down on the coffee table and said, "David, you make it sound like I manipulate the man, pull his strings like he was a puppet."

Strauss leaned forward and said, "What is the proverb about a shoe fitting?"

Cooper smiled and rubbed his droopy eyelid.

Strauss said, "Do not interpret what I just said as an insult, Jerry. It is not. It is more a statement of admiration mixed with envy and curiosity. There you are, a rather unremarkable person with pedestrian credentials, who operates from no constitutional or congressional authority, who sits in the shadow in the Oval office until everyone leaves, and then whispers in the ear of the President who abides by the voice in his ear. It's an historic job description, Jerry, following a lineage from the bible through viziers throughout the ages. Some serve for power and all the benefits power provides. A few—fools in my judgment—serve out of conviction, a firm belief in the thing worth doing. So I ponder: Why does Jerry Cooper serve Albert Packard? The question is enigmatic, Jerry, not hostile."

Bull shit, Cooper thought. *Your true question is: Why not me? Why don't I have the ear of the President like Cooper has? Not that you're not doing everything you can to get it, you wily bastard.*

Rather than be helpful, Cooper intuitively opted for the understatement.

"We all do the best with what we've got, David," he said, half-smiling.

Strauss swigged the last of his brandy.

Cooper wanted to get to his Camp David experience. Under normal circumstances, "David, we've got a problem," would be his opening sentence. However, the distress in Strauss's demeanor changed the dynamic. Cooper sensed a frustration that went beyond Strauss coveting his role. He sensed it went beyond him. There was something else. And so Cooper tread lightly so that he could turn and walk away if necessary.

"Did the President seem alright when you met with him?" Cooper began.

Strauss laughed for an instant. He said, "Yes, more or less. The President seemed preoccupied when I broached the subject of Belov and the interview with him. When I told him who would be the interviewer the President acquiesced. As I said, Jerry, you set him up for my presentation beautifully as usual."

"Thank you," Cooper said, although the phrase "set him up" somehow offended him, even though in its purest definition, it was true.

Strauss's expression changed. He appeared almost frightened. Addled.

"Then, Jerry," Strauss said, with more intensity, "an inexplicable thing happened. Packard said it was okay with him for Bernie Frank to interview Belov because—and these are his words— 'Bernie Frank and you'—meaning me— 'are from the chosen house.'"

A chill rippled through Cooper's body.

Strauss continued. "When I inquired as to the significance—or perhaps I said the definition of his statement—the President got a strange look in his eyes and replied, 'Your lineage to The House of David, Dr. Strauss, was far more influential in my selecting you for your current position than any of your academic, philosophic or intellectual credentials.'"

Cooper sat numb as his mind over-laid Packard's absent countenance at Camp David over David Strauss as he spoke.

"Then, Jerry, and I swear this is absolutely the truth, the President took on this...this voided appearance, and said to me, 'But I want you to know, David Strauss, that even membership in the house of the Lord does not excuse you from the sin of incessant fornication.' He seemed to be looking straight through me without seeing me. Jerry, I have never seen the man like that. Have you?"

Cooper's body had not quite warmed from the sudden chill of seeing again—even by proxy—that not-of-this-world stare of Albert Packard. He downed the rest of the brandy and refilled his glass. He understood what was tormenting Strauss that morning.

"Yes, I've seen him like that, David."

Strauss's eyes widened. "You have?"

Strauss wasn't posturing; he was genuinely puzzled. He could play games of wits where the stakes were the survival of the planet with the best in the world, however this Machiavellian was helplessly run aground by the unanchored mind of President Albert Packard.

Cooper stood and moved a few steps to the fire and sat down on the brick foundation with his back to the warming flame.

He said, "He was like that Friday night at Camp David."

Strauss's cheek flinched—a nervous reaction Cooper had never seen from him before.

Then clasping his hands in supplication, he said, "Ah, such madness! And with the Summit just days away! What kind of fool is this man, Jerry? What's all this business about House of

David—Camp David? What is it? The dominating issue on his mind was clearly my alleged sexual encounters rather than how we need to deal with Pavlovsky and how to save the world from nuclear holocaust!"

Cooper said firmly, "That is exactly what Packard wants to do, David."

Taken aback, David said, "What?

"He wants to save the world!"

Strauss cocked his head in bewilderment.

"He told me so Friday night at Camp David. He wants to save the world—not in the diplomatic sense—in the evangelical sense. Specifically, your President believes the devil is responsible for the world's problems. He believes Pavlovsky is the Anti-Christ, sent to serve the devil. Therefore, your President and mine intends to give Pavlovsky a two-part ultimatum: One, renounce atheism. Two, to accept Jesus Christ as his personal Lord and savior. Pavlovsky will have twenty minutes to decide yes or no."

Wild eyed, Strauss asked, "And if chooses no?"

Cooper's hands pantomimed the release of something in to the air, and replied, "Boom."

Strauss said, "You mean?"

Cooper repeated, "Boom."

"He can't," Strauss said beseechingly, "there are fail-safe measures in place."

Cooper replied, calmly, "He's had them removed and had the code reprogrammed to accept the detonation command upon his order, which, I assure you, David, he will give precisely twenty minutes after he gives Pavlovsky the ultimatum. That's what I wanted to talk with you about today. And now that you have had a taste of how fucked-up his mind is, you can understand how mortified I was to discover what Packard has been thinking about all these years.

"And that is…" Strauss left it open-ended for Cooper to complete.

"That converting Pavlovsky is the only thing he's cared about since we got to Washington—shit, maybe even before, back in Iowa. David, the stupid bastard's a Christian Khomeini—*Jihad* had and all."

Cooper then told Strauss about his experience with the President at Camp David, Packard's fascination with Strauss's reported sexual exploits, speaking in tongues, all of it in graphic detail.

He closed with, "And, David, he told me that his sole mission at the Summit was to convert Premier Pavlovsky to Christ."

Strauss shook his head and exclaimed, "Jesus Christ!"

"The same," Cooper said.

Almost as if to himself, Strauss said, "Now I am beginning to understand his indifference to my briefings. They were extraneous to his mission."

"Bingo!" Cooper said. "We thought we worked for a man dedicated to paving a road to world peace. The truth is that the President was re-paving the road to Damascus for Dmitri Pavlovsky! Would you say that's carrying the art of personal diplomacy a bit too far, David?"

Strauss refilled his brandy glass and then Cooper's. His hand trembled.

"I am unabashedly a bit shaken, my friend," he said.

"Understandably, David," Cooper replied. Then added, "my remorse is worse, David. All these years that this "rather unremarkable fellow," as you characterized me earlier, was—as you said—"whispering in the President's ear," he was never hearing a word I was saying."

Cooper paused, then added, "Do you still covet my position, David?"

Strauss stood and moved to the window behind his desk and drew open the drape just enough so that he could look out and watch the noiseless traffic slowly cruise by. Heads in every automobile curiously turned toward his house in hopes of catching a glimpse of the most flamboyant character in the Packard administration stepping into his limo to be rushed to

Andrews Air Base and flown to Russia, or China, or wherever the *Washington Post* rumored he was going to practice the art of realpolitik. Muttering something under his breath, Strauss forcefully yanked the drape shut as if pulling a gallows rope. He tightly held on to the cord for a few seconds and then shook his head and sat down behind his desk. Perhaps some idea, some scheme, some contrivance would flick on in the complex circuitry of his brain and grant to him that which he craved above all else: control of events.

He drummed his fingers on the top of the desk and said in a low solemn voice, "Jerry, has he been like that since you've known him?"

Almost in a whisper, Cooper replied, "Maybe. I'm not sure. Not in the beginning, I don't think. Not to this extent, anyway. I don't know. Perhaps."

Pausing a moment, Cooper leaned forward and said, "Damn it, David, I staged most of that crap that won him the backing of those religious right wingers! Not only did I stage it – I exploited it! Hell, the liberals used the blacks; I used the evangelicals. We needed them to get elected. Then we could do good things. And you know what? We did some good things. True, Packard signed the bills I crafted, but—and David, this is the critical part that I want you to understand if you possibly can: Never, never did I ever advise or otherwise influence Packard on any position that was not consistent with his own central core of conviction. And from day one, with the exception of his religious beliefs, my beliefs and Albert Packard's were the same. Do you understand that? Unfortunately, what I didn't see, or maybe I ignored, was the religious cancer growing in his brain. On top of that—and get this too, David: I liked the guy!"

Strauss straightened up and put his arms on his desk. Looking at Cooper as a teacher to a pupil who needs special instruction after class, he said, "Don't castigate yourself, Jerry. What we have is a political problem requiring a pragmatic solution rather than an emotional dilemma. I, too, served his interests. I feel no guilt or contrition. I was appointed to serve the President—this President. That I did, and that I will do. Now, we have a complication—one that begs for clear and incisive judgment—not breast-beating. We must treat the illness as we find it, Jerry, without currying the comfort of recrimination. Perhaps, if we now view our assignment as serving the Presidency rather than the President, we will become more alert to opportunities for a proper course of action when they present themselves. Now, may I suggest you go home and get some sleep?"

Cooper swallowed the last drop in his brandy glass sensing that in the recent moments Strauss seemed to have regained his cherished control. Somewhere between yanking the cord of the window shade and drumming his fingers on his desk, whatever was eating at him before then was gone.

Cooper was bewildered how Strauss seemed to have recovered his power. The President's Special Advisor had forgotten, or was unmindful of the fact that his wily colleague interpreted a deleterious effect after one's exposure to a shocking emotional experience as a flaw in one's psyche, and thus a personal psychological advantage from which he derived strength. To David Strauss, the paradox of Jerry Cooper was unraveling and no longer a threat and that energized Strauss.

Feeling drained, Cooper stood up to leave. Strauss remained standing behind his desk. He appeared back to normal size.

Then, trying to imitate Al Packard, Strauss said, "Ya know, as my daddy used to say, 'fatigue is the mother of error.'"

"You know, David, you do a lousy Packard," Cooper said.

Strauss smiled his smile, and replied, "Perhaps it's an omen; that's what they used to say about my Ford."

Chapter Thirteen

There was never a better Millard Hampton than the one that went to the Russia to uncover Yuri Belov. The old pro, with a rediscovered joie de vivre, was a new and improved edition of the previous model.

The Hampton journey began a few days after breakfast with the Franks. Freda rode with him in the cab to La Guardia Airport while hurriedly taking down a glut of instructions on a steno pad. When they pulled up in front of the international concourse, he kissed her goodbye.

He asked, "Clancy, do you have any idea how much I love this?" gesturing to the world that made up the world he was about to re-enter.

Freda thought he looked twenty years younger. His eyes sparkled and energy pulsated from him.

She closed her eyes, said a silent prayer, and said, "Take care," then watched him swagger to his flight to Russia.

All Hampton had to go on was a five-year-old clipping from the *Jerusalem Post* saying Yuri Belov was arrested in Red Square. He had made numerous calls to contacts in the press, the Red Cross, humanitarian groups, and people he knew who played in the shadows and margins of governments. No one had anything that might lead him to Belov.

It was Freda who remembered.

"Sugah," she said the night before the trip, "remember when we did the research on the dissidents, we came across a man named Litvak, Father Dmitri Litvak. Wasn't he arrested five years ago in Red Square?"

"Clancy, you are indeed a gem!" Hampton said.

A quick telephone call to a contact in the Vatican confirmed that Litvak was still alive, still active in the freedom movement, and, best of all to Hampton and Freda, Litvak would see Hampton.

Hampton didn't wait to check in to his hotel when he arrived in Moscow. Instead he headed for Father Litvak's apartment immediately. He was greeted with suspicion by a short, balding man well in to his sixties.

"May I see some identification, please, Mr. Hampton, " Father Litvak politely asked.

Hampton was somewhat taken aback. Nonetheless, he produced his press credentials and World Broadcasting identification along with his passport.

Father Litvak studied the documents, and then said, "Forgive me. I mean identification to verify your association with Mr. Frank."

"Sir, I told you, I am here on Mr. Frank's behalf to develop…"
He stopped. Father Litvak held up one hand, and said gently, "Please, Mr. Hampton."

Totally unexpecting that development, Hampton reached into his travel worn leather brief case, and pulled out a photograph of he and Bernie Frank. It was autographed, "to my godfather, Millard Hampton, with appreciation, Bernie."

The priest turned to examine it carefully. Then he smiled, and said, "Ah, yes. Unmistakable."

Immediately, Litvak's demeanor changed from suspicion to warmth. He said, softly, "Yes, I knew Yuri Belov. I'd be pleased to offer you what I am able."

Hampton wanted to cut to the chase. Therefore, he did not dwell too long on the unanticipated incident.

After offering Hampton tea, Father Litvak told him of his eight years spent in a Soviet labor camp after his arrest for writing religious poetry.

"I'll spare you the gory details," Litvak said. "After my release, I began to hold a series of seminars at the Church of St. Nicholas in Moscow. Generally, my theme was the decline of morality and spirituality in the Soviet system. It seemed to resonate with the young people, especially the well educated.

At every session," Litvak continued, "one man wearing the clothes of a beggar but with the bearing of a nobleman, stood out. His questions were probing, his rebuke of the system even more harsh than my own. By the fourth session, he became as much an attraction as I. His name was Yuri Belov."

Father Litvak told Hampton that the KGB finally brought an end to the meetings and arrested him again. "This time the punishment was more severe," Litvak said, with his face looking at the floor as if to avoid revisiting his ordeal.

Then he regained composure, and said, "Belov continued to preach to the remnants of the St. Nicholas group outside of the church after they took me away until he, too, was arrested. After that, I lost track of him. I heard rumors he had been sent to Cristopol, God help him. It's one of the worst prisons in the Gulag, not that the others are any picnic, you understand. I had also heard he spent some time at the Serbsky—forgive me—another hell hole."

Hampton nodded his head to indicate he understood, and then said, "Father, I am confused. If the Soviet Union represses religious freedom, how did the churches exist?"

Father Litvak smiled, and said, "The answer is the essence of our plight. The Communist leaders in the Kremlin have not banned religion, they merely keep a record of those who attend services. Those who attend are harassed, fired from their jobs, or, worse, arrested. It's the death by a thousand cuts rather than the Nazi way of Final Solution. Each achieves the same result."

Father Litvak stood. He looked weary. "Belov was born in Lithuania," he said. "Go to Vilnius and look up my friend Asa Bobek. He and Yuri were arrested, tried, and sent to prison together."

"I will do so, Father. I cannot thank you enough for helping me." Hampton extended his hand.

As Father Litvak took Hampton's hand with both of his, he said, "You can thank me by helping Yuri, Mr. Hampton. May God bless your journey and keep you safe."

Rather than depart immediately for Lithuania, Hampton decided to find out what he could at the Serbsky Institute of Forensic Psychiatry.

"To be there is to be inside the mind of Kafka," he recorded that night into his small tape recorder. "I have seen the worst of war and tragedy. Neither had ever given me nausea until the Serbsky Institute. Clancy, you know your expression 'ugly air?' My dear, in that place the air is vile."

Using the Hamptonian combination of intimidation and chicanery, he was able to secure an appointment with Dr. Georgy Morozov, the Director of Serbsky.

Hampton was surprised to find him affable.

"Sure, I'll tell you about Yuri," Morozov said, with almost American-style informality. "Either he has excellent protexia— that is, influence—with the Central Committee or the Politburo, or he is totally worthless, and thus barterable."

"Which do you believe to be true, Dr. Morozov?" Hampton asked.

The doctor leaned back, thought, and then said, "I think he had help somewhere high up." He went on to say that only the most tricky, borderline cases from all over the country are normally sent to the Serbsky, and he estimated that no more than about fifteen percent of the inmates are ruled "not responsible."

"Not responsible," he said to Hampton, "was Soviet psychiatric dialectic for 'dissident.'"

Hampton got the impression that Morozov was imagining himself on American television.

Morozov continued: "Belov was without the hostility that one detests in so many of the so called dissidents. So many of them have an intellectual arrogance. Belov tended more toward the esoteric than the political. Yes, he would lecture his fellow patients about the sinfulness of the denial of human rights. He wasn't speaking so much about political rights as he was about the right of the mind to expand, inquire, reach, and develop. I found him quite fascinating, frankly."

"Go on." Hampton said. "Your insight is remarkable."

Morozov ran his hand across his hair. "We would have lengthy conversations—Belov and I. There was something compelling about him. Honestly, at times I felt as if our roles were reversed."

"Conversations about what?" Hampton asked, as if enthralled with Morozov's performance.

"We'd discuss all sorts of things. Mainly the relationship of the mind to the body. Belov insisted that all mental disorders were the result of spiritual disorientation that triggered chemical impulses within the body, manifesting in abnormal behavior. He complained that as long as Soviet science functions in the Godless political system, they will never get to the root causes of mental illness. Naturally, I disagreed and told him we had the most advanced drugs in the civilized world with which behavior could be altered. Belov said he agreed with the word *altered*, however he asked if the motive was not to cure? A very engaging fellow, Belov."

Hampton asked if Morozov minded if he smoked.

Not wanting to offend his guest's attempt at courtesy, Morozov replied, "I hear it's bad for your health. But since you are in the Serbsky Institute for Forensic Psychiatry, if you suddenly fall dead, we'll find out if it's true and what compelled you at the same time. So, go ahead. In the interest of medical progress, by all means, smoke."

They both laughed. Hampton enjoyed the dark Russian humor. Satisfied that his pipe was lit properly, he asked Morozov if drugs were a part of Belov's treatment.

"At first, yes, of course," Morozov said confidently. "As a 'not responsible' schizophrenic, we administered Aminazin, which I believe is Thorazine in the West, and Haloperidol, which you call Serenace. Oddly, they didn't faze him. No matter what level of dosage or frequency we administered. Nothing! Never have we seen anything like it," Morozov said wide-eyed. "No painful side effects, no nausea, no mental or emotional alteration, nothing! After several months, we stopped injecting. A waste of good drugs."

Hampton asked if Belov explained his resistance to the drugs.

Morozov smiled, lit a cigarette and said, "Yes, he did. At least he offered an explanation. He told me that he could will—I assume by a kind of hypnotic suggestion—his body to reject the properties of the drug, thus nullifying its effect. He told me that when he was being 'physically rehabilitated' at Cristopol, he felt no pain because he psychically disassociated himself from the beating. In fact, I remember his words because of their psychiatric implications. He said, 'I watched the beating from the ceiling.'"

Hampton had heard such tales from tortured POWs before. On matters beyond reason, he was consistently agnostic.

At that moment, he needed more information from Morozov while Morozov remained willing to give more. Hampton tamped the ashes in the bowl of his Dunhill, and said, "Dr. Morozov, you've given me the impression you had more than a formal doctor-patient relationship with Yuri Belov. Am I correct?"

Morozov smothered his cigarette, reflected several seconds, and said, "Yes, I did. Truthfully, I'm glad he made it out of here.

Many do not. He said he would not die here. But may I tell you something that I have not said to anyone?"

"Yes, of course." Hampton said.

"He told me I would."

Hampton remained silent—an invitation for Morozov to continue.

"Belov told me I was dying from guilt. He said that it started when I accepted the directorship, and consequently the responsibility, for the institute. He said that in exchange for comfort and prestige, I sold out the commitment of my early years to become a physician to help people. He said the worst part of it is that I know it and can't bear it. Belov said I freely chose to turn aside from what I knew inside I was supposed to do in this life for a softer path. He told me my dereliction was of the worst kind: the kind that does harm and inflicts pain. He told me I had two alternatives—either one of which would save my life: One, I could become a dissident myself and actively oppose the system. Two, I could fully and totally accept and forgive what I have become. He said that I should make a free and unrelenting choice of either course. According to Belov, if I maintain my present course, I will continue to inject myself with hourly doses of toxins which will eventually kill me."

Hampton let several seconds go by, then said, "I was right. You two did have a profound relationship. That's quite a story, Dr. Marozov. Obviously, our Mr. Belov is quite a mental Houdini. The patient tells the doctor he's dying! That's a first."

Dr. Morozov looked at his watch. Hampton took the cue, thanked him for his time and information.

Morozov looked at Hampton seriously, and said, "You seek an unusual man, Mr. Hampton. He spoke so often of his desire to go home. I can't understand why he didn't, and went to Israel instead."

Hampton thanked Morozov again and told him he hoped they would meet again under different circumstances.

"I doubt that we will, Mr. Hampton," Morozov said. I have cancer. It's terminal. Three months at the most to live."

Suddenly shaken, Hampton left the Serbsky Institute of Forensic Psychiatry as fast as he could walk.

Hampton had dinner that night with some Moscow bureau chiefs from CBS, Newsweek and the Associated Press. The conversation was mostly shoptalk and old war stories. Hampton was careful not to disclose why he was there or what he had learned. "Old pals," he sarcastically told Freda on the telephone later that night, "will sell their first born for an exclusive." She laughed. "Besides," he continued, "I assume I'm being monitored by the little General's boys as well as his Soviet soul mates."

"Well, you take care, sugah, and remember to stay off the sauce." Freda said.

"Don't worry, my dear. That's past history. I'll call you tomorrow," Hampton said, imagining both the CIA and the KGB agents listening in and saying in unison, "From where?"

The train ride from Moscow to Vilnius was drafty, bumpy and long. Hampton loved every minute of it. He thought of Sidney Wade, how much he would enjoy this journey, how the ambiance would inspire his creativity. He buried the thought, and thought of Freda, and then the job he needed to do.

Professor Asa Bobek lived in two small rooms adjacent to his academy. Hampton rang the bell, and was greeted by a rather tall man with skeletal facial features guarding deep sunken eyes. Hampton introduced himself and gave him a gift of a bottle of wine. Professor Bobek thanked him profusely, exuding a warmth that belied his physical appearance. Bobek offered Hampton a seat in what appeared to be the professor's reading chair. Like counting the age of a tree, Hampton noted the layers of blankets and other cloth covering the seat and arms and wondered how many owners it had until someone gave it to the school. His host sat in a wooden hardback chair that resembled its occupant. Like the weather that day, everything about the place appeared drab.

After brief opening platitudes, Professor Bobek seemed satisfied that Hampton was not an agent for the secret police or had other covert motives.

"I will do something that is unseemly these days, Mr. Hampton," Bobek began. "I am going to trust you."

"Thank you, Professor. I hope what I do with what you tell me merits your trust."

"Mr. Hampton," Professor Bobek began as a teacher to a student, "You represent Mr. Bernie Frank. That merits my trust, and the trust of those who are praying for him when he introduces Yuri Belov to the world. It is quite an amazing and wonderful turn of events."

Hampton noted that Professor Bobek's near veneration for Bernie was similar to the disposition Father Litvak portrayed. Hampton wondered why an American TV personality—a newcomer never seen on communist controlled TV—would be so revered?

Hampton nodded agreement. "I'm certain Bernie will live up to your hopes," he said, without completely understanding the meaning of Bobek's remarks.

Professor Bobek seemed pleased. He took a deep breath, and said, "Now let me begin to assist. You want to know about Yuri Belov. How to begin? Hmm. You see, Yuri Belov saved my life. He and I have known each other since we were young. You may find that hard to reconcile: Me, a devout Catholic; Yuri a devout Jew." Bobek paused, noting a look of surprise on Hampton's face.

"Something I said?" He inquired.

Hampton said, "I'm somewhat surprised. Yuri a Jew? I just assumed from what Father Litvak told me about Belov's preaching at St. Nicholas Church and sending me to you, one who was arrested with him, that Belov was a Christian."

Professor Bobek looked squarely at Hampton and said nothing.

Hampton lit his pipe, settled back, and said, "Sorry, Professor. Go ahead, please."

"As a boy and on into manhood," Bobek began, "Yuri had an insatiable thirst for knowledge about the partisan days of World War Two. He would seek out people who survived—Jews mostly—but anyone and pick their minds to learn this and that about his father and others. Well, my father, a devout Christian, was a physician. During the terrible days of the Vilna Ghetto, he performed a surgical procedure on some Jewish men who looked Aryan. At the risk to his own life, he saved several Jewish lives.

Hampton had heard the story about the Christian doctor who performed reverse circumcisions on Jewish men. He had thought it was another myth from a time ripe with fable. He was not only pleased that he was verifying the tale, the corroboration was a first person source: the son of the doctor of valor.

Professor Bobek continued, "When Yuri was the acting Rabbi in Vilna, he would often come by our apartment and talk for hours with my father about those days of the Vilna Ghetto. My father often told me that Yuri desperately wanted to know as much as my father could remember about Lev Belov – Yuri's father. Lev was killed during the fighting just before Yuri was born."

The professor paused a moment to allow his pupil time to assimilate and process the information. Then he continued:

"It was about that time that a rumor circulated around Vilna and the countryside that Yuri had performed a miracle. According to the rumor, a woman named Bluma Ketsherginski, who was blinded at Auschwitz, had her vision restored by him. Suddenly everyone was flocking to the Belov place to be cured of everything from diarrhea to dropsy. Reports of miracle cures performed by the young Vilna Rebbe spread like wildfire. I must admit that when my father took sick, I considered taking him to visit Yuri, however I quickly dismissed the thought after indirectly proposing it to my father. He, a physician and a Christian, would have nothing to do with such 'non scientific antics,' as he called them."

Professor Bobek hesitated, smiled a bony smile and said, "Perhaps this is a good time to discover what wonders lie captive in that bottle you brought me, Mr. Hampton."

Hampton leaned forward, and said, "Professor Bobek, it would give me great joy for you to enjoy its contents. I would dearly love to share them with you, however, my days of libation terminated recently, and I promised someone dear to me that I would refrain."

"I understand, Mr. Hampton. I will save the bottle for later, and make us a cup of tea."

As the tall, gaunt man poured the water from a pitcher into the kettle, and took a pinch of tea from the tin on the table, he said, "Frankly, it was difficult for us to think of Yuri Belov in the terms of what was being said about him. Many times, when I saw the line of people lined up in front of his home waiting for instant healing, the thought crossed my mind that Ksana's boy, Yuri, might not be as straightforward as he appeared to be."

By that time Hampton, too, had begun to wonder if he were searching for a mystic, a magician or a madman.

"I shall never forget the incident when my father died," the Professor said as he stood by the stove, "Yuri suddenly appeared by my side at the funeral and said Kaddish, the sacred Jewish prayer for the dead, at the gravesite. Imagine: Kaddish for a Catholic! Then, as we walked away from the burial ground, Yuri put his hand on my shoulder and said, 'Your father is already at a special place in Heaven.'"

As he poured tea into a glass for Hampton and himself, he told Hampton about the underground newspaper he published that served as a rallying point for the religiously persecuted of Lithuania. In time, he was arrested by the KGB and was sentenced to two years in a prison camp at Praveniskes. There he was tortured and beaten by sadistic guards.

"As I lay ripped and bloody on the floor of my cell, writhing in pain, I felt a hand on my head. It seemed so warm and gentle. I thought I was either dead or hallucinating. Certainly, it couldn't be the touch of anyone at Praveniskes. My eyes opened and there, as if in a mist, was Yuri Belov. I couldn't believe it! I blinked several times to make sure I was seeing correctly what my mind said was so; and the image remained. Yuri Belov, there in the squalor of my cell, at a time when my soul and body were in the pits of a nightmare. Yuri Belov! How did he get in? He had that look of peace about him that I saw at my father's funeral. Only this time it seemed to almost permeate the space around us so that I began to feel immediate strength. Then, he gently put his arm under my head and held me to his bosom. I felt energy flowing into my body as if I was plugged into an electric current. I looked at myself. My hands and legs were nearly unrecognizable. I can imagine what my face looked like after being beaten for so long. Yet, I was feeling strong, stronger and stronger as each second went by in his arms. I heard him whisper in my ear, 'Believe in God's healing. He's healing you now. Trust in Him now and always.' Holding me for several more minutes, he then picked me up, laid me on my cot, and gently brushed his hand over my eyes. I slipped into a deep sleep. He must have left me then, and I never saw him again."

Professor Bobek paused, sipped his tea, then said, "I was released shortly after that and returned to Vilnius."

Hampton finished his tea, then asked, "How do you explain what happened, Professor?"

Bobek stood, and said, "I have told you what happened."

He escorted Hampton the few steps to the door and opened it. He said, "There, down the street and three blocks to the left, is a marker telling where the Vilna opera house was located. You'll find Yuri's mother living in the house by the marker.

Read the marker, Mr. Hampton. I will tell her about our visit and recommend that she visit with you—perhaps tomorrow, say around mid-day?

"Thank you Professor Bobek. You have helped a great deal. Be sure to enjoy the wine."

"I'm sure I will, my son. And you keep your resolve *not* to enjoy it."

"Oh, by the way," Hampton said, turning back toward the dour man standing in the doorway, "that woman, the one who was blind, can you direct me to her?"

Millard Hampton's visit with Bluma Ketsherginski was brief. A feisty heavy set woman whose voice could rattle dishes. She raised a few chickens and hogs on a small plot of land located several miles from Vilnius, at a place called Lida.

She told Hampton in the coarsest of language that it was unimportant whether he, or anyone else, believed her. "What is true," she said, "was that Yuri Belov made my eyes see again."

Hampton asked her how he did it. At first, she refused to respond. Then, she folded her hands over her bosom, looked upward, and said, "I'll tell you if you give me an photograph of your boss with his signature."

"My boss!" Hampton exclaimed.

Resolute, Bluma said, "Yes. The American television star you work for. I want his picture. Then I'll tell you how Yuri fixed my eyes.

Hampton plunged his hand into his briefcase, and brought out a glossy photograph he carried for emergencies, which Bernie signed, "Best wishes, Bernie Frank" and handed it to Bluma.

She studied it, and said, "I'll be damn. It looks just like him!"

Mystified how she would know, Hampton said, "Yes, it does. Now, Miss Ketsherginski, about Yuri Belov and your eyes."

Bluma tucked the photo under her arm, sighed and said, "Oh,

what the hell. You seem like a nice fellow," she smiled broadly, exposing the absence of one tooth near the front of her mouth.

"Yuri placed his hand over both of my eyes and whispered in my ear."

"What did he say?" Hampton asked.

Again she paused a second or two, then said with a more rapid delivery than before, "Yuri told me that God approves of choosing life over death; and that I should feel no guilt about doing what I did in order to stay alive. He told me what I saw was not my fault, and that God wants me to see again if I want to see again. I told him I believed what he said was true, and that I wanted to see again. And just then, I could see. My eyes could see! His face was the first face I saw since Auschwitz."

As he was leaving, Bluma told Hampton that a Mr. Viktor Abramov, the "Soviet's son-of-a-bitch in Vilnius," was responsible for Belov having to leave Vilnius shortly after he restored her sight.

She never thanked Hampton for the picture.

Hampton drove back to the center of Vilnius and parked in front of the Vilnius Headquarters of the People's Republic. The office had a spartan appearance with Premier Pavlovsky's portrait dominating the room.

"I'm in a huge hurry, Mr. Hampton, nonetheless I always try to accommodate the American press when I am able, " Abramov said.

Looking straight in his eyes, Hampton said, "I am grateful for whatever time you may provide, sir. As you are aware, I am seeking information regarding Mr. Yuri Belov. Our program has been selected by our governments to interview Mr. Belov. My job is to provide background on the man for our journalist."

Abramov considered Hampton's statement several seconds, then said brusquely, "Mr. Hampton, the file on that hooligan Belov was closed, and I have nothing more to say about him or the case."

Then Abramov jotted a note on a small pad, ripped off the page, and crumbled it in his hand. Hampton noticed that several fingers of his left hand were missing. Again, more loudly than before, he proclaimed his disavowal of any knowledge or interest in helping Hampton know about Belov "or any other reactionary."

Abramov abruptly stood up in a way that said the meeting was over. Hampton thanked the Vilnius Communist Party Chief for his time and extended his hand for his. The crisp paper crushed into Hampton's palm as he briskly shook hands goodbye.

Hampton was a safe distance from the Party headquarters when he finally unraveled the note that he kept clenched in his fist. Abramov had written one word: Gershon.

Hampton dined alone in his hotel room that night. He had no idea what the significance of the word Gershon was other than the knowledge that it was a rather common Lithuanian surname. He spent a quiet night refining his notes and recording them on tape with some added color commentary as he had done from the outset of his journey. The tapes would be sent to Bernie in New York prior to his departure for Israel. Bernie would frame his questions for Yuri Belov from those tapes. Hampton kept the original notes on his person at all times just in case.

After several hours of trying to get through to Freda on the telephone, he abandoned the effort and fell asleep in anticipation of tomorrow's visit with the mother of Yuri Belov.

The bronze plaque was fixed to the side of an old building. It was designated and maintained as a Lithuanian Historical Site. Across the street was another building. It was dilapidated and coming apart. All ornamental markings of its former life were either ripped off or otherwise removed. Its last Rabbi was Julian Zoya.

Hampton paused to read the inscription on the plaque of the

historical site as Professor Bobek advised him to do. It read, "Site of the Vilna Opera House. It is dedicated to the memory of its last director, Michael Frankel, who was martyred by the Nazis in Ponary Forest in September 1942."

Hampton's mind raced as he walked to Ksana Belov's residence half a block away. He rang the bell. The woman who greeted Millard Hampton accomplished a unique feat: She took his breath away.

"The tea is about ready," she said, while excusing herself to go to the kitchen.

Hampton took the opportunity to hastily write a note so that he would not forget his instant impression. "Bobek description conservative...tantalizing/disarming woman met my life...gentle incandescent beauty...penetrate you...essence of grace: beauty wit sense of sadness."

"Ah, Mrs. Belov, here, let me help you," he said, as she brought a pot of tea from the kitchen.

"Thank you. I can manage. Careful, it's hot. Take some sugar if you like."

"No, I take mine plain. Thank you."

She asked, "Your journey –was it tiring?"

"Yes, quite tiring indeed. I can imagine how tired your son must have been when he came home," he replied.

She smiled.

"Does the tea taste good, Mr. Hampton?"

"Delicious, Mrs. Belov. Quite excellent."

"That is good," she said.

A slight pause, a sip, then she said, "Tell me, Mr. Hampton, why suddenly so many people interested in my son?"

Hampton looked curiously at her. "Interest? Have you been interviewed — that is, I mean — have you been asked by others about your son?"

The reporter's fear of being scooped surged through Hampton's veins.

"Yes, of course Yuri has always been of interest to the

authorities for long time. I don't mean that kind of authorities. Others – like you – foreigners want to know this and want to know that about Yuri. Why, Mr. Hampton?"

"Do you mind telling me who has been to see you asking about Yuri, Mrs. Belov?" Hampton inquired.

Ksana shook her head, and said, "No, I do not mind. One man – two, three days ago – says he is from American film company – wants to make movie about Yuri. I say, movie about Yuri? Why? Who would go see it? He says he is not sure they will make film. If they do, he will pay me lots of money. All I have to do is tell him everything I can remember about Yuri—his friends, his activities, what he thinks, what he has written, everything. He says if his, how do you say, his boss—yes, his boss, likes what I have told him, then they will make movie of Yuri."

Hampton breathed a sigh of relief while noting how gracefully animated she was when she spoke. Better than a well-directed actress, Ksana's movements were natural. He wished he had a video camera.

Ksana continued: "Well, Mr. Hampton, I am a simple woman from a simple town, yet I have seen much of life, and much of people. What I am telling you is that man was not telling the truth. I know that for certain. He must be from the police, I thought. Not our police—I recognize them right away after all these years. Anyway, our police do not play games. The man was American. That I knew. And here he was, pretending to be filmmaker so to find out information about Yuri. Why would American police care about Yuri when they know Yuri went to Israel?" Ksana asked innocently.

Hampton took a sip of tea, and said, "Our police like to play games, Mrs. Belov. They wanted to find out about your son because they suspect some evil reason for his release from prison."

Ksana braced her back. "Evil? Yuri evil? This is what they think?" She said indignantly.

Hampton gestured puzzlement with his hand, and said, "Quite frankly, Mrs. Belov, they don't know what they think. Just like Russian police, our police think all people are considered bad people until they are proven good. Our government is divided over the purpose for your son's sudden release. The American police, called the CIA, suspect an evil purpose. Do you understand what I have said, Mrs. Belov?"

"Yes, yes I do," Ksana said nodding her head. "They think maybe using Yuri is a trick,"

"Exactly," Hampton said.

Ksana leaned forward in her chair, closer to Hampton. Searching his eyes, she said, "And you, Mr. Hampton. Why do you want to know about my son?"

He replied, "I told you, Mrs. Belov, I am the producer of an American television program and the information you provide me will be used to formulate questions when Yuri is interviewed on television."

"I see," she said, softly. "And will you pay me lots of money like the other man said he would if my answers are good?"

With some of the old Hampton hubris, he said, "Now, you know better than that, Mrs. Belov. The other man was pretending to be a filmmaker just to get information about Yuri for the authorities. He was a liar."

"Oh. And you? You are not liar?" she asked, in mock disbelief.

"Not now, Mrs. Belov," Hampton replied resolutely. "I lie sometimes. Trust me, I am not lying now. I am Millard Hampton, a producer of..."

"Shhh. Enough, enough. I'm sorry. Here, have more tea," she said, as if to say the game was over.

"Thank you, Mrs. Belov," Hampton said, deferentially.

Ksana paused to allow the mood to pass. She toyed with her spoon in her cup, looked over at Hampton to make sure his was full, and gave him a warm smile. Then she said, "Tell me, Mr. Hampton, why would you want Yuri on American television?"

Hampton looked in Ksana's eyes in the way he had coached so many TV hosts to do to the camera, and said, "Mrs. Belov, from the information about your son that I have gathered so far, I believe he is a very special man. I believe that the Soviets do not have any idea who has been in their midst, and in their cities, and in their prisons, and who they have exported to Israel. And, I believe there are only two people who know how special he is: One is your son; the other is the beautiful woman who just poured me another glass of tea."

"I see, I see." Ksana said reflectively.

Hampton couldn't detect by her body language or her eyes if he had scored points on the believability meter. For an instant, he felt a pang of guilt for even trying his phony theatrical chicanery. Such was the spell cast by the lovely woman before him.

"Tell me, Mr. Hampton, are you married?"

"Why, no…no I am not," replied Hampton, non-plussed

"Have you ever been married?" Ksana persisted.

"Well, no…yes, I have," he responded, more uncomfortably. "It only lasted a few months during the war."

"Pity," she said.

"Pity?" he asked.

"Yes, a pity. You are an attractive man – quite unlike most American men. You have a European bearing about you. You could have made some woman proud to be your wife. She would have looked at you a lot—quite uncertain at times that she is really your wife—other times to see how you feel. Ah, you have missed so much, Mr. Hampton, but some woman has missed more," Ksana said, warmly.

Hampton chided himself for allowing what he preached against: the guest taking control of the interview.

Resigned to go with the flow, he said, "I'm afraid my work and marriage do not get along well together, Mrs. Belov."

"Nonsense," Ksana admonished. "She would fit herself to your work. Lev, my husband, may he rest in peace, might have looked like you now. Bigger, perhaps, with golden hair, athletic—with fire inside. Time would soften him—like wine, perhaps as time softened you. Still with the fire," she said, her hands spreading apart, her face glowing.

Ksana's mention of her husband's name opened the door for Hampton to drift back on point, to regain control. He asked, "Was your husband killed during a battle, Mrs. Belov?"

But Ksana would not be conducted.

She said, "You have been in love? Haven't you, Mr. Hampton?" She leaned closer to him and lowered her head to connect with his downward cast eyes. "Yes," she said, gently, "I see somewhere in your eyes that you loved —deeply loved— and lost your love. I'm sorry you lost; I am not sorry you loved."

Hampton nodded, as the strains of "Precious One" floated through his heart. At that point, he was grateful a camera was not present.

Ksana reached for his hand, and said, "Always remember that life is a gift from God. He gives it for us to use, to cherish, to fill it with love. Use it, live it, never reckless, but as you would a precious gift."

Ksana withdrew her hand from his, and had a look of joy. She had once again given of herself.

Hampton said, "I can see where Yuri gets his sensitivity, Mrs. Belov."

"Can you?" Ksana asked as if pleased.

She turned, and said, "That is Yuri there—on the table—the photograph. It was taken the day before his bar mitzvah. A beautiful child, yes? All mothers think their sons are beautiful—especially on their bar mitzvah. I'm no different—a proud mother."

Hampton turned to the table, looked at Yuri's photograph, and said, "He does look handsome."

He noticed there were two other photographs on the table. He cast his eyes on the one to the right. The light in the room was dim, however he could make out a bearded man with a prayer shawl around his neck and a prayer book held to his breast. His face was stern, yet his eyes were warm, a hint of Ksana in his expression.

"The man, was he..." Hampton began.

"My father, may he rest in peace, Rabbi Julian Zoya" she said, emphasizing each syllable as if savoring the sound.

"He looks like a wonderful man," Hampton said, gratuitously. Ksana nodded with a gentle smile.

Ksana reached for Yuri's photograph, looked at it, and said, "Ah, that day—his bar mitzvah. Eleven people. Imagine, in Vilna—the Jerusalem of Europe they used to call us—eleven Jews left. Yuri spoke that day a message of freedom and of God. Eleven people heard him. One went to police. From his bar mitzvah to today, Yuri was watched."

Pleased that he was now back on track, Hampton quickly said, "I thought his trouble started when he restored Bluma Ketsherginski's eyesight."

Ksana shook her head, and said, "No, it began the day he became a man. Or," she paused and said reflectively, "perhaps the day he was born."

"I don't understand," said Hampton, quizzically.

With a wave of the hand, Ksana replied, "A foolish statement. I'm sorry. It means nothing,"

Hampton honed in. "The reports of your son's ability to heal the sick are fascinating. When did he acquire that ability?"

With noticeable anxiety, Ksana replied, "Mr. Hampton, I am unable to help you with more information. I'm sorry. I cannot."

Hampton persisted, "Have you heard from him since his release from prison?"

"Yes," she answered.

"How is he?"

Ksana eyes took on a distant look, as she said, "Yuri is in good health. Lev and I dreamed of going to Israel after the fighting. We didn't get there. Yuri sees it for us."

"Will you be able to join him there?" Hampton asked.

With a tone of sadness, Ksana said, "I can tell you no more, Mr. Hampton. I'm sorry."

Sensing he'd struck a nerve, Hampton said, "Certainly you want to be with your son?"

"Of course. Doesn't every mother?" Ksana replied, as if to a silly question, yet obviously unnerved. Then she added, "Yuri will fulfill his destiny with or without his mother."

Hampton bored in. "His destiny?"

"Perhaps his responsibility would be better word," Ksana responded delicately.

"To do what, Mrs. Belov?" Hampton asked, knowing her answer would solve the riddle.

"I'm sorry. No more," Ksana replied.

Hampton pleaded, more emphatically, "Responsibility to do what—just that, please, Mrs. Belov!"

Ksana looked at Hampton sitting on the edge of his seat and smiled a knowing smile. Then she turned and placed her son's bar mitzvah photograph back on the table. Hampton followed the action. Curiously, his eyes focused on the third photograph. He froze.

"Oh my God!" Hampton said.

He stood up, went to the table, and picked up the framed photograph to get a closer look. It was a theatrical picture—a head shot—used for publicity. To the side, an inscription, "To Ksana, with love, Michael Frankel." The resemblance is...it's him!" Hampton shouted.

Ksana watched Hampton's reaction. Then said, "Mr. Hampton, with all due respect: Did you really think all of us spoke with you because of your charm?"

Hampton turned and looked curiously at Ksana. She continued, "Your Mr. Bernie Frank is quite a legend here in Vilnius. We have never seen him, of course, however when word that Herbert Frankel's son—Michael Frankel's nephew—has become a big television star in America, we all rejoiced in the irony. Bernie Frank became what Michael Frank dreamed. He is the completion of his uncle's song that night on the death march."

Ksana went on to tell Hampton the story of that frightful, fateful, Ponary Forest night.

When she finished, she studied Hampton and said, "Tell me, Mr. Hampton, is Mr. Frank a *mensch*?"

He knew the meaning. "His uncle would be quite proud of him, Mrs. Belov," Hampton said with conviction.

"Good," she said, sweetly. "Give him our love."

Hampton stood, and held out his hand. Ksana placed hers in it. It felt warm and soft. He brought her hand to his lips, and gently kissed it. Then, he said, "Thank you, Mrs. Belov."

She smiled and said, "I am glad we met, Mr. Hampton. May God be with you."

He turned toward the door, stopped and said, "I will see your son in a few days. Is there any message you want me to take from you?"

Ksana hesitated, and then said directly to Hampton's eyes, "Tell him not to worry about his mother, and to do what he must do. Tell him that I love him with all my heart and soul."

"I'll tell him," Hampton said. "Good-bye."

"Shalom," Mr. Hampton.

Hampton knew he was being followed since leaving Ksana's house. He also knew it would have been a paradox if a foreigner—let alone an American journalist with a mission as circuitous as his—were not followed. Accordingly, both the CIA and the KGB had followed Hampton since landing in Russia. However, the man who followed Hampton from Ksana Belov's house to his hotel was neither an agent of the U.S. nor the Soviets. Hampton knew the person was not a professional by the clumsy manner he was being tailed. His predator was thin and wore a dark blue wool seaman's jacket—P coats they were called during the war—and had difficulty staying hidden. Hampton concluded there were two possibilities: Either the man wishes to make contact and is waiting for a safe moment or he is in physical danger of being attacked and beaten or killed by the man.

Just as Hampton was considering his options should he be attacked, there was a soft knock on his door. How he wished he had a gun, but it was too late for wishing.

"Who's there?" he hollered, as he positioned himself to the side of the door so as to get in the first blow if the door busted in.

There was no sound from the other side.

Again, "Who is there?" That time with more *profundo* to mask his anxiety.

Nothing. Inadvertently, Hampton looked down. There, partially visible, was a brown envelope that someone had slid part way under the door. A fleeting thought that it might be a letter bomb flashed across Hampton's brain, but he intuitively dismissed it.

Before taking hold of the exposed end of the envelope and pulling it through, Hampton flung open the door and leaped out of the way in case the envelope was a ploy to gain access to him. He carefully stepped outside the doorway and quickly looked both ways. No one was there; the hallway was empty.

He bent down, picked up the envelope, went back into his room, and withdrew several sheets of paper handwritten in English. He raised one eyebrow after reading the first sentence.

"Ah ha," he said, as he reclined on the bed, lit his pipe, and read the letter.

When he was finished, he decided to omit the contents of the letter as well the story of Michael Frankel from the recording sent back to Bernie. He needed to convey both items to Bernie in person in Israel.

Chapter Fourteen

"Freda, are you positive they said the Orange Terminal?" Bernie asked, for the third time.

Freda looked at Peggy and rolled her eyes as if to say, "If he asks me that one more time I'll pop him."

Peggy smiled, knowing all the time Freda's impatience was pretended, that her tolerance for any of her husband's moods was infinite.

"Bernie, the chick in the Israeli Ambassador's office who made our travel arrangements told me we should go to the Orange Terminal at Kennedy International Airport and from there we would depart to Israel. That's all I know. But I know what she said—and that's what she said."

Bernie thought a second, then said, "Yeah? Well, only the Israelis would hide a terminal that couldn't be rhymed."

Peggy and Freda looked at him quizzically.

Several people passed by and noticed him. The whispered, "Isn't that, what's his name?" and louder to his face, "Say, aren't you...?" turned his TV smile on. Freda ignored it. Peggy hated it—not the fans—the phony smile.

To provide as much protection from hijacking as possible, the Orange Terminal was isolated nearly one half mile from the main Kennedy airport complex. After complete body and baggage searches by security agents, the trio finally entered a bus that swiftly drove them from the clandestine terminal on to the airfield. There the bus stopped abruptly at the entry ramp of the El Al airplane bathed in searchlights.

For seven thousand miles, the three flew to the accompaniment of American students—one of whom, of course, brought her guitar—singing Israeli folks songs. The kids only knew five songs, which drove the rest of the passengers batty. In the morning and evening, several Hasidim and other religious Jews chanted their morning and evening prayers, rocking themselves and stretching their necks upward.

During the flight, Bernie wrote questions for the Belov interview while listening to the tapes of Hampton's notes. Hampton had wangled the State Department's approval to carry the tapes from Russia back to the U. S. by diplomatic courier. From Washington, they were hand delivered to Bernie in New York. He had begun to work on the interview immediately. The more he listened, the more he concentrated on his subject. Hampton's tapes convinced him that Belov was not your ordinary celeb. Bernie began to feel an odd sensation, as if he existed on two dimensions; one apparent, the other ethereal. In flight, he felt a strange connection to Yuri, like a gravitational pull toward and connected to Belov.

Suddenly, the theme from the film *Exodus* blared boldly through the airplane's speakers, and the pilot instructed the passengers to look below. There, as if beamed through the time tunnel, was Israel.

In a voice calmer than his emotion, Bernie leaned to Peggy, and said, "I promised my parents once that I would see Israel for them."

She squeezed his hand. He was referring to the Yiddish legend, which claims that when one member of a family visits Israel, he sees it for all his ancestors who didn't have the opportunity, and that they see it through his eyes.

The inevitable passenger van pulled up to the ramp of the

plane at Lod Airport, as it did at Kennedy; but this time two machine-gun-toting Israeli soldiers guarded the van. The fifty-foot trip to the terminal and through customs, with the predictable question about someone giving something to deliver to someone, was performed with humorless efficiency.

"These folks mean business," Peggy said to Freda.

"I wouldn't mind that one frisking me," Freda replied, as she looked at a swarthy Israeli soldier standing by the door leading to the lobby of the main terminal. His sharp eyes scanned her body, which was obviously not concealing a weapon, or anything else.

As the trio walked through the entryway, Freda's lascivious thoughts vanished abruptly when she spotted the gray haired form clad in a tweed sport coat, white shirt with the collar unbuttoned smoking the familiar smelling pipe, smiling as the threesome shuffled exhaustedly in his direction.

"God, I'm so glad to see you," Freda cried, as she threw her arms around the lined and ruddy neck of Millard Hampton. "God, Sugah, I've missed you so much!"

Bernie was somewhat surprised at his mentor, knowing how he detested "pedestrian emotional demonstrations." He seemed to be savoring this encounter.

"I'll confess to somewhat missing you too, Clancy," Hampton said.

"Somewhat!" Freda shouted as she backed away—but only far enough to see that unique smile which brought her to tears and back into his arms.

As Bernie and Peggy watched, Hampton and Freda held one another accompanied by the cacophony of the muffled whine of jet engines, motor vehicles, varied costumed passengers shouting in assorted languages amid the incessant public address system. Lod is a microcosm of Israel—a mixture of cultures groping to survive in the Holy Land .

Hampton disengaged himself from Freda and politely embraced Peggy and, more warmly, hugged Bernie.

"You are both well, I trust? Jet lag can be debilitating," he said.

"We're just fine, Millard," Peggy said.

"Good to see you, Millard. How've you been?" Bernie asked.

Hampton answered, "dandy, folks. Just dandy."

"Millard, I've never seen you look better," Freda said. "You're one groovy hunk."

"I beg your pardon?" He gibed.

"She thinks you look great, Millard," Peggy said.

Bernie echoed, "I agree. Travel must agree with you." He wished he hadn't used agree twice—especially talking to Hampton.

Tapping the ashes from his pipe into a cylindrical container of sand, and putting it into the breast pocket of his sports jacket, he said, "We'd better go. Let's get your bags."

"If they made the plane it's a miracle," Freda said. "After they got done with me, they really did a number on my bags. I mean, they went through everything piece by piece. Even took apart my stopwatch!"

Taking Freda's arm in one hand and Bernie's with the other, Hampton said, "I think the baggage counter is over this way."

Peggy felt a twinge of intended slight.

They slipped through a group of Hasidim, with their broad hats and beards and side-locks and dangling fringes, who were in animated conversation with each other and obviously distressed about something.

"You should have seen this young dude when he came to my bikini panties, Sugah. He looked at them, and then up at me, then felt them slowly in his hand—and all the time grinning this shitty grin. By that time I was so pissed off at the whole deal, I said, 'Look, honkie: if you want to try them on, go ahead. Otherwise, put 'em down.'"

Hampton smiled almost condescendingly.

As they stood waiting for their luggage to appear on the circling baggage conveyer, Freda noticed a large Yemenite woman nursing her baby. Looking at the intense face of Hampton concentrating on the circling baggage, Freda poked him in the ribs and motioned with her head for him to look next to her. Hampton looked at the nursing woman disapprovingly. Freda laughed and said, "Wanna be next?"

Hampton laughed loudly. "Clancy, you are truly a woman unique."

Outside the terminal, the Egged busses waited with their black pollutants pouring out of their exhaust and seemingly non-stop babbling, pushing and shouting passengers elbowing for a front place in line by the door. This was more than your usual metropolitan, anywhere airport. This was Israel—the womb of the world.

Hampton flashed something in his billfold to a cab driver who seemed to snap immediately to attention. Untypically servile, he held the door open until Peggy, Freda and Bernie had seated themselves in the rear. Then the driver placed their bags in the trunk and briskly took his place behind the steering wheel. Hampton was already in the command seat beside him. The cab sped away to the highway, then to the narrow winding rock-strewn road leading up to Jerusalem, 62 kilometers away.

"And you thought the Smokies were mountains, right, Clancy?"

"Yeah, well, I thought I had boobs until I saw that Yemenite mother."

Hampton shook his head. "My dear, for five thousand years, man has been awed, awakened, inspired and uplifted by the loftiness of these mountains. For you to even attempt to correlate them with…"

Hampton glanced back at Freda who was giving him that innocent "tell me Daddy" look, and threw his hands up in feigned surrender.

Peggy laughed, as did Bernie, at the Millard and Freda Show; however both wished for a little less shtick and a little more blend of behavior with environment.

From the first kilometer, it became obvious that Hampton would play tour guide.

"Every tree along the way from Tel Aviv to Jerusalem was planted by man," he announced to his audience in the back seat, "over ninety million of them."

The driver drove as the Israeli lives: with daring confidence. Peggy and Freda ooh'ed and ah'ed as he took the sharp curves at high speed which, if mis-negotiated, would have sent all of them tumbling down any one of the deep ravines jutted with ancient rocks.

"Notice the hillsides," Hampton barked as he pointed. "The Arab method of farming on a hillside is to terrace the hill. They've done it that way for thousands of years."

"Over there is En Kerem—where John the Baptist was born."

"Now you can see Jerusalem—about fifteen miles away."

"How have you fared with the tapes, lad?"

Several seconds of silence passed.

Hampton turned around to look at Bernie, "Lad, I said how have you fared with the tapes?"

Bernie had missed it the first time. As he gazed out the window, his mind had floated to John the Baptist and Yuri Belov. Peggy nudged him.

Jolted back to reality, Bernie said, "Super...ah, excellent, Millard."

Hampton hated the over-used expletive "super."

"And, the books? Did you get through any of them?" Hampton asked.

Bernie answered smartly this time. "As a matter of fact, I studied every one."

"Especially the New Testament?" asked Hampton.

"Especially the New Testament." Bernie affirmed.

"That's my good lad," Hampton responded, with a smile of approval.

Along with the tapes, Hampton had sent Bernie a suggested reading list. Included were books about the Soviet prison system, esoteric and parapsychological subjects and, on the bottom of the list, in big bold letters, he wrote, "IF YOU READ NONE OF THE ABOVE, READ THE NEW TESTAMENT."

Panning his eyes to Freda, Hampton said, "Clancy, we're going to have to do this shoot in one take. The Israeli technicians are costing us a fortune. Any mistakes, glitches or whatever will stay in. We'll fix them in postproduction. We'll keep rolling, no matter what. No busts."

"Gotcha," Freda said.

Peggy wished for a role in all this besides dutiful wife and friend. When her husband was with Hampton, he was Hampton's. Now that Freda had a thing with Hampton, she, too, was Hampton's. An unsettling feeling nagged her as the cab drove up to the Inter-continental Hotel at the top of the Mount of Olives.

It was sundown. The sound of the Moslems in the Old City praying in mosques drifted upward seemingly with the instinct of migrating birds.

"Tomorrow I'll show you Israel, folks." Hampton said proudly.

Tomorrow came sooner than jet lag left. After breakfasting on plates of herring and white fish, cheese, fresh vegetables, rolls, pita, Turkish coffee and very sweet juice, Hampton and yesterday's dutiful driver took Bernie and the ladies on the Hampton guided tour of Israel.

Starting with the museum, from there to the Shrine of the Book—where Bernie stared spell bound at the Dead Sea Scrolls—the group drove the short distance up to Yad Vashem, the memorial to the six million killed by the Nazis. The path leading to the Holocaust museum is lined with small carob trees fronted with a stone marker with the name of a Gentile who risked his life to save a Jew.

"There are not many trees here, are there?" Bernie commented, softly.

"No," Peggy said, "there aren't."

Freda wondered *how many trees there would be at a museum for whites who tried to save a black's life in the South*, but she kept her thought to herself.

In the center of the main room, about four inaccessible feet below, cast in shades of gray, are the names of all the concentration camps built and run by the Nazis. Only the flame of an eternal light above the display illuminates the area in a surreal reminder of the horrible suffering endured by those guilty only of being Jews.

As the group leaned silently on the railing looking at the names of the camps on the stone markers, Bernie whispered through his tears to Peggy, "Dad told me his brother had a beautiful voice. He sang in the opera in their town."

Bernie softly recited the Kaddish for his uncle Michael.

After seeing the exhibition hall in another building where the tools of torture, photographs of once human beings and other artifacts from the camps are displayed like relics from a pre-historic barbaric civilization, the group felt drained of energy. Dabbing at tears, they headed back in silence toward the parking area.

Hampton said, "I would like a moment alone with Bernie, ladies. Perhaps you would like to take a brief walk, or sit here on a bench and rest."

Bernie was caught off-guard, fearing something has changed or gone wrong. Peggy was grateful for the opportunity to alter her mood. Freda knew what Hampton wanted with Bernie. He had divulged it to her the night before.

Hampton entwined his arm around Bernie's and guided him to a bench. A soft breeze coaxed the small white and purple flowers to point the path before them.

"Lad, your name was Frankel before you changed it for show business, right?

Bernie had no idea where he was coming from or where he was going. "Yes," was all he said.

"And the prayer you said in there," Hampton said, pointing to Yad Vashem, "it was for your uncle, right?"

Bernie looked like a sixteen-year old boy who got caught driving the car without permission. "That's right, Millard. I think his name was Michael."

Hampton took out his pipe and Zippo lighter. The breeze tried to keep the flame from scorching the tobacco, but Hampton's experience won out. The familiar aroma drifted back to Peggy and Freda who were inspecting a small garden. The scent made Freda look over toward Hampton who was focused on the moment and didn't notice.

"Lad, there are two items I did not memorialize on tape for you. I wanted to talk to you in person. The first item is about your uncle. Yes, his name was Michael. And I want to tell you about him and the incredible connection to our mission here," Hampton said with a mentoring manner.

Bernie listened stoically to the tale of Michael Frankel. At the end, tears welled in his eyes. He asked no questions. He simply said, "how incredible."

"I agree, lad, I agree. Remember our conversation around your breakfast table about predestination versus happenstance. I say we need another breakfast after we wrap up this venture. Don't you agree?"

Bernie wiped his eyes with his handkerchief, and nodded agreement.

Hampton puffed his pipe, and said, "Are you ready for more?"

Bernie had forgotten Hampton said there were two items not on the tapes. He sighed, jerked his head in a "lay it on me" gesture, and said, "Sure. What's the rest?"

Hampton reached in the breast pocket of his jacket, withdrew several sheets of paper, and handed them to Bernie.

"This letter was slid under my door my last night in Vilnius. I will see to the ladies while you read this. Join us when you are finished."

Hampton got up, took a few steps, turned back to Bernie, and said, "Oh, lad."

Bernie looked up, and said, "Yes, Millard?"

"I saw a photograph of your uncle. You look exactly like him."

Bernie gave Hampton a weak smile, then nodded, and started to read.

"My name is Gershon Spetzler." the letter began, "I have been told that you are in Vilnius seeking information about Yuri Belov. Because you represent the nephew of Michael Frankel, G-d rest his soul, I will help you. And, because Mr. Frank is a member of the American free press, which is the best hope for we who fight for human rights, I will help you. Accordingly, I want Mr. Frank to be aware of the following information:

First, to appease the American President, the wily masters of the Kremlin reach into the barrel of apparently valueless hooligans, pluck one itinerant preacher named Yuri Belov, and set him free. One worthless nobody to drown the debate.

Ironically, fate had other plans. What the Soviets do not know is they have released their most dangerous dissident of them all. The Soviets have set free the one hooligan who could bring them all crashing down.

Yet, the Soviets remain true to their nature: Soviet sailors always wear a life jacket even when their boat is docked. In the Belov case, they have insured his worthlessness through his mother. Yuri Belov was told, prior to his departure for Israel, that if he uttered any statement counter-productive to the best interest of the Soviet Union, his mother would be arrested."

The letter went on to say that the author was in love with Ksana Zoya before the war. Then the Nazis came. He told the horror of her father's torture and martyrdom in his synagogue, the deprivation of the Vilna ghetto, the Yom Kippur march to Ponary and the Kol Nidre chant of Michael Frankel. When Ksana broke from the death march and ran into the forest, Gershon wrote that he, too, ran into the forest in the opposite direction to be a decoy. After his rescue by Lev Belov's group, he lived as a partisan with Ksana, Lev and the rest of the group.

"One night, Lev ordered an attack on a SS command site. Included in the group were Victor Abramov and myself. We crept within a few meters of the site when suddenly blazing lights illuminated our small group and SS, who had lain in waiting, immediately pounced upon us. To this day, I do not know how the Nazis knew we were coming.

As we were herded into the cellar, Lev shouted to each of us, 'Tell nothing! Tell nothing!' We were stripped of our clothes by four burly Lithuanians and told to sit, stark naked, on the stone floor of our cell. We did as they ordered.

Within moments, a tall, blond SS officer entered with another tall, blonde SS officer. A woman. I recall her terribly pockmarked skin covering a fierce canine looking face. Her jaws never closed, exposing long white teeth which I remember thinking were too many for one human mouth. Her eyes glared.

Lev was told to stand up. They brought a bench in, and he was told to lie down on it. Quickly, two of the Lithuanians each held one of Lev's arms straight out, and two more held his legs. Several times Lev struggled free, only to receive a crashing blow to his stomach or to his neck by the male SS officer. The more he struggled, the more blows he received until he was finally held, exhausted, while a trickle of blood seeped from his swollen mouth.

Viktor Abramov and I were then told to stand. Viktor was sobbing like a baby. At least six bulky Lithuanians began to beat us. The blows were furious and landed like clubs, although they used their fists. When we fell under the onslaught, they kicked us again and again in the groin. On command from the SS officer — the man — they stopped beating us. We lay like heaving lumps on the floor.

'Who is the leader of the partisans?' the officer screamed. We said nothing. Again, he screamed, and again we remained silent. Lev was still being held spread-eagled on the bench, his eyes pleading with us not to talk. The male SS officer then motioned, with a nod of his head, to his female colleague. She told the Lithuanians to hold up Viktor's hand. They nearly yanked his arm from his shoulder. From her tunic pocket, she withdrew a pair of sterling silver surgical sheers. In a surprisingly soft voice that clashed with the viciousness of her face, she asked Viktor to tell her who the leader of the partisans is. He shook his head. With that, she clipped off one of his fingers. It fell to the gray stone floor without a sound. Viktor screamed. Again, she asked. He refused. Another finger fell. Then a third. Viktor's face was purple with agony. She asked again for the name. He refused with one jerky nod. With that, the female surgeon leaned down and whispered something in Viktor's ear. Instantly is face turned from purple to ashen, and his mouth dropped open with fright. Fecal matter oozed from him. The male SS officer screamed at the Lithuanians to mop it up.

Viktor laid in the fetal position, shivering and sobbing in fear. Again, the female officer asked for the name. Crying with the pain of many sources, Viktor pointed his blood-covered hand to the prone Lev Belov. The surgeon smiled a smile that would only please the devil.

Slowly pacing to Lev, she eyed him from head to toe. His chest and stomach heaved in and out from the effect of the beating as the bulky Lithuanians gripped his wrists and ankles tightly. 'Such a good specimen,' she said softly. With her right hand still gripped the surgical sheers, she gently, with a circular motion, rubbed Lev's chest with her left. Then her hand slowly moved down to his abdomen, then to his groin. As if following some hideous ritual, she held his penis with her left hand and slightly pulled it so that his testicles rose from his scrotum. Then, without saying a word or changing her fowl expression, she castrated him.

Lev regained consciousness the next morning. Three days later, the dawn we were to be shot, the three of us escaped thanks to a diversionary action by our comrades. How Lev made it back to the Rudnitska Forrest in his mutilated condition, I'll never know. Somehow he did.

Upon our return, Viktor was tried by our partisan council and convicted of treason. He was sentenced to be shot, but Ksana intervened and convinced the tribunal that the greater punishment for Viktor would be to live. She was right.

I don't know if Ksana knew what the Nazis did to Lev. She stayed with him constantly upon his return. Even though we were constantly on the move, she provided him was as much comfort as was possible. He lost strength with each passing day. She cared for Lev, and I, as best I could, cared for Ksana.

Lev lived for six weeks. During that time, he talked constantly to me and to Ksana of going to Israel. The dream kept him living for as long as he did.

One evening, while lying in Ksana's arms, Lev died.

That is the end of my story. I have told you nothing about Yuri. Yet, I have told you everything.

With hope for eternal justice, Gershon Spetzler."

Bernie remained seated on the bench for several moments starring out into the distance. Five thousand years of history lay before him. The Lev Belov information contained in the letter impacted his professional approach to tomorrow's interview; the Michael Frankel story impacted his soul. He tried to imagine the kind of courage, the kind of fearlessness his uncle mustered on that horrible journey that Kol Nidre night. He looked inward. Like his uncle, he was talented. Would he have had the courage to do what Michael Frankel did? The answer his heart gave brought him to tears.

Then a voice spoke to him, as if delivered by the gentle breeze. Somewhere inside his head, he heard a voice say, *It is not about saving your show or an audition for another job. Tomorrow is about bringing forth what is within you to enable people to see and hear Yuri Belov.*

Bernie took a deep breath, folded the letter, closed his eyes, and said softly, "Thank you."

He walked up to where Peggy and Freda were sitting. Hampton was standing a few feet away pointing to some place in the distance and talking. Peggy was so relieved to have Bernie disrupt the lecture and rejoin her. Hampton had told her about Michael Frankel while Bernie read the letter. He left out the Lev Belov story. She stood and ran to her husband's arms.

"Are you okay?" she asked.

"I'm fine, Peg." He answered.

"I love you," Peggy said.

"I know. I love you too," Bernie said.

Hampton walked the few steps back, and said, "How are you, lad?"

"Never better, Millard. Thanks."

Freda noticed it. For the first time ever, Bernie had looked Hampton in the eyes when he spoke to him. She hoped the knowledge of his uncle's courage had a similar effect on Bernie as her father's courage had on her.

Hampton announced, "Come on, folks, it's time I show you the Holy Land."

From Yad Vashem they drove to the Old City of Jerusalem. They paused at the Dome of the Rock—a holy spot for Jews, Christians and Moslems—and proceeded through the semi-darkness of the narrow streets and enclosed market places where Arabs drew smoke through the glass bowl of the hookahs, and bearded Rabbis and Talmudic scholars walked briskly past the earnestly silent nuns and priests.

Then a short drive south to Bethlehem. Stopping at the Tomb of Rachel—where women pray for fertility—Peggy turned to Bernie and kiddingly said, "Shall I pray, honey?"

To her delight, for the first time in weeks, he laughed a natural laugh.

The pace picked up. The driver sped to Tiberius as if he were in trial runs for the Indy 500. From there on to Bet Shean, where

Hampton instructed the driver to pull over beside the ruins of the Roman amphitheater. Hampton got out, ran down row upon row of stone steps, stood in the center of what was the stage, whereupon he bellowed a few lines from King Lear.

"Perfect!" he extolled, to Freda's applause above. As he reached the top step after jogging back up, he said, with excitement in his voice, "What superb natural acoustics! Wanna try it, Bernie?"

"Freda's jaw dropped open and Peggy cheered as Bernie bound down the steps, stood where Hampton stood, and sang the familiar aria from Pagliacci. When he came back up, he asked, "How'd I do?"

Freda gave him a thumbs up and a look of pride. Her hope manifested.

Peggy said, "Encore."

Hampton added, "I know one opera singer who would be proud, lad." Bernie looked at him, and smiled knowingly.

Inside, Bernie was getting anxious. His spirit was keying up for the interview with Belov and pumping out the juice only those about to enter the arena understand.

"By the way, Millard," Bernie asked as they wearily got back into the cab, "have you had contact with Yuri?"

"No, not personally," Hampton replied. "I've been handling that through a PR person in Mayor Teddy Kollek's office. They've been surprisingly cooperative. Then again, they love American TV and film properties shooting here. I understand Belov is staying with some friends in Jerusalem. I've been assured that he'll be at the location by eight tomorrow morning."

"If we live till tomorrow morning," Freda said, with exhaustion. "My feet won't do their thing no more, Millard."

"Just a few more stops and we'll head back. I want Bernie to see two more sights for background."

Peggy marveled at the seemingly infinite endurance of the oldest member of their group. Hampton seemed as fresh and exuberant as when they started.

They drove to Bet Alfa.

"I want to show you a strange discovery made at this Kibbutz while they were bulldozing a new area," Hampton announced.

On the floor of fourth century synagogue was a beautiful mosaic and, in the center of the floor was a sign of the Zodiac.

"Astrology is contrary to Jewish belief," Hampton said. "Why then, in this synagogue in lower Galilee, do we find the Zodiac?"

He left the question unanswered.

"Damn," Freda said, "and I thought Jean Dixon invented astrology."

Peggy didn't even offer a polite laugh. She had assisted Freda's comedy relief role for Hampton's benefit throughout the day. By then, however, the sun was setting and so were her spirits. Cramped in the back seat, she felt resented by Hampton, like excess baggage to her husband, and unable to compete with Freda. Her usual good nature and emotional resilience plummeted in antsy despair. How she longed to be back in Atlanta with people and places that made no exceptional demands upon her. Even their apartment in New York would have been better. There, in that place, in that time, with those people, she felt unnecessary.

"We must have dinner on the shore of the Sea of Galilee," Hampton proclaimed.

After finishing their huge portion of St. Peter fish—which Hampton insisted they all order—he asked Freda to join him for a stroll along the shore. It was the best announcement Peggy had heard all day.

After Hampton and Freda hand-held their way down to the rocky shore, Peggy said, "You didn't eat much, honey."

Bernie replied, "Neither did you."

She hesitated, and then asked, "Where are you?"

Looking at her in mild exasperation, he said, "Honey, you know after all this time, I don't like you to ask me that."

She picked some fish from the bone and said, "Worried about tomorrow?"

Bernie looked from his plate to her eyes. "Not worried; anxious, I guess. There're two things going on here, Peggy: One is the interview; the other is me. I feel confidant about the interview, more confident than this morning. As for me, I feel something deeply being here; I don't know what it is. It's almost like..."

"Like what, darling?"

"Like I know this place—these places really. Maybe it's just Israel, you know, all that it means to me and to my family. I mean, here I am, the first Frankel to see it, and I'm seeing it for all of them, the ones who survived, the one's who didn't. Now, finding out about my uncle, it's pretty overwhelming. Then again, it's more than that, honey."

"Déjà vu?" she prompted.

Bernie thought, then shook his head slowly. "Well, perhaps in a way, but not really. It's more like, this sounds weird but there were times today—and even now looking out over that sea—that I feel as if I am reaching into another place for something, something I should take, or maybe learn. Sort of like being aware, or prompted by a kind of voice inside yet not actually hearing what it is saying. There's something going on here, honey, I feel it's about me. I can't put my finger on what it is."

Peggy smiled gently. "I understand, darling."

It seemed the thing to say. Actually, Peggy believed that Bernie was on emotional overload from the pressure applied by Hampton to save their show and finding out that there was a connection between his family and Yuri Belov

"Do you, Peggy, because I really don't."

"Yes, honey. I do."

He put his hand on hers, and said, "And you? You're awfully quiet."

"I'm fine," she lied. "Just enjoying being with you."

"I love you, baby," Bernie said.

"And more than anything in this world, I love you too, darling," Peggy said.

"You know," he said, dabbing his mouth with his paper napkin, "this Belov interview could be the biggest thing that's ever happened to us."

"Whatever will be, will be," Peggy said. "It's in God's hands."

Down by the shore, Hampton had been giving Freda some instructions on how he wanted the show to go.

"The boy was telling me the truth, wasn't he, Clancy? He did study the tapes and read the research material, didn't he?"

Freda put her hands on Hampton's gray, hairy forearms and said, "Millard, Bernie told you the truth, and has always told you the truth. In fact, I don't know if you noticed it, but since he read that letter, he's like gotten a self esteem transplant."

"I didn't notice," Hampton said, "but I'm glad to hear it. It will make him better tomorrow."

Freda looked Hampton in the eye, and said, "No. It will make him better. Period."

Hampton thought a second, and then nodded approvingly.

Freda intuitively knew that Hampton wanted to walk because he wanted a drink. In the weeks since he had been on the wagon, there were times, especially at the end of long working days, when he desperately craved a drink. Walking helped in New York; and she hoped it was helping him where Peter and Andrew cast their nets.

"Clancy," he asked, almost innocently, "what did you think of the tapes?"

Freda considered, then immediately dismissed any humorous reply. His tone and eyes refuted any cue for comedy.

"I thought you'd never ask, Millard, because I've wanted to tell you but didn't want to embarrass you. I know how you find flattery suspicious. The truth is that all those Millard Hampton stories—you know, the ones people tell about you—how Hampton did this and how Hampton did that, years ago? Let me tell you, my darling, none of them matches what you did in Russia. The tapes—and all of you that went into them—are magnificent." She put her hands on his face so that what she was about to say would go right in. "I'm so proud to know and be a part of Millard Hampton today."

For a few seconds he didn't say a word. The only sound between them was the mild splash of the Sea of Galilee upon the ancient rocks.

Then, softly from him: "Thank you."

They walked slowly back up the hill to the restaurant. Before reaching the top, Hampton said, "Clancy, do you know what the toughest part of the Russian trip was for me?"

"Locating the people?" she said.

"No. That came relatively easy."

"Then, what was it?"

"The Vodka!" he roared. "All that bloody vodka everywhere, and I shunned it all! Nearly busted my bloody bladder on all that tea I drank!"

Freda's white teeth glistened in the twilight as she laughed.

Peggy slept on Bernie's shoulder most of the way from Galilee to Jerusalem. The brief, intimate table talk with her husband eased most of the feeling of displacement and excess baggage she had felt since arriving in Israel. For the first time in twenty-four hours, she relaxed.

Bernie and Freda listened to Hampton's on-going colloquy of anecdotes and apocryphal tales about Israel. Freda marveled at his stamina; Bernie marveled at his knowledge.

"Too bad we don't have the time for me to take you to the South," Hampton said with passion to his drowsy audience. "Some day I'll take you to Elat, where the purple-orange desert meets the blue Red Sea. It was once King Solomon's port, you know. It's a voyeur's paradise, I tell you. Strong young boys and ample young girls sun and stroll along the beach—some in bikinis—some a la natural. I have a friend down there, Ralphy Nelson. He set up shop about twelve miles down the beach— away from the tourist traffic—about twelve years ago. Ralphy was sick of the city and the pressure. So Ralphy escaped. He spends his days lounging near his thatched hut on the remote section of the beach with special invited friends—young boys and girls, that is—drinking beer and talking about nothing that matters. If you look for him, you can find him. Ralphy's always garbed in an orange bathing suit, a blue yachting cap, sunglasses and holding a can of beer. He is the official host to those seeking revelry. Many a burned out businessman seeks out Ralphy for aid and comfort and surcease from strife via the pleasure derived from drink and flesh. I tell you honestly, Clancy, had I not recently found a renewed purpose in life, I believe I would have sought the intemperance and decadence offered by my friend Ralphy Nelson."

A sudden wave of nausea and panic gripped Freda as she realized for the first time since their encounter in his apartment how vital she was to Hampton's survival. Her body's chemical change both surprised and annoyed her. Nausea and panic were the components of "ugly air."

She took a deep breath and changed the subject.

"How long will we stay after the interview, Millard?"

"Glad you brought that up, Clancy," he shot back. "Bernie and his wife can go back right away if they want to. You and I will stay here for another day, wrap the business up, and do the necessary amenities." He was all business again.

"Then, Clancy, you are going to personally escort the tapes back to New York. I don't want you to check them at the airport or let them out of your sight. I'll put you and the tapes in a cab, and I want you and the tapes to get on that airplane, and I want you and the tapes to go directly to our office."

"You're not coming with me?" she asked.

"No, unfortunately. I'll be going to London, Paris and Tokyo and possibly West Germany to tie up world rights for satellite transmission."

"Satellite transmission!" Bernie yelled. Peggy squirmed but didn't wake up.

"That's correct. That's why it is crucial, Clancy, for you to mother hen those tapes of the interview back to New York. The stakes here are enormous, but I think worth it. Don't you?"

"Yes, Millard," Freda said. "I'll guard them with my life."

Chapter Fifteen

Before leaving the Soviet Union, Millard Hampton knew that the interview with Yuri Belov must take place in the Garden of Gethsemane. It was an olive grove when Jesus affirmed that God's will be done. Now pines, cypresses and eucalyptus trees grow below the domes of the Russian Orthodox Church. Opposite it, there are olives still that the Arabs harvest with long poles by hitting the branches to make the fruit rain down.

Bernie arrived before anyone else—even before the contingent of Jerusalem police that Hampton had commandeered to cordon off the area from tourists or local fanatics of any genre. All night long, he mentally rehearsed, visualizing the flow, the feel, and the careful mix of ingredients leading to the culmination of the Belov interview. Having established in his mind where and how he would take the interview, Bernie psychically prepared for contingencies in case Yuri turned out to be a screwball, or if he turned hostile. Without having any sleep, he felt surprisingly energized and primed.

Slowly, he walked the sloping terrain, occasionally pausing to take a deep breath as if trying to assimilate with the environment. He needed that time alone in Gethsemane to hear what was not being spoken; to feel what he couldn't touch.

Yuri arrived next. Alone. Bernie extended his hand and Yuri

accepted it with both of his and held it firmer and somewhat longer than is customary. Belov's hands felt warm, his fingers longer than Bernie's yet not disproportionate with his rather lean frame. He was not as tall as Bernie had visualized him. His triangular face, with its prominent nose slightly curving at the bridge, was framed with a brownish close-cropped beard. His eyes were deep blue, compelling, almost translucent, giving Bernie the feeling of being transparent before him! Rather than feeling disarmed or vulnerable, Bernie felt an inner calm, a feeling of being balmed with love.

Bernie selected a navy blue blazer and gray slacks with an off-white open collared shirt for the shoot.

Yuri wore a dark turtleneck sweater—more like a jersey—and dark nondescript slacks. His hair, a slight tone darker than his beard, parted in the middle and grew in thick wavy locks over his ears and the back of his neck.

About 8:00 A.M., the television remote truck invaded the peace, bearing lights and cables and sound equipment and cameras and technicians and Millard Hampton and his Clancy.

After dealing with video's supplication that a high quality picture was impossible with Bernie wearing white and Yuri wearing dark, audio's lamentation about the bells from the Russian Orthodox Church drowning out the voices, lighting's wailing about creeping shadows, and camera personnel bemoaning his edict that no one smoke during the session, Hampton instructed Bernie and Yuri to take their places in the ancient garden.

A member of the crew attached Yuri's lapel mike; Bernie fastened his own.

They sat in director's chairs facing one another without speaking.

Standing on the steps of the truck, Hampton finally roared through a bullhorn: "Take One—and only one!"

After a thirty second Hampton written intro, Bernie got right to business.

Responding to Bernie's first question, Yuri confirmed that the Soviets threatened they would arrest his mother if he publicly criticized their government. He ripped them saying, "They will find a charge; perhaps being the mother of a hooligan."

So, why, then, was he speaking out?

"Because I must," was his answer.

Paying homage to the price his fellow dissidents pay for their courage to stand up to Soviet oppression, Yuri described the brutality of the Soviet prison system:

"It is not worked out witlessly," he said. "At its core is a reality grimmer than their torture and more confining than the walls of their cells."

He continued: "Isolation, silence, a world unaware that you even exist year after year—and you realizing no one is aware—will make you sign anything just to be noticed by someone.

Bernie asked if the upcoming Summit offered hope?

Yuri scoffed, then replied, "Your president is a fool and Pavlovski and Molenski and that whole gang of thieves in the Kremlin are playing him for one. They have something up their sleeves."

Then turning his eyes from Bernie and looking directly into the camera, he said, "But I tell you this: Like the Roman Empire, the Soviet Union will collapse of its own rot at the core before the end of the millennium."

Seated beside Hampton in the cramped confines of the control truck, Freda leaned over and whispered, "the kid's cookin'." Hampton was pleased that Bernie and Yuri were interacting so well. He was slightly agitated, however, by the nonchalant attitude of the crew and technicians. In New York he could bellow and bark; in Israel he could merely suggest and request. These were unionized government employees.

Bernie set up the Bluma Ketsherginski incident and asked Yuri to explain what happened.

After saying that, like medical treatments, spiritual healing requires specific treatment as well, he said, "In Bluma's case I helped her restore her faith in herself. I provided energy—in her case, by assuring her that she should love herself just as God loves her."

Yuri further explained that he didn't heal everyone who came to him afterward because "there are those who suffer who say they want to become well, but do not really want healing. They find some satisfaction in their suffering, although they won't admit it to anyone, especially to themselves."

He compared spiritual healing to electricity:

"Spiritual healing taps into that negative thought that triggered the illness and implants a positive thought in its place. It is actually a re-circuiting of the thought process with God as the power source. If the circuit weakens from lack of intensity from either pole, the healing fails."

Bernie asked if a spiritual healer is interfering with God and His will, and Yuri replied that there is a real difference between God intending and God allowing.

"God never intended for people to suffer," he said. "Man does that to himself in various ways. God allows man to suffer, and patiently waits for man to heal himself or be healed by another."

Hampton heard a technician in the truck snickering. The Hampton glare stopped it cold.

Then Bernie told the hero story of Lev Belov—which temporarily quieted the crew—concluding with his castration and escape to Ksana.

Yuri said, "When I found out about the events of my birth, it was as if I had confirmed a premonition. Knowing of the manner of my present incarnation certified my past. Once again, God wanted me to know who I am."

Bernie suggested another explanation: "Perhaps you were conceived out of wed lock before Lev Belov was captured; perhaps your mother had intercourse with another man other than Lev Belov," Bernie said boldly.

Hampton and Freda both prepared for Yuri to bolt the set,

perhaps lash out physically or verbally at Bernie. He didn't. Oddly, he didn't so much as squirm, or shift positions in the chair. Studying him on the small monitor in the control truck, they watched him remain unruffled, his eyes still relaxed.

"That's been suggested before, " Yuri replied, with a slight smile.

While Freda was captivated by Yuri's presence, she was as much moved by Bernie's seemingly new sense of himself, with just a slight hint even of a swagger. It became him.

"You said God wanted you to know who you are." Bernie asked.

"This is going to sound egotistical," Yuri began, "and at this point, that is the last impression I want to make lest I be set back a notch. But souls as highly developed as mine usually appear in a body for only a brief time, usually to guide or deliver a message. Sort of the way it was my last life. That's why I'm here talking with you."

Hampton instructed the director to slowly tighten up on Yuri's face. The technicians in the truck were all smirking, some making comments under their breath. Cussing sounds like cussing no matter what the language. However, Hampton got his tight shot, which was all he cared about at that moment.

"And who were you in your last life?" Bernie asked.

"I was Jesus." Yuri replied, calmly.

Bernie didn't flinch. It happened as he visualized it would. The crew on the set squirmed. The technicians reacted with a combination of groans, laughs, and cussing. One pretended to throw up.

Hampton turned to Freda, and said with pride in his voice, "He laid it in there beautifully, didn't he?"

Freda nodded, her pride showing as well.

"And you came back," Bernie said, with a hint of cynicism. "Last time in occupied Palestine; this time in occupied Lithuania. Why?"

"To rectify," was Yuri's answer.

Bernie, said, "Oy vey! You mean we're in for two thousand more years of such paradise?"

The Israeli technicians in the truck erupted in cheers, hoots, foot stomping and thumbs up.

Yuri leaned in closer, and said, "The gospels are not the gospel, Mr. Frank," he said, with a smile.

Citing an extensive litany of discrepancies and contradictions within and between the gospels themselves, Yuri concluded by saying, "Mr. Frank, would a perfect Father, dictating a perfect book, about His only Son, bollix and bungle so badly the events of His birth, His life, and His death?"

Yuri went on to say the purpose for the distortions were for what he called "The Three Ps": The pagans, prophecy, and persecution of the Jews.

By then Hampton was getting better cooperation on the shots he was calling.

Bernie put his hand to his chin, thought a second, then said, "And the unabridged, unaltered message of Yuri of Vilna is…"

"The same as it was as Jesus of Nazareth: To show people the way to live so that they evolve closer to the Light of God when they die. The measure of love you give on earth is proportionate to your distance to the Light in heaven."

Yuri said that he returned to Israel as Yuri Belov to repeat that message.

"This time, it is being recorded. Thank God no one can do what they did with it before," he said.

Bernie was given a six-minute cue.

Yuri sensed time was running out. He cocked his head slightly to one side, his eyes narrowed with intensity.

He said, "Last time I was sent to the Jews; this time I am sent to the Christians. I want them to know that God is of no religion. Religion is created and managed by man. Therefore, religion has the potential for choices good and bad. And Christianity has made some bad choices. Denominations of a religion I never established compete for revenue and audience as your program competes for sponsors and viewers. Evangelists, who misquote me, grow rich cheating poor, unfortunate souls, while clashing with one another for social and political prominence. How many of the world's hungry and suffering could be fed and clothed and comforted by the wealth of gold and silver, vast landholdings and countless business enterprises accumulated by the church that prays to God in my name? The moneychangers have returned to the Temple, only now they traffic in the name of Jesus! Christianity has converted him into a product whose intrinsic value appreciates in proportion with the degree of perversion in his message. Christianity, as it is marketed today, is as much a stranger to me as is its doctrine. Did Jesus ever ask that those who don't believe in him be abused socially, emotionally or physically by those who say they do? I tell you that those who have done such things are further from the Light than those who have never heard his name! The Christian who proclaims his faith with self-righteousness and arrogance mocks Jesus, and shames God. I want to affirm, as I did before, that the Lord God is One. And we should love Him with all our hearts, minds and spirit. And that we should love one another. Love one another! No other prescription advances the soul."

Yuri eased back in his seat from the edge.

Bernie allowed several seconds of silence.

Hampton praised his reaction, saying softly, "Nice."

Freda's eyes were filled with tears.

The technicians previously heckling behavior transformed, becoming as theatrical support people behave when they realize they are present at a special event.

Drawing a deep breath and exhaling, Yuri said, almost to himself, "There. It is done."

Noting a one-minute cue, Bernie said a short thank you to Yuri.

Yuri replied, "It is I who thank you."

Bernie looked into the camera, and said, "From the Garden of Gethsemane in Jerusalem, Israel, I'm Bernie Frank. Good night."

Freezing the pose until he was certain the camera stopped rolling, Bernie reached over and shook Yuri's hand. "You were fantastic," he said.

Yuri smiled warmly, and said, "May we have a word alone?"

Bernie looked as drained as he felt. "Sure. How about up there?" he said, pointing to a bench under an olive tree about twenty yards up the slopping path. Give me a minute to thank the crew, and I be right there."

Inside the truck, Hampton shouted his customary, "That's a wrap! Thank you everyone!" He embraced Freda then extended his hand to the director and the others in the truck while offering the obligatory "terrific job…great to work with you…thanks for everything " platitudes.

"Was it what you wanted it to be, Millard?" Freda asked.

"And more," Hampton replied with a contented smile.

Hampton had already written a disclaimer to appease those viewers who would be offended. He'd have Bernie voice it in New York when they edited in background video, commercials, and other pieces of the show. He instructed Freda to remind him to write a plea to the Soviet government not to arrest or harm Yuri's mother after the show aired.

After extending his appreciation to each member of the crew, a weary Bernie Frank strode up the path to join Yuri.

Yuri said, "I know how tired you are, so I'll just keep you a minute. But I have something important that you need to know."

"No problem," Bernie said. "What is it?"

Yuri searched Bernie's eyes, and then said, "Just as we determine our own state of being in the next life, we determine our state of being in this life. As above, so below. It is no accident I am here with you or that you are here with me. Perhaps you have felt an unusual sensation since learning of our meeting.

People about to rendezvous with their destiny often feel an inner vibration."

Bernie nodded. He understood.

Yuri continued, saying, "You see, Bernie, in another dimension, we made an agreement, a contract to come back under circumstances favorable toward accomplishing what we did during this hour. The state of your life is exactly as it should be because you ordained it. Those people in your orbit also agreed to their role in this dance. Each played a part that enabled me to bring my message of spiritual salvation to the world once again."

Bernie asked, "And where and when did we make this agreement?"

Calmly, Yuri answered, "In heaven, a little over thirty years ago. You had just arrived. I had been there for some time, waiting for another opportunity. Right before you arrived you were a fine singer – a tenor. You lived to be 68 years old. One night you were rounded up by the Nazis, along with others. It was the eve of Yom Kippur. You were marched from Vilna, which was your hometown, toward Ponary, where you and the others were to be shot. On the way, you suddenly were inspired to chant the Kol Nidre, which gave inspiration to the others. Included among them was a young woman named Ksana Zoya. You were beaten to the ground by fists and rifle butts. Still you tried to sing. Then you were shot. Your name was Michael Frankel."

Bernie startled eyes widened. Then welled with tears,

In a loud whisper, he said, "Michael Frankel, my uncle?"

Yuri slowly nodded, then said, "As often happens after sudden martyrdom, one reincarnates into one's own family almost immediately. It's part of the law of reciprocity, karma."

The two sat silently for several moments. Bernie thought of how he felt at Yad Vashem, the voice that spoke to him after reading Gershon Spetzler's letter, his strange feeling of connectedness and inner strength, and his attempt to explain to

Peggy the night before his odd feeling of something he should learn.

Without asking another question, he turned to Yuri, who was looking up at the sky deep in thought. Bernie asked, caringly, "Tell me, Yuri, what will happen to you now?"

Yuri dropped his head and smiled introspectively, then said, "God only knows? I have delivered my message, thanks to you. Let's wait to see what happens."

Below, the TV remote truck and several vans carrying crew and technical personnel drove off to another shoot.

Hampton, his battered briefcase full of paraphernalia, sauntered off to his now familiar cab and driver. He held the door open for Freda. Freda's satchel containing the tapes and Hampton's instruction and notes was flung over her shoulder. She waved broadly to Bernie and Yuri, and blew them a kiss.

Bernie turned around to watch Freda and Hampton drive off, leaving the Garden of Gethsemane to absorb its latest chronicle.

After waving back to Freda, Bernie turned again to say goodbye to Yuri.

But he was gone.

Chapter Sixteen

The two buzzers sounded within a second of each other in Jerry Cooper's apartment. The first signaled that the two TV dinners in the microwave were as ready as they would ever be; the second meant that the White House was calling. The oven clock said 11:07 PM. As he had been home barely twenty minutes, hadn't finished his second Jack Daniels on the rocks, Cooper muttered an "Oh, shit" and grabbed the receiver.

"Cooper," he barked to the receiver.

"Mr. Cooper, the President wants to see you immediately."

"Okay, Mrs. Thoman. I'll be right over."

In and of itself, such a late night summons was not irregular. What was disconcerting was Mrs. Thoman's verbiage. By design or by chance, Albert Packard's long time secretary enabled Cooper to assess the degree of urgency of her boss's nocturnal problems throughout all the years they had worked together by the phrasing of her message.

"Jerry, sorry to disturb you; the boss wants you to come over," was, on a scale of 5, a 4 priority call.

On the other hand, a 2 was something like: "Jerry, drop by tonight if you can."

As Cooper hung up the receiver and pushed the off button on the microwave, he concluded that "Mr. Cooper, the President wants to see you immediately," was Thoman for "Get your ass over here right now." For sure, something was up.

Cooper considered all possibilities, from nuclear missiles streaking toward Washington to some of Strauss' porno pictures accidentally turning up in Packard's summit briefing book, as he strode into the Oval Office.

The President was seated behind his desk reading something. He didn't look up or say the customary "Hi, Jerr." His face was ashen, his nostrils occasionally flared and his lips slightly quivered as his head followed the words across the line of the white page.

Strauss and McKenna were there also, ensconced in what appeared to be the pages of a lengthy memo. No one acknowledged Cooper's presence except Mrs. Thoman, who briskly followed him into the Oval Office and handed him a copy of what engrossed everyone.

Cooper sat down, withdrew a fresh yellow legal pad from his briefcase and glanced quickly at the President—who appeared close to cardiac arrest—then at Strauss—whose head was shaking slowly back and forth in dismay—and then at McKenna—whose dark beady eyes were emitting a laser beam straight back at him. Cooper winked his good eye at the General who took a deep breath, held it, and silently fumed.

Cooper's moment of personal one-up-manship fled swiftly, however, when he read the heading on the red cover of the document resting on his lap. In large bold black type across the top it said, "CLASSIFIED TOP PRIORITY—NSC EYES ONLY." A white sticker in the center of bore the title of the document: "TRANSCRIPT OF INTERVIEW WITH YURI BELOV."

Strauss finished reading the document and waited for the rest. McKenna, who had read it several times prior to the meeting, waited also. Then Cooper read it and waited for the President, who had always been a plodding reader.

Finally, Packard looked up, his hands gripping the sheaf of typed pages as if to strangle the life out of the words.

No one spoke. Then Cooper asked, "How'd we get this?"

In a low voice, Strauss said, "One of McKenna's people infiltrated the Israeli TV crew posing as a technician and taped it. It was immediately flown back by CIA courier plane and transcribed when it arrived."

"Correction, Strauss," McKenna interrupted. "It was transcribed en route."

Puckishly, Strauss glanced at Cooper. "My mistake," he said, rolling his eyes.

They didn't have to wait long for Packard's reaction. Like an erupting volcano, he exploded, hurling fire and brimstone out in every direction of the Oval Office.

With his hands outstretched to the ceiling, he looked up, and cried, "Dear Lord, forgive me for what I have been made to read. Satan rejoices at the sight of your humble servant reading the poison of that blasphemer, that emissary of Beelzebub, that wickedest of all false prophets, that devil in the skin of a dissident. Oh Lord, would that I but had the courage to pluck out mine eyes that have just read the Gospel of Satan. But no! I will not pay that vile serpent even that tithe. Satan, you get no part of me! I serve the living Son of God, Jesus Christ— born of the Virgin Mary—conceived by the Word of God— to save that sinful mass of rotting flesh called man from Abadon's power of darkness. Lord, that mongrelizing Russian devil will not have his way! His is the path to the bottomless pit! He will not be seen! He will not be heard! Thy will be done!"

Perspiration coursed down the flushed face of the President of the United Sates as the last echo of his diatribe ricocheted off the ceiling.

McKenna was perched at the edge of his seat, and Strauss was viciously picking at the raw skin around his fingernails.

Cooper sat wondering if Hampton knew what Belov would say in an interview when he called that night at Camp David, or was it just another Hampton hunch that paid off?

After a silent several moments, the President calmed to

where he could hold up the transcript and, in a more subdued tone, asked: "Who is responsible for this?"

Strauss answered, "General McKenna secured the information by covertly..."

The President interrupted, saying emphatically, "I did not mean how did we get a copy of the interview. I'm well aware of General McKenna's fine piece of work, and I pray that he is aware of my eternal gratitude."

Springing to his feet, McKenna saluted, and said, sharply, "Thank you, Mr. President."

"At ease, General—please sit down. What I want to know is who is responsible for arranging this interview in the first place?"

No one spoke for several seconds.

Then, McKenna again sprang to his feet. "Mr. President," the reedy voice began, "There's the man who arranged the whole thing," he said, rapidly stabbing his finger toward Cooper. "He did it for his former mentor and close, shall I say, intimate friend Millard Hampton. Hampton produces *The Bernie Frank Show*. The program is about to be taken off the air, and they rigged up this scheme to save it."

Cooper glanced at Strauss, who was deliberately ignoring him by pretending to be re-reading something in the transcript. He silently pleaded with Strauss to remind the President that both he *and* Strauss recommended the interview and that the President personally approved it.

The sick bastard doesn't remember, Cooper thought, and *Strauss is plotting fifty ways to cover his own ass.*

After a typical brief interlude of silent reflection, which followed whenever Packard was presented with startling information, he said, starting soft, building with the crescendo effect of a tent preacher, "They would have a man pretend to be the second coming of our Lord and utter everything despicable to Christ's servants to save a television program? They would have a Russian atheist call the Word of the Lord inaccurate to save a television program? My most faithful and trusted aide would conspire with Millard Hampton and allow an imposter to rebuke God and His only begotten son in order to save a television program? In order to save a television program! Why Jerry? Why?" He boomed.

Again, Cooper looked over to Strauss, silently pleading with him to say something to explain his role, to manipulate or rearrange the pieces of the dilemma swirling in a frenzy around the Oval Office. However, Strauss, remaining hidden in feigned preoccupation with something in the text of the transcript, ignored Cooper's pleading eye.

Cooper glanced at McKenna, whose lips were pursed in a diabolical smile.

Cooper began cautiously, "Mr. President, to me Yuri Belov was a low level dissident to be released by the Soviets. Millard Hampton called me and asked me if I could help him arrange an interview with Belov. Aside from the dubious benefit Hampton would receive, I saw merit in the proposal for the administration. Bernie Frank's interview would satisfy our media obligation without offending the Soviets and thus endangering the Summit. Everybody wins. I ran it by you and you, sir, signed off on it. I ran it by your National Security Advisor who agreed to its merit as well. He then appraised the Soviets and they agreed. Again, sir, you approved the strategy."

He paused, gained his composure, and continued:

"Granted, you may have been preoccupied with the Summit agenda you shared with me at Camp David. Regarding Millard Hampton: he's a friend. If you'll recall, it was Hampton who arranged for me to work for you way back when. And, if you don't mind me saying, that hasn't worked out so badly for either of us. Had I known or suspected that advising you to approve the Belov interview was anything except a positive for our administration, I assure you I never would have proposed it regardless of my relationship with Millard Hampton. I think you ought to know that after all these years. I had no idea Belov had delusions of Messiahship or anything else. I regret that has happened, and I'll express our disappointment to Hampton. But there was no conspiracy—overt, covert, or anything in between."

Strauss looked up at Cooper, nodded approval, and returned to his hiding place in the document.

Just as the President began to say something, McKenna stood took a few steps toward Cooper, and said, "Ah, Mr. President, perhaps another piece of information that I have uncovered will add yet another dimension to the compelling willingness of Cooper here to save the career of his close, intimate friend, Millard Hampton, at all cost!"

Cooper glared nonplussed up at McKenna.

The President asked, "What's that, General?"

Salivating profusely, McKenna swallowed, then licked his lips like a hyena about to have at a rabbit.

"Millard Hampton is, and has been a homosexual. Or do you prefer I use the term 'gay', Cooper?"

Cooper bolted out of the chair, lunged toward the diminutive CIA director and screamed, "McKenna, you no-good dirty mother fucker, I'll kill you!"

McKenna adroitly dodged Cooper's clumsy attack while priming his right hand for a judo chop. However, a counter attack proved unnecessary as Jerry Cooper lost his balance and found himself sprawled out on the blue carpet floor in the center of the Presidential seal.

The President stood up, strode from behind his desk over to the panting Cooper, kneeled down, and asked, "Jerr, are you a homosexual?"

"For Christ's sake, you know better than that, Mr. President!" Cooper said, looking up at the Commander in Chief.

"Please, Jerr, refrain from using the name of the Lord in vain. Now, just tell me, straight to my face, man to man: Are you a homosexual?"

"No." Cooper said emphatically.

The President said, simply, "Good," as his lips instantly broke into that phony campaign smile, and reached out his huge hand to help Cooper up.

"Damn, I don't believe this!" Cooper implored, as he got to his feet and found his bearings. "David, will you get your fucking face out of that fucking transcript and straighten this fucking thing out!"

Strauss looked over his glasses and said quizzically, "In what way, Jerry?"

"Oh my God!" Cooper said, with his arms and eye to heaven.

Walking slowly back to his desk, the President said, "Now, one more thing, Jerr: Is Millard Hampton a homosexual?"

"Sir, I don't know. I never slept with him. And frankly, I don't care."

Inwardly, Cooper was stunned by the accusation. Nothing, in the years they worked together, offered the slightest reason to suspect Hampton was attracted to anything other than his work.

McKenna plowed in: "Mr. President, Millard Hampton's boy friend for many years was a tin-pan-alley song writer named Sidney Wade. Wade died of cancer a few months ago, of the prostate I would presume. Lately Hampton has one Freda Tucker for a companion. She is a production assistant on *The Bernie Frank Show*. Our conclusion is that Miss Tucker, a stunningly attractive Negro woman, who bedded down with most of the male faculty and student body at the University of Georgia, is used willingly by Hampton to procure men for their mutual gratification."

The President slowly sat down, reclined and closed his eyes. His face looked tortured.

Cooper's mind replayed scenes from his boyhood and the unexplained jokes between his mother and father when Hampton's name appeared on the TV screen.

Was that what they were laughing about? he wondered. *Is that why he and his mother divorced?*

McKenna stood and briskly paced back and forth with his hands behind his back and said, "It could very well be that the Yuri Belov interview is a Millard Hampton creation—a ruse, if you will—conceived, written, directed and cast by that legendary closet-queen. It would not surprise me if Belov is nothing more than an itinerant Russian actor—or, more likely, to please Hampton's palate, a member of the Bolshoi Ballet—and not a dissident at all!"

Instantly Cooper's mind flashed to Hampton impersonating the voice of Israeli Prime Minister Amos Gavron on the phone at Camp David, and a hundred other devices he employed to get a story.

Could it be? He thought, *Could the Belov bit be an ingenious Hampton hoax*? Staring incredulously at McKenna, Cooper said to himself, *I hate your guts, you dirty bastard, but you just might be right!*

Without stirring, the President said slowly, "If you are correct, General, Hampton's transgression becomes even more despicable."

Just then, Strauss surfaced. "Mr. President?"

"Yes, David," Packard said, his eyes still closed.

"After careful reflection on this matter, I believe that there is an element in this unfortunate drama that we may be overlooking."

"Yes, David. Go on. I'm listening," the President said.

"It is quite possible, Mr. President, that the Soviets want to sabotage the Summit."

Packard's feet flew off his desk, his chair jolted him upright. Eyes open now, he said, "Sabotage the Summit! How? They mustn't! Explain what you suspect, David."

"General McKenna's hypothesis regarding the authenticity of Yuri Belov may have foundation," Strauss began using a slow cadence. "However, as to motive, it is within the realm of possibility, Mr. President, that they released Yuri Belov precisely for the reasons we presumed, that is, as a show of good faith to the world prior to the Summit, and to nullify or neutralize your valiant human right position as a warranty should the Summit take place."

Strauss hesitated, awaiting his cue, which he knew would come with a roar.

"Should the Summit take place!"? The President roared, his face begging for clarification.

Pleased with himself, Strauss continued: "Mr. President, it is possible that the Soviets veritable purpose for releasing Belov is to create such domestic havoc in America so as to make a Summit meeting at this time politically intolerable, and thus force us to cancel at the last minute."

McKenna, who was having such a field day until Strauss finally made his play, sat down and began rapidly drumming his fingers on the arm of the sofa.

"In what way, David?" the President asked.

Strauss' eyes checked his audience to make sure they were watching him.

Then he said, "Perhaps they arrested some poor insignificant dissident-preacher, or Rabbi, or actor, General, whatever—used their mind-altering drugs and brainwashing techniques on him and produced a man who thinks—actually believes—he was Jesus Christ and has come again as Yuri Belov. And when they explode their Belov bomb on television, the people of this country—especially your core constituency, Mr. President— will become so outraged they will demand you abort your plans for the Summit."

McKenna shouted, "That's it! That's it, Strauss! And Hampton's probably involved with them right up to his fairy neck. I say he's in on it. I felt all along Belov was a Soviet agent. I'm glad you've finally come around to your senses."

While Strauss was pontificating, Cooper was arching and flexing his back, which ached terribly since his *klutzy* attack on McKenna. In a voice that sounded like his back felt, he said, "Why don't they just cancel it?"

Strauss looked at Cooper surreptitiously, and said, "I beg your pardon, Jerry."

"The Russians," Cooper said, while continuing to pamper his back, "If they don't want a Summit, why don't they just cancel it? Say Pavlovsky's sick or something. I mean, you all have them going to a hell of a lot of trouble, when all they'd have to do is pick up the phone and say, 'Sorry, not now; maybe later.'"

McKenna blurted, "If that isn't typical of your pink-eyed view of communism, I don't know what is. This is not an invitation to a tea party, Cooper! This is a battlefield where the stakes are freedom or slavery! Are you so blind that you can't see that the wily communist rulers in the Kremlin will do anything, contrive anything, concoct anything, in order to gain an inch of ground in their quest for world domination?"

"McKenna," Cooper said with a smirk, "you sound like a caller on a late night radio talk-show."

Turning to Strauss, Cooper said, "What I'm asking you, David, is if the Russians don't want a Summit, why go to the trouble of programming a Yuri Belov? Why not just RSVP no? I'm not refuting your theory; it just seems...well, silly!"

Strauss bristled. "Silly?"

"Well, let's say, a dubious machination." Cooper responded.

"Jerry," Strauss began in his lecture mode, "although I take issue with General McKenna in some respects, I must concur generally with his assessment of not only the prize at stake in the contention between the U.S. and the Soviet Union, but also with his presumption that Soviet strategy is unconstrained by any principle—including truth. Thus, any machination, however dubious it appears, must be considered viable when dealing with such an insidious adversary."

Cooper replied, "Okay, they're rotten. You've both convinced me. They've got a lousy system; it's contrary to all we believe. I've got no problem with that and never have. Now, scratch your stock speech to the VFW and tell me, David, why would they go through the intricate scheme of building a Yuri Belov in order to get the Summit cancelled at the last minute?"

"World opinion," Strauss replied, without missing a beat. "Think it through, Jerry, as if you were one of them, not as one of us. We cancel because a poor, unfortunate dissident preacher, speaks his delusional mind through the free American press, and the millions of evangelical Christians—the President's core supporters—of this country become so enraged that they demand the President not only cancel the summit, they demand he cancel our nuclear arms treaties with them as well. To the world, the United States appears as the hawk; the Soviets as the dove—the willing but rejected peacemaker. And they'll play their role to the hilt, finding substantial and sympathetic reward from the Moslem nations of the Middle East and some of the Third World. Can't you see, Jerry, the Soviets have far more to gain from the propaganda value in the aftermath of the Yuri Belov program than they could ever hope for across a Summit negotiating table?"

"David," the President began, with a look of confidence, "that is exactly what I suspected all along. It took you a while, but you finally caught on!"

Strauss paled. He knew what was coming: A retelling of his idea packaged in a Packard wrapper.

"Sure!" Packard began. "They select some rebel, and set him loose. 'Hooray for Russia' says the world. He's a nobody, so they don't lose a scientist or someone smart. To top it all off, they brainwash the poor maverick into thinking he is the Second Coming. Are you all with me? Next, they fill him so full of nonsense and blasphemy so that when he proclaims it on American television, our people go berserk and demand cancellation of the Summit—which is what the Ruskies wanted to begin with! Ha! Nevertheless, just to hedge their play—in case all their shenanigans don't take and we do go to a Summit—Belov's release neuters our human rights argument. How about that, David, Jerr? General? Ya' all follow me? The Ruskies have it every way!"

"Brilliant, Mr. President," Strauss said sheepishly, his stomach knotting.

McKenna darted over to Packard, grabbed his hand and shook it furiously.

"Right on target, sir. Not only perceptively and analytically adroit, but a lamp for our feet as well."

The President looked at McKenna quizzically.

McKenna continued: "Sir, now that we know the Bear's method and motive, we can plan our strategy accordingly."

"Oh, yes. Yes, of course," the President said.

"That is a touchy situation, Mr. President," Strauss interjected.

"What is, David?" the President asked, looking bleary-eyed

"Well, obviously you are going to try to halt the airing of the Belov interview in order to nullify the consummate Soviet strategy."

"I...I was. Yes, I...I was thinking of that. Yes," the President said.

Strauss added, "Well then, in the first place, World Broadcasting would scream denial of First Amendment Rights to high heaven. Others would join the chorus which would portend all manner of negative political fallout for you."

"Even if I convinced them it violated national security?" The President pleaded.

Strauss shook his head. "That excuse is an open invitation for an investigation by a special prosecutor, sir."

The President implored Strauss saying, "But in this case, it is true! It would wreck the Summit!"

Strauss held his position. "You could never convince the network of that. Not even if you gave them a complete and detailed briefing of the issue—which, of course, you wouldn't."

"No, I suppose not," Packard said, dejectedly.

"In the second place," Strauss added, "if you called World Broadcasting and said that the White House would prefer that the Belov interview be preempted, it would be their lead story on their evening news. Then every news service would pick it up, every columnist, every talk show, and the result would be an audience fifty times larger for *The Bernie Frank Show* than it would normally have. Thus, you would be assuring the success of the ultimate Soviet plan."

The President ran his hand through his hair, and said, "Then how do we handle it, David?"

Strauss thought for a moment, then said, "The apparent options are: One, to appeal to World Broadcasting to not air the program; Two, to avoid any interference with the program whatsoever."

"And what is your assessment of both options?" the President inquired.

Strauss replied, "The first option would be politically disastrous. If we take our chances and opt for the second, we run the risk of dancing to the Soviet's tune."

"Hmm. Option one, I lose the public; option two, I lose Pavlovsky."

Strauss nodded in agreement.

The President sighed, and said, "I'll never forget what my daddy used to tell me when I got myself between a rock and a hard place: 'Son," daddy would say, "always keep a can of lard handy; you never know when you'll get in a tight squeeze!'"

Strauss grimaced, cleared his throat, turned towards McKenna, and said, "Notice, Mr. President, that I categorized those two options as apparent options. There is, of course, another alternative—one that would fall more appropriately within the purview of General McKenna."

McKenna flicked his head in Strauss' direction; his lips creased, forming that Mephistophelean smile.

Cooper had been following the flow of dialogue assiduously since Strauss seized center stage in the Oval Office. However, the emotional and physical buffeting he had suffered earlier at the hands of McKenna rendered vague his normally keen perception. He was less wounded from McKenna's personal insinuations than he was from the allegations about the sexual proclivity of his mentor. Consequently, Cooper couldn't get a handle on whether Strauss actually believed his hypothesis about who Belov was and the Soviet's motive for using him, or whether he was manipulating the issue and Packard to suit his own intention.

Worse, Cooper untypically allowed Strauss' third option—one that seemed to delight McKenna—to linger without qualification or disclosure. Cooper was physically and emotionally rocked, not at all himself.

As for David Strauss, he was savoring the gutting of the President's first among equals—the one whose favor he never understood. He now considered Jerry Cooper politically vanquished.

The President stretched his huge arms above his head expanding his massive chest. Then he said, "Jerr, we haven't heard much from you lately. Are you on board, or did we leave you waiting at the station?"

Without hesitation, Cooper answered, "A few moments ago I didn't know if I still owned a ticket, Mr. President."

"What's that, Jerr? What do...oh, oh, I see. The Hampton business. Forget it. It's over. I asked you if you were a faggot, and you said you weren't. That's good enough for me." Packard laughed.

Cooper looked around the Oval office. Suddenly, he felt a strange compelling notion. It said, *This is no longer your place.*

He wasn't sure why he did what he did next. Years later, he still wasn't sure why. Casting his good eye squarely at the President, he said, "And if I had told you I was gay? What would you have done then?"

The President ran his fingers over the days accumulation of stubble on his chin and said, "Then I would have told you that you are reprehensible to me and an abomination to the Lord."

"I see." Cooper said pensively.

Packard added quickly, "But, of course, you're not; so don't worry, Jerr. Now, the Belov thing. Any ideas?"

During the President's exchange with Cooper, McKenna and Strauss were engaged in whispered conversation in the back of the room. Apparently, they were boiling some lard.

Cooper answered, "Yes, yes, I have an idea, Mr. President. After reading the interview and hearing your advisor's evaluation of the Soviet's motives and our options, I believe we ought to just stay the hell out of the way and let World Broadcasting run it."

Cooper said it loud enough so that McKenna and Strauss couldn't miss it. They caught it all right. They both strutted back to the President's desk on the double, leaving the out-of-shape Strauss puffing.

Strauss spoke first: "Mr. President, I believe we have sufficiently demonstrated the potential for diplomatic counter-productivity, that is to say, the public outcry in opposition to a Summit if the interview is aired."

"Over and above that," McKenna screamed, "If Belov—a programmed Soviet operative—succeeds in appearing on American television, there is no assessing what encouragement that will give the KGB to attempt even more adventurous schemes to infiltrate or disrupt our institutions."

Packard listened, and then he reflected for a moment.

Then looking at Cooper, he said, "Jerr, I've shared with you why I want this Summit to take place. Allowing this program to get on the air might stop the most significant event of our time from occurring. In addition, I would violate my covenant with our Lord and Savior if I permit one word of that vile interview to be heard by anyone. Therefore, quite honestly, I am puzzled by your recommendation."

McKenna spoke: "Perhaps Cooper feels a greater sense of loyalty, for whatever reason, to his bosom buddy, Millard Hampton, than to our nation, Mr. President,"

"McKenna, go fuck yourself," Cooper erupted.

Packard's eyes widened in disbelief.

Cooper continued: "Mr. President, my loyalty to you and to this country is beyond reproach. I say let the show go on for several reasons, neither of which will go down well with either that asshole standing at attention or your National Security Advisor."

McKenna shot back saying, "Mr. President, I will not permit this person of questionable character to..."

Hoisting his middle finger at McKenna and stepping on his line simultaneously, Cooper said, "First, I am not convinced that Yuri Belov is a Soviet robot, or that their bottom line purpose is to force a cancellation of the Summit. It is an intriguing plot—one that tickles the fancy of diplomatic and intelligence officers—but is inconsistent with current world conditions. The United States and the Soviet Union are in a nuclear arms race; and they are losing. The Russians need the Summit more than we do, Mr. President."

McKenna shot back: "That's typical of the naïve and dangerous..."

Interrupting again, Cooper added, "Secondly, I don't know for a fact whether Millard Hampton likes sex with boys, or girls or Koala bears—and I couldn't care less. All I know is that he has assembled a dynamite program, and it deserves to be shown."

McKenna wagged his finger and beseeched, "Mr. President, don't forget Hampton's black woman assistant who procures..."

"And thirdly, I didn't read anything that Belov said that diminishes or profanes either God or Jesus. As a matter of fact, I found it rather inspirational."

Strauss started to say something, but the President waved him off. Turning his chair to face the huge window behind him, the President watched the distant dots of lights from automobiles heading up and down Pennsylvania Avenue. By then, it was nearly 1:00 A.M. Most of America was asleep, in a bar, making love or watching TV. An hour earlier, Johnny

Carson had probably kidded the President in his monologue; editorial writers had racked their brains for something to take him to task for, and young children were dreaming of being him. Throughout the length and breadth of the United States, President Albert F. Packard was a very popular and beloved man.

He swung his chair around slowly and placed his hands together. Looking straight at Cooper with that blank, distant stare, which brought back images of the glossolalia episode at Camp David, he said, "Inspirational? You found the message of the devil inspirational? You found reincarnation—the infernal anathema of Christianity—inspirational? You were inspired to read a man debunking the gospel, reducing the Lamb of God to a scientific principal, defiling and vilifying the Christian—that inspired you? Jerr, I'm worried about you."

Cooper fired back: "Mr. President, I'm worried about you! And I'm worried about the ilk that supports you, and the dreadful things that could happen in this country if you and that mob of moralists ever completely closed the already narrowing gap between church and state. Christ, how many times in how many speeches have I heard crowds cheer you when you promised to 'establish the America the founding fathers intended.' The truth is that you and your self-righteous following are the antithesis of the dream of the founding fathers."

The President raised himself and stood behind his desk.

Cooper continued: "And, Al, as for your perverted plan to convert Pavlovsky to Christ when you meet with him in Moscow, or you'll become the 5th horseman of the Apocalypse, allow me to quote one of *my* heroes."

With deliberate enunciation, Cooper recited, "Millions of innocent men, women and children, since the introduction of Christianity, have been burnt, tortured, fined, imprisoned; yet we have not advanced one inch towards uniformity. What has been the effect of coercion? To make half the world fools, and the other half hypocrites."

The President raged, "Which of your heroes were you quoting: Lucifer?"

"No. Thomas Jefferson, Mr. President."

The President gazed at Cooper for several seconds, than at Strauss—who was looking at the floor, and then at McKenna—whose beady eyes were piercing Cooper's head.

In a calm voice, the President said, "My order is the following: I do not want the interview with the Russian to be shown on television. I must have my meeting with Pavlovsky."

Then he walked slowly over to Cooper and stood inches from him as he gazed downward at Cooper's seated and immobile body. Placing his two huge hands firmly on his Special Council's face, the President gently tilted Cooper's head backward so that his one eye was frightfully staring up at the President.

The President closed his eyes, and bellowed, "In the name of the Father and the Son and the Holy Ghost, I ask that this vessel be rid of whatever demon possesses it. Be out! Be gone from this vessel, Satan!"

The President yelled so loudly, that Strauss glanced toward the Oval Office door thinking that the Secret Service might come rushing in with Usies drawn.

Cooper—his head locked in the vise of Packard's huge hands—had no thoughts except those produced by the panic to free his head from Packard's grip. Packard was whispering a prayer to him. However all Cooper could hear was the roaring sound in his head like a ball hitting all the pins a bowling alley.

Suddenly, Packard shouted in a thunderous voice, "In the name of Jesus Christ, I command you to come out!"

President Packard held Jerry Cooper in his grasp for a few moments longer. Then, gently, he removed his hands from Cooper and joined them together in the prayer pose.

Packard said, "Thank you, Lord Jesus, for freeing this man of his corruption."

Cooper felt like his belly was twisted into knots. Bolting out of his chair, a sharp pain seared through his injured back.

Grabbing at the hurting place, he screamed, "Packard, you're sick! David—even you, McKenna—if you know what's good for you, you'll get the fuck out of this loony bin!"

Calmly sitting back down behind his desk in his Presidential pose, Packard said, "David, you and the General get on about carrying out my orders by whatever method or means the situation requires."

Turning his head toward Cooper, he said, "Jerr, your services to me and to this government are terminated as of this moment." Pausing an instant, then he said, "However, I shall continue to pray for you."

Tossing his copy of the Belov transcript inside his briefcase and slamming it shut, Cooper said, "Pray for yourself, Mr. President!"

The meeting adjourned.

Seven thousand miles away, at that very moment, Freda Tucker and Millard Hampton were sitting across a breakfast table from one another at the Plaza Hotel in Tel Aviv. Hampton was at the top of his form, laying out plans for publicizing and promoting the airing of the Belov interview as if he were about to launch an invasion.

"Clancy, I predict that the impact from the Belov program will be the most resounding broadcasting event since Orson Welles convinced radio listeners that Martians landed in Princeton, New Jersey," he boasted. "Only this one might mark the beginning of a new age," he added.

Both of them hadn't slept the night before. They had hit most of the spots on Diezengoff Street and a few in Jaffa until dawn with Bernie and Peggy. Then they said goodbye to the Franks, who took an earlier flight home, and went into the coffee shop to talk until it was time for Freda to leave for her mid-morning flight to New York.

Every now and then, Hampton would peer to the side of Freda's chair to make sure the videotape was still there.

"Honey, you sure your checkin' that tape? Couldn't be my legs, could it?" Freda kidded.

Hampton looked at her with a half-smile, and said, "Clancy, will there ever come a time when you will cease in your effort to corrupt me?"

"You want that time to come, sugah?" She asked with a doubting look.

"All right, here's the plan," Hampton said, wanting to digress to business.

"Again!" she asserted. "Tell you what: let me run through it. Then, if I have it right, I'll let you look at my legs under the table all you want, and I won't jive you about it. Okay?"

Hampton tapped his pipe in the small ashtray, and said, "You're impossible, Clancy."

"No, I'm not," she flirted. "I'm very possible."

"Yes you are. You're impossible. Impossibly, you've given me—me," he emphasized, —"the best me I can be. Impossibly, I find myself, old duffer that I am, being comforted by the mere thought of you. You're more than a friend, less than a lover. Yet, in some unique way that my logical mind cannot fathom, I...I dearly love you, Clancy. And that's impossible."

Freda dabbed at her eyes with the edge of her napkin. She started to say something when the waiter appeared.

"More coffee?" he asked, somewhat abrasively. They had been sitting there for at least three hours.

Hampton looked at his watch. "Goodness, it's nearly ten o'clock. No, no more coffee, my good man. Here, this ought to take care of breakfast and any inconvenience we may have caused you by lingering at your station so long."

Hampton signed a twenty-dollar traveler's check and placed it in the waiter's palm. He bowed away.

Freda got into the cab outside the hotel and rolled the window down. Hampton stuck his head through the opening.

"Ah, good. Right by your side," he said with satisfaction.

Freda smiled and said, "Sugah, I'm really worried about you and this leg fetish you've suddenly developed."

"Clancy," he said warningly.

"All right. If it'll make you feel better, I promise that this here tape will not leave my body till it and I park ourselves at World Broadcasting Headquarters. Believe me, baby, I know how important it is to get there safely."

Hampton nodded, and said, "I know you know. And it's important that you both get there safely. I'll do what I have to do setting up the distribution network and the rest, and I ought to see you in about a week. Well, I suppose you better shove off. Goodbye, Clancy."

Hampton leaned in the window again, kissed her on the cheek and backed away.

Freda looked at him through her misty eyes, and said, "Take care, precious one."

As the cab drove off, Freda turned to watch Hampton wave and walk briskly back into the hotel.

When they got outside the Oval Office, Strauss invited Cooper down to his office for a drink and to "see how the real world works."

Feeling shaky, Cooper fumbled for a cigarette and said, "That'll be my pleasure."

Strauss replied, "I'm not so sure, Jerry. We'll see."

Inside Strauss' office, Cooper flopped into one of his low-backed easy chairs, forming a kind of extended hypotenuse. Normally disheveled, he now resembled road-kill. He closed his good eye, and attempted to mentally evacuate. Allowing himself to be aware of nothing except for the slow steady beat of the throbbing in his head, a voice severed his reverie. "Jerry," the voice standing over him said, "Here, take your drink."

Cooper opened his eye and blinked a few times.

Noticing his guest's hand was shaking, Strauss mercifully placed the glass on the table beside Cooper, and said, "I cannot begin to tell you, Jerry, how much in awe I am to have you sitting here. That the first man ever to be personally exorcised by a President of the United States graces me with his company is a tribute far exceeding my worth."

"Strauss, shove it," was all Cooper could weakly muster.

With intensity matching the President's hand lock on his head a few moments earlier, Cooper clasped the whisky glass with both hands and chug-a-lugged it empty. Without comment, Strauss refilled the glass, which was cupped in Cooper's hand like a beggar for alms.

Three more ounces of Jack Daniels and another cigarette made the storm subside with sufficient calm allowing Cooper to orderly contemplate the events of the morning while Strauss was going through some papers on his cluttered desk.

As Cooper analyzed the facts listed on his mental legal pad, he pondered: *Why was Strauss trying to save the Summit knowing Packard's plan for Pavlovsky rather than seizing upon a golden opportunity to scuttle it? Why didn't Strauss support me when the President and McKenna were attacking me? And what is the plan that Strauss said falls more appropriately within the purview of General McKenna?*

Not daring to attempt standing, Cooper did manage to straighten himself up in the chair, cross his legs and assume some semblance of composure.

He said, "David."

From behind the massive desk, the familiar voice said, "Sorry, Jerry, the bar is closed."

"It's not another drink I want, pal. I need some information," Cooper said.

A slight pause, then Strauss said, "Ach, you have had too much to drink. You've forgotten that you are no longer the President's Special Council. I'm afraid you'll have to receive your information like everyone else does from now on."

Without hesitation, Cooper said, "Look, Strauss, you know as well as I know what lunacy Packard is up to—why he wants the Summit at all cost. Why the fuck didn't you stop it? And why in the hell did you just sit there and let that bastard McKenna accuse me of being a queer and a traitor when you had just as much to do with arranging the Belov interview as I did? What's with you, Strauss? And what's this secret plan to keep the interview off the air? Tell me, for Christ's sake, David. What the fuck is going on?"

David Strauss said nothing nor indicated any particular interest in Cooper's frantic appeal for an explanation. He scrawled a few notes, signed his name to a sheaf of letters and skimmed over a memorandum, all of which took about four minutes, while Cooper waited.

Just when Cooper was about to demand the bar reopen, Strauss reached for the red telephone.

"Get me Ambassador Anatole Molenski, please. Have him awakened if necessary."

Reclining his chair to the right, he propped his scuffed shoes on top of his desk and hummed a little tune while he waited for the Soviet Ambassador to get on the line. It was around 2:00 in the morning.

"Anatole, forgive me for disturbing you at such an ungodly hour, however I must consult with you about a rather urgent matter." (pause)

"Oh, you've seen a transcript?" (pause)

"How interesting! I wonder if anyone in the Israeli television crew was an Israeli!" (pause)

"No, not at all. Naturally, we are all shocked at the impudence of your Mr. Belov." (pause)

"Yes, yes, that is true, however the United States, unlike the Soviet Union, cannot censor nor infringe upon the right of the press to print or televise whatever they please." (pause)

"No, no, not even for that." (pause)

"Quite a stir, yes. You can well imagine what the reaction will be." (pause)

"I would presume so, yes. But we are committed to the Summit no matter what public opinion suggests. Oh, by the way, you know President Packard is a very devout Christian and is terribly distraught with the sacrilegious statements of Mr. Belov. Of course as the person who is sworn to uphold the Constitution of the United States, the President would do nothing personally to prevent the televising of Yuri Belov's interview with your favorite American journalist, Bernie Frank." (pause)

"Yes, he is good on it, I agree. However the point is, Anatole, the President told me just a few moments ago that as an act of redemption for Yuri Belov's sacrilegious statements, he intends to tell Premier Pavlovsky the he has twenty minutes to decide whether to publicly renounce the policy of atheism and accept Jesus Christ, or suffer annihilation of the Soviet Union from American nuclear missiles." (pause)

"Anatole? Anatole? Are you there, Anatole?" (pause)

"Oh, I thought we were disconnected. Isn't that marvelous of our President to feel so deeply about his religion to attempt such cataclysmic event!" (pause)

"Anatole?" (pause)

"Oh, I thought I lost you again. Anyway, I thought you would like to know that. I realize your estimation of President Packard has been less than lofty, nonetheless you must respect and admire a man with such spiritual dedication, even at the expense of his personal fortunes. Am I correct?" (pause)

"Oh, yes, as I said, the American people will demand we cancel the Summit when they see and hear Mr. Belov; however the President has just informed me that we will have the Summit regardless. And President Packard is personally committed to having his Armageddon moment with your Premier."

Strauss raised the telephone receiver closer to his lips, and said, "Anatole, only an act of Congress could prevent it. Well, good night, Anatole. Sleep well."

Cooper tried to put it all together, but it wouldn't stick.

Strauss, still reclining, and appearing very much at peace with himself, said, "Do you care for some food, Jerry?"

For the first time since he put two TV dinners in his microwave, Cooper remembered he hadn't eaten.

"Yes," Cooper said. "Anything."

Strauss pressed a button and ordered some bacon, eggs, and coffee from the White House mess.

After several more attempts at clarification, Cooper became convinced that neither coercion, pity, nor reason would compel Strauss to reveal his plan or his motive. He alternately ignored, humored or artfully dodged the former Special Advisor.

Perhaps feeling the need, for whatever reason, to oblige his bewildered guest with something near substantive, Strauss offered, "The difference between your world and mine, Jerry, is that, in my world, two plus two equal six, minus three, plus one."

He immediately reached for the receiver of the red telephone.

"Would you connect me with Foreign Minister Yizthar, please."

Again he hummed an indiscernible tune—this time to the accompaniment of the tapping of his stubby fingers, with their raw tips, on his desk—as he waited for his Israeli counterpart to come on the line. Several moments elapsed.

Then, "Yigael, how are you this fine morning?" (pause)

"Good, good. Yigael, no doubt you have heard about the interview given by Yuri Belov?" (pause)

"I understand. In fact, I would have been disappointed in the Mosaad had they not provided you with a tape." (pause)

"Oh, yes, I agree. Naturally, Yigael, you understand that the government of the United States will do nothing, and can do nothing, to prevent that interview from being aired." (pause)

"That's right, but ostensibly there will be an outcry from the American public against any nation connected with Mr. Belov in any fashion." (pause)

"No, we will attend the Summit regardless of public opinion." (pause)

"That is correct. It would take an act of Congress to stop President Packard's mission to Moscow." (pause)

"That's true. As a matter of fact, I believe that the Soviets will make a strong effort to have Mr. Belov returned to the Soviet Union." (pause)

"Precisely. I want you to know that even though the evangelical Christian lobby in the United States will demand not only a cancellation of the Summit, they'll demand an end to any financial aid whatsoever to your nation, as long as Mr. Belov is harbored in Israel. Of course we will do our utmost to resist that pressure, which I admit, however, is quite formidable." (pause)

"Yes, I agree. Tourism will suffer immediately." (pause)

"His reaction? In all honesty, I must tell you that the word is 'furious'. That would be the only way to characterize the President's reaction and I may be understating it." (pause)

"Yes, he is an evangelical Christian. You are correct. Although I feel fairly certain that he will not permit his religious convictions to influence his political judgment, one never can be perfectly sure about such things." (pause)

"I was thinking the same thing. Your people have indeed had all the problems you need with one Messiah! Just goes to prove, Yigael, things can always get worse! Well, nice to hear your voice, Yigael. Have a good day." (pause)

"Thank you. Shalom."

Strauss made a small mark on a pad just as the White House waiter entered with a tray of bacon, eggs, English muffins and a pot of coffee and placed it on Strauss's circular dining table.

Right after shoveling a forkful of scrambled eggs into his mouth, Strauss looked at Cooper, and said, "Rather symbolic, isn't it, Jerry?"

"How so?" Cooper asked.

Strauss chewed several times, and said, "This is your last supper."

Instead of acknowledging the Strauss wit, Cooper said, "Quite true, David. And how do you see your role? As Judas, perhaps?"

With that, Strauss tossed his fork onto his plate where it splattered a slice of bacon into bits. Forming both hands into pudgy fists, he riled, and said, "What I do, I do. And I do it without apology, without remorse, without contrition. Nations and men survive and fall according to their ability to be pragmatic. Dreamers, moralists, idealists and prophets, true believers, liberal or conservative, maintain the course of neither ships of sea nor state. I keep my own council consulting with neither heaven nor hell, with God nor the devil. I have given you a rare opportunity, Jerry, to witness the artful weaving of a tapestry of which moralists condemn and weep, yet within whose strands the world holds together."

The ringing of his red phone interrupted Strauss' deep-throated monologue. He grabbed the receiver, and said, "Yes?...I see...Yes...Thank you, General."

As a master deliberately and delicately moves a chess piece, Strauss placed the receiver back in its cradle. Then he said, "I have just been told some tragic news, Jerry."

Cooper looked up quickly, and asked, "What is it? What happened?"

"A terrorist threw a bomb in a taxi cab in Tel Aviv moments ago, blowing up the cab and killing the driver and the passenger—an American woman named Freda Tucker—Millard Hampton's associate. Mr. Hampton was not in the cab. He's being treated for shock. Miss Tucker had the videotape of the Belov interview with her in the cab. Unfortunately, it was completely destroyed along with everything else."

Cooper pushed himself away from the table slowly and walked to the door. Pausing, he shook his head in disbelief.

Then, he turned and gazed at the little man sitting behind the massive desk peering at him over the top of his glasses.

Although he was shaking his head sadly, Cooper clearly detected a twinkle in his eye.

Saying nothing, Cooper opened the door and got out of there.

Several days later, two divisions of Soviet military forces landed in Iceland, as Millard Hampton had forecast. Iceland's Ambassador became the hottest newsmaker in Washington. Appearing on all three major news networks, he pleaded with the U.S. government to help his people stand up to Soviet aggression. Opinion polls indicated he had the overwhelming support of the American people. Nevertheless, President Packard insisted he would meet with the Premier Pavlovsky.

The next day a Special Act of Congress was passed prohibiting a Summit while the Russians were on Iceland's soil.

President Packard suffered what was officially described as "nervous exhaustion." The Vice-President served out Packard's remaining term in office.

Ksana Zoya Belov was placed under house arrest in Vilnius pending the return of her son to the USSR.

A special squad of KGB flew to a remote airfield in the Negev where the Israelis handed over Yuri Belov for extradition to Russia.

He was never heard from again.

Epilogue

When Jerry Cooper clicked the shut down button on his odious computer that night at the Jefferson Institute, he knew what to do next if he were going to put a symposium together on the Packard affair. It would have to wait until the next day. It was getting late.

He wished there was someone to have dinner with, talk politics, gossip. However, Nashville was an early to bed family town. He had even thought of inviting a couple of the interns who were still hanging around to go out with him. The thought didn't linger long.

"Hell, it would be just my luck for being a nice guy I'd probably get some god damn law suit thrown at me for some kind of harassment."

So he threw his notes of his recollection of the Packard affair into his beat up briefcase, turned out the light, and walked back to his efficiency apartment. After tossing two TV dinners into the microwave, he poured himself a root beer, flipped on the TV and cursed Jay Leno for not being Johnny Carson.

When he got to his office the next morning, he placed a call to New York, and to his surprise, the man he wanted to talk with got right on the phone after Cooper told three secretaries who he was.

"Jerry, is that you?" The familiar voice asked. In spite of all that happened, it made Cooper feel good to hear it.

"It ain't Donald Duck," Cooper replied. "How are you, David?"

"Very well. I hope you are the same."

Cooper knew Strauss was very well. After remaining National Security Advisor for a while for Packard's successor, he left the government and formed an international consulting company. His services were for sale to any country—friend or foe—that could pay him his fee.

"I'm just fine. I'm down here in Nashville with the Jefferson Institute. They want me to organize a symposium on the Packard affair."

There was silence on the other end of the telephone.

Cooper continued: "Now I realize that is one subject with which you have absolutely no knowledge, David, but how about coming down here and tell us what you can?"

"Jerry," Strauss began, "I am gratified that you have not lost your ingratiating manner. Seriously, if you believe I can be of some historical value to the event I will be happy to appear. Understand, of course, there have been all sorts of rumors regarding the nature of my involvement with respect to Belov and all the players in that unfortunate drama. Therefore, as a pre-condition, I must tell you that nothing I will say will validate any of the conspiracy theories. If that is agreeable, I will attend and participate."

"David, even if you told everything, I believe you would still not be telling everything. I accept your condition."

As Millard Hampton taught Jerry Cooper many years before, you've got to hook the fish before you put him in a pan to fry.

"Fine. I will put one of my assistants on the line in a moment to apprise you of my requirements. Tell me, who else will be attending?" Strauss inquired.

"You are the first I've contacted, David. I want to invite Bernie Frank, Millard Hampton, maybe even McKenna. Know where any of them are? I never heard a word from Hampton since the incident."

There was a pause, and then Strauss said, "Frank is in Atlanta on the radio. McKenna, that *schmendrick*, last I heard he was in Nicaragua helping the Contras. As far as Hampton, I have no idea where he is."

Cooper thanked Strauss, who put him on the line with one of his assistants. She faxed Cooper Strauss's fee, travel and accommodations requirements. The laundry list of perks befits the king of an Arab emirate country.

Cooper asked one of the Jefferson Institute's secretaries to find out what station Bernie Frank works for in Atlanta, and to get him on the line.

Bernie said he would be happy to appear, and would do it without charge in the memory of Freda Tucker. When Cooper asked if Bernie had any idea where he could locate Millard Hampton, Bernie said he had no idea—that he had not heard from him since that terrible day. "He just dropped out of sight," Bernie said.

"Well, he trained us both," Cooper said. "If you think of anything, anything he might have said, what ever, call me, please."

Five minutes later, Bernie called back.

"It's a long shot," he said, "but when the four of us were in Israel and Millard was giving us the tour, near the end of the day, he talked about a place, a beach, I think it was a place called Elat. The way he told it, it sounded like a lot of drinking and screwing around. Some guy, I think he said his name was Ralphy—I remember because the whole scene sounded like Alphi—you know, 'what's it all about?' He said if it hadn't been for Freda, he probably would have wound up there. Again, it's a long shot, but somehow it stayed with me all these years."

Cooper thanked him, and booked the next flight to Israel.

The flight over was non-eventful other than Cooper's annoyance with a group of teenage girls—one of whom, of course, brought a guitar—who kept singing the same five Israeli folk songs over and over. When Cooper asked one, "Don'tcha know another song?" the kids said they learned them from their mothers who made the trip twenty years ago.

From Tel Aviv, Cooper flew on a small plane down to Elat, a vacation spot on the southern tip of Israel, where the purple orange desert meets the blue Red Sea.

Sweating profusely through his wrinkled dress shirt and khakis, his jacket slung over his shoulder, his maroon knit tie askew, Cooper asked a young woman in a topless bikini if she knew of a fellow named Ralphy something. The girl smiled, and pointed down the beach.

"It is approximately twelve miles to Ralphy's place," she said with a wink.

Wiping his brow most of the way, a cab took Cooper to a remote area away from the tourist traffic. The driver stopped where the narrow road ended, pointed in the general direction to a spot about fifty yards away, laughed and said, "I hope you have fun!"

Trudging slowly in the sand, he finally came upon a conclave of strong young boys and ample young girls, some in bikinis some nude, along with about a dozen middle-age runaways. Presiding over the group was a jovial older man lounging near a thatched hut wearing an orange bathing suit, a blue yachting cap, sunglasses and holding a can of beer.

Cooper approached him, and the man gave him a hug, and said, loudly, "Welcome! My name is Ralphy Nelson. You look like you could use some refreshment, and some R and R."

Panting like a beached porpoise, Cooper said, "Do you know where Millard Hampton is?"

Nelson looked Cooper up and down for several seconds, then nodded to a lean-to several yards away.

"How did you find him?" Nelson asked.

"I'm psychic," Cooper replied, and walked toward the hut.

Sprawled inside was Hampton. He was a shadow of his former self. Emaciated, his full gray beard matted like a cats fur becomes if not brushed. He was nearly dead drunk, but when Cooper said, "Hello, Millard. Remember me? Jerry Cooper," he simply dropped his head on his chest.

They sat together without saying a word for the rest of the afternoon. Hampton took an occasional swig of liquor, which didn't seem to alter his level of intoxication. Apparently, he could no longer pass out.

After about four hours of just sitting together, the sun began to set over the Red Sea. Cooper took the cue to tell Hampton why he had come. When he asked if he could take him back to America and tell the story, Hampton spoke his first words to Cooper:

"Hell no."

Cooper made another attempt, evoking the name of Freda Tucker and Bernie Frank.

Hampton raised his head slowly. His answer was spoken through his blood red, tormented eyes.

Cooper let it drop, wistfully mindful that failure to secure an interview with a primary source for a story was a capitol crime according to Hampton's law back in his glory days.

After sitting awhile longer, Cooper said it was time for him to leave.

Hampton nodded and dropped his head

Cooper stood and gazed for several seconds at the remains of the legend, the wizard, the man once his idol.

Then he said, "I need to know one thing before I go, Millard: Belov. Yuri Belov. Was he a Soviet invention? Was he a

Hampton ruse? Or was he who he who he said he was? Who was Yuri Belov, Millard?"

Hampton cracked open a can of beer and took a lengthy swig.

Wiping his mouth with the knuckle of his bony hand, he looked straight up into Cooper's eye, took a deep breath, sighed, and said, "What difference does it make?"

The End

Printed in the United States
38588LVS00007B/277-279

9 781413 787078